THE WITCHES OF WYLDEDEN
CHRONICLES

THE MARK FOR THOSE UNBOUND

ALEX CLIFFORD

THE MARK FOR THOSE UNBOUND

BOOK 3 OF THE WITCHES OF WYLDEDEN CHRONICLES

ALEX CLIFFORD

ALSO BY ALEX CLIFFORD

THE WITCHES OF WYLDEDEN CHRONICLES

The Mark of Things Unwanted

The Mark of One Unending

THE WITCHES OF WYLDEDEN NOVELLAS

A Tale of Scars and Rebels

A Love of Books and Leather

BEFORE

"Ry! Lunch!"

If the old wooden floors had been polished, Ryson's boots would have squealed as he skid to a stop. As it was, the leather scuffed black marks into the floor that he'd have to scrub out later, lest the three of them lose their security deposit. The landlord was one of the better humans, willing to lease the decrepit apartment to newly freed demi-kin, but not so good that he wouldn't jump on an opportunity to steal their money.

Sheepishly, Ryson jogged back across the small room to where Edwina held out a paper bag. He was running late, but three years of freedom was not long enough to forget how it felt to be hungry. These days, between Eddy working at the palace as a maid and Rad working nights maintaining streetlamps, they rarely missed a meal.

"Thanks, Red," Ryson said as he took his lunch and kissed her on the cheek.

Her nickname brought a smile to Edwina's tired eyes.

The three of them had been the only children kept by Master

Ackford, and after Ry and Rad had bonded, Eddy often felt left out. In their youth, the solution was simple: put an R at the front of her name too and call themselves the Triple R Threat. The adult demi-kin had played along, and the three of them had been inseparable ever since.

"I'm back at the palace for the next few nights," Edwina reminded him as she wiped clean the tiny kitchen bench with a dishtowel. "Make sure Radley bathes."

A quick nod and a glance to where their brother was passed out on the floor, empty liquor bottle still clutched in his fingers, spoiled his mood. Three years they had been free; three years since Master Ackford's daughter had ended her relationship with Radley, and he still wasn't over it. Ryson didn't understand, but he couldn't resent Radley his misery either. His brother had suffered a lot to be with the master's daughter, but the moment the demi-kin had been freed, the excitement of being with a slave—the forbidden nature of it, the power trip—was over. She'd lost interest.

"I'm late," Ryson said, fixing the blanket over Radley's snoring form in front of the dark fireplace. "But I'll see you later, okay?"

"Ry." Edwina rushed to catch him by the wrist before he could dart for the door. At seventeen, he was finally as tall as she was, but that didn't stop her from finding a way to look down her nose at him. "It's been three months. You've had your fun. Quit and go back to school before you're caught."

They had a version of this conversation at least twice a week. His older sister and brother insisted training for the royal guard was too risky, but he hated school—he was no good at it—and the extra income he received as a cadet meant they could save for a better apartment.

Not only that, but being at the palace, surrounded by others who understood his gratitude toward Princess Aisling for freeing the Hyrschan demi-kin, felt like finally belonging somewhere. Yes, he had to be careful, but it was a risk he would take if it meant he could do his part in protecting their new ruler from humans who hated her for taking away their slaves. In the three years the princess had been in charge, over a dozen assassination attempts had been reported, and Ryson would let the city fall back to old ways over his dead body.

Which meant never.

"Get some sleep before you have to go back, Red. I'll be fine. And I'll make sure Rad bathes and gets up for work."

He pulled his wrist from her grip and ran for the door, closing it quietly. Down the rickety exterior stairs on the side of the building, Ryson made it to the street and sprinted for the palace gates.

The city was changing.

Ryson grinned as he dodged the early risers already wandering Westgate, taking first pick of the day's produce. Only impoverished humans or small business owners lived on this side of the city, but it was getting harder to tell the difference between them and the demi-kin who now lived among them. The slightly paler strip of flesh around their throats gave them away, but it was less noticeable than the metal collars that used to be clamped there.

Ryson's cadet uniform meant people rushed out of the way as he pounded the cobblestone roads, receiving just as many tired smiles as annoyed glares as he made his way to the center of the city. The architecture changed the closer he got—polished, clean and grand—but as the morning bells chimed, he didn't spare a glance for it, nor the suspicious looks wealthier humans gave him.

The guards at the palace gates saw him running and shook their heads, opening the wrought-iron doors for him.

"You're late, cadet!"

"I know!" Ryson panted as he slipped inside.

"Porter is going to kick your ass!"

"I know!" he repeated, laughing as he skirted the outer structures, making his way to the training fields.

He wouldn't be allowed to step foot inside the actual palace until he graduated, but as towering spires of dark stone came into view, he broke into a grin. One day he would get his chance. He would kneel before Princess Aisling and swear his loyalty. Spend his days and nights ensuring she could continue her work to better the city in peace.

On the far side of the grounds, beyond the stables, were rows of sparring cadets. Ryson put on a burst of speed, tossing his paper bag on the pile of personal possessions before weaving between the others, coming to a stop before Commander Porter.

One hand on his heart, he saluted. "Ryson West reporting for duty, sir."

Unlike his sister, who'd taken her position as maid as a surname, or his brother who'd used Lighter, Ryson had chosen his new *free* name after the home they shared in Westgate.

"You're late, cadet."

"Yes, sir."

"Reason?"

It was a question only the demi-kin cadets were ever asked. Humans didn't get to have excuses, but demi-kin—or in Ryson's case, supposed demi-kin—were given a little slack. Yes, it had been three years since their collars were removed, but time wasn't all it took for those enslaved to find their feet.

Commander Porter was one of the few humans the demi-kin

4

trusted to integrate them into the ranks of the royal guard, but Ryson, for one, didn't want his lenience.

"No good reason, sir."

Porter narrowed his eyes dubiously but sighed, pointing to the edge of the field. "A hundred push-ups. Over there."

A hundred. Porter was going easy on him.

Compared to the human cadets, Ryson was small. Most demi-kin were. Underfed and worked to the bone their whole lives, there was an obvious discrepancy between them. Or most of them. The demi-kin who successfully graduated into the royal forces seemed to pack on muscle in a way Ryson desperately wanted to.

Edwina was still frail, and Radley had never recovered from the deprivation he'd endured, joints always hurting, body struggling to hold sustenance. Ryson was different. His body had healed, and with every passing year he grew a little, but he was still stunted. Shorter and thinner than he wanted to be.

But a hundred push-ups? When he knew the humans who showed up late were given two hundred? It was insulting.

Your mind will break before your body does.

It was a point that had been driven into him from the earliest days he remembered. He couldn't recall his mother's face, nor the sound of his father's voice, but their words and lessons would be with him always. If he could shut down the part of his brain that told him he couldn't keep going, he would be unstoppable.

He would do two hundred push-ups; not to spite his commander, but to spite the human cadets who sneered every time the demi-kin were treated differently. Even stunted, he would be twice the guard they would ever be.

Up and down, up and down; he focused on his form and posture, making every rep perfect. A whistle blew, and he risked a glance across the field to where the senior cadets had finished their march around the palace, standing at attention in front of their commander. When the whistle blew a second time, the cadets retrieved weapons from huge sacks they'd been made to carry on their backs.

Ryson couldn't wait to get his hands on a steel-and-silver sword. To begin *real* training instead of sparring with wooden weapons. But it wasn't a sword the senior cadets pulled out today. Instead, most struggled under the weight of the compact crossbows, cursing as they tried and failed to pull back the string.

Reaching thirty push-ups, Ryson had to turn away. His shoulders and abdominal muscles burned, arms shaking. Every breath trembled as he focused on the individual blades of grass bending in the breeze. His body would not fail. Even as his uniform dampened with sweat, biceps cramping, lower back straining from his rigid posture, he knew his body would not fail unless he let it. Torn muscles, sprains, even broken bones would heal eventually.

Unstoppable.

If he could conquer pain and fear, he would be unstoppable.

And when his parents decided to show up, he would prove how strong he had become. He would make them proud.

Up, breathe in. Down, breathe out. Up, breathe in. Down, breathe out.

He lost track of how many he'd done. He always did once he got into the fifties. In Master Ackford's house, there had been no reason for slaves to learn to count that high, and even after, when he'd been at school, he'd never really gotten the hang of it.

So he just kept going. Even under the threat of bile in his throat, he kept going. Even when he couldn't manage controlled breaths, when his bones had turned to jelly, he kept going.

Kept going until, nose to the ground, he couldn't push back up again.

It's all in your head, he reminded himself, trying to force his quaking body to rise. *You can do it. There's nothing stopping you.*

His knees hit the ground and he cursed.

"Cadet!" Somehow, Ryson knew Commander Porter meant him.

Turning his head, he caught the look of amusement in the commander's eyes.

"Get some water and join us for the next round."

He didn't know if he could stand, but Ryson nodded and rolled into a sitting position. Paid servants had set up a water station between the junior and senior cadets and, after climbing to his feet, Ryson managed to drag himself to the barrel. A servant filled a cup and passed it with a smile.

"Shit!" The curse sounded at the same time the order rang through the field: "Get down!"

Without hesitation, everybody dropped to the ground.

Everybody but Ryson.

He turned toward the commotion just as something slammed into his throat. Sprawling back, hot pain speared through his head as he hit the ground, red splattering his vision.

The servant screamed. Orders were shouted. Ryson couldn't understand any of it as he lay there, stunned. And the pain . . . gods, the pain. He couldn't breathe. Whenever he tried, he choked, liquid iron burbling against his lips.

Commander Porter skidded to his knees beside him, color bleached from his face.

"Hang in there, cadet," he rasped, pushing down on Ryson's throat.

"Who shot that fucking bolt!" someone else roared.

"It slipped!"

"It was an accident!"

A bolt, Ryson realized, fear finally soaking through the pain. He'd been hit by a stray bolt.

This was bad.

Not because it would kill him, but because it wouldn't.

Seeing the panic widening Ryson's eyes, Commander Porter forced a stressed smile on his pallid face.

"Medics are coming. Just hang on. If anyone can survive this, it's a demi-kin like you, alright? You'll be okay."

No, not even a demi-kin would survive a wound like this.

As blood pumped furiously from Ryson's throat, his body going cold, Commander Porter's reassurances followed him beyond consciousness.

He wasn't shackled, but the guards at the door made it clear he was not free to leave.

After waking in the infirmary to the wide-eyed stares of medics, nothing but a soiled uniform and bloodstained face as evidence he'd been injured at all, guards had collected him and taken him to the parlor to wait.

The parlor. Inside the palace.

He was *inside* the palace.

There wasn't room for excitement as he sat carefully on the edge of the settee, trying not to stain the beautiful cream-and-gold cushions with his filth.

Nobody had said the word yet, so maybe they hadn't realized what he really was, but they had to know he wasn't a normal demi-kin. Someone would be coming to ask questions, and he had no idea what to say when they did.

Truth was off the table. His parents had made that abundantly clear.

"Our kind are not welcome anymore, Ryson," his mother had warned him. *"Don't ever get caught. You'll regret it."*

It wasn't like he'd done it on purpose, but that pride he imagined his parents having when they came to find him would be tarnished if they knew he'd been caught.

All he could do was hope whoever came to question him didn't know about Kinner. Or at least bought into the lie that they were mere legend; a story the demi-kin made up to make themselves feel special.

Perhaps he could say he just had very strong genes. Say that he *could* have died, and in fact, it had been a close call; he'd felt the cold grip of death around his heart, but the medics had pulled him back in time.

Ryson shook his head. Nobody would believe that.

The door creaked, and he turned.

Paled.

Princess Aisling Aurnia stood in the doorway, grey eyes wide and staring. Both soft and sharp, she was so beautiful with her sleet-grey hair braided in a coronet, a small tiara balanced delicately on her head. The fabric of her dress was more luxurious than anything Ryson had a name for, and he sat in stunned awe as she stepped inside the room.

"You may leave us," she said mildly to the guards.

The sound of her voice broke the spell over Ryson; he slid off the couch to his knees, bowing so deeply his nose brushed the thick pile carpet.

"Your Highness," one of the guards started warily. "I don't—"

"Look at him," Princess Aisling said. "The boy is a loyalist. I will be fine."

Ryson kept his head low, so he didn't see the guards leaving. The door snipped closed, and the heavy silence returned.

"You may rise. Make yourself comfortable."

Ryson didn't move. He didn't know how. Words came out in breathy disbelief. "Your Highness, I am honored by your presence."

Her perfume sweetened the air as she approached, fingernails brushing the back of his neck. He shivered under her touch.

"It is I who is honored," she said. "Please, I beg of you. Rise."

Ryson balked at the words. The princess should beg for nothing.

Quick as he could, he stood, heart stuttering at her proximity. Self-conscious of his bloody, stinking uniform, he stepped back until his knees hit the settee.

The idea of his filth tainting her was unbearable.

As was the prospect of lying to her, yet he managed to choke out, "I am not worthy of such honor, Your Highness. I'm just a demi-kin cadet."

Princess Aisling lowered herself into one of the plush armchairs across from him, the noon sunlight bringing out a little color in her face. Knowing it was rude for a servant to stand higher than their master, Ryson also sat.

Though her face was a mask of indifference, her tone hinted at deep amusement as she said, "You and I both know that isn't true. Ryson, is it?"

Swallowing the lump in his throat—the echo of the bolt still jammed in there—he nodded.

"My staff believe they witnessed a miracle from Sanni, the Spirit of Healing. Or the god of it, as the humans and demi-kin call her. Do you believe in the gods, Ryson?"

He didn't know. His parents were vehement believers, but he didn't remember much of what they'd said about them. The teachers at the school he'd briefly attended from fourteen to fifteen had tried to explain the seven minor and two . . . Three? Four? He couldn't remember, but the major deities, as well, though he'd never paid much attention. It didn't matter to him. Gods blessed witches. They weren't interested in demi-kin or humans. Did nothing to intervene in their lives. Didn't do much of anything, as far as he understood. They simply existed, passing on magic to those they deemed fit.

"I don't know much about them," he admitted. "I'm sorry."

"Please, don't apologize to me." She averted her eyes and frowned. "I am the one who should apologize. I am so greatly sorry for what has been done to your children. The demi-kin should never have been subjected to such cruelty."

Ryson blinked, a question escaping before he could think it through. "My children?"

The princess's frown turned wry. "I know you're a kinner. There's no point lying about it to me. Even if you had not healed from a lethal injury, the silver of your mark in lieu of brown identifies you for what you are. The Sparrow Coven knows how to recognize a kinner, even if most of them, along with the rest of the world, don't believe you were ever real."

Shit.

"You don't need to be scared," Princess Aisling promised, leaning forward to reach across the little table between them to offer her hand. "I'm not like the rest of my coven. I wasn't lying when I said I am honored to be in your presence."

He didn't deserve to touch her, but it would be rude to leave the princess reaching. Trembling, he took her hand.

Her smile was radiant as she squeezed gently, but Ryson had spent enough time watching his siblings' fake smiles to know the happiness Princess Aisling portrayed was a lie.

"May I ask a few questions before you go home?"

He started at that. She was going to let him go home?

"Anything," he promised.

Sitting back, she folded her hands in her lap and blushed. "Sorry if it is offensive to ask, but I've never seen one of your kind in the flesh. Do you all appear so young?"

Ryson frowned. "Um, I don't think so. I'm not sure."

It had been ten years since he'd seen another kinner, and even then, he only knew his parents, who he didn't remember well enough to say.

As if reading his mind, her face softened with pity. "Has it been a long time since you've seen any of your own?"

He nodded, once again too overwhelmed to control his tongue. "I was only seven when I saw my parents last."

Something in Princess Aisling's eyes sparkled at the words. "When they were captured by the Sparrow Coven?"

His body stiffened, a warning bell chiming in his head. Princess Aisling could be trusted, he knew that, but he also knew better than to admit there were kinner who escaped the Sparrow Coven. Her stare had him wiping sweaty palms on his pants. There was something about the tilt of her head, the perfect stillness of her face as she waited for an answer, that reminded him of a ravenous predator waiting to strike.

He nodded.

Her eye twitched.

"You know," she said, remaining far too still. "Our peoples haven't had the best history."

Ryson didn't know much about it, but he nodded anyway.

"But it only takes one person to reach out their hand, to offer peace, for a second chance to be possible. I would like that for us."

"Me too," he agreed, hating the way his voice cracked around his nerves. "It would be an honor to be allowed to serve in your royal guard."

She blinked, a strained smile breaking her face. "I would like that, Ryson. But what I really need from you first is a way to find the other kinner. Despite my family and the consequences, I want to help them, just like I helped the demi-kin."

He might not know much about what had happened between the Sparrows and the Kinner, but he knew they did need help. And Princess Aisling had done such wonderful things for the demi-kin, even if another of the key lessons his parents had given him was to *never trust Sparrow witches.*

"That would be amazing, but I'm sorry," he said, looking down at his shoes as he scuffed them on the carpet, a stone in his throat. "I don't know how to find them. I was too young when we were separated, and I don't remember anything about them. But if anything comes to me, I promise to let you know."

The silence between them lingered. When he dared to meet her gaze, he flinched at the cold, hard look on her face.

"Perhaps you simply need some time to think on it."

PART I

HIRAETH

CHAPTER 1

CINN

My name is Cinn. I cannot speak and I only understand Nirnish. I am looking for Moyra Thorne. A witch named Yomra sent me. The witches of Wyldeden support me if you require trade.

EAON BLEW ON THE INK TO DRY IT BEFORE TUCKING THE NOTE into Cinn's pack.

{Thank you.} He never could have gotten this far without Eaon, and he had no idea how to manage now that he had to leave him behind.

"You can do this," Eaon said in earnest, as if sensing Cinn's uncertainty.

{You'll be here when I get back?}

"I promise."

And that was something to focus on. Getting back.

Releasing a shaky breath, he hugged Eaon, chin resting on his shoulder. There was so much Cinn didn't know how to say; words could not express how much he didn't want to walk away. Especially after the night before last, sleeping soundly in the hammock together. Or in the hall just now, when the dark had threatened to crush him and Eaon sent it running with the bare brush of lips against Cinn's temple.

The waiting Qiri witch cleared her throat.

Eaon's grip tightened. In a silent promise they would both be okay, Cinn returned the gentle kiss to Eaon's cheek.

It wouldn't take much for his resolve to falter, so he didn't look at Eaon as he pulled back and turned to hurry after the Qiri witch, quickly disappearing into the narrow crack in the mountainside.

The dark was absolute, and the tight squeeze scraped and bruised as they slid along the passageway. Even though such things were fleeting on his body, Cinn recoiled from the temporary pain of broken skin. Not outwardly, as there was nowhere to recoil to, but in the numb place in his head where things weren't so overwhelming.

Stop it, he scolded himself.

It was this place. He'd come so far from the terrorized, instinct-driven shell of a person he used to be, but ever since arriving at the Northern Mountains he'd regressed. It was being underground again; the lack of escape routes, of open air and sunlight.

Eaon made it bearable, enjoyable even, but Cinn was alone now.

Alone in the dark. Confined to a cramped stone cell.

"We're coming up to the wards," the witch muttered in her thick, rolling accent. "It will be uncomfortable passing through, and you will not be able to return without a Morvish guide."

Her voice ever so slightly soothed the panic building in his chest. He wasn't entirely alone, but he also didn't know this woman. Impatient, reluctant . . . What if she left him behind? What if he was stuck down here forever?

He needed to get out. He needed to get above ground. To breathe.

He wanted Eaon and Puddles. Sarah and William.

He wanted to go home.

But that was why he was here. The Copelands' farm had been taken from him, just like everything else, and he didn't know how to get it back. Didn't know how to get back anything he'd lost.

Moyra did. Whoever she was.

Moyra Thorne had the answers, and even if he wasn't convinced he was brave enough to get them for his own sake, he would do this for Sarah and William. They'd lost their home, too. Because of him.

The witch stopped suddenly and Cinn walked right into her.

Snarling, she elbowed him in the rib. "Back off."

Biting his tongue—*It isn't my fault I can't see in the dark*—he took a step back and focused on getting air into his lungs.

Not that he needed to breathe to stay alive, as he had unfortunately discovered time and time again, but that wasn't the point. He had a job to do, and he wasn't going to be able to do it if he couldn't keep his shit together.

"Put this over you." The witch pressed something against him—a heavy, dank length of fabric that didn't seem to have an end no matter which way he turned it.

Muttering under her breath with a cadence Cinn recognized as incantation, she wasn't going to wait for him to figure it out. Hurriedly, he pulled the fabric over his head any way he could.

"Move," she snapped.

The air was thick and bitter against the roof of his mouth, and every inch of skin not covered by fabric blistered the farther he followed the Qiri witch into the wards. It didn't last long, the burning replaced with a healing itch, skin smoothing back to flawless in a matter of seconds.

It's how he used to tell time down in the dark and cold. A cut would only last a minute, a broken bone maybe ten. Growing back an organ could take an hour, limbs a little more. The longer he was down there though, the longer things took to heal, and soon, keeping track of time became impossible. And irrelevant, since he was never getting out.

I am out, he reminded himself. *I am out, and I am never going back.*

After a night of dancing by the bonfire instead of sleeping, his legs complained at the upward slope. The path narrowed and twisted around and around in an imperceivable maze, and only the labored breathing of the witch ahead kept his sanity from splintering.

Finally, sunlight bounced off a stone wall ahead, the crevice cutting to the right. Stepping into the day, dry air scorched Cinn's throat as he squinted against the sun's glare.

He'd never seen so much open space. The desert was limitless. Dunes irregularly interrupted the flat expanse of golden sand blending seamlessly into the bright, cloudless sky, but otherwise the world seemed endless.

The witch who'd led him through the gap in the wards—though what the magic felt like where there wasn't a gap, he couldn't imagine—didn't give him time to adjust to the sudden blinding light before snatching the fabric from his shoulders, bundling it up with her own.

"Hurry up," she called, leading the way to a horse-drawn wagon waiting in the shade of the mountain.

Cinn broke into a jog, tossing his pack among the array of wooden crates in the back before climbing aboard. Most of the crates were stuffed with sacks of grain and fruits he didn't recognize, but the witch slipped a crowbar under the splintering lid of a barrel toward marked "water," easing it back.

"In."

Cinn frowned at the empty barrel and the expectant look on her face until it dawned on him. Stumbling back, he shook his head.

"I'm not going to prison for bringing in Southerners, so either get in or get off."

There was no way he was getting in that barrel. None.

His adamance must have been clear because the witch slammed the lid and smacked the nails home with the butt of the crowbar. As she approached him, she reached for a velvet pouch at her hip.

"Off, then."

Before he had a chance to do anything, she pulled out a pinch of black dust and threw it in his face. Twisting away, he fell onto the hard-packed sand, coughing hard. The witch tossed his pack and jumped down, crouching to look him in the eye.

"Forget my face," she commanded, the words filling his head with such undeniable force that everything else became secondary. "Forget how you got here."

By the time Cinn found his feet, the horse-drawn wagon was almost out of sight.

He really shouldn't be so shocked that the witch had abandoned him. The Copelands had been an exception; most people didn't risk their necks for strangers.

Eyes finally adjusting, he spun in a slow circle to get his bearings. He couldn't remember which mountain he'd come from, nor could he recall any details about the passage through. Only the dark, and that he wished Eaon could have come.

Pausing, he looked along the mountains again.

Would Eaon have tried to follow? Was he stuck in the crushing rock, or hurt by the wards?

No, Cinn thought as he shook his head at himself. Not after that goodbye.

But another question chilled the sweat beading on his brow. How was he going to get back?

Moyra will have the answers. It was the only thing he had to hold on to. The only thing keeping him from sinking into the numb place or panicking at the sudden reality that he was alone.

Very, very alone.

He didn't know which way to go. How far to Ahrenhale it was.

Think. He pushed a fist against his forehead. *Think positive*.

It made sense to follow the tracks the witch had left in her wake, and surely there would be other people along the way—who didn't want to lock him inside a barrel—who could point him in the right direction.

Nodding to himself, Cinn hiked his pack onto his shoulders and set a brisk pace along the mountain range's shadow. One way or another, even if he had to walk for weeks and weeks, he was getting to Ahrenhale.

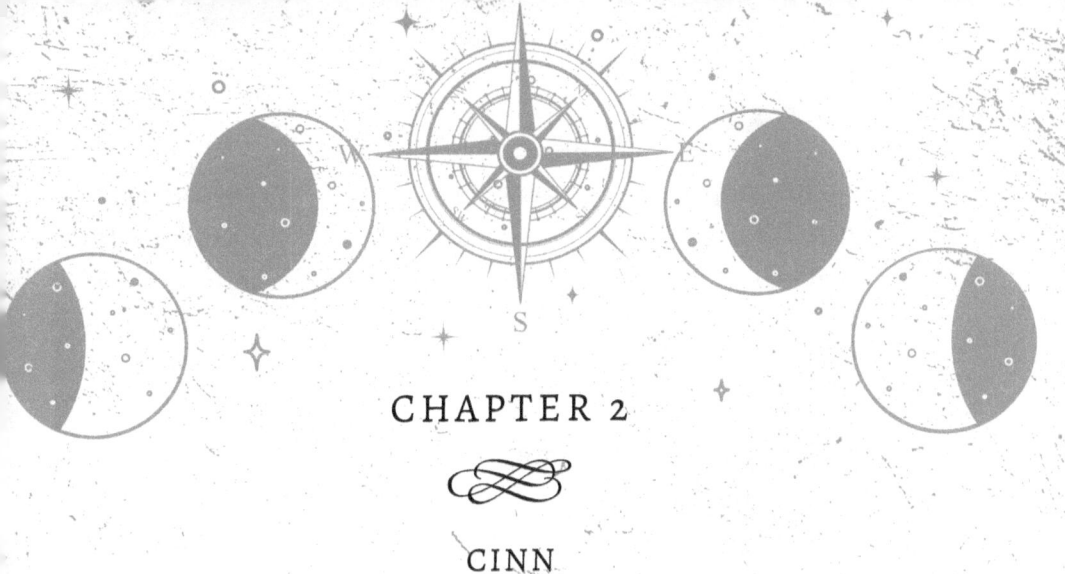

CHAPTER 2

CINN

NOTHING WAS AS BEAUTIFUL AS A DESERT SUNSET AND nothing lonelier than its vastness at night—his total singularity in this empty place. In all the long hours of walking, he'd seen nothing else living. Not even a tuft of grass. There were only dunes and sand all the way to the horizon.

Blanketing clouds had moved into the sky, and without the stars, darkness crept in so absolutely that he could not see his own feet. At the peak of a dune, beyond tired, he sat down and emptied the gritty sand from his boots before blindly rummaging through his pack for his trinket box. The one William had bought for him. His fingers slid over the grain to find the latch, hinges creaking in the still night as he opened the lid. The first thing he found was the blue-streaked pebble, cold and hard. Pulling it out, he pressed it to his lips.

Home.

He'd made it back once before; he could do it again.

His collection usually distracted him, but tonight that pebble and what it represented wouldn't soothe his thundering heart.

He couldn't stop thinking about how he'd not been this alone since the Oford forest those initial weeks after escaping, but even that was not the kind of alone he was now. There had been beasts and fae and wildlife in the forest; the sounds of the Copelands working their farm, oblivious to his presence in their barn.

The desert was utterly empty.

Without the moon or the stars to remind him he was outside, it was too easy to remember the kind of alone he'd been in that cell—the world too small, walls pressing in on every side, suffocating and crushing.

Tingles rushed across his scalp, tension shuddering from his body. His hands fell limp at his sides, the pebble rolling from his fingers. A hollow ringing quieted his head.

The darkness was everything.

He was nothing.

Nothing but breath and skin and blood.

He existed, because there was no choice to do anything else.

When the world greyed, he frowned. The movement reminded him he had a face as he tried to understand why the dark had color.

A breeze brushed his bare arm. He flinched, turning to see who had breathed on him.

The lump to his left confused him until he recalled what it was: a pack.

His pack.

And the grey . . .

The sky.

Desert.

Qiri.

Sucking in a sharp breath, he looked down to his numb hand to see the pebble was gone.

No.

Pins and needles flushed his legs as he moved them for the first time in hours, scrambling, desperately searching for a flash of blue in a field of loose sand.

There. Halfway down the dune.

Surprised by the strength in his weak body, or the weakness of his healthy body, he wasn't sure which anymore, he dove after his treasure.

The two grooves the smuggler had left in the sand were gone. He should have gotten in the barrel. It would have been better than being lost in the fog of his head. A fog he wanted to both push away and wrap himself in, a comforting blanket of forgetfulness.

How quickly he'd slipped into it now that Eaon wasn't there to squeeze his hand. Now that the Copelands weren't there to keep him present.

Rubbing the pad of his thumb over the pebble, he closed his eyes and forced himself to remember how it felt to find it all those months ago. A solid feeling. A good memory. Something real to hold onto.

Returning to his trinket box, he traded the pebble for the feather, tickling his own ears and eyelids until he felt it. Until he connected with his face again.

Nobody knew what creature the feather had come from. It was strange. Unique. The only one of its kind in the world, as far as they knew.

Alone. Like him.

Don't think about it.

Shaking his head, he put his things away and got his pack on his shoulders. All traces of the smuggler had been blown away during the night, but as long as he kept the mountains to his right, he'd reach civilization eventually. Hopefully.

∾

His skin hurt.

His feet hurt.

His lips hurt as he tipped the canteen, a pathetic dribble of water soothing the dry cracks in them.

The night's clouds had dissipated, allowing the ruthless sun to cook his brain. Rest would help but that meant stopping, and if he stopped, he wasn't sure he could start again.

Besides, it wouldn't help the sunburn. That wrathful ball of fire in the sky burned each fresh layer of skin the healing mark on the back of his neck provided.

A constant cycle of itching.

∾

There were still no clouds when the sun went down again, the stars bright enough to light the way as Cinn kept walking.

He couldn't stop. Didn't want to stop. He didn't want to sleep when he was so sure there were only nightmares waiting for him, and he didn't want to sit alone and lose himself in the dark again. Or worse, sit lucid, ruminating on everything that had led him to this stupid desert.

He hated the desert.

So he walked.

∾

The clouds didn't return the next day, and the heat welded his cracked lips so tightly he couldn't bear the pain of pulling them apart to eat. Not that he could have, with his mouth drier than the sand swallowing every step.

His vision blurred, even as his feet kept moving. Every now and then, the path he followed would disappear and he had to blink until it came back. Which hurt, because his eyes were so dry.

Spots bloomed red and black. He blinked, and the path was gone again. Blinked a few more times and realized it was because he'd strayed, his wobbling legs taking him a direction he hadn't meant to go.

Stopping, his knees buckled. The hot sand scalded his palms as he caught himself, but even that pain wasn't enough to make him stand again.

Laying down, fingers stiff as parchment, he worked the latch of his pack and pulled out a spare shirt to cover his head. Maybe it would be enough to let the sludgy mess his brain had become recover.

He woke to darkness. Fighting the cloth over his face and grimacing at the metallic taste on his teeth as he tore his lips apart, Cinn panted heavily. At some point, he'd stopped breathing; the familiar ache in his lungs slowly eased as the mark healed them.

The stars were hiding again, bar a few, low on the horizon. They twinkled dully, pale orange instead of the crisp white that had blanketed the sky the night before.

As he stood, his head throbbed, stomach lurching. Gods, he hated dehydration.

Stop complaining.

It was counterproductive. Pain was a part of life, inevitable and inescapable, but, if he took deep breaths and retreated into the quiet recess in his mind, it was also endurable.

Too tired to put his pack on, he dragged it across the sand as he stumbled along. It took no effort to find that quiet place. To slip into it and let the agony of each step, each breath, become a vague monotony.

It wasn't until he was practically in it that he realized he'd found a town. A small one, but it didn't matter. People lived here, which meant there was water.

The pathetic stars he'd spotted were lanterns hanging in doorways, lighting the way as Cinn struggled down the lone street. The small houses built from adobe blocks—a mix of clay, sand, straw and water that he had vague memories of mixing in his pre-Hyrsch days—were dark and silent inside, except for one. Horses were tied out front while drunken chatter buzzed inside.

Cinn forced his body to climb the single step onto the porch. His hand trembled as he pushed open the rickety door and squinted into the brightly lit tavern.

The chatter died.

A long table lay the full length of the room, two bench seats on either side where humans sat with bowls of stew and pitchers of ale. At the far end, a man stood behind a makeshift bar made of barrels and an old door. He'd been pouring amber liquid into a cloudy glass but stilled at the sight of a stranger in the doorway.

Dropping his pack, Cinn pulled out Eaon's note. His feet dragged as he approached the bar, and he had to force himself to lift his aching head to meet the barkeep's eye as he passed the scrap of parchment.

The man glanced at it too briefly before giving Cinn a thorough appraisal.

"You a tourist?"

Cinn frowned, unfamiliar with the word. Or if he did know it, he couldn't think of its meaning as the smell of stew and ale sent his head spinning.

"Are you going to Ahrenhale?" the man asked slower, as if that would help.

Cinn nodded, the movement exacerbating the throbbing in his temple.

"You got money?"

He shook his head, reaching for the note to show him the part that promised Wyldeden would compensate anyone who required it, but the man tossed the parchment back at him.

"What about the dagger? Looks nice."

Cinn's heart stuttered, hand dropping to the scabbard at his hip.

No. Never.

The barkeep saw the answer in Cinn's eyes and inclined his chin toward the door. "Then get out. I ain't a charity."

One of the other men at the table stood. "Daryn."

"No, I'm sick of this!" The barkeep slammed a hand against the door-turned-bar, ranting in a language Cinn didn't understand.

Holding onto the door to keep his balance, he looked to the patrons, hoping one might help him. Loan him some coins, or share their drink, or *something*. But as the barkeep went on, each of them ducked their heads. The man who'd stood up resumed his seat, refusing to meet Cinn's eye.

"Get out," the barkeep repeated in Nirnish.

The words rang hollow in Cinn's ears, their implication taking too long to sink in. At his hesitation, the man stormed around the bar and grabbed Cinn's arm.

It was all he could do to keep his feet under him, snatching the note off the counter and his pack from the floor as the barkeep dragged him to the door and threw him out. Landing on top of his pack, the sharp corner of his trinket box rammed his ribs hard enough to crack them, breath leaving his body in a pained wheeze.

The door slammed, low muttering breaking out inside.

Cinn rolled onto his back and pressed a hand against his fractured ribs, bones already shifting back into place.

The Copelands had spoiled him into forgetting that humans were usually raging assholes.

One of the horses trotted the length of its leash to stand over him, its long face blocking out the light from the tavern.

Please don't kick me, he begged silently, closing his eyes.

The animal's hot breath huffed against his face, but it decided to leave him be and return to the hay piled against the tavern wall.

Relief made Cinn dizzy as he watched the gentle beast, but as the muttering inside shifted back to drunken chatter, he scowled.

He could be an asshole, too.

Grunting as he climbed to his feet, Cinn hobbled toward the horses. They were still saddled. Watching him carefully as he approached, they let him brush a hand against their hide all the way to the saddlebags. Inside the first he found a sack of sunflower seeds to add to his shrinking traveler's rations, as well as a pair of thick socks, a checkered red-and-white cotton scarf, and finally, an empty waterskin.

Maybe it was petty, but he bit down on the leather and chewed until he wore a decent hole before putting the waterskin back.

The second horse's bag contained strips of jerky wrapped in muslin and a loose copper coin that he quickly pocketed.

A new sound stilled his hand. Turning to where the second horse had its head ducked low in the shadows, Cinn's eyes widened at the sight of a rusty trough filled with cloudy water.

Dropping to his knees, Cinn plunged his hands into the lukewarm liquid and brought some to his lips. The first touch on his parched tongue elicited a crackling cry. Tempted to dunk his whole head in, Cinn drank as much as his distending stomach could hold, then filled his canteen, regretting his pettiness with the waterskin he could have stolen if he'd noticed the trough a moment earlier.

The door swung open. Cinn froze.

Quick enough not to be seen but not so quick he'd draw attention, Cinn crawled into the shadows behind the trough and made himself as small as possible.

The porch creaked. Boots scuffed the sand. Cinn peeked over the lip of the trough to where one of the tavern's patrons had halted in front of Cinn's pack which he'd stupidly left in the middle of the road.

Leave it and go away, he begged silently.

"Kid?" It wasn't the barkeep; the voice belonged to the man who'd spoken against Daryn. "Look, I don't have any money, but I've got some water and I can take you to Ahrenhale in the morning."

Chewing his lip, he leaned out farther, trying to decide if this was some new human trick or whether the man looked trustworthy. The closest horse shuffled back, eying Cinn nervously. The movement caught the man's attention, his gaze sweeping the shadows.

Cinn shrank back again, but as heavy boots plodded in his direction, he knew he'd been caught. Shifting his weight, he pulled the dagger from his hip.

The man's boots scuffed as he came to a quick stop. Cinn

peeked again, only to find him far too close, hands raised, and eyes locked on the dull glint of the steel-and-silver weapon.

"Hey, kid."

With his tone soft and wary, Cinn was reminded of the way William had spoken to him that day he finally came out of the forest—like he was a spooked horse, to be approached carefully. Maybe he looked as wild and feral as he had back then. He was certainly as desperate.

"Sorry about Daryn. He's got *feelings* about Ahrenhale tourists." The man took a step closer. "Looks like you've had a rough trip so far. Like I said, I'm riding out in the morning. I can take you on the back of Pretty, if you like."

The man slowly reached inside his vest and pulled out a waterskin, holding it out for Cinn, whose eyes flickered quickly to the trough.

Wrinkling his nose, the man put the waterskin away again. "That desperate, huh?"

When Cinn didn't answer, the man went to his horse. It only took a moment to realize his jerky was gone.

"Helped yourself, I see."

Cinn knew what happened to thieves. Lunging from his hiding place, he made a dash for his pack.

The man swore. "It's fine! I was going to give it to you anyway!"

The shout was swallowed by the empty night as Cinn snatched his pack from the ground and fled back to the desert. Or tried to. A heavy body tackled him from behind, dagger slipping through his fingers to skid across the sand.

Instinct took over: elbows, knees, teeth.

The man grabbed hold of any part of Cinn he could, grunting and cursing as Cinn hit all the tender places.

"I'm not— Stop, would you? Ow! Did you— Did you just bite

me?!"

The man pulled his hand back and Cinn managed to squirm out from under him.

"Fine! Mother above, you can walk another week for all I care!" The man groaned as he got upright. "I'm not stopping to bury your body when I pass it."

Another week.

The thought stopped him mid stride.

Obviously he would survive it, but . . . A week with nothing but his own head for company? A week just to get to Ahrenhale, and then gods knew how long to track down Moyra. To get the answers he needed, then all the way back to Eaon.

Clutching the willow charm around his neck, Cinn didn't think he could do it. He'd lose his mind.

Sheepishly, he turned back and grimaced at the man fussing over his bleeding arm. After retrieving his knife and sliding it away, Cinn approached slowly, bringing out the muslin-wrapped jerky. The man stilled as he noticed, raising an eyebrow at the peace offering.

"You know, not a lot of people out here give help for free. I should make you walk."

Cinn sighed, dropping his arm with a nod.

Yet the man didn't leave. Narrowing his eyes, he blew out a harsh breath through his teeth before extending a hand.

"Donnivan."

Cinn touched his mouth and shook his head before taking Donnivan's hand in an embarrassingly weak grip.

"You don't talk, huh? Well, that's preferable to some of the company I've had in the past. Keep the jerky, kid. Put something in your belly and I'll meet you back here at sunup. Alright?"

Cinn smiled, hoping Donnivan hadn't noticed his lips were already healing, soft and unbroken again.

CHAPTER 3

CINN

In the early daylight, Cinn almost didn't recognize Donnivan as he came to wake his horse. Face leathered from a lifetime in the sun, it was hard to tell if the human was the oldest Cinn had ever met or just looked it. His bleached hair sat under a wide-brimmed hat, a white cotton scarf pulled up around his mouth and nose; the wrinkling around the man's eyes was the only sign he was still happy to see Cinn waiting by the water trough.

"Let's get going before the other folks realize you've robbed them blind, shall we?" he said with a deep chuckle.

Hoisting himself into the saddle, Donnivan's grip was strong on Cinn's forearm as he helped him up. The saddle wasn't comfortable, the height dizzying and too reminiscent of riding Kaelean's lupanis form for Cinn's liking.

When Pretty started moving, Cinn had to grab the back of Donnivan's vest to keep himself from sliding off.

"Plenty of time to find your sea legs, kid. Hold on tight."

~

It took an hour for Cinn to find the courage to let go of Donnivan's vest, and even then, it was out of necessity. The horse's hooves kicked up loose sand with every gallop, and at the speed they travelled, every grain was a shard of glass against his face. Pulling the checkered scarf from his pocket, he wrapped it around his mouth and nose.

Noon brought with it another ramshackle town. Another tavern. Cinn stayed with Pretty at the water trough while Donnivan "made his rounds." The desert was beginning to change; some kind of tall, leafless shrub was baking in the heat, a rabbit carcass rotting underneath. It wasn't much, but it was life adjacent.

A few more hours of riding and they stopped again, the road increasingly defined as the towns grew larger. Only in physical size, though. The lack of people, of noise, was poignant, many of the adobe-block houses beginning to crumble from lack of upkeep. Of the few humans remaining, all had deep age lines creasing their weary faces.

"You'd never believe these places used to be thriving," Donnivan broke their companionable silence as the sun moved lower in the sky. "When witches lived in the desert, people would travel from all over the bay to get their palms read or whatnot. Future telling, ailment tending, fixing up little spells to keep a stray home. Now look. Place as barren as my old lady's womb."

Cinn wasn't entirely sure what he was talking about, glad his position on the back of the horse meant Donnivan couldn't see his face wrinkle in confusion. The man went on, oblivious.

"Must have been fifty or fifty-five years ago, thereabouts. One day, just all the witches packed up and left. All of them! Big storm brewing, people said. Nothing else could do it. Now, Ahrenhale gets the tourists that used to keep these towns alive. Only the stubborn ones stayed. Like my folks. And when they passed, I stayed too. But my old lady convinced me to make the big move. Not inside the city, we ain't got the money for that, but a town just outside will do us fine."

Cinn let out a breath. No wonder the barkeep had a stick up his ass about "tourists."

"Old lady has a friend who's a witch; said the path is set now, or something of the sorts. You know how them witches talk. Told us staying south was a death sentence, and she wasn't keen to see us end like that. So, I sent the missus up a few weeks ago with most our things while I finished up business. Guessing you must have heard something similar. Then again, you don't really look like you're from these parts. Too pale. You over from Phara? Only place that makes sense with you being this far west."

Cinn shook his head and found the note jammed in his pocket, passing it over Donnivan's shoulder. The human took it, read it, and passed it back.

"Can't say I ever heard of Wild-ened-en. And I don't think that note's gonna get you much in Ahrenhale. Don't know how things work where you're from, but here, we bleed gold, silver, and copper."

Even if he could find a way to speak, Cinn didn't know what to say. Donnivan settled back into silence, at least for a while. As the sky shifted into a quilt of pink and lilac clouds, he started humming a tune that only made Cinn more homesick.

Just as night truly settled, they reached yet another town. This one was different. Busier, livelier, but not in a good way.

Cinn would know what a guard looked like no matter what they called a uniform.

Horse-drawn carts like the one he'd refused to ride on wove through the streets, coming and going down the many intersecting roads. Stopping each and every one was a guard covered head to toe in white linens, silver-and-steel weapons strapped to every limb.

"This has been getting worse," Donnivan said quietly. "Ever since the witches migrated, the powers that be got real strict about checking people coming from the south. Ain't nobody been turned away, as far as I know, but best to just do what they say."

Everything about the witch who'd gotten him to Qiri was fuzzy, but he remembered something about going to prison for bringing in southerners. Not people like Donnivan, but people like *him*.

Mouth dry, Cinn tugged on the man's vest.

"Easy, kid. We're stopping soon."

Cinn tugged more urgently. Donnivan turned his head, raising a brow at the panic Cinn didn't try to hide.

"Ah."

He didn't say more than that, and he didn't stop Pretty's cantering as they moved through the thoroughfare.

He was going to turn him in.

Shuffling back, Cinn prepared to jump from the saddle.

"Easy," Donnivan repeated, voice hushed as they passed a stopped cart, three guards checking it over. "Don't get twitchy on me again. You're alright."

Cinn wasn't convinced, but he kept still a little longer, one hand wrapped tightly around his knife.

Outside what appeared to be an inn, the horse slowed. A guard approached. Speaking in that same curling language Daryn the barkeep used, the guard asked a sharp question, to which Donnivan answered calmly. He jerked his thumb in Cinn's direction before dismounting, pulling a wad of folded parchment from his pocket.

As the guard read, Donnivan looked back at Cinn and winked.

More conversation Cinn didn't understand. It was one thing when he was in Wyldeden with Eaon—he was safe there, even if he had no idea what was going on most of the time—but this was different. He was not safe at all. Nerves frayed, it took all he had to remain seated, especially when the guard turned their gaze to Cinn and extended a hand expectantly.

Donnivan began arguing in a soft, beseeching voice before lowering his scarf and removing his hat. After a pointed look, Cinn let go of his knife and lowered his scarf too, sweaty hands shaking. All Cinn could see of the guard was their narrowed eyes, but exposing their faces seemed to have an effect; their next words didn't need translation, the dismissive gesture universal.

Cinn waited until their back was turned before closing his eyes against the burning relief behind them. Taking Pretty by the reins, Donnivan led the horse to where a dozen others were being brushed down before helping him off.

Standing there awkwardly, Cinn didn't know how to thank the man for not turning him over. All he could do was reach into his pocket and retrieve the copper coin he'd stolen, offering it back.

Donnivan raised a brow. "Keep it."

Turning the coin in his fingers, Cinn didn't quite dare to pocket it again. He waited for the questions, the suspicion, the blackmail.

"I wasn't lying last night. I ain't got money for a feed. Not even for me. We're only staying long enough to fill up with water, then we ride through the night. Pretty's a tough horse—gotta be out here. She can make it, and we'll be at the city gates by morning. You gonna last till then?"

Cinn blinked. Twice. Then nodded. Maybe, just maybe, there were good humans in Qiri, too.

CHAPTER 4

CINN

THERE WERE NO WALLS AROUND AHRENHALE. BRIDGES OF stone lay over a glistening moat too narrow to provide any real security, while the banks were crusted in a shimmering mosaic of green and blue that Cinn thought may be actual gemstones. Not that he had experience with such things, but the gleaming silver of the city guards' armor and the jewels glinting on their scabbards heralded the kind of wealth he hadn't even seen during his brief glimpse inside Hyrsch's palace walls.

There had been precious stone imbedded in the walls at the bleeding mountain as well, but they were there naturally, not cleaved from the bedrock the way these ones were. Such decoration would never last in Hyrsch; thieves would have picked the banks clean within days.

At the fork where a bridge met the road, Donnivan brought Pretty to a stop.

"This is where I leave you, kid."

Sliding off the back of the horse and straightening his pack, Cinn placed a hand against his chest in thanks.

"Don't go telling people I do favors for free," Donnivan warned.

With a wink, Cinn pretended to lock his lips. The man laughed and shook his head, giving a two-fingered salute before trotting away, following the path toward a bordering township.

A decent human. Cinn smiled to himself as he watched Donnivan for a while, hoping he found his way safely, but locked the feelings away when he finally turned to face the city. To assume his luck would continue would be foolish. Briefly, he considered whether he could pry loose a few gemstones to trade with, but there were too many guards nearby. And even if there weren't, it would be suspicious for someone as raggedy as him to be carrying such things. Offer them to the wrong person and they may turn him in. Not to mention the strangeness of the gemstones existing in their pretty mosaic at all; if they were worth anything to the people living in Ahrenhale, they would have been taken already.

Trailing a group of travelers in better condition than he, Cinn kept his eyes on his dusty boots as they passed patrolling guards. It was a miracle he could hear anything through the blood pounding in his ears, but he could have sworn one was making a joke, the other shaking with building laughter. Relaxed. At ease. So different to the guards who'd searched them in the outer towns, as if the idea of a threat reaching the city never crossed their minds.

Nobody stopped him as Cinn reached the other end of the bridge and took his first step into Ahrenhale.

Stalls bordered the streets, selling colorful souvenirs that screamed for Cinn's attention. Behind them, sea-weathered limestone houses with patterned banners hanging over doorways were so tightly crammed together that the alleys between would barely let a stray cat squeeze through.

The travelers he trailed shot suspicious looks over their shoulders, whispering, so Cinn fell back to peruse the trinkets at the nearest stall. Masses of people meandered by, a large number sporting shimmering constellation tattoos on their foreheads. The sight took him back to the prison beneath Pirevia. To that horrible moment Prince Nevan had threatened Eaon and Eavha, and Cinn had been made to choose between them and his silence. Back to Yomra, who had called him by his name. Not only the given name he'd left behind in Hyrsch, the one that belonged to a boy who didn't exist anymore, but also the surname his mother had given him. The one nobody in the world should know.

Cinn clutched his pack straps and kept his eyes on people's hands, wary of thieves as he followed the breezy sound of flutes deeper into the city.

The residents of Ahrenhale frowned as he passed, sweat- and sand-stained clothes worn and smelly. As was he; it had been a while since he'd had the chance to bathe properly. Still, nobody accosted him. Nobody called for guards. They simply averted their eyes and gave him more space on the sidewalk.

As the stalls and houses gave way to official storefronts, Cinn looked in the crystal-clear windows of a bakery with ravenous envy. After the tavern debacle, he wouldn't bother trying his note here, opting instead to squeeze down the narrow gap between buildings that let out into a backroad alley.

Considering the places he'd roamed in Hyrsch, Ahrenhale's alleys were obnoxiously clean. Yet, even here, trash had to go somewhere. Large bins lined the sea-weathered walls and, after lifting a few lids, Cinn grinned at the bakery rejects piled inside. Easing his pack down and keeping one eye on the back door of the bakery, he loaded it with as many burnt pastries and broken biscuits as he could fit. Too many years scavenging for meals in dirtier places than this meant that, even as he took his first bite of a charcoal-crusted fruit bun, a moan escaping at the sweetness of it on his tongue, he didn't turn his back to the door. A baker could come out any moment and he had to be ready to run.

Holding the bun between his teeth so he could once more shoulder his pack, Cinn returned to the main street as fast as his tired feet could take him.

For such a busy place, there was a noticeable lack of urgency among its civilians who frowned at Cinn's rushing. Buskers played peaceful music while stall owners gently encouraged passersby to try their products. Wide-eyed children gawked at the crystals and colorful desserts on display, and none of the owners shooed them away.

Cinn forced himself to slow, growing accustomed to the easy pace, when a chorus of angry shouts rang through the street. Dropping his bun and reaching for his dagger, Cinn put his back to the nearest wall.

"One people! One Nir! One war!"

The chant repeated, the crowd parting to make way for a large group of protesters marching in the middle of the road with large poles. Not weapons, but banners.

Furrowing his brow, Cinn tried to read a few words: 'down' was one, while another looked like 'war' but with a 'd' on the end. War-d?

"Fools!"

Cinn flinched against the wall as a man pushed through the crowd to stand in front of the cloaked demonstrators. Crouching low, Cinn kept his eyes trained on the scene and searched for his dropped bun.

"You want to see this city burn so bad, keep it up!"

"One people!"

"Those of us smart enough to keep the only thing protecting us from what's brewing down south aren't—"

"One Nir!"

"—going to just let you bring down the wards!"

"One war!"

The man who'd stepped into the street didn't move as the front lines reached him. The demonstrators didn't stop. Cinn flinched again at the meaty sound of bodies colliding, then shuffled farther down the wall as other bystanders called out in anger, a brawl breaking out.

Those who didn't get involved muttered under their breath in that same language Cinn didn't know, making way for the converging guards who were drawing batons.

Cinn knew better than to wait around.

Whatever drama Qiri had going on was none of his business. He only needed to find someone to ask about Moyra.

Guards roamed the streets in pairs, and Cinn waited until he was far enough away from the protest that the ones he approached seemed relaxed. Plastering a shaky smile on his face, he clutched Eaon's note in his hand.

"Est vu rama trchasty?" one of the men wearing purple brocade asked as Cinn stopped directly in their path.

Swallowing nervously, he held out the note. The one who hadn't spoken took it, read it, shrugged, and handed it back. Without another word, they continued their patrol and didn't look back.

Cinn's smile faltered as he watched them go.

Not holding on to a lot of hope, he continued down the streets. Most civilians wouldn't meet his eye, and those who did quickly darted away in fear of being approached. One man gave Cinn a nod before averting his eyes, so Cinn quickened his steps after him.

Tapping the man on the shoulder, Cinn tried to hand him the note.

"Ni, ni." The man shook his head and hands, backing away. "Ni dusha. Ni dusha."

Letting him go, Cinn swallowed his frustration, searching the faces of the crowd for anyone willing to help.

After hours of wandering around, face flushed and eyes burning, only one person stopped to read his note.

"Nirnish?" they asked, raising an eyebrow.

Cinn's breath shuddered in his chest as he nodded, clasping his hands together. *Please.*

"I wish I could help, but I don't know any of these names. You could try asking a way-finder, but . . ." The woman gave him a purse-lipped appraisal. "Their services can be expensive. I'm guessing you don't have dusha. Money."

A way-finder. Cinn didn't know what that was, but it was a lead. It was *something.*

Pointing to the part of the note that said Wyldeden would compensate them, Cinn wasn't surprised that the woman simply shook her head.

"Never heard of it, and honestly, nobody here will work for a promise. You'll need gold coins. A lot of them."

Taking a long, steadying breath, Cinn nodded. This place wasn't so different to Hyrsch, and he knew how to make money if he really needed to.

The woman started to walk away, but Cinn reached for her, a deep frown on his face.

"Please don't touch me," she said firmly, eyeing his dirty nails. But she stopped walking.

Cinn raised his hands in apology but didn't know how to communicate his question. Pointing at the woman, he made the sign for "speak," which he hoped was obvious enough. Then, silently, he enunciated the words "way-finder."

"Way-finder? Where in the world are you from if you don't know what a way-finder is?" She wrinkled her nose, glancing around the street, eager to be on her way. "The houses with the blue banners and a compass insignia. That means a way-finder lives there and is open for business."

Clasping his hands together to express his gratitude, he let the woman leave.

The sun burned a deep orange as it inched lower on the horizon, heavy clouds a shield against its oppressive heat. Leaning against the nearest building, Cinn shivered at the dropping temperature. Night was coming; he needed to think about shelter, but without money, his options were limited.

Heading down another narrow alley where workers were depositing the day's waste into bins, he lurked in the shadows, waiting. He had enough burnt rolls in his pack to get him by for a while, but as he eyed the vegetable scraps in the nearest bin, he knew they would give him more lasting energy.

The alley grew quiet.

Finally, he slipped out of the shadows and pulled back the lid of the nearest bin.

"Hey!"

That's all it took. The lid clattered to the ground as, without waiting to see who had spotted him, Cinn ran.

Down the alley, he took a left at the fork and sprinted to the next gap between buildings. The main road had emptied out too, so he ran and ran until his lungs burned and his knees threatened to snap. Another gap, another backstreet alley. Fleeing until he rounded another bend, he glanced back, the winding alley dark and silent. He hadn't been followed.

Slowing, laughter swelled in his chest. He swallowed it as he turned to grin at Rad and Eddy.

It took a heartbeat for the shock to register.

Wrong city. Wrong time.

Grief hit him like a hammer to the gut. Crouching low, he tucked his head between his knees and focused on catching his breath.

Why did this keep happening?

Why couldn't he keep his head straight?

Why couldn't he shove everything away like he used to?

He still couldn't believe he'd told Eaon about them. Couldn't believe he'd allowed himself to recall their names. To let them become more than distant figments of imagination. To let the questions wringing his heart raw crowd his thoughts.

What happened to them? The princess couldn't have discovered them, or they'd have been used against him; but were they safe? Were they still in Hyrsch? Did they remember him, or had they accepted his disappearance and let him become a figment of their imaginations, too?

Why couldn't he stop thinking about them? For months, everything from *before* had ceased to exist. There had been nothing but *now*, this moment, this breath, this immediate problem to solve in order to stay free. But now . . .

Now his entire life was trying to squeeze back into the very narrow space in the forefront of his mind.

How many times had he slipped the flimsy restraints keeping Master Ackford's slaves in the house at night? How many hours had he spent crawling the streets with his adopted siblings, ransacking trash cans for scraps? Lumps of stale bread, moldy vegetables, meats with a slimy film—the kind of spoil that was no issue for a kinner. Nor an issue for starving demi-kin, who'd spend an hour or two with cramps then be alright, enough food in their bellies to keep from fainting the next day.

But at certain times of the year, the bakery would have more than stale bread for him to take back to the others—broken shortbread, burnt ginger snaps, and misshapen cinnamon biscuits deemed unworthy for sale. The adults had feasted on the shortbread and ginger snaps, but the Triple R Threat had curled up together in front of the kitchen fireplace, making themselves giddy on cinnamon biscuits as they listened to the carolers outside.

For a fleeting moment, only those perfect nights existed. For a second, he thought he could hear the carolers again. Could feel the warmth of the fire and the knobby bodies curled up against him, the smell of sugar and cinnamon on their breath.

It made him think of the jar in Sarah's kitchen.

Of the reason he'd been in Sarah's kitchen to begin with.

No amount of swallowing could loosen the knot in his tight throat. No amount of blinking could clear the hot prickling behind his eyes.

It was easier to let himself forget than to think of the people he'd left behind, but every day that went by, the self-imposed amnesia became harder to hold onto.

CHAPTER 5

CINN

"HEY!"

Instead of the sun or morning sounds of bakers, Cinn startled awake to a shout and a kick to the ribs. Eyes crusted and head foggy with sleep, the late morning heat baking his scalp, he scrambled to his feet and found himself cornered between a guard, the wall, and a bin. Behind the guard, a sweaty baker scowled. Cinn's stomach twisted at the sight of his pack in the baker's arms.

"His bag is full of stolen food."

The guard's brow furrowed. One large, hairy hand came up to shield his eyes against the bright sun, the other drifting toward a set of shackles hanging from his belt.

Ice flooded Cinn's veins, breath freezing in his lungs. His own fingers twitched, brushing against his hip where his dagger ought to be.

Gone.

The guard's tone was soft as he said, "It's alright, kid. Let's get you somewhere we can talk. Find out where you're supposed to be."

Cinn struggled to drag in a breath. To clear his screaming head. There would be trouble if the guard realized he was from south of the wards, but maybe . . . Maybe this guard would help him.

With the edge of the bin digging into his shoulder blades, Cinn pointed at his pack with one hand and pressed the fingers of his other to his lips, shaking his head and hoping they understood that he couldn't speak. If he could just show them the note in his pack . . .

The guard lunged for his wrist, pulling the shackles from his belt.

Cinn ducked, heart in his throat, and rammed his entire body into the guard. Shock sent the bigger man sprawling. Scrambling to his feet, Cinn dived for his pack, but the baker didn't want to give it up, grabbing a fistful of Cinn's dusty shirt instead.

"Thieving little—" he started, but the insult was cut short by Cinn's forehead smashing into his nose.

Blood sprayed everywhere and the baker cried out, releasing the bag to clutch his face. A punch to the man's wrist convinced him to let go of Cinn's shirt, but the guard had recovered and snatched his arm, twisting it up behind Cinn's back.

Cold metal clamped around his wrist. The world went still. A high ringing echoed in his ears until he could taste metal on his teeth.

Wrenching his body around, oblivious to the crack of his bones breaking, the socket dislocating, tendons snapping until the limb was useless, Cinn clenched his other fist and jabbed it into the guard's throat. The man's horror-stricken face blanched, releasing Cinn's arm to hold his throat, wheezing haggardly.

To be safe, Cinn kicked out the guard's knee. Spotting his

scabbard tied to the man's belt, he took it back and turned to the baker, who was halfway down the alley, calling for help.

Leather scabbard scraping the canvas as he scooped up his pack, Cinn sprinted the opposite way.

Out the alley, down the street; he was blind to the civilians who screamed and jumped out the way, numb to the pain of his broken bones scraping against each other.

Darting into another alley, he dropped his knife, dumped his pack, and took a moment to catch his breath. To twist his arm back into place, the socket *popping* loudly. The itching started immediately as torn ligaments repaired themselves, bones welding back together. At the sight of the cuff locked around his wrist, the length of chain dangling to where a second cuff waited to imprison him, Cinn's vision went spotty, the world spinning.

Succumbing to gravity, he dropped to his knees, then onto all fours as he gagged on the bile at the back of his throat. There were no rocks laying loose in the alley, so he shifted around until his booted foot hovered over his splayed hand.

Gritting his teeth and turning away, he stomped down.

Again, and again, and again.

Fragile bones shattered until his hand was mangled and flaccid, enough so to squeeze through the cuff.

Vision blurring, he spat at the chain and kicked the contraption across the alley, cradling his itchy hand. The crawling of a thousand fire ants beneath his skin was almost worse than the breaking, but he didn't let it distract him. He had to move. The guard and whoever else the baker rallied would be looking for him.

~

Slipping down alleys, avoiding the public as much as possible, he wound his way through the maze of Ahrenhale until the sun began its descent. There was a deeply shadowed alcove on the side of a building that seemed like as good a place as any to stop. He didn't know or care what the building was, just that there were very few people around.

His hand and arm had healed, but every time he looked away from the perfect skin of his wrist, he swore he could still feel the shackle there. The phantom sensation a steel-and-leather muzzle across his cheeks persisted even as he wiped at his sweaty face. Scratched it raw.

A white and ginger streak sent him flinching back into the alcove, choking on his breath. It was just a mangey cat hunting a mouse, but the sight of it exacerbated the ache in his chest. The yearning for home. For the empty fireplace and cinnamon biscuits, and for Puddles, who always knew when he needed company, and whose steady purring always calmed his frantic heartbeats when he woke in the middle of the night.

More than anything, he yearned for the low drone of Eaon's voice as he read aloud, in part to himself because he too couldn't sleep, but also in part for Cinn, who'd never felt safer than he did when he was with Eaon.

Pulling the willow amulet from around his neck, Cinn rubbed his thumb over the carving and forced himself to think about those weeks last spring. Of the forest, and Eaon's cool hands showing him how to sign. Of Eavha's gentle smile and Kaelean's watchful stare. Even Dearmead's solid presence had been a comfort, the way Radley's had been growing up.

Squeezing his eyes shut, he shook his brother's name from his head. Or tried to, but it was lodged there like a splinter. Right beside Edwina's.

Did they know he was out? Did they hate him for leaving

them? For leaving Hyrsch and everything to do with it as he fled for his life?

Still fled. Would he be running forever?

If he abandoned this mission Yomra had given him and just kept running, would they forgive him? Would Eaon?

Was there even anything beyond Qiri? Or had he put himself in another cage by coming here?

The thought set him heaving again, and when he finished emptying his stomach and rinsing his mouth with a sip of his rapidly depleting supply of water, he got to his feet.

He had to keep moving. He had to get out of this place.

How many times had he started a new life? Three?

He'd last seen his parents in the snow when he was only seven and found a new, albeit awful, life as a demi-kin slave in the city of Hyrsch. Once freed, he had started over in that tiny apartment that leaked and groaned with Rad and Eddy. When he'd come out of that hole in the ground, when he'd crawled and bled his way through the forest to somehow end up at the Copelands' farm, he had been given his third chance.

Every time, he pushed his past selves farther away, burying them so deep that only sleep reminded him of what he'd lost.

He could do it again. A new name, a new self, a new life.

Cinn looked at the willow amulet cupped in his hands. Pressed it to his lips.

Just once, just briefly.

I'm sorry.

Flipping open the top of his pack, Cinn found his trinket box and buried the amulet among his treasures. Then he secured his knife to his belt once more, wiped his face, and started walking.

Heading north, he had no goal in mind except to get as far from the southern border as possible. To keep walking until he was far enough away that he could start over.

As he stepped into the street, another band of demonstrators paraded past.

"A separate Nir is a safe Nir!"

"No wards, no way forward!"

Above all the other voices, one boomed so impossibly loud it couldn't have been natural.

"Morvia sees the bigger picture! If she wished to see us reunited with the south, she would have shown us in the stars! But she hasn't! She gave us the wards to protect us from Chaos, and those who want to see them fall are heretics!"

Just like last time, someone from the crowd stepped into the path of the protest, red in the face with rage.

"She *has* shown us we are needed in the south! You deny the truth because you are cowards!"

"Unifiers twist the visions to suit their cause!"

"That either of you think Morvia cares at all is idiotic!"

Cinn could taste violence in the air. Another fight was about to break out. Creeping along the walls, he stayed out of the way as the shouting swelled.

"Ryson!"

Cinn froze.

The name had been called as if someone was searching rather than to get his attention. Not that it mattered, because they couldn't mean him. Nobody here knew that name.

Yomra knew it, he reminded himself. And this was her homeland.

"Ryson Tacenda!"

Well, shit.

Before he could duck into an alley, a woman came shoving

her way through the crowd with wide, frantic eyes. Unlike everyone else he'd met in this city, she looked . . . unkept. Her clothes, while unnaturally bright and colorful, were dirty and torn, her feet bare. Body frail, hair matted down her back, there was no focus in her eyes as she headed right for him.

"You're here! You're here, you're here, thank the stars you're here. This way now. This way. Come on. Come this way now. This way. Come on."

He tried to walk away, but she grabbed his wrist in a viselike grip, stepping so close he could smell the sour milk on her breath.

One hand dropping to his knife, Cinn ground his teeth to keep himself from killing her right there and then. She was not a danger to him, even if her grip on his wrist was unbearable.

"You're late. So late," she continued. "The stars said you have to come now. Now, or it will be too late. *Late.* Come on. This way now."

She pulled on his wrist. His grip tightened on his dagger as he wrenched his arm away. Desperately, she made to grab him again, but stilled before she could.

"No touching," she whispered, blinking furiously. "He doesn't like the touching. No, no, no more. No more. Tell him. Okay. I'll tell him." She raised her chin, even though her eyes were looking somewhere above his head. "I should have been a way-finder. You have to listen to me."

Cinn didn't care. Not anymore. He had made his decision.

"*Please!*" Borderline hysterical, she sucked in a sharp breath. Her eyes rolled back, exposing the whites, and her voice took on a calm, patronizing quality. "Those who flee across the sea only change the sky upon them."

Shattering glass and the meaty smack of fists meeting flesh as a full-blown riot broke out in the street didn't distract the woman, who was more focused without pupils than she'd been with.

"Come."

Not a command. Not a plea.

A promise.

And maybe he hadn't really made as firm a decision as he'd thought, because that was all it took for him to take her outstretched hand.

Not so far from the riot that they couldn't hear the guards shouting for peace and order, the woman—the witch, Cinn corrected himself—stopped and pointed to a store with a horse-drawn wagon waiting out front. Her eyes had righted themselves, but the blue was so bright they were almost glowing.

He'd noticed the strangeness of some of the Ahrenhalians before—hair gold as the sun, eyes green as lime. It was usually the ones also bearing the constellation tattoos who seemed unnaturally vibrant, and not the way that could be faked with cosmetics.

He knew the difference. Had seen up close the way lips looked with false color on them, eyes darkened with kohl. The memory made him want to vomit again.

No, these peculiarities had to be magical, yet the witch before him bore no tattoo.

"This one," the witch said, wiggling her finger toward the wagon. "This is the one. This is the path to the truth. To the answers. The wagon will take you to her."

Cinn had never been truly convinced of the gods until he'd gotten to know Eaon and the others, but *this* . . . Only the divine could have sent this witch, as mad as she was, just as he was about to quit.

Nodding to the witch, Cinn bowed his head. She sagged, smiled, at his silent promise.

His moment of weakness was a humiliation he was glad nobody had witnessed. He didn't recognize the thoughts that had led him to put away the amulet. Did, but didn't; as if there was another version of himself just beneath his skin that cared nothing for love, for friendship and family, loyalty and promises. A version that was only motivated by fear.

Cinn didn't like that side of himself. At all.

As inconspicuously as possible, he approached the small wagon just as a man finished loading wooden crates, bolting the rear upright before mounting his horse. Considering how the last week in Qiri had gone, Cinn doubted asking for a ride would go well, but there were too many people around for him to sneak aboard unnoticed.

As if she knew, and Cinn suspected somehow she did, the mad witch began screaming at the top of her lungs, cursing the cloudless sky. Everyone in the vicinity turned to stare.

Without wasting a second, he shoved his pack in first, then climbed over the back of the wagon. Pitched like a tent, the sheet of taut canvas enclosing the space provided both shade and privacy as he tucked himself between two crates and peeked back out. The witch was still screaming at the sky, but the crowd was moving on as if this happened every day.

A part of Cinn wished he could help the witch find the aid she so obviously needed, but she wouldn't accept it. He'd promised to go. And besides, he was barely capable of helping himself.

CHAPTER 6

CINN

YOMRA'S INSTRUCTIONS HAD BEEN VERY CLEAR: "GO TO *Ahrenhale. Find Moyra Thorne,*" but it wasn't until the wagon left the bright city, all its noise falling away, that Cinn realized those were two separate sentences. Two separate instructions. There had been no promise that Moyra would be in Ahrenhale.

Sweat slid down the narrow groove of his spine, sticking to his already crusty shirt. How far would the wagon take him? Where was he going? How would he get back?

Making a conscious effort not to fret as the hours passed, Cinn snacked on another burnt pastry, sipping at water that would have to last him gods knew how long. The man talked to his horse the whole time, but Cinn didn't understand a word. Which was fine, because there wasn't room in his head for words anyway.

The wagon tilted and began to rock, path deteriorating as they descended a gravelly hill. Trees shaded the canvas in an intricate shadow pattern, while the pungent smell of algae and stale water wrinkled Cinn's nose. Peeking over the lip of the wagon, the world had softened—a comforting quiet, muffled by dull foliage and a blanket of gum nuts.

The man called for his horse to slow. Before he could be caught, Cinn shouldered his pack and leapt off the wagon, rolling into a nearby bush.

A thorny bush.

Fuck. Everything.

A tinkling high-pitched laugh made him freeze.

Eyes narrowing, he scanned the thick bushland, but there was nothing but dry leaves and thistles under the patchy canopy. He carefully disentangled himself, picking thorns and splinters from his skin, but aside from the wind rustling a stray dandelion, the bushland was quiet again.

On high alert, Cinn moved farther down the hill to a cluster of briny boulders. From there, he could better take in the village he'd been brought to.

No, not a village. It wasn't big enough to be called that.

Four desolate houses sagged in the sand bordering a murky green lake that rippled all the way to the horizon. Brown ducks paddled in the water alongside a single swan, but otherwise there was a stillness to the scenery that was both comforting and perturbing. Nature undisturbed. Even the crumbling mud-brick houses with their mossy verandas and lichen-crusted steps had surrendered to the wild.

The delivery man stopped outside the nearest house, dismounted his horse, and hauled a crate from the back. The front door opened. A woman stepped onto the porch.

Moyra. It had to be.

Dressed in a sleeveless white blouse tucked into a long homespun skirt, she appeared no older than a thirty-year old human. Her frizzy hair was cut short, blunt, as if it had been hacked off with a dull blade. The color made him think of the dirty straw he once slept on in the Copelands' barn, the musty, phantom smell cloying his nose as he watched Moyra take the crate from the man. They held a brief conversation, and after he left, Moyra dragged the crate inside and closed the door. Cinn waited until the wagon was well on its way back to Ahrenhale before brushing his hands on his pants and retrieving the note Eaon had written for him.

This was it.

Moyra would know how to help him. How to get him home again. The thought of this awful journey nearly being over left him trembling as he navigated the eroded path down to the lake's edge.

The steps creaked under his weight as he climbed the veranda. Smoke and mold tickled his nose, barely disguised by the thick and tangled herb garden. Raising a shaking fist, he knocked on the door.

One breath. Two, and her footsteps padded along wooden floors. The door opened.

Cinn couldn't stop staring at her eyes. Two rose-quartz irises framed in golden rings. Eyes like that weren't normal. Weren't human. The constellation on her forehead confirmed it.

"Qies?"

Her voice was soft but her tone clipped, as if his mere presence annoyed her. Clearing his throat, Cinn handed her the note.

Frowning suspiciously, she took it. Read it.

Twice.

"Gah! Nirnish." She handed the note back. "A tourist then. Tell me, are you lost? Does this look like Teller's Avenue to you? No. Nobody is stupid enough to think this is there. So, you must believe it's okay to knock on strange people's doors asking for things. Well, it's not. It's rude. You are rude, and you can get off my porch. Right now. Go. Shoo."

Cinn frowned, shaking his head, pointing to Yomra's name.

"I don't know who that is. And I don't know what a Wil-did-dideden is either, however you're supposed to say that ridiculous word. And even if you were a paying customer, I would still tell you to *go away*."

With that, she stepped back and slammed the door in his face.

Cinn's breath rushed out of him, not quite sure what had just happened. Clearly, she didn't understand why he was here.

He knocked again and the door flew open.

"You entitled, presumptuous brat!" Her wrath was palpable. Cinn stepped back off the veranda and raised his hands. "How dare you. I said, *go away*! Knock on my door again and I will curse you until . . ."

She trailed off at the sight of Cinn pulling his knife from its scabbard.

He didn't know what to do, but he refused to believe he had made it this far, had been guided here by so many witches, for nothing.

Dropping to his knees, he offered her the dagger. With his other hand, he desperately searched his pocket for the copper coin he'd stolen from the drunks in the dessert. They were the only things of worth he had.

Moyra blinked. "Onribleq."

The force of the slamming door sent a tile sliding off the roof to shatter at the bottom of the steps.

～

Sitting on the sand where water lapped at the land, Cinn stared at the horizon and the sun slowly setting behind it. From the moment the door had shut in his face that final time, there had been nothing but silence in his head, not a single part of him having any clue what to do now.

Untethered in every sense of the word, there was nobody to turn to. Nowhere to go. Was he supposed to turn around and walk all the way back to that crack in the mountain just to tell Eaon he had failed? That there were no answers in Ahrenhale, only civil discord and struggle?

The Northern Mountains felt like a dream. A figment of his imagination; like the brush of Eaon's lips on his cheek. So did the Copelands, who he'd uprooted and ruined before abandoning in witch territory. He wasn't sure he remembered their faces. Did Sarah have blue eyes or brown? Were William's hands warm or cold when he mussed Cinn's hair after a day in the fields?

Had he made them up entirely? Had he imagined this whole new life? The forest, the witches, the magic—what if none of it was real? What if the truth was unbearable; that he was still beneath the palace dungeons in Hyrsch, completely insane.

No. The brine coating the back of his throat as he drew deep breaths of humid air, the lake water creeping up to soak his worn-out boots, was too real. It wasn't something he could make up.

But what if this was what Yomra had meant? What if her instructions to come to Ahrenhale, to find Moyra, was so that she could turn him away and he would be far enough from everything to see a different way out?

Not this again, he scolded himself, burying his head in his knees, trying to banish thoughts of running away again.

That mad witch, or whatever deity had spoken through her

at that moment, was right. No matter how far he ran, it wouldn't change anything that mattered.

It wouldn't stop *her* from finding him.

He couldn't outrun her. And he couldn't fight her. He'd tried for several years, and it had gotten him nowhere. Bound together in pain and fear, she had his life in her fist, the blood she drew spilling onto everyone he cared about.

He had abandoned them before. In the field in Vertlyn, when Kaelean had betrayed them, Cinn had turned his back on Eaon and Eavha and fled. It hadn't been a conscious decision, and they'd never spoken of it, but he knew what he'd done. What he'd almost done again in Ahrenhale.

It wasn't who he wanted to be, but he didn't know what to do.

And as the sun kissed the water, Cinn went around and around in circles, getting absolutely nowhere.

CHAPTER 7

MOYRA

IT WAS TELLING OF HOW OVERDUE SHE WAS TO CLEAN THE windows that, as Moyra peered through the lacy curtains in her kitchen, the tourist sulking by the lake was nothing but a blur of black hair and dirty linen. She scowled at him as she moved to fill the kettle at the sink, turning the tap with a little more force than necessary. A single drop of water balanced on the edge of the rusty steel pipe before falling with a pathetic *plop*.

"Nena," Moyra hissed, moving the kettle so she could dip her head and peer up the pipe. "Stop messing around."

A high-pitched chitter echoed through the pipe before the plumbing began to groan and rattle.

"Nena! Out!"

The pipes rattled again, and Moyra barely moved her head out of the way as water gushed from the faucet. Before the sprite haunting her plumbing could block it up again, Moyra filled the kettle, slammed it on the stove top, and found the fresh box of matches from the monthly delivery sitting on her dining table.

It had been days since her last cup of tea, and the lake-sprite knew it. Was risking Moyra's wrath by delaying her even a moment.

As the water began to simmer, she peered out the window once more and grumbled under her breath at the tourist still sitting there.

"Ugh," she spat before returning to the crate, digging through it for tea leaves and a jar of honey.

After being trapped in the house for so long, one would think she'd be better at rationing her supplies, but even in Ahrenhale some things could not be predicted. Like the pettiness of a certain faerie who, after destroying the last of her tea in a petulant fit, had been smart enough to keep their distance the last few days. But, with Gatty gone, the sprites were running rampant, using up the very last of Moyra's patience.

After brewing her tea, she took the porcelain cup to the veranda where she could sit in her wicker rocking chair to watch the sunset. And the tourist pacing morosely along the shore.

It had been a long time since she had spoken to a sensible person besides the delivery man. Fae made poor houseguests, and her clients were not usually lucid, so as she sipped her tea she wondered if she had been too harsh with the boy.

The hot brew warmed her belly, relaxing the tension in her shoulders. As she rocked herself, she wracked her memory for the name Yomra. It was an old, distinctly Qiri gem, but wasn't one belonging to anyone she knew. Or at least she didn't think so. The twenty-two years she'd lived as a free citizen were clouded with grief, and the fifty-five years she'd spent stuck in this house since then had done nothing to keep her mind sharp.

Did it really matter if she knew the witch who'd sent the tourist looking for her, though? The fact of the matter was that *someone* had sent him. Someone who thought she, out of all the Morvish witches in all the world, was the one he needed to see.

"Lover damn me," she muttered, drinking deeply. "No. I don't care. We're not doing this."

A breeze cooled summer's bite on her cheeks, the low sun reflecting off the water in ribbons of gold. The silence lasted a moment longer before the familiar call of cicadas begun to swell.

"No," she insisted, shaking her head at the darkening shore. "Absolutely not. We are not getting involved. It never ends well for us, and Mother knows we have suffered enough in this lifetime."

The tourist was lost in his head, kicking absently at the shallows. If she were lucky, the selkies that lived beneath the rippling surface would grab him. Remove the problem before she could convince herself that *not* finding out why Yomra sent him was a mistake.

"If Gatty were here, he would say to ignore him. Let him wander back to Willy-whatever. So that is what we're going to do."

It was a lie. If Gatty were here, he would be sticking his nose into any bit of gossip he could find. For fifty-five years, he had stuck by Moyra's side, looking at the same old view day after day. A stranger with a mysterious note was the kind of entertainment Gatty was always nagging for.

Draining the dregs of her tea, she placed the cup on the deck and rocked herself again, tapping her fingers on the wicker arms of the chair.

What to do.

"What to do, what to do, what to do."

By the time the tourist paced back around to the house and noticed her sitting on the porch, she had almost made a decision. They stared at each other with only the cicadas between them, until finally, Moyra stood and gave him a more thorough appraisal than she'd bothered with before. He didn't give off any bad vibes, so, with an exasperated huff, she retrieved her teacup and inclined her chin.

"Well, don't just stand there. Are you coming in or not?"

PART II

SCIAMACHY

CHAPTER 8

MOYRA

WHILE THE TOURIST WASHED HIMSELF, MOYRA THORNE LIT A few lanterns to beat back the night. She had not had a new client in fifty-five years and technically wasn't meant to be practicing her craft at all, but the other unifiers had smuggled tarot cards and crystals to her when she'd first been sentenced to this stinking cabin. After moving the crate delivered earlier, she arranged her cards in preparation and put together a bunch of holy basil and jasmine from the garden, laying them in a clay dish to burn.

By the time the boy emerged, she was ready to get this over with. The plainness of his depthless black hair and mottled green-blue eyes marked him as human, and she hadn't worked with humans since . . . well, ever. They were boring, and she had been too well off during her youth to warrant fleecing them of coins for promises of an average life and mediocre success.

"Stand still and let me look at you," she told him, drawing in deep lungsful of the floral incense designed to focus her crown and third eye.

He held perfectly still as she assessed him, almost to the point of not breathing, and without the smell of his unwashed body permeating the cabin, it was easier to concentrate on his aura.

So much red.

Her eyebrows rose at the dark color—not the shade that emanated between lovers, but the shade that marked the kind of violent-tempered client Moyra usually steered clear of. There was a little pink flushing his hands, promising some joy in his life, but around his throat and chest flickered the pale grayish yellow of fear.

"Hmm," she hummed, pursing her lips. "Sit."

He did so with surprising grace. There was both a youthfulness and weariness in the way he stared at her with precarious hope.

Taking her own seat, Moyra cleared her throat. "Do you have anything in particular you came to see me for?"

Again, he pulled the note from his pocket and pointed to the name Yomra.

"As I said, I don't know who that is. I can do a general reading but it's not going to be anything more special than what you would have gotten from any trained witch in the city. Not without some direction."

Cinn moved his finger to point at the part of the note that explained his muteness. Moyra sighed.

"Yes, I can read. Thank you. I don't know what answers you expect me to give you without a question though."

His lips parted in mild surprise.

Pinching the bridge of her nose, Moyra grumbled under her breath, "Please don't tell me you came here without a purpose." Then louder. "Why did Yomra send you?"

With pained anticipation, Cinn shrugged.

Onribleq. Unbelievable.

She had not had nearly enough tea to deal with this.

Leaving him to ponder what he'd even come here for, Moyra went to set the kettle on the stove again. By the time she returned with a fresh brew, the boy had fetched a charcoal nib from his pack and was scratching illegibly on the back of the parchment.

Perhaps this was some new punishment sent by the council. Leaving her to rot in this festering pit wasn't enough, they had to drive her mad with this nonsense, too.

Her scoffing was cut short. With Cinn bent over his paper so intently, she spotted the shimmer of unicorn blood on the back of his neck.

"What is that?" she asked, teacup stilling halfway to her mouth.

Cinn's head whipped up, looking for danger before realizing she was staring at him. The way he immediately reached for the back of his neck, the grayish-yellow aura around his bobbing throat flaring, suggested he'd been asked about it before. Despite his reluctance, he turned his back and moved the tangle of hair obscuring the mark.

"What a strange witchmark." Moyra frowned, tilting her head. "And you can bear it? As a human?"

It was Cinn's turn to frown as he faced her once more. Slowly, he shook his head.

"You can't bear it? Is that why you're here?"

He blinked rapidly, waving a hand from side to side while also shaking his head again. It took Moyra a moment to realize what he was trying to say.

"You're not human."

Putting her teacup down, she took another whiff of the incense and leaned forward. "May I see your palm?"

He hesitated, the fear in his aura growing until it overshadowed the joy, pushing out most of the anger too. But he held out his hand, trembling as she took it.

Turned it over. Flipped it back.

"You have no lines."

It was clear from the vacant way he stared at her that he did not understand how bizarre that was. She released his hand, surprised by the ferocity with which he withdrew it.

Not just a boring human after all.

Taking the parchment he'd been writing on, she could barely make out sensible letters let alone a word.

"You did not write the other note." She pulled it closer, squinting at the scribble. "Was someone with you?"

Cinn nodded.

"Where are they now?"

Taking up the charcoal nib again, he took back the paper and drew an X, pointing at the ground. As if that established anything, he went on to draw with a wobbly line underneath it.

"Is that meant to be the city's moat?" she asked.

Cinn shook his head and frowned at his terrible drawing.

Lover take her, this was excruciating.

After a sip of tea, Moyra tilted her head as Cinn drew over the wobbly line more forcefully, creating peaks and valleys before stabbing the paper beneath it.

Not a moat, then. Perhaps the X wasn't meant as a marker for the shack, but for Ahrenhale. Yet even that didn't seem right. He didn't speak any of the bay's languages, and Moyra had never heard of the place representing him. Perhaps the X was broader. A marker for Qiri, which was surrounded by ocean in almost all directions.

But the shape of the line didn't look like waves—rather, mountains.

Working to unclench her teeth, she met his stare. "South of the wards?"

He nodded.

"Is that where you came from? Where this Wilder-dilly place is?"

He snorted, pink flushing against the fear in his aura as he nodded again. Leaving him for a moment, Moyra went to fetch more parchment from the cupboard by the window.

"Why did your friend not come with you?" she probed.

Taking the fresh pages, he ducked to draw again. Moyra took the opportunity to inspect his neck more closely. Not human, but definitely not a witch, either; she sensed no blessing on him. It was obvious he wasn't fae, nor one of their half-breeds—the Fair Folk—as even they had telltale signs.

On the table, Cinn had drawn a childish picture of a tall tree and a bird.

"Lover take me," she cursed aloud this time, resuming her seat and sipping her tea.

At her words, Cinn sat up straighter, eyes alight.

"The Lover?" Moyra guessed.

He snapped his fingers three times, shaking his hand in excitement.

"Spirits?" She looked at the pictures again. "The bird . . . the sparrow was Mother's first gift to the Lover. The person you travelled with was Lover-blessed? And whoever brought you through the wards would not bring him."

Cinn sagged, nodding.

"And the tree . . ." That one was harder. It had been a long time since she'd bothered with any of the minor Spirits. "Terra?"

Cinn nodded again.

"Alright, we're getting somewhere. Give me a moment to think. We don't really have the minor Spirits up here."

Before she could close her eyes to search inwards for information she had not needed since first hearing the nature Spirit's name, Cinn hastily scribbled question marks on the page.

"They're contained by the wards as well," she explained offhandedly, about to roll her eyes when it dawned on her—he was from the south. He wouldn't understand.

A chill ran down her spine.

Regardless of why he had come to Qiri, there were truths he deserved to know.

Five decades of isolation couldn't keep the fire in her heart from flaring. No matter what the council did, the part of her that wholeheartedly believed in unifying Nir would not die. That a southerner had found their way past the wards was a sign, and that they had come seeking her, of all people . . .

"I have to show you something." Her voice came out low, heart sinking. "Bear with me."

Crouching at her cupboard once more, she found a map of Tryce Point Bay and brought it back to Cinn, who stared as if he'd never seen the world laid out like this.

"You think the wards are here, yes?" she asked, drawing a circle with her finger around Qiri.

Nervous, Cinn nodded.

"Well, they're not. They're here." She traced another loop around the rest of Nir, leaving out Qiri. The entire spans of land beneath the mountains and east of a place labeled Phara, as well as everything north of a land called Yvar, was trapped under a dome of magic. "It's an enormous faerie ring. Those trapped inside, forget. It keeps them from growing curious about what lies beyond the western border. From wondering why ships who sail too far are always lost at sea. Why their messages to us go nowhere."

Cinn's eyes widened, his body so rigid that Moyra second

guessed herself as to whether he was fae or witch after all. It was difficult to tell what he was thinking, his aura shifting in ways she didn't understand.

"What are you?"

He blinked, then shook his head, inching the map closer and tapping on it. He wanted to know more, and though she knew better than to strike a deal with faeries, no matter how innocuous, she was completely certain he was not one.

"If I explain everything, will you . . . communicate, somehow, what you are?"

Cinn nodded.

Though she would have liked to use the dreamscape to weave the story visually, she didn't dare invoke it until she knew it was safe.

"The wards were erected during the Great War to contain Chaos, one of the four High Spirits; a deity of destruction, lawlessness, and savagery. But, since the minor spirits were birthed afterwards and within the confines of the wards, they are trapped inside too. Their realms exist alongside our own, but their influence cannot pass the ring. The rest of the bay learned about them from seers, and we study them a little at the academies, but they're not a part of our lives."

Cinn was a pillar of concentration as he waited for her to continue.

"Ahrenhale has known for a long time that Chaos will find strength again. There are many in Tryce Point Bay who think we should break the wards and aid those trapped inside. Help to suppress him once and for all. We call ourselves unifiers. For decades, the bravest of us have been slipping through, preparing for the inevitable fight."

Every inch of her body ached with grief as she thought of

that crack in the wards. Of what it had cost to pierce such potent magic.

"Unfortunately," she went on, her voice thick, "there are also many who don't want to risk it. Who are desperate to find the crack and repair it. Separatists think taking down the wards will unleash Chaos upon the entire world again, but with the wards intact, should Nir fall, Chaos is still trapped. Unless he binds himself to a physical form and locates the crack, he will never get out."

Cinn had lost what little color he had, his fingers tracing places on the map that weren't labeled. Places inside the wards where he no doubt had family and friends oblivious to how much danger they were in. The devastation about to be unleashed upon them.

Any day now, according to the seers.

In the dreamscape, Moyra had seen their predictions. Saw the riots breaking out in the streets as fear took root. The Lover would soon have millions of gifts awaiting embrace.

Every day, the devout prayed to Morvia for guidance, to show them the best of the billions of potential timelines. Moyra didn't bother.

"Do you have any more questions?" she prodded gently, taking a sip of her still scalding tea.

Cinn snorted as he rested his elbows on the table, head in his hands.

Only a few, then.

"While you figure out which is most pressing, would you answer mine?"

His gaze flicked up, and the ugly yellow consumed his conflicted aura once again. But he nodded, looking to her teacup and holding out a hand for it.

Reluctantly, she handed it over, just to watch him dump the boiling water over the inside of his wrist.

"Mother's sake! What—" She stopped squawking as the blistering skin began to heal before her very eyes.

Not everything was known about what happened inside the wards after they went up, but this . . . she had seen this in the dreamscape, too.

"Kinner," she breathed. "Of course."

Cinn nodded solemnly.

It took a moment for her to collect herself, but as Moyra took back her empty teacup, she scowled.

"What a waste of perfectly good tea. Next time, just stab yourself or something."

That Cinn didn't even crack a smile, his gaze already falling back to the map, told Moyra all she needed to know about how hard the news was hitting him.

CHAPTER 9

CINN

Eaon.

It was his first thought—Eaon, trapped in Nir with something called Chaos, where apparently millions of people were going to die.

Despite the overload of information and all that it meant, there was only room in his heart to care about the small group of people waiting for him to come home.

William and Sarah, who'd cared for him in his moment of greatest need with more patience and kindness than anyone had mustered for him before. Who had let him claim their cat as his own comfort creature. Who'd given him everything and asked for nothing in return.

Siobhan. His savior. The human woman who'd risked her life to find him in the darkest part of Hyrsch's bowels, coaxing the feral thing he'd become out if that cell with gentle words and even gentler hands. She fought for freedom in a city that would hang her for it if caught. Had witnessed the murder of her friends for their roles in helping him.

Then there was Kaelean. Nobody infuriated him as much as the high priestess of Wyldeden, and yet despite what he too often said, he couldn't hate her. Not when she had saved his life . . . gods, how many times now? Four? Five? Nor could he truly hate her after she'd given his friends back their home; Eavha, who had one of the most beautiful souls he'd even encountered, and Dearmead, who'd faced all his fears to find them in Pirevia. Though Cinn could not in good conscious like Dearmead *too* much until he and Eaon worked their shit out, he would make a great friend one day.

Speaking of Eaon . . .

It scared Cinn how much he missed him. How afraid he was for him. How much he wanted to run back to the Northern Mountains right now and drag his friend through the wards, consequences be damned. To find somewhere quiet and safe together and just . . . live.

A small, dank apartment came to mind. A fireplace that never had enough wood to last the winter, and platefuls of cinnamon biscuits they didn't have to steal from the baker's trash anymore. The first home he'd ever really had. The first family he'd ever loved.

Edwina and Radley.

He'd abandoned them. He should have sent word that he was out. Free. He should have asked them to come to the Copelands' farm so they could run away together and start fresh somewhere else.

But for so long, they had not existed. They had been relegated to imaginary friends he talked to when the days and weeks and months alone in his cell were endless. And when he could not summon the mirages anymore, and talking became something he'd banned himself from doing—a ban he had yet figured out how to remove—his adopted sister and brother had become nothing at all. His life from before became nothing. The past and future were *nothing*. There was only the dark. Only loneliness and pain. Forever.

To let himself remember them, to think their names, was to remember all that had been stolen from him, and that . . . that was more unbearable than all the rest combined.

The more he dwelled on what Moyra had told him, the deeper into the dark his mind tumbled. Fuzzy memories surfaced of a similar lecture about Chaos and war from another ill-tempered witch.

The shadows in the room deepened until his vision was murky and muted, his skin tightening as the room pressed in. Pressure on his face—cold steel and sweaty leather. His wrists and ankles were raw beneath the shackles.

In Master Ackford's house, he had not endured the beatings doled out to slaves. Not after Edwina and Radley discovered what he was, insisting on taking the blame for every mistake on his behalf. A shield, to keep his secret safe. Before that, the things his parents had done to prepare him for the cruelty of the world had not been enough for Cinn to find the courage to fight his restraints in that cell the way he should have. To shatter his hands and feet to crumbs.

"I trust you've had enough time to think about what you want to tell me."

He sucked in a sharp breath as that voice rang through his head.

"It dawned on me that I didn't really make it clear why I need to know what, exactly, my coven did with the rest of your kind."

The moment the muzzle was off his face, he'd confessed he was second generation. That he didn't know where his parents were. All he remembered was them telling him to run, the knee-high snow slowing his seven-year-old legs as he fled down the mountain. He'd waited in the little cave they'd been using as shelter, but after three days, his parents still had not returned. He'd been out looking for food when a stranger found him and dragged him to the city to sell into slavery.

He'd told her a hundred times as she'd laid him out on her table of horrors, but she didn't believe him. It wasn't the answer she wanted.

"You must know something. I know your people's instincts are not to trust Sparrows, but I am not like them. I want to help the Kinner. I need their help in return. Everything they worked to build, everything we have, will once more be reduced to Chaos's toy box if I can't find them. Help me, and you'll be saving the world."

Her words were fanatical, and he'd been too overwhelmed by the agony of his body to listen properly.

A physical weight fell over his shoulders as Moyra wrapped him in a blanket, her strange pink eyes solemn as she sat down again. There was a cup of tea in front of him.

"You're in shock."

He said nothing. The depth of cruelty a single witch was capable of still haunted him every moment of every day, and if *she* was afraid of Chaos . . .

"You're unwell." Moyra interrupted the inward spiral his panic-soaked brain was taking him down. "The dreamscape blurs with your consciousness."

He didn't know what she was talking about, and he didn't care. There was blood in his mouth, his ribcage peeled open, the hollowness of his chest cavity proving the flesh of his body was just another restraint, trapping him.

"Cinn." Moyra's voice was a distant echo. "I can help you through this. I'm a dream-weaver, it's my specialty. But I need your permission."

She was talking nonsense, her silhouette blurring. Both the

pink of her eyes and the color of her hair was greying, the straw-coated barn floor now soaked in blood. She was still speaking, but he couldn't hear her through the ringing in his ears. His head was floating, his body somewhere far away. Everything was dark and cold and rough and smothering, and he couldn't breathe through the acrid piss and stale blood and burnt skin and bitter bile and . . .

Rosemary. Lavender. Peppermint.

He opened his eyes, not remembering closing them. Moonlight flooded the warped wooden shack, his body heavy and real. Whole.

Moyra crouched beside his chair, a fistful of herbs clutched in her hand. Snatching them, he shoved them under his nose.

"Breathe deeply," she said, low and soft.

She didn't need to tell him twice. He would happily sit there for the rest of his life and breathe, breathe, breathe.

CHAPTER 10

MOYRA

SHE WISHED SHE COULD SAY PEOPLE COLLAPSING ON HER FLOOR was a novel experience, but it wasn't. Cinn's rigid posture began to sag to the side, so she reached out to help him safely to the floor. At her touch, he jerked back and dropped the bouquet, snarling and reaching for his knife.

It was too much too quickly, his weight shifting too suddenly. He toppled off the chair, the furniture sliding out from under him into Moyra's knees.

She swore in her native tongue as she hit the floor, eyeing the teacups on the table as they rattled. If he wasted another drop, she didn't care how unwell he was, she would throw him in the lake.

And he *was* unwell. She'd seen it often enough while training at the academy. Trauma often left a psychic scar that pierced the barrier between this realm and the dreamscape, and judging by the way it had descended on Cinn, his wound was still wide open.

The sweat beading down her neck had nothing to do

with the humidity as she watched his fingers twitch around the hilt of his knife. She didn't dare speak as her magic continued to wrestle between Cinn's mind and the nightmare sinking its claws into him, trying to disentangle the two enough for Cinn to get a hold of himself. But without permission, it was like prying apart the teeth of a bear trap.

Something got through to him though. Slowly, he let go of the knife and picked the bouquet of rousing herbs that she'd ripped from the garden the moment she'd seen the dreamscape enveloping him.

Releasing the tension in her body with a heavy sigh, Moyra climbed to her feet and offered Cinn a hand up. Sheepishly, he took it, but he was still unsteady.

"What do you need?" she asked before remembering he couldn't speak. "Food? Water?"

He shook his head and righted the toppled chair, leaning on it as he continued to breathe in the herbs.

"Rest, then."

Again, he shook his head, but the grey yellow that had flared so violently in his aura just a moment ago throbbed once more. He did need rest, but he wouldn't take it.

"Sit down," she told him, taking her own seat. Though her hands were shaking, she brought her teacup to her chest, more for comfort than a desire to drink it.

Once Cinn had settled, pulling the blanket she'd given him tighter around his shoulders, she asked, "Did you hear me tell you that I'm a dream-weaver?"

He blinked, then nodded.

"Well, I want to offer my services to you. I used to treat people afflicted as you are and I'm rather good at it, if I may say so myself."

Again, Cinn blinked absently, still not fully present. He wasn't ready to talk about this.

Sighing, she didn't know what to do. He wasn't ready to talk about dream-weaving, nor was he in any state to do an effective card reading. She couldn't check the tea leaves in his untouched cup, his palm was blank, and his aura wasn't giving her much else besides fear. The longer she sat with him, breathing incense, the clearer it became how much he needed her help, but she didn't know how to approach such a challenging situation. Gatty would usually guide her with things like this, but the faerie still had not shown his face after their spat.

She couldn't simply go to bed, but she couldn't sit there and wait for him to snap out of it, either. Since the dreamscape wasn't looming presently, she left him so she could retrieve more herbs from the garden.

The supplies she was given each month weren't enough to get by on, especially not if she wanted to continue her work, so after a trial-and-error period to see how far from the shack she could venture, she'd staked out a perimeter with twigs and twine and begun cultivating her own flowers, herbs, and vegetables.

In her youth, she'd hated gardening. In truth, she still did. Hated all the menial tasks involved in keeping a bountiful crop, but it was a necessary evil now she was banished from the city. And though it bored her to tears, it also made her smile. Fond memories of her brother often surfaced whenever she tended the herbs—her brother, who had loved nature and gardening, always running barefoot, covered in mud.

Filling a watering can from a pipe she'd wrangled from the house, she wandered about, trickling a drink to clusters of thirsty plants. Some looked ready to brown, and honestly, Moyra was half convinced the garden would be an utter failure if it weren't for Nena and her friends.

As if thinking their names summoned them, a light giggle alerted her to the trio of palm-sized sprites dancing around a ginger lily. The tiny fae creatures had driven her to the brink of insanity when she'd first moved into the shack; without salt to throw or rowan berries to string around her neck, their mischief couldn't be contained. Blocked pipes, cold drafts, and thorn-riddled shoes had all been daily occurrences. Gatty negotiated a cease-fire on her behalf, but Moyra liked to think they'd become friends since then.

The three sprites caught her staring and squawked, chittering hysterically before making their way to another plant. Nena's voluptuous form was pure liquid, tinged green like the lake she'd been made from. Dida, on the other hand, was a slight thing made of twigs and a dandelion puff for a head. She didn't spend as much time around the house as the other two, especially during colder months when a strong wind could blow her away. The third sprite, Lula, was at risk of being stood on every time Moyra left the house, her red-capped mushroom body blending into the garden.

"I don't even want to know what you three are up to," Moyra grumbled as she finished her rounds and looked back through the kitchen window at where Cinn was yet to move. "Any chance you want to try getting him out of that chair?"

She worded it carefully so the faeries knew they weren't helping her, thus no favor was owed. Dida made her way to the window, pressing her face against the glass until the fluffy white dandelion florets around her face were smooshed flat.

"What do you think?" Moyra asked, then rolled her eyes as the sprite put a twiggy hand to her forehead and swooned. "Of course. *Him* you like."

Dida chittered and went back to the others, a seed escaping from her puff as she spun in circles, gesturing animatedly.

Excitement bubbled as the three of them made their way to her door and slipped beneath the gap between it and the floorboards.

Mother have mercy.

Brushing the dirt off her hands, Moyra quickly followed them, leaning in the doorway as she watched Lula toddle to Cinn's pack and wriggle under the flap. Nena swirled her way up the table leg, leaving tiny wet footprints on the map as she wandered to Cinn's tea and slipped inside. Meanwhile, Dida floated to Cinn's shoulder and tugged on a strand of hair. Startled, he flinched and swatted at the critter, who simply cackled and tugged again. Excited squawking came from the pack and Moyra had to cover her mouth to contain her laughter as Lula came tumbling out with a blue-streaked pebble in her mushroom hands.

A distressed noise cracked in Cinn's throat. Forgetting the dandelion on his shoulder, he chased after Lula, who sprinted for the door as fast as her tiny legs could carry her.

Moyra moved to the table, rolling up the map. With as close to a "thank you" as Moyra dared, she whispered to Nena, who was still soaking in the spoiled tea, "I'll leave some honey out for you all later."

Dida's cackling grew louder as she perched on Cinn's head, holding strands of his hair like reins as he dove to block the door, scrabbling after the mushroom sprite. Catching her in a gentle fist, Lula screeched in dismay as he pried the pebble from her hands.

Moyra hid her amusement as she put the map away, watching Lula make grabby hands for her stolen treasure. Cinn only scowled silently, putting her down on the threadbare furniture and pocketing the stone.

His next problem was Dida.

Watching a nearly six-foot-tall boy struggle with the dandelion sprite tangled in his hair, all while trying to avoid stepping on the mushroom faerie darting between his feet, trying to tie his shoelaces together, was too much for Moyra. Easing herself to the floor, she laughed in great wheezes, glad it wasn't her suffering for once.

"Alright, alright," she finally said. "Leave him alone."

They didn't listen right away, so Moyra went to fetch the fresh jar of honey from the crate.

That got their attention.

All three heads snapped in her direction, Nena clambering out of the teacup while the other two stilled so thoroughly they could have been mistaken for real plants.

Twisting off the lid, Moyra scooped out a teaspoon of honey and placed it on the bench. Screeching with joy, the sprites rushed to the kitchen, leaving Cinn to rub his scalp and smile gratefully.

"They're territorial," she told him, putting the jar away in the cupboard, equally smug and guilty for encouraging her little friends. At least it had gotten Cinn out of his state. "They'll warm up to you in time. Which, I'm assuming we have. After how desperately you wished to see me, you don't have intentions of running off before we get to the bottom of things, do you? Did you have plans as to where you're going to stay?"

His face warmed as he glanced to the door and shrugged, waving a hand toward the lakeside.

Moyra sighed. "If you think these three are terrors, you would not enjoy meeting the things that lurk out there at night. It's not much protection, but you may stay in the house. I'm guessing you'll require feeding, too?"

Flipping open the flap of his pack, Cinn pulled out a squashed lump of burnt bread.

"I'll take that as a yes."

His cheeks warmed even further as he shook his head, grimacing at the crate in the kitchen that she was yet to unpack. Placing one hand on his chest, he patted his pack with the other. But, as he glanced between the Moyra and the door, his throat bobbed nervously. She waited, and eventually he pointed to himself, then her, making a question mark with his hand.

"Yes." She sighed again, already exhausted. "I'm going to help you."

Once again, he pulled that copper coin from his pocket and offered it to her.

"I don't want your money. I have no use for it."

He mouthed an "oh," then pulled the dagger again. She couldn't help but flinch back, and he bit his lip before offering her the handle.

"I don't want your knife, either."

He quickly put it away. Next, he offered her the pebble.

She shook her head. "You don't need to compensate me. Not for this."

Lula noticed him holding out the pebble and made a move for it. Cinn saw her coming and stashed it, narrowing his eyes at the sprite. Moyra couldn't help but smile, though she quickly lost it as she assumed the soft, gentle voice she used with all her dream-weaving clients.

"It would be one thing if all you wanted was a tarot reading to better your chances of the girl down the street taking well to your advances, but I will never charge someone who needs help with the dreamscape." She held his gaze as he shuffled uncomfortably. "You are welcome here, Cinn. And I will help you."

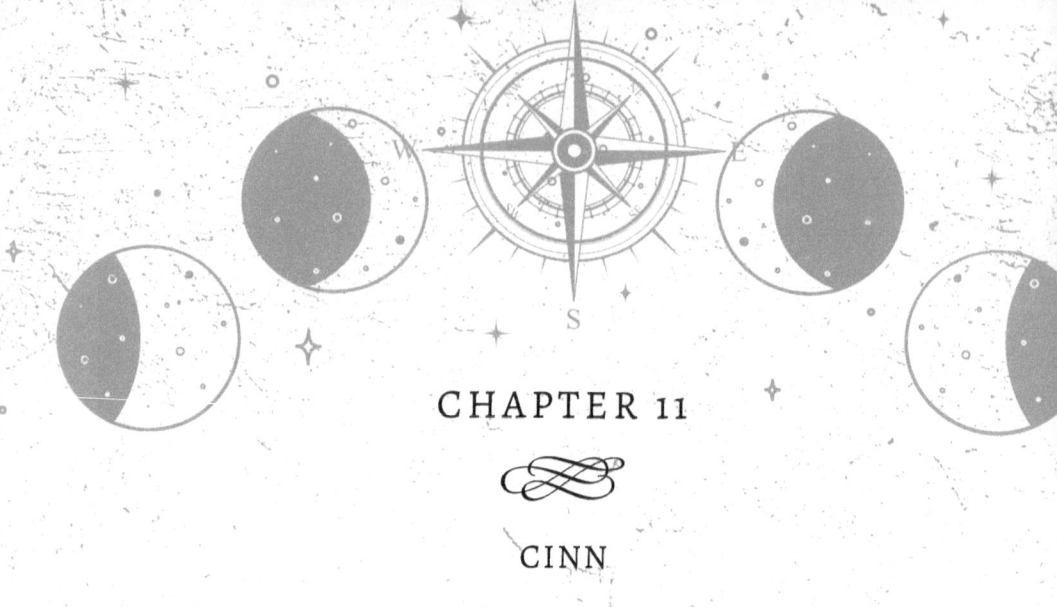

CHAPTER 11

CINN

EVEN IF CINN WANTED TO SLEEP, EVEN IF THE CICADAS AND frogs quietened down enough to let him, the whirring in his head was never going to allow it. With his clothes washed and hanging up to dry, the itchy fabric of the sofa on his bare skin was worse than the mosquito bites that only lingered on his skin for a few seconds. Not to mention the pack under his head was far from comfortable, but even though the sprites hadn't shown their faces since Moyra had gone to bed, he didn't trust that mushroom one not to try and steal his stuff again.

All those peeves were secondary to the dizzying whirlwind of questions and concerns spinning inside his skull.

He still hadn't figured out how to ask Moyra about how to get the Sparrow Coven off his trail, but considering everything she'd told him today, it didn't seem the most pressing issue. There was a large possibility there wouldn't even be a farm to go home too soon.

The impulse to go back to Eaon *right now* was strong, but even if he returned with the news about Chaos, about southern Nir being trapped in a faerie ring and cut off from aid, what good would it do? There wasn't much to be done about it. Not without Morvish help to get people through the wards.

Not to mention, he didn't even know how to get back.

The weight of this revelation was enough to make him nauseous as he rolled to his side, staring at the cabinet under the window. A window covered with sheer curtains, no drapes to block out the moonlight or the flickering shadows of creatures passing by the shack.

He didn't want to know what was out there. A phantom ache spread through his throat as he remembered the shtryg that had attacked him twice; first in the forest, then again at the Copelands' farm. He hadn't seen any silver around to ward off the beasts, and clearly there wasn't protection against the fae, either. Every time a shadow passed by, Cinn found his hand moving to his dagger.

How Moyra slept at all was a mystery.

She had promised that when the "dreamscape"—whatever that was—descended, and his nightmares consumed him again, she would be there waiting to help. As long as he gave her permission. How he'd do that while asleep, he didn't know. Whatever Morvish magic was, he didn't understand it.

Moyra was abstract, whereas at least with Kaelean, he could see what happened when she used a spell.

Ugh, Kaelean.

Blowing out a harsh breath through his nose, he rolled to face the back of the sofa.

He had stopped trusting Kaelean the moment she'd betrayed them in Vertlyn—the moment she'd helped put him back in a cage—and nothing she'd done since had convinced him she was anything less than a conniving, manipulative snake.

A snake he owed his freedom to, fivefold. A snake he knew, deep down, had reasons.

Ugh.

It would be easier if he could truly hate her instead of lying to himself that he did. It only added to his permanent state of confusion that he disliked someone he respected—mistrusted someone he could rely on to come running in a crisis.

Because she *had* come running the day Eaon died on the farm.

The thought of it chilled him, sweat breaking across his skin.

All because of this stupid mark on the back of his neck.

Rubbing at the shiny mark, he remembered what Moyra had said about it. Despite everything that had happened, that tidbit of information had not been missed. Moyra had asked if he couldn't bear it. Did she know how to nullify the mark? If so, the next time some beast dragged him into the shadows to make an eternal feast of him, he might not have to endure such unending torture. He could be free.

It wasn't the right time. Not with everyone he loved in mortal danger. But one day, he could be human. He could live a simple life, no longer hunted by every power-hungry—or just plain hungry—asshole in Nir.

Her.

Cinn's breath caught in his throat. Sitting up, he looked to the window. The door.

No locks. Nothing stopping him from leaving if he wanted to. The lacy curtains swayed in a breeze creeping through gaps in the window frames, but other than that, there was nothing obstructing his view of the clear night sky with all its stars, the waxing moon so close to full.

Still, he got up and unsheathed his knife, checking the shadows before peering out each window. Though he couldn't see anything, he knew there were creatures out there, peering back at him. Knew none of them were *her*.

Returning to the couch, he lay down and tried to focus on the exposed beams and clay-tile roof above, the smell of burnt herbs and charcoal permeating the room. But he was too aware of his pulse as it beat through his body, his stomach digesting his pathetic dinner. Of his eyelids grating against aching eyes. Of his teeth. His nails and knees.

Knees crumbled to dust. Nails pulled from his fingers and toes. Teeth ripped from his gums.

Strapped to the table in that dark, cold room, Cinn was too weak to fight it anymore. Barely had the strength to open his eyes when commanded. He wouldn't have bothered at all, except the last time he had defied her she had cut off his eyelids and sprinkled salt in the wounds to slow the healing.

Pulling his jaw open, she tipped water down his throat. He choked on it, resenting the relief it brought his tongue, sitting like a stone in his mouth. She only ever gave him water so he could speak.

"What is your name?"

Cinn gasped and looked up at the woman standing over him. Sarah's hair was braided down her back, cold and grey.

Whatever scraps were left of his heart shattered as the woman who had been a mother to him rested a meat tenderizer on his protruding ribs.

"Where's Eaon?"

No.

He would never tell her. She could break his body a hundred different ways and he would never tell her.

Cinn. A soft voice—the sea washing against the shore, cooling the sweat on his skin. *Let me in.*

A trap. Radley had told him stories when they were children

about witches who could get inside your head to make you see and hear things. Who could control your mind and body. Could make you kill your family.

I can help you. I can make it stop, but you're blocking me.

Sarah was gone. Siobhan stood in her place, belly swollen, and face twisted with rage.

"Talk!" she shrieked as she brought the tenderizer down on him, destroying bone and puncturing the lung beneath. Blood burst up his throat, out his mouth, splattering her in it.

How did she expect him to talk when he couldn't even breathe? This wasn't an interrogation anymore. It was punishment.

Inch by inch, he retreated from his body. Knowing what was coming, that he didn't want to feel it, didn't want to be present for it, he fled to the only place he could.

A chipped hearth and a banking fire, sugar and cinnamon on his fingers.

A giant tree in a mist-shrouded forest.

A farmhouse surrounded by silver and salt.

A bonfire, and a hammock.

The smell of eggs coaxed him from the shadows, and slowly, the warmth of the sun on his bare chest thawed the shield he'd built around himself. His crusty eyes peeled open and Cinn cursed himself for falling asleep twice in so many days.

"I'm not brewing you a tea unless you swear you'll drink it. You've wasted enough."

Clawing upright, he peeked over the back of the sofa dividing the room to where Moyra stood in the kitchen, scrambling eggs in an iron pan. Barefoot and dressed in a cotton shift, her hair was tangled around her face like a cloud, heavy bags under her pink eyes.

If she was comfortable in her sleepwear, then he didn't bother with a shirt as he stood from the couch. It was too humid. Even pulling his trousers on was unpleasant as he shuffled into the kitchen, already damp with sweat.

Though that could have been the nightmares, too.

Even though she wouldn't understand, Cinn began signing an apology for the rough night. Raising a hand, she pushed his face away.

"No. Not before tea."

She already had the kettle boiling, two cups ready. When it began to whistle, she left the eggs, so Cinn took the wooden spoon and poked at the rubbery consistency. Not as bad as the ones Eaon had tried to make for him once, but still, perhaps he could convince Moyra to let him cook while he was staying. It was the least he could do.

Edwina had taught him how to scramble eggs. Radley was better at it than she was, but their brother had been busy licking his wounds after being caught flirting with Master Ackford's daughter again.

The memory stuck in his throat. He turned to cough in the crook of his elbow.

"Could you not hack all over my breakfast? Onribleq. Wolves have better manners than you."

Cinn raised an eyebrow and made a mental note that Moyra was not a morning person. In fact, he had the sneaking suspicion that, if she was not actively drinking tea, she was going to be in a bad mood.

As she took the two cups to the table, Cinn separated the eggs into the two bowls she'd laid out and joined her. They sat in silence over their food, staring blearily at the morning birds bragging their success to each other as they scavenged their own meals. Birds that matched the delicately painted black-and-white renditions on the cups and bowls. Magpies, Eaon had once called them.

"I get bored," Moyra croaked. Cinn looked up to see her watching the way he brushed his thumb over the painting. "And I kept dreaming of them, so I painted them."

He smiled, nodding his appreciation. Waving a hand around the room, he wondered what else she might have painted.

"Hold on," she said, draining her teacup before going to the cupboard under the window. After rummaging around for a while, she returned with a framed picture, her grip on it white-knuckled.

Inching closer, he raised his brows again in appreciation of the depiction of three people. The witch on the left was clearly Moyra, the likeness perfect. Another female stood to the right of the male in the middle, all three with similar features—the same noses, chins, and crooked smiles. Either an artistic limitation or the three of them were related.

His question must have been evident. Moyra took her seat and stared at the picture wistfully.

"My brother and sister. Olyvia was barely matured when she died, fifty-five years ago. My brother . . . almost a year ago, in autumn. I hadn't seen him since Olyvia died, but I felt his passing." Her hand rested over her sternum. "Do you have siblings?"

Cinn nodded.

"Are they still alive?" she asked, chin dimpling.

He waited until she looked up before shrugging. It was reasonable to think Edwina was alright—she knew how to keep out of trouble. But Radley . . .

"How long has it been since you've seen them?"

He remembered the way Eaon helped him figure out how long he'd been down in that cell. How old he was. He didn't know his actual birthday, but his parents had told him to count the years by the first blooming flower after winter.

It had been autumn when he'd been caught, and he'd been seventeen, which put him on the other side of twenty now. All that time . . . Lost. Too much time, but also somehow not enough. He'd lived an eternity in that cell.

"Where's your head going?" Moyra asked gently.

Blinking rapidly, he held up two fingers to answer her first question, not even sure how to answer the second one.

"Two . . . Oh, your siblings. Two weeks? No? Months?" When Cinn shook his head again, she sat back in her chair. "Two years?"

Cinn finished his tea and took a steadying breath.

"And how old are you?"

Flashing all ten digits twice, he grimaced at the pity on her face.

"Two years is a long time at that age." She seemed to look at him without really looking, the way she had when he'd first arrived. As if there was something just behind his ear. "Can you tell me why you separated?"

No, he couldn't. Even if he could figure out how to speak again, he wasn't sure he could explain everything that had happened and why he'd left his adopted family behind.

"Something happened to separate you," she said, taking his teacup and peering at the dregs he'd left behind. "Those two years . . . They changed your path. Led you here."

She tilted her head, looking up to fixate on his neck.

"They left a blockage in your mind. Your throat."

Cinn swallowed nervously. Moyra smiled, placing the teacup back down.

"Don't look so spooked. I'm Morvish. My specialty might be dream-weaving, but we learn all the basics at school." Perking up suddenly, her words seemed to have given her an idea. "Since last night was . . . unsuccessful, perhaps we should start with something easier."

As always, he couldn't remember his dreams bar that they were horrible, but he did recall Moyra wanting to help. In the dream, he had forgotten her. Hadn't trusted her.

"After we're both ready for the day, and if you're comfortable, I would like to try a reading."

Wrinkling his nose, Cinn didn't know how to explain that he wasn't very good at reading. Sarah had helped him learn a little, but he'd rather do just about anything else.

"It's not intrusive," she went on, "and it's the best way for us to get on the same page about what it is you need from me.

And just like that, Cinn didn't think she meant the kind of reading he was familiar with. Blinking at her with absent confusion, Moyra smiled and collected the dishes.

"I'll show you."

CHAPTER 12

MOYRA

CINN INSISTED ON FIXING THE DISHES WHILE MOYRA CLEANED herself in the washroom. She supposed she was lucky the council had banished her to a place that had basic plumbing, though only cold water came from the tap to fill the wash trough, and the soap supplied each month left her skin dry and itchy. She had the dignity of a latrine as well, but since the water came from and went back to the lake, she always checked for nasty critters that may have snuck through the pipes.

When she was done, Cinn took his turn while Moyra reset her deck of tarot cards and selected fresh herbs from the garden. The morning held a weight, and as it settled on her shoulders, she couldn't help but feel that Morvia was watching. Using the ash from last night's incense, Moyra marked her forehead and hands with spellmarks, encouraging the magic in her blood to clear her mind. To guide her.

By the time Cinn returned in semifresh clothes, damp hair plastered across his brow, she was ready.

"Don't be nervous," she said as he took the seat across the table.

Her tarot cards were fanned out, their energy pulsing. She had painted them during her training at the academy, infusing her very essence into each stroke, the exact image divined during star-reading classes. The unifiers had taken an incredible risk getting them to her—one she hoped to pay back someday.

Worrying his lip, Cinn shifted as he looked at them. It was unlikely he could sense the power she had placed in them. While the true magic in card reading came from her, using tools crafted specifically for the way she wished to use them made it easier. The traditional ways worked well, but Moyra had her own methods of divining.

"This is what we're going to do. I'll ask you a question, and even if you don't know the answer, I want you to embrace whatever it makes you feel. Select a card, and we will see what Morvia knows."

He nodded, but he seemed almost afraid of the cards.

"All I'm trying to find out is what Yomra sent you here for, and how I can best help you. They're not going to tell me all your deepest, darkest secrets." She tried a teasing tone, but he only managed a twitch of the lips in response.

He was as calm as he was going to get.

"Alright, Cinn." Breathing deeply, she let the incense fill her head, honing her magic. "Why are you here?"

Eyes roaming the cards, he tentatively reached out and tapped the corner of one in the middle of the spread. Pulling it out, she flipped it over to face Cinn and worked to keep a straight face.

The eight of swords was not unusual in her line of work.

Judging by Cinn's rigid posture, he was prepared for the card to leap off the table and bite him.

"You feel trapped," she started. "This card is upside down, which can mean you've overcome what restrains you, but in your particular case I don't feel that is right. Upside down, it can also mean you feel your options narrowing, and that freedom is beyond reach on your own."

It wasn't a great start, but the relief in Cinn's face as he slumped back in his seat, covering his face with his hands, suggested she was on the right track. Often, the prison represented by this card was self-made, but again, Moyra got the impression that wasn't strictly the case for Cinn.

"My second question is," she began, waiting until Cinn had gathered himself before letting her third eye choose the words. "What stands between you and freedom?"

This time when Cinn went to select a card, there was less hesitation. Her magic reacted to the sudden presence of the dreamscape pressing in, but Moyra was fed up with its obsession with Cinn, banishing it before it could brush against him.

Flipping the second card over, the Emperor in reverse stared back. Her stomach dropped.

"The Emperor signifies authority, structure and logic. In reverse, tyranny or entitlement." Again, she didn't sense that this stemmed from Cinn himself, rather an outside force. "Someone, or multiple people, in a position of power in your life have forsaken boundaries. Considering the eight swords, they seek to entrap you. Control you."

The shock and devastation on Cinn's face as he nodded threatened her composure. The Emperor was major. This was not a small problem Cinn faced, and reaffirming his boundaries was not going to be a simple task. A novice may have skipped right to asking for the solution, but Moyra had done this enough to know there was always more at play.

"Think about what circumstances led to this current

situation. Again, you don't have to know exactly, but let the feeling into your heart."

Being understood was boosting his confidence, the shift in his aura proof. She had been scoffed at by the wounded before, especially males, who either didn't want to or didn't know how to let themselves feel things, but Cinn was different. As she watched him select another card, he was so open and willing. The boy had his heart on his sleeve.

Just as his fingers were about to brush a card, his aura darkened. His face froze, a flash of fire behind his eyes. The dreamscape flickered nearby with a dark, feminine energy, but didn't stay as Cinn changed which card to draw.

"You weren't thinking of yourself just now," she commented, waiting to reveal his selection. "Something changed your mind."

Throat bobbing as he smothered the rage festering inside, he pointed to the upside-down Emperor. Looking between the second card and the third, she felt the connection.

"Unusual," she muttered to herself. A tarot reading was meant to give insight to the person drawing the cards, but something strange was happening today. Magic thrummed through her veins, the whispering of stars echoing in her ears. This draw was not for Cinn, but it was vital.

Turning it over, Moyra frowned. The Chariot was upright.

"It's not your past that formed the circumstances you wish to escape, but that of the Emperor," she explained while trying to listen to what the stars were telling her. "She is determined, focused . . . desperate for forward movement. Even positive cards can have shadows. Her determination is all consuming, her grit overbearing. Too focused on her goal, she has forgotten that the journey to accomplish it is just as important."

Strings of color flickered between the cards. Between Cinn

and the Emperor. Drawing a deep breath, guilt settled in her chest as she explained the connection to him.

"Your fates are intertwined. As your prison is in part formed by the Emperor's overflowing drive, it is her claiming of accountability that will form the key."

He didn't like that. Blowing a harsh breath through his nose, he stood, the chair toppling over from the force of it. Fists clenched and tucked under his arms, he began to pace.

Giving him time, Moyra placed the Chariot beside the Emperor. She wasn't proficient in *seeing*, the way true seers were, but her blessing swelled until she closed her eyes to *see* what it wanted to show her.

A mirror.

A young queen peering into it while an older one, cold and swollen with child, snarled back from the other side. Not the same person, but related, both dressed in the garb of the Emperor. Both rode the Chariot, both desperate for the kinner boy.

But their hearts were different.

The old queen turned, red eyes looking right at Moyra.

Gasping, she opened her eyes, returning to the shack. Cinn had stopped pacing, eyes wide with concern as Moyra shook off the feel of those eyes finding her.

"Just a vision," she promised, blotting the sweat beading on her forehead with the back of her hand. The red-eyed queen hadn't actually seen her. That wasn't possible. It was just a sign; one she would analyze later. "Come. Let's continue."

Cinn collected two cups of water and brought them to the table, taking a sip. Moyra smiled. His anger may be hot and violent, but she could not doubt his true self was kind. A self in need of freeing.

"Deep breaths," she said, wafting the incense to her nose.

Cinn copied her calming routine as they readied to delve back into divination.

"When the opportunity to be free arises, it is important you are ready to seize it. What needs to be resolved so you are in the right frame of mind?"

He drew the six of cups, again, in reverse. Unlike the Chariot, this was not a surprise. The six of cups was common in her line of work.

"You're stuck in the past. Nostalgia for happier times is an escape but dwelling there keeps you from living life in the present. Painful memories also plague you, and while these often bear lessons to keep old mistakes from being repeated, they also prevent you from moving forward. If you wish to be free, you must seek closure."

Chewing on his thumbnail, Cinn slouched in his seat. The news was not a surprise for him, either. As he met her gaze, he shrugged and waved a hand around: *how?*

"Ask the cards."

Straightening, his brow puckered in concentration before reaching for a card. As Moyra turned it over, she smiled.

"Ten of cups. Family. Home. There is much of this in your life, and it's time to reconnect with these things." Meeting his pained gaze, she was glad she had already asked about his family. "It might be time to find your siblings."

He smiled back apprehensively. There was more to the story.

Putting aside her assumptions, Moyra let magic guide her tongue.

"There are other familial relationships it is time to reconnect with. You have chosen a family that gives you love and support, and they will be instrumental in fulfilling your desire for a safe home, but bonds of blood and magic are also important." Something sickly churned in her stomach, which was a strange response to the ten of cups. "Perhaps these relationships are not loving in the conventional way, but they are loyal. There is compassion to be found on both sides."

Moyra couldn't say she understood, but Cinn clearly did. His aura had shifted into a sad blue, with the same fear flaring at his throat.

"You won't ever truly be free until you clear that block in your throat," she told him, immediately regretting it.

Face blank, his swirling emotions tightened, closing in. Cutting himself off emotionally, he retreated from the conversation, the reading, and her.

They were done.

Fetching a cloth she'd intended to make a new skirt from, she covered the spread for when they were ready to continue.

Without meeting her eye, Cinn rose from the table and went outside.

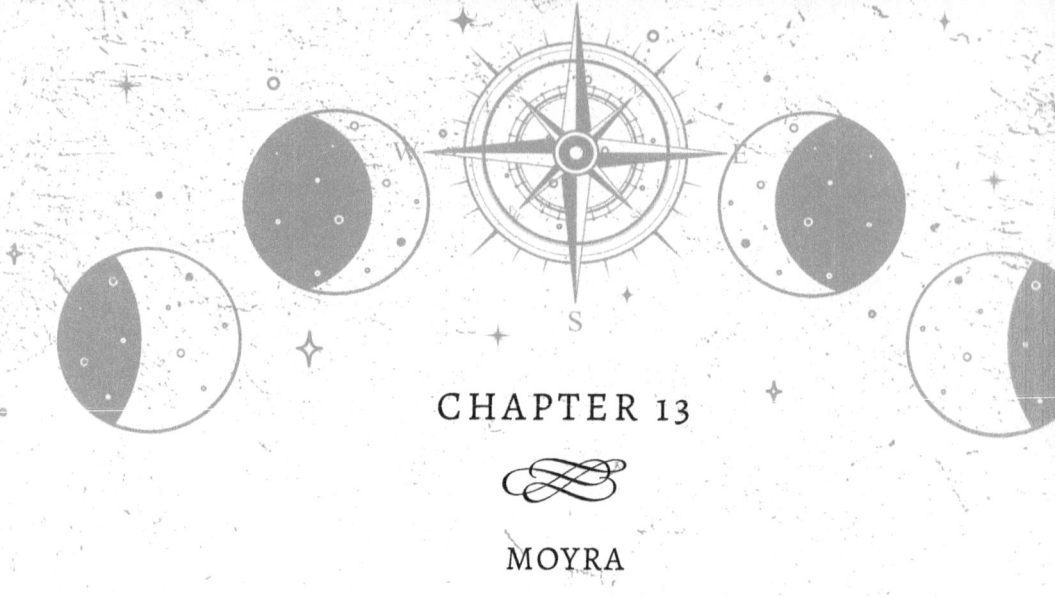

CHAPTER 13

MOYRA

Brewing some chamomile tea, Moyra stood at the kitchen window and watched Cinn tossing pebbles mindlessly into the shallows by the lake. He was just a young boy looking for peace and safety, but considering the reading, what he was, and who was after him, on top of where he came from, it seemed fate had other plans. When he was ready, she needed to finish the reading. The conclusion may have good news for him, which meant good news for everyone.

Steeping the flowers in hot water, her mind wandered back to the vision Morvia had gifted her. The mirror and two queens. The one with red eyes had looked at her, dark intentions pulsing in their heart. That whoever it was might have actually sensed Moyra was impossible, but so was the sign such an action suggested: that Moyra was in their sights, a part of what fate had in store. Impossible, because the red-eyed queen was in the south while Moyra was stuck in this shack for the rest of her life.

Perhaps she could paint their faces and ask Cinn who they

were. It might give her some idea as to how they were connected.

~

The day was long and hot, but that didn't seem to bother Cinn, who avoided coming back inside by taking long walks around the lake, inspecting pebbles and leaves. Moyra set herself up on the porch with her paints, watching the three sprites follow him at a distance.

On his second lap around the lake, Cinn found something that piqued his interest. A high-pitched battle cry sounded, and before he knew what was happening, Dida was in his face, twirling and blowing seeds in his eyes while Nena got inside his boots, soaking his socks. Lula waited on the ground, making grabby hands at the shell Cinn had found. As he swatted at Dida, he dropped the little treasure and Lula squawked in delight as she snatched it up and fled into the trees.

Cackling manically, the other two chased after their friend while Cinn was left rubbing his eyes and shaking his boot.

"I wouldn't if I were you," she called as he prepared to go after them. "That's not a fight you'll win."

Cinn scowled, but marched to sit beside her on the porch, pulling his boot off and peeling the wet sock from his foot.

When he saw what she had painted, he froze. Paled.

"You know them?" Moyra asked gently.

With a trembling hand, he pointed to the younger queen. The one Moyra had felt pure intentions from. The fear and anger in his aura burned so brightly she had to avert her eyes, frowning at the pale figure on the canvas.

"This might not be a bad thing," she said, putting the

painting aside so Cinn could calm down. "I get the impression this queen may be capable of—"

Cinn huffed loudly and leaned across to snatch the painting from the porch. Moyra flinched back at his sudden movement, mouth agape as he ripped her work, over and over, then took the pieces and stormed down to the lake, throwing them in the water and stomping them until they were buried in the sand.

"Well, that was mature," she muttered, sitting down to wait as Cinn began to pace again.

It was at least an hour before he returned, charging up the bank, anger still too bright. Stopping only a foot away, he pointed a shaking finger at her.

"Get that out of my face," Moyra snapped, slapping his hand away.

He bared his teeth, fists clenched at his sides. Moyra stood, squaring her shoulders.

"I understand you're hurt, but I am trying to help. Don't like it? Feel free to leave. Otherwise, calm yourself and sit down."

Nostrils flaring, he held her gaze, indecision warring. Just as he wasn't the first to collapse in her care, he wasn't the first to lose his temper either. Moyra was a pillar of steel.

Finally, he took a long, deep breath. Another. The red in his aura wavered as he sat down, relaxing his fists one finger at a time.

Straightening her blouse, Moyra sat beside him. When she was sure he was calm enough, she asked, "What about the other queen? Did you know her?"

Stoically, he shook his head.

Curious, indeed.

Moyra made to pack up her paints, but the movement made Cinn flinch.

"I'm not going to hurt you."

He only sniffed, staring back at where the sun was getting low again.

This was going to be a problem. If his trust could be broken by a simple painting, she couldn't help him.

Leaving the paints, she crossed her ankles and turned her body to him. "I know there aren't really Morvish witches in the south, but have you ever tried to see a healer?"

Petulantly, he rolled his eyes and flourished a hand over his body.

"That mark on the back of your neck may keep you indefinitely alive and unmarred, but it's not going to keep you healthy in here," she tutted, poking his forehead. "That is where your injuries fester. That is where I need to do my work. That is where you need to let me in."

The constellation tattoo on her forehead tingled again, and as she gave his defensive posture an appraisal, she knew what to do.

She reached for his wrists.

As soon as contact was made, he flinched away, the swirling colors of the dreamscape appearing like mist above his head. Rallying, she held it at bay, bracing herself against the violence within.

"I am not here to hurt you."

She'd done this exercise with so many clients the steps were second-nature. Watching his body language, reading his aura, his emotions and thoughts; it was her most prized skillset. She knew the response each of her actions was meant to elicit, and she waited for them calmly.

It took a moment, but Cinn finally heard her, relaxing his arms and letting her reach for them again. The fear in his aura was neon by the time she wrapped her fingers around his wrists, grip firm.

"Pull away and I will let go," she promised, watching the dreamscape take form.

Shackles. Restraints. A prisoner. The eight of swords had been *literal*.

Breaths quickening, Cinn tugged.

Moyra released him.

Eyes wide in surprise, it was his turn to appraise her demeanor. Her gentle hands between them, open and waiting. It took almost ten minutes of staring, but Cinn raised his shaking hands. Offered his wrists.

"Pull away and I will let go," she repeated as she took them.

Convinced she wasn't lying, he sat still and controlled his breathing. Only the rapid blinking, the quick dart of his gaze to the knife at his hip, gave away his stress.

Carefully, Moyra eased her hold on the dreamscape, letting it come closer. He immediately flinched, tugging on his wrists. Moyra let him recoil.

Wrangling the dreamscape was easier when it loomed like this rather than after it had taken hold of his mind. Which it wanted to do. She felt the realm pulling against her leash, urging him to fight harder, and trying to remind him what it would be like to be a prisoner again, unable to escape.

This function of the dreamscape had its purpose—a place to process waking life, to take the hard lessons learned and turn them into future warnings—but here and now, Cinn was not in danger. The warnings were too eager, his memories too potent. The line between waking life and remembered terrors too blurred.

She couldn't change that. She couldn't reprogram his subconscious. What she could do was help Cinn do it. He had come looking for freedom, and she had more than one kind to offer.

Of his own volition, Cinn put his wrists directly in her waiting palms. She closed her fingers over them again, watching the dreamscape roar. With magic thrumming through her veins, she held it back, but as Cinn adjusted to the turmoil in his head, deciding for himself if this moment was dangerous, she backed off inch by inch. Let him make that choice over and over.

Over and over, he chose to trust her. The memories were still there, but given enough space to separate past from present, Cinn regained an element of control.

When he realized it, breath rushed from him.

Dipping into the pool of her power once more, Moyra banished the dreamscape entirely and let go of his wrists. Birds sung their goodnights as the two of them sagged on the porch, sweating so profusely it looked like they'd taken a swim in the lake.

To anyone watching, all that had transpired was Moyra holding Cinn's wrists while they stared at each other awkwardly. Only she had seen the dreamscape come for him, and only he had felt the shift in himself as he learned it was safe to be touched in the place that had caused him so much pain. That not everybody who held his wrist intended to harm him.

Cinn's smile was wobbly, eyes glassy as he stared at her. Moyra gave him a warm one back, pushing her sweaty hair from her forehead.

"Tea?"

CHAPTER 14

CINN

BY THE TIME HE WAS READY TO FINISH THE READING, THE SUN had set on another day and Cinn wondered how many more he would spend here before making his way back to Eaon.

"I want you to remember what I said you should do if you want freedom. I want you to remember how hard that seemed. The next card you choose will show the short-term consequences of choosing the easier path."

Neither option seemed easy, but of course, he didn't say that. Seeking closure with Eddy and Radley was one thing, but the rest of what Moyra has suggested . . .

He picked a card, and when she turned it over, nausea rolled in his stomach.

"It's not as bad as it looks," Moyra promised. "The Death card signifies endings of all kinds, but reversed like this, it can mean resistance to change or clinging to the past."

The look she gave him was pointed.

"When we cling to things that no longer serve us, we become

stuck. Without closure, without doing the work to heal, nothing will ever change."

Chewing his lip, Cinn nodded. Deep down, he knew that already, but surely there was more to getting back his home, his life, than making things right with his family and moving on from everything that happened. None of that would get the Sparrow Coven to stop hunting him.

"There are always other forces at work that can affect the outcome of our journey, and these need to be considered when making choices. Are there external influences to overcome?"

A hundred, at least. Swallowing nervously, he looked over the cards and once again wished there was some kind of magic pull to assure him he was choosing rightly. Selecting one at random, he waited for her to explain.

She took a moment, muttering to herself, "So many major cards. So many reversals."

From the corner of his eye, he spotted the sprites sneaking under the door. How anything so cute could rouse so much rage in him, he didn't know.

"The upside-down Wheel of Fortune suggests either you or someone influencing your life is fighting fate. In the academies we learn that most people have multiple possible destinies, but the choices we make at pivotal moments can set us on a course that, once on, cannot be changed. Not unless there is another pivotal moment in your future that could change it again. Or if Morvia directly intervenes, which, in all of time, she has only ever done once during the Great War. Fighting a set course is pointless and only causes more pain when fate inevitably arrives."

Was he fighting fate? He didn't even know what his destiny was, let alone be knowingly resisting it.

An echo of a memory ran through his mind—Yomra's prophecy, but not the one directed at him.

You are exactly who you need to be. Stop fighting it.

Eaon.

"It's okay not to know what it means right now," Moyra said, watching his face. "Fate and time are the trickiest parts of Morvia's realm for witches to get a handle on, so I wouldn't expect you to. But it's something to be aware of going forward."

Swallowing against the worry knotting in his throat, he tried to clear his thoughts again, wanting this reading to be over with. He'd barely done anything all day, yet he was exhausted.

"What are you not aware of that may need to be overcome?" Moyra asked, repressing her own yawn.

He chose a card quickly. This one didn't look so ominous, yet Moyra frowned.

"The five of wands suggests there are hidden conflicts going on that may affect your journey." She closed her eyes, the tattoo on her forehead glowing brightly again. "Everyone has their own agenda, and oftentimes the actions that lead to one person's success causes the failure of another. Too much time is wasted while nobody can agree on anything—the best chance you have depends on whether you can integrate all these diverse standpoints."

When Moyra opened her eyes, she scanned the cards already laid out on the table.

"Considering the players on the board, you may have to consider whether you can come to some sort of compromise with the Emperor."

His teeth snapped, knowing who she was referring to. There would be no compromising with *her*. But as he thought it, Moyra tapped on the Death card. His resistance to change.

She was interpreting it wrong. That was all there was to it.

He'd rather run forever than face *her* again. Or, if forced to, there was a better chance of him ripping her into a thousand tiny pieces than listening to a word that came out of her mouth.

"We're nearly done," Moyra interrupted the violent dissention of his thoughts. "Looking at this spread, what kind of impression has it given you?"

She had laid bare his inner turmoil, his fears and hopes, the impossible odds he faced. She'd told him finding his family—all his family—was in his best interest, along with coming to peace with what *she* had done to him. She had told him the consequences if he couldn't. None of it came as any real surprise, but having it laid out cemented it somehow.

Drawing a deep breath, he chose another card.

"The Magician." Her smile was unexpected. "You know your own agency and choices. Found strength in your willpower. Understanding that your fate is not yet set, that you can still create your destiny, and that it is in fact *your* decisions that will set you free, has empowered you. This is promising, as long as you know when to fight and when to get out of the way of fate."

Cinn nodded. He still wasn't sure he could follow all Moyra's advice, but he did feel less like a finch in a hurricane. There was hope.

"Last card," Moyra promised. "Given all that we've seen in the cards and your feelings about them, the likeliest outcome will be shown in this final draw."

No pressure then. Closing his eyes, Cinn let his truest hope surface. Then he reached out and chose a card.

"The Fool," Moyra said.

Cinn's heart sank. His disappointment must have been apparent, because Moyra smiled reassuringly. "The Fool is always you. In this position, it promises a blank slate. A new beginning."

Jaw falling slack, Cinn wasn't sure he believed what she said. It wasn't exactly what he had wished for, yet it was.

A new name for a new beginning. He'd been tempted by it in the city, and now it was almost a promise. But whether that was a good thing, what that meant for the people he loved, he didn't know.

The knowledge that he was dreaming buzzed like a blowfly, sometimes close enough to swat at while other times so distant he couldn't be sure he heard anything at all. It hummed in his ear now, reminding him that no matter how real the grass felt beneath him, how warm the sun was on his face, he wasn't really home. He was not at the farm, and that was not Eaon looming over him with pitch dark eyes and a stoic expression.

Cinn tried to speak but couldn't. His mouth wouldn't work. He tried to sign, but his limbs were deadweights as he lay limp in the grass.

Then he saw them. Skin peeled from their faces, his family lifted him from the ground and carried him toward a deep hole.

William and Sarah didn't care as he silently begged for mercy. Edwina and Radley were blind to the pleading in his eyes. And Siobhan, with an umbilical cord wrapped around her throat, a grey lump dangling from it like a pendant, ignored the welling of tears in his eyes.

Eaon watched vacantly as the others threw Cinn into the grave.

"Wait. Wait, wait, wait. Please. I don't know anything. I don't know anything. I don't. Please. Wait."

He had begged. The first time he had seen the cell *she*

planned on leaving him in, he had begged. He did so again now as the first shovelfuls of dirt landed on his chest and face.

Before that day, he hadn't been afraid of the dark. Of small spaces or being alone. He hadn't feared anything.

Conquer your mind, and you'll be unstoppable.

Even enslaved and shackled, he had thought himself unstoppable—escaping every night to rummage through trash for scraps, sassing the adult slaves until not even the grumpiest demi-kin could help but smirk. And after, when they were free and Radley was spiraling into drink and rage, not even his brother's threats to sew his mouth shut had frightened him. Nothing had stopped him from doing everything in his power to lift Rad's spirits.

But as *she* closed the hatch on his cell and secured the bolt, as he broke his hands over and over trying to get out, Cinn realized his mother had lied to him. He was very stoppable.

He couldn't breathe.

Dirt cascaded into the grave, filling his mouth and nose. Ribs creaking under the weight of the earth piling on his chest, nothing could drown out *her* commands.

"Talk."

Suddenly, the compression was gone. Color bloomed across his vision like ink, the grave vanishing into periwinkle clouds and glittering mist. Flying through a sky of blue and purple—weightless and buoyant—he looked down to see his body replaced by pure light. It no longer felt like a dream, that vague sense of unreality replaced by a keen alertness.

This space he found himself in was boundless. If the fleshless faces of the people he loved weren't still plaguing his mind, he might have enjoyed the kind of glee a bird must feel as it soared the limitless sky. Images flashed briefly among the formless clouds as he hurtled by, come and gone too quickly to see.

Except one. Clearer than the rest and directly ahead, Cinn flailed as collision became imminent. He couldn't slow down, couldn't stop himself from tumbling into the image.

The expanse of color and mist was gone, but so was Cinn's body. He was nothing but a bright orb floating in what was undeniably a dungeon of some kind.

Just not his.

He didn't know this room. Didn't know the haze of it, the oppressive heat. There were windows set in one wall, a familiar limestone city sprawling far below with a border of glimmering gemstones in the distance. This dungeon may not be underground, but that didn't change what it was; he couldn't bear to look at the restraints bolted to the walls, the table laden with potions and tools he knew in his soul were not for benign purposes.

There were two women occupying the space. The one tied to a chair in the center of the room had her back to him while the second stalked in a slow circle, forehead tattoo blazing.

"I don't require you to talk, but I suggest you do. It's less painful that way."

If Cinn had teeth, he would have bared them at that tone. It curdled his blood—the suggestion that what was about to transpire was *his* fault, and she resented him for it.

"Dig away, Pearl," the woman in the chair spat. "You won't learn anything."

He knew that voice. He shouldn't be here, because *he knew that voice.*

Moyra's hair was longer, her braid half falling out, but as she raised her head to level those pink eyes—hard as real quartz despite the tears staining her cheeks, her own tattoo molten silver on her forehead—there was no mistaking who's dream he had fallen into.

The other witch, white hair coiled and pinned intricately at the base of her skull, stopped pacing directly behind Moyra. Tipping her head back, the older witch placed hands on either side of Moyra's face and began to chant.

Clenched fists on the arm of the chair, Moyra readied herself. Then stilled.

Whipping her head to the side, looking directly at Cinn, her mouth fell open.

"No."

Cinn looked behind him, but there was only the polished stone wall.

"Mother above, Cinn, I'm so sorry."

An intense vacuum pulled him out of the dungeon, tossing him back through the weightless landscape of rainbow clouds where he hurtled by at dizzying speeds.

Weight returned to him. Rather than flying, he was suddenly sinking with such velocity his stomach rose into his throat. The clouds parted below, and he saw himself asleep on the couch, Moyra skidding to her knees at his side, hands on either side of his face.

"*Wake.*"

PART III

ZEMBLANITY

CHAPTER 15

CINN

CHOKING, HE ROLLED TO HIS SIDE AND VOMITED. Candlelight pushed back the shadows as Moyra knelt on the floor, rubbing his sweat-soaked back. She wasn't the only one there to witness the flush in his face; Lula the mushroom sprite perched on the arm of the sofa, mewling.

"You're alright." Moyra's tired voice cracked around the promise.

He didn't feel alright. Cold shakes wracked his body, his stomach twisted in knots.

"I'm so sorry, Cinn. That has *never* happened before. I . . . I . . ."

It wasn't just him shaking, he realized. Patting Moyra's hand, both in comfort and forgiveness for whatever just happened, he slowly sat up and breathed through the nausea. While his head spun, Moyra left to fetch a glass of water, then began to mop up his mess on the floor with a towel.

"It's not your fault, but I just . . . I think it's just been so long since I've done so much magic, and I didn't exactly get much sleep last night . . . I lost control. I can't believe I lost control of the dreamscape like an *amateur*."

The dreamscape. Sipping at the water, he frowned until she noticed. Dabbing her sweaty forehead on her nightgown, she sighed and sat back on the floor.

"The dreamscape is a part of Morvia's realm," she explained. "The way the Lover has both the void and the after-realm to look over, Morvia has many domains. The dreamscape is where the conscious and unconscious mind meet, where we go when we're asleep. It's where our dreams form, and it's what descends on you when you have vivid flashbacks while awake. One of the many things a Morvish witch may specialize in is dream-weaving. We learn to manipulate the dreamscape. I was so tired that, while I was waiting for you to go to sleep to see if you'd let me into your personal unconscious space, I fell asleep myself. But I have *never* pulled someone into my own dream before. *Never*. And I am so sorry."

Most of what she said was gibberish to him, the concept of realms and unconsciousness too much to wrap his head around right now. But he thought about his own dream, and the moment he'd been pulled out of it and sucked into hers. The similarities.

Sighing, he gave Moyra's shoulder a gentle squeeze and forced a smile. Whether he had triggered the switch somehow, or whether it was just a lapse in control on Moyra's behalf, he didn't blame her. He knew how it felt to be out of control, to not know which way was up or what was real.

Drawing in the deepest breath he'd taken in hours, he got off the couch and padded through the night-cloaked room to his pack. Pulling out his trinket box, he brought it back to her and found the blue-streaked pebble inside.

This was real. The feeling of going home, of being welcomed, was real. Pressing it to his lips, Cinn focused on the coolness of the pebble until there was no doubting the sensation.

Moyra stayed on the floor, watching, but Lula toddled over to peer inside the box. The sprite didn't try to take anything, so he let her stay as he returned the pebble and brought out the feather. Leaning across the space between them, he brushed it down Moyra's nose. Too startled to do anything but scrunch her face, she continued to stare, pulse throbbing in her neck.

Her dream might have been real once, but it wasn't now. The tickle of the feather on her face, the humidity frizzing her hair . . . This was real.

When she finally swatted him away, he returned the feather to his box. It was enough, but his eyes snagged on one of his other strange treasures. Carefully withdrawing the cracked eggshell, he inspected it in his cupped palms. Remembered finding it in the Copelands' barn and being overwhelmed by a grief he didn't understand. William found him sobbing, and though utterly bewildered, he'd sat beside Cinn and comforted him for hours.

Unlike everything else, Cinn didn't know why he kept the eggshell. The feather made him feel seen, the pebble comforted him, the leaf he'd given to Eaon had been a reminder that even when he was tired of hanging on, someone would catch him. And the button with only one hole? He hadn't initially known why he'd been obsessed with that either, but he did now.

Now that he believed in Spirits—in fate.

Anyone else would think a one-holed button was useless, but regardless, it was precious to Cinn. He'd given it to Eaon so his friend would know that, even when feeling worthless, he mattered.

But the egg was still a mystery. He put it back, heart squeezing as he traded it for the most precious treasure of all;

pressing the willow amulet against his lips, he breathed in a scent that didn't actually linger, then tied it back around his neck. He never should have taken it off, and he never would again.

His dreams might try to trick him into believing the people he loved would hurt him, but he knew better. All his little things reminded him what was real.

"That's very beautiful," Moyra croaked, watching him tie the string.

Cinn smiled and showed her the paper fox, letting her turn it over in her hands. A gasp of hope, and Lula was reaching for Cinn's pebble once more.

He snapped the lid of his box closed, narrowly missing her little mushroom fingers. The sprite growled and bit his hand.

"Tss!" Cinn hissed, yanking his bleeding thumb away.

Ignoring them, Moyra sniffed and asked, "You like foxes?"

With a huff, Cinn clicked his tongue and shook his head with a smile. Of all the things Siobhan had made for him during those quiet months on the farm, passing the days folding paper into birds and flowers when pregnancy wouldn't let her do much else, Cinn had chosen the fox to keep safe. When Siobhan had made it, they'd shared a look over the Copelands' dining table, knowing exactly who it represented.

The cunning fox who had orchestrated Cinn's escape from Hyrsch, just so she could betray him in Pirevia, *then rescue him again*. Eaon had told the story with more respect for the shapeshifter than Cinn would have managed. When the Sparrows had come for him and Kaelean had shown up, he'd been half convinced she had yet another ulterior motive.

The paper fox was a reminder that not all who appeared as friends could be trusted, but not all who break your trust are enemies.

"My brother's familiar was a white desert fox," Moyra reminisced.

Cinn frowned, which seemed to confuse Moyra. Handing back the paper fox so he could slip it quickly inside his trinket box, Moyra mimicked his frown.

"Do witches south of the wards not have familiars?"

In all honesty, he didn't know.

"Well, out here they're quite common amongst witchlings growing into their power. A fae will appear and vow to guide the them until they're no longer needed, in exchange for a drop of blood. You must be careful what sort you allow to be your familiar, because a drop of blood is powerful. Some fae use it for nefarious reasons, but many use it to spawn Fair Folk or Sidhe— a child of fae and mortal blood, or fae and witch blood."

Cinn's eyes widened, both fascinated and terrified. Why would anyone take such a risk? What was so great about having a familiar? Moyra could not read his mind, so she went on, the explanation distracting her from the awfulness of their dreamscape experience.

"The sort of fae who approaches you depends on the blessing received. Gatty is a cat sith and is still with me, which is very uncommon, but he seems to think he is still needed." She looked out the window and bit her lip, worrying it before mumbling to herself, "Well, I hope he still thinks he's needed."

Cinn waited, glad for the distraction, too.

Moyra chuckled at some thought, then turned back with a bashful smile. "I was so young when he came to me that I didn't know what he was. I thought he was just an oversized cat, and my toddler tongue made the word came out as 'gat.' So that's the name he lets me use for him out loud. I wouldn't dare use his real name for anything less than a life-or-death emergency. He'd kill me."

Shivering, Cinn wasn't sure what was so funny about that.

"But my brother Kai was approached by a sand sprite presenting as a fox. He called her Eve. They're both gone now."

The laughter that brightened her face a moment ago disintegrated into such a profound sadness Cinn's own heart squeezed from it. Slipping from the couch, he sat beside her on the floor and patted her hand again. A tear slid down her cheek, and she let it, turning back to the window again.

"Sorry, Cinn. You didn't come here to listen to me mope."

Shaking his head, he squeezed her hand until she looked back. Placing his other palm to his chest, all he could do was nod and hope she understood what he couldn't say.

Again, she worried her lip for a moment before asking, "Would you like to know about them? My siblings? Maybe knowing more about me will help you trust me with your own . . . stuff." She waved a hand about his head.

Cinn couldn't help but smile—Stuff. Yeah, he had some stuff.

Taking that as a yes, she turned to face him.

"Would you trust me to show you instead of droning on? I can manipulate the dreamscape so you can see it all for yourself. It's a much better experience when I'm actually in control, I promise."

His stomach clenched, but if that was easier for her than talking right now, he would manage it. Gods knew he understood being too tired to talk anymore.

So he nodded. The tattoo on Moyra's forehead began to shine and the world once more dissipated into violet clouds.

CHAPTER 16

MOYRA

I<small>T</small> <small>WAS ABOUT MORE THAN BEING TOO TIRED TO TALK OR</small> wanting to share her family history with him—to talk about what happened with someone other than unsympathetic faeries. She had lost control of the dreamscape, sucked Cinn inside her own head, into one of the worst days of her life; how was he supposed to trust her help after something like that?

No, this was about showing off her skill. Showing what she could do, rather than leaving the bilious taste of her failures in his mouth.

Bathing in magic until she could taste it on her tongue, she summoned the dreamscape to envelope them.

It was not a physical place, and thus they did not exist in physical form. Cinn's soul shone brightly, undulating nervously as he returned to this place of shifting color. The first thing she did was summon him a body, a mirage to ease his mind, along with something to stand on. Once corporeal, Cinn relaxed a little, marveling as Moyra transformed this shapeless place into her childhood home.

Average. Just another limestone building crammed along the city streets, their home, her family, unremarkable in every way. The furniture was decent, their clothes fashionable; Mama and Papa had accrued enough loyal patrons with their healing tonics to keep the kitchen full.

It had never been enough for the Thorne children. Up in the attic with a stolen library book, the three of them were going to triple their power.

Moyra stood beside Cinn and watched her younger self standing in a ring with Olyvia and Kai, their hands joined, a soft chant passing their lips.

"In our youth," Moyra explained to Cinn, "we formed a coven. Many cultures have appropriated the term to define their chosen families, but to the Morvish it has always been more than a bond of love. It's a bond of magic."

They were too young to be doing it. If they were caught, they would all be thrown in jail. But, with their power pooled, they would not struggle through their final years at the academy. They would graduate top of their respective classes, be offered top-tier jobs, paving the way for their climb to upper society. There would be galas and parties, and none of them would ever again have to brew tonics for a living again.

"My abilities leaned toward dream-weaving, Olyvia was a strong spell-cleaver, and Kai was a natural way-finder. It's normal for witches to have strengths and weaknesses, even though we technically have the capacity to do all forms of Morvish magic. Once we achieved coventry, my ability to spell-cleave and way-find improved significantly. My dream-weaving skills were unmatched."

Cinn had a deep crease between his brows as he watched the trio, head tilted.

"Something wrong?"

Slowly, he shook his head.

"Well, a few years later . . ." She willed the dreamscape to shift again, the library at the academy taking form around them. The three Thornes were huddled around a study table, but there wasn't a book in sight. Olyvia had graduated the year before, Moyra the year before that, both sporting their constellation tattoos proudly. Kai was due to graduate in a few months but had summoned them to his boarding school with an urgent message.

"*You don't understand,*" Kai implored, fists clenched on the table. "*This fate line is brighter than the rest. It's magnetizing. The purest silver I've ever seen. If I didn't know better, I would say Morvia herself is pulling me south.*"

"*Like, to Ewich?*" Olyvia wrinkled her nose.

"*No.*" Kai leaned closer, lowering his voice to a bare whisper. "*Like, south of the wards.*"

Moyra remembered the way her gasp ripped her throat. She watched her younger self press a hand there, as if she could ease the shock.

"*That's impossible.*"

"*It's my destiny, Moyra.*"

"*Well.*" Olyvia tossed her frizzy brown hair over her shoulder. "*Looks like you're out of luck. Those wards are solid.*"

"*Maybe.*" Their brother met Olyvia's eye and held it. Waited for her to piece together what he was really asking.

"*You want me to cleave the wards,*" Olyvia breathed. Her forehead began glowing as she pulled on the pool of magic.

"*What are you doing?*" Kai hissed, looking around the library. As was Moyra, waiting for the high seer to come traipsing in to arrest them. All three were unifiers, but having beliefs was not illegal. Acting on them unsanctioned on the other hand . . .

"*Putting a kill order on the magic that lets seers see us right now, lest we all end up in prison just for thinking the idea. Mother forbid.*"

"Will that work?" Young Moyra whispered.

Olyvia grimaced and crossed her fingers. She was training under the high cleaver himself, such was her ability, but even so . . .

It was Kai's turn to draw on the pool, peering at the lines of fate connecting them all. *"I don't see any immediate departure, but some weird stuff is going on right now."*

"Probably because you're planning on literal treason!" Moyra hissed at him.

"Please," Kai begged, leaning farther across the table. *"You don't know what this feels like. I'll never sleep another night until I find what lies at the other end of this fate line."*

"It's insanity!" Moyra argued, but Olyvia had a gleam in her eye that promised trouble.

"The council is never going to vote in favor of uniting with the south. Maybe it's time we took matters into our own hands."

"No." Moyra shook her head. *"No, we're not messing with the wards. I won't be a part of this."*

Olyvia and Kai exchanged a long, loaded look, then rose as one.

"Stay here then," Olyvia said.

Kai nodded. *"I need to do this. I can feel it."*

Mouth hanging open, Young Moyra watched her brother and sister turn their backs and stalk for the door. Her stunned paralysis only lasted a moment before she was running after them.

"Olyvia, stop!"

They didn't stop.

"Kailevi, listen to me!" she used her brother's full name, mimicking Mama's scolding tone.

They had not listened to her.

And she had not followed them.

"I was the oldest," she explained to Cinn, who watched the two witches scurry down the hall of the academy, hatching the ultimate rebellion. "But they'd never listened to me a day in their lives. So I did the only thing I could."

Once again, she changed the dreamscape until the two of them stood in the Prayer Temple. Cinn gaped at the enormous ceiling. Moonlight filtered through tall arched windows, mirrors set at the base to guide light upward. Imbedded in the stone ceiling were opals, sparkling like stars. Pillars decorated with precious stones made a runway to a statue lording over rows of disciples on their knees.

Young Moyra was among them.

"Praying to Morvia is pointless," she told Cinn, shaking her head. "She does not intervene. But it was better than wringing my hands at home, avoiding Mama and Papa's questions and waiting to see what would happen when Olyvia and Kai reached the border. I knelt there for days, until I felt it."

The serene quiet of the Prayer Temple was broken by a scream of such agony that a disciple wet themselves. Only two witches ran toward young Moyra as she collapsed on the ground, fists in her hair as she screamed and screamed. The rest scrambled away as fast as their hands and knees would take them.

"Olyvia died cleaving the tiniest gap in the wards." Moyra's voice cracked, eyes burning as she stared at herself, the pained cry spiraling into a mournful wail. "I felt it through the coventry bond. Like a limb being cut off. Worse, I could still feel her magic in the pool. In that moment before death, it's normal for a witch to draw on every ounce of power she has access to in order to save herself, but if she died with it in her veins, the power died too. Olyvia knew she was burning out, but she left the power with Kai and I rather than try to save herself. Rather than risk failure, leaving the pool empty."

She couldn't look at Cinn. Couldn't bear the pity that would be in his eyes. Her sister was gone, but a little piece of her lived on, deep in the well of power residing in Moyra. A reminder that, once, she had not been so alone.

"I never saw Kai again, either." She sniffed. "But I felt it when he died too. I was alone in the shack when this sickening, severing pain exploded through my chest. But he left his power with me, too."

She should have gone with them.

In the Prayer Temple, guards were running in. At first they tried to help her, but then every witch still lingering began screaming. Terror washed through the building, out into the street and through the city like a tsunami. It swallowed Ahrenhale whole before devouring all of Qiri, feasting across the bay to take root in Phara and Erve. Within hours, reports came in from Yvar that their witches had felt the cosmic shift, too.

A shift that changed all of fate.

A shift the high seer didn't see coming.

She didn't show Cinn what happened next. The interrogation. Nobody had seen the crack coming, but once the act of treason had been committed, the high seer *knew* who had been involved. Guards dragged Moyra, still wailing, from the temple right to Pearl's feet.

The high seer had done everything she could to force Moyra to admit where her siblings had committed their crime. How they shielded their intentions from her. Moyra knew the answers, of course. Olyvia had left a note in case Moyra changed her mind and wished to join them, but she had burned it and gone to the temple instead.

She would not betray her coven, though. If cleaving the

wards was something Olyvia thought worth dying for, Moyra would honor her decision. And she would not let the council's bloodhounds go after her brother. Would not let them find and seal the gap, because as soon as she could, Moyra would go after Kailevi. She would tell other unifiers how to get through, too, and they would do what they could to help the south with Chaos.

Unlike the high seer, who would never risk binding herself so intimately to others, Moyra had the power of three at her disposal. They were matched, and she'd learned a few spell-cleaving tricks from her sister. Every attempt to pull the information directly from her head was met with a mental blade, cutting through the magic. No spell, hex, or curse could touch her.

Letting the dreamscape fade away, Moyra and Cinn sat on the floor of her shack once more.

"I should be in prison, but instead, they banished me here. Perhaps they hoped the fae would get rid of me, or perhaps they knew that living with my loss, alone and in poverty, was the perfect punishment. I would *rather* be in prison."

Cinn winced, and perhaps she should have kept that part to herself. Rising, she helped him up and the two of them went to the kitchen to brew some tea. It was highly unlikely she would get any more sleep tonight, and dawn was only an hour away.

"But, now you know who I am. Why I'm here." She prepared two cups and lit some incense to clear the room of all the negative energy the two of them had brought in. "Maybe it will help you not be so afraid to show me who you are."

CHAPTER 17

CINN

STIFFENING, CINN FOLDED HIS ARMS OVER HIS CHEST. HE wasn't afraid to let her help. After what she did yesterday while holding his wrists, somehow making it possible for him to function through his panic, he'd have been more than willing to let her in his head tonight. To get him out of that grave.

Probably.

Maybe not.

He just . . . He didn't know what the problem was.

But he also did.

It wasn't distrust or shame or residual fear of Moyra that made him hesitate. It was fear of something else. Fear that if she got inside his head . . .

He couldn't think it. Swallowing, he shifted on the dining chair and pressed a hand to his throat.

Moyra narrowed her eyes as she waited by the kettle. "Where did your head go just now?"

It was none of her business. She was never really going to be able to help him because no matter how he may want to, he could never really let her in. Not the way she had let him in tonight, her pain and secrets on display. He couldn't let her mess around in his head.

What he needed was a way to ask for the answers he'd really come here for. The reading may have shed some light on things, but he needed to know how to protect his family. As long as they were south of the wards, they weren't safe. Not because of the Sparrows, or because of *her*, but because of Chaos. So he knew his first steps. He had to go back and convince them to come north, then find a way to get them through the wards.

That was his question. Finally, he had one.

Standing quickly, he fetched a bit of parchment from Moyra's cupboard, trying to write legibly.

Moyra watched him for a moment before asking another question, the weight of it leaden.

"Why can't you speak?"

"*Why won't you tell me?*"

He flinched, waiting for pain, but this time the dungeon didn't descend. His body remained strong and steady—present, even if memories knocked loudly against his skull. Memories he didn't want to look at. And words. They fizzed like bubbly wine, pushing at the cork in his throat. They might as well have been pushing at the solid door of a cell, so deep underground that even if he released them in a scream that tore open his throat, nobody would hear.

The worst part was that he knew he was the one holding that cell door closed, but even if his life depended on it—even if his family's lives depended on it—he couldn't make himself let go.

"It's okay to admit you're scared," Moyra said gently, but the accusation raised his hackles. He wasn't scared, he was determined.

But if that were true, why was he sweating?

Maybe it started as pure defiance, refusing to give *her* another word . . . but she wasn't here now. To speak bore no consequence.

A shiver ran down his spine, as if deep down, he didn't believe that. As if, should he breathe so much as a single syllable, *she* would hear it. Would appear before him in blood and shadows to snatch him away, back to her dungeon where nobody would ever find him again.

A gentle nudge against his mind.

Cinn flung open his eyes. He hadn't even realized he'd closed them.

"It's alright," Moyra soothed, sitting across from him, tea forgotten. "It's just me."

No matter how hard he swallowed, Cinn couldn't dislodge that cork in his throat. Wasn't sure he wanted to, content to choke on it forever.

Moyra nudged at his mind again, and for the briefest moment, an image flashed behind his eyes.

Eaon.

"I'm just tugging at happy thoughts right now, but if you let me in, let me see, I can do more."

Cinn couldn't concentrate on Moyra's words as he remembered Eaon's furious face, his words drowning out the voice that haunted his every sleeping moment.

"You tell her that if she doesn't leave the kinner alone, I will make what happened in Pirevia look like a scratch compared to the lashing I will unleash upon her city."

Even if Cinn's worst nightmares came true, Eaon would come for him. He knew that truth in the very deepest parts of his soul. Eaon would not leave him to rot. Eaon would ruin himself and the world to find him. Free him.

Eaon would keep him safe.

As if that knowledge was some kind of key, Cinn's defenses fell and Moyra enveloped him.

"This wasn't exactly what I had in mind, but let's go with it. Take my hands," she told him, reaching across the table between them.

With his eyes closed, he could easily imagine he was back in the little cottage he'd shared with Eaon at the Copelands' farm. Could see his dearest friend shuffling silently from the bedroom, rubbing his weary eyes. See the morning sun gilding his bronze skin and mousy hair, alighting the amber in his eyes.

He wanted to thank him. Cinn clutched a sleeping Puddles to his chest and opened his mouth, the words on the tip of his tongue.

A loud bang shattered the illusion.

Who flinched harder, he didn't know, but Moyra was quick to lunge across the table and clamp a hand over his mouth, eyes wide.

"Disappear. Now," she hissed, then shoved him out of his chair.

Cinn didn't need to be told twice. Snatching his pack off the floor—the only evidence a second person was in the house—he scurried to Moyra's bedroom and dived beneath the narrow bed. The threadbare woolen blanket wasn't long enough to curtain his hiding place, and besides a chest of drawers by the window, there was no other furniture in the room. Under the bed was the only place to hide. Whoever was at the door would easily deduce where he was.

He shouldn't have caused such a scene in Ahrenhale. No doubt the city guards had somehow tracked him, or, considering the kind of magic that existed in Qiri, someone had *seen* that he was here.

At his hip, he curled a fist around the hilt of his dagger. With his heart pounding in his ears, it was a miracle he could even hear the creak of the front door as Moyra opened it.

She gasped. Cinn drew his knife.

A stranger's voice, wild and desperate. "Please."

"Mother above," Moyra wheezed, then called out, "Cinn! Get some oatstraw from the garden! Now!"

He hesitated. It could be a trap. If he was quick and quiet, he could get out her bedroom window and disappear into the trees before they got tired of waiting for him to emerge.

Sliding the knife home again, Cinn loosened his grip one finger at a time. He licked the sweat from his upper lip and clenched his eyes against the urge to run. Moyra wouldn't do that to him. They'd only known each other a couple of days, but he had to believe she wouldn't put him in danger.

Rolling out from under the bed, he approached the living room warily. The front door was still open and Cinn's eyes widened at the sight of a witch on his knees, clinging to Moyra's bare feet. Both his skin and clothes were dirty, oily hair limp across his brow. He may have latched to Moyra like she was salvation incarnate, but his gaze followed something around the room that only he could see.

"It's alright, Jonah. Get up for me." Moyra struggled with his weight, half dragging the witch to the couch. The male was too busy clawing at his head to keep his feet beneath him for long, muttering the same word—*please, please*—repeatedly.

Desperately.

"Cinn, now," Moyra hissed.

Snapping out of his shock, Cinn rushed to the little garden out front of the house and hunted down the herb Moyra had asked for, grateful for Eaon's lessons during their travels. The babbling from the insane witch was getting louder, enough so to draw the attention of the fae. As he surveyed the shadowy glen, he swore he saw large shadows moving, eyes shining in the moonlight.

"Hush, Jonah. It's alright," Moyra tried to sooth him.

Shutting the door firmly, Cinn met her in the kitchen and traded the oatstraw for another knife, slipping it into the waist of his pants. Moyra eyed him as she rushed around the kitchen gathering ingredients, so he explained by pointing to the door and making little flapping motions. She only pursed her lips and nodded.

"There's so many of them," Jonah gasped, curling up on the couch. How he hadn't been eaten alive out there, Cinn had no idea. "Everything. Everything touches everything. Your eyes are glowing with everything you've seen. The connections. The fate lines. Oh, Lover spare me, the fate lines. There are so many. I can't see. It's too bright."

"I know, Jonah, I know. You'll be okay. I'll make them go away," Moyra promised before urging Cinn closer. "Stir the ground lavender in the water until I tell you to stop, then sieve the diffusion into this vial with the oatstraw."

He took the wooden spoon as Moyra went to Jonah, kneeling on the floor beside him.

"Jonah, can I put you in a dream?"

"You have six lines beside yours," he said instead of answering. "So dark, and golden shimmers. One so close, the others so far away."

"Jonah, I need you to focus. Look at my face." She took his cheeks in her hands, holding him firm as he wrenched back and thrashed his head. "It's me. It's me, Jonah. Tell me I can put you in a dream until your tonic is ready."

"Sevens. Sevens everywhere."

"Jonah!"

He stopped, and for a moment his bloodshot eyes focused solely on Moyra. "A dream?"

She gave him a comforting smile and Jonah nodded. Within seconds, his body went limp, eyes fluttering closed. At first his sleep was fitful as he continued to mutter about colors and fate, but, as Moyra took him deeper into the dreamscape, he began to settle.

Sighing deeply, Moyra left him and came back in time to sieve her own lavender, praying over the solution in a way that reminded him of how Eavha prayed while brewing for Eaon.

The hair at the nape of Cinn's neck stood on end as he waited for an explanation for who this male was, because all of this was eerily familiar. Too like the way Eaon sometimes talked when he was in a state.

"Just another shining example of Ahrenhale's failure to its people," Moyra muttered. When her gaze lifted to Cinn's, his confusion evident, she sighed through a yawn. "Morvish magic is only a blessing to those who can afford to manage it. For those who can afford to attend an academy. Too poor? Too bad. And magic as strong as Jonah's? Without training? It takes over. It's sending him mad. I've talked to him about binding it, but he's afraid to lose the magic completely. So all I can do is suppress it with tonics; try to give him some peace. This is a family recipe. My parents' life mission is to treat those too poor for schooling, and fifty-five years of estrangement doesn't stop them from sending clients to me when they're overwhelmed."

She collected the vial and whispered a few more words of prayer before taking it to where Jonah slept deeply.

A family recipe.

Something had nagged him while he'd gone with Moyra to see her siblings, but now it slapped him in the face why her brother's name was so familiar. Why he'd looked familiar, too.

Her brother, who'd gone to find his fate south of the wards. And as Cinn looked from the witch passed out on the couch, driven mad by his untrained blessing, to the magic-suppressing tonic in Moyra's hand, Cinn cursed himself for taking so long to see it.

Moyra Thorne was Eaon's aunt.

And Eaon was Morvish.

CHAPTER 18

MOYRA

MAGIC SUPPRESSION TONICS HAD SOME UNPLEASANT SIDE effects when used long term, but if Jonah wouldn't let her bind his blessing, then it was better than leaving him to his affliction.

Her parents had worked on all sorts—dream-weavers who couldn't anchor themselves, tumbling through the dreamscape endlessly; star-talkers who couldn't filter through all the whispers, unable to find a moment's peace; time-watchers and seers, spell-cleavers and way-finders, there wasn't a single specialty immune to the consequences of going without training.

The evidence was laying on her couch, drifting in safe and comforting dreams. Jonah was worse every time he came to see her. She'd brewed him a whole case of tonics only last week but, judging by his distress, he wasn't taking them. It broke her heart to see the state of him, so unraveled compared to the young way-finder who'd initially knocked on her parents' apothecary door. That he'd even had the sense to find her again was a miracle.

Or fate. That the lines had led Jonah to her just as she and Cinn were having a breakthrough was not a coincidence. Such a word didn't exist in the vocabulary of Morvish witches. But what would be the point? Was she not supposed to help Cinn after all? Or was the kinner seeing Jonah in such a state important somehow?

Considering the shade of grey Cinn had gone, the latter was possible.

"Help me sit him up," Moyra said as she approached the couch.

Perching on the edge and holding the tonic between her knees, she took hold of both Jonah's wrists, ready to pull him upright. When Cinn didn't move, she sighed.

"You're mute, not deaf. Get over here."

Sucking in a sharp breath, he took a step back toward the door.

"Don't you dare."

He blinked a few times, finally meeting her eye. The terror there silenced Moyra as he took another step back, turned for the door and left.

It made no sense. The dreamscape was nowhere near him.

Since Jonah was happily asleep, she left his tonic on the floor beside the couch and rushed after Cinn. The first rays of daylight were greying the clouds, but it was still too dark to see much. Standing on the porch, she listened for him. Nothing but the lake's gentle waves washing the shore, both a lullaby and a threat.

"Cinn?" she called, squinting into the surrounding bush. Her heart galloped as she searched, knowing the fae were out there. The crumbling brick of her shack had never been much protection, but Gatty had marked his territory early on and they rarely disturbed her. But Gatty wasn't here. Sweat slicked her back. "*Cinn!*"

The sun rose a little higher just as the sound of boots kicking water set the hair at the back of her neck rising. She spotted him, finally, already ankle deep in the shallows, hands in his hair.

"Not so close to the water!" she shouted, descending into her garden. Not at night.

Cinn turned back, then stumbled. Frowning, he bent to pick up a long, heavy cloak from the water.

A wrathful shriek rattled the tiles of her rook.

"Get out of the water," Moyra wheezed, hitching up her skirt as she rushed through her garden. "Cinn, get out of the water!"

It was not a cloak he had found.

The selkie came barreling from beyond the trees faster than a whipped horse. Humanoid on land, its spindly legs were a blur of moon-white flesh, wet feet slapping on the sand as it shrieked again and dived for Cinn.

To hold the coat of a selkie was to have command of them, thus the places they left their seal-like skin while prowling the land were aggressively guarded secrets. This one had grown lax; nobody but Moyra lived at the lake.

The monstrous faerie tackled Cinn down into the shallows, wrenching her coat away. Baring rows of tiny teeth, she screeched in his face. Cinn spluttered water and tried to scramble back, but two more selkies came roaring from farther along the shore. The dawn light turned their moon-white skin opalescent as they joined their sister, one grabbing Cinn by the hair while the other bit down on the hand reaching for his weapon.

"Cinn!" Moyra screamed as they began dragging him into the lake's depths, wrestling his flailing limbs.

She raced to the edge of her garden, trodding everything in her path. She didn't know what she was going to do, but she couldn't just—

The moment her foot passed the twine perimeter, she fell.

The breath she'd been saving for a deep-water dive became a throat-ripping scream as streaks of lightning burned through her body. Blind with pain, she dragged herself back into her garden.

"Moyra?"

Heart leaping into her throat, she whipped her head to where her familiar stood, brushing his fluffy tail against the doorway. She didn't care if it meant he won their little spat, she sobbed with relief at the sight of the cat sith.

"What's wrong?" Gatty asked, whiskers twitching. "I sensed your pain."

"The lake," she panted through labored breaths, echoes of pain lingering in her bones. Pointing to where the surface rippled, there was no other sign Cinn had been there at all. "Selkies took him."

Slowly, the knee-high black cat with eyes like starlight padded from the porch. The weight of the muscle in his tightly coiled body bowed the step as he descended. "One of your clients?"

"Please. I know you hate the water—"

"It's alright," he interrupted before she could finish asking for a favor. Ears flattening, his tone dropped. "I was in the mood for seafood this morning anyway."

Sweating and trembling, Moyra forced herself to sit upright, helpless to do anything but watch as Gatty loped to the water's edge, easing into the water with preternatural grace.

From under a trampled marigold, Lula whimpered.

"Oh no."

Guilt ripped her chest open as she leaned over and pulled the mushroom sprite onto her lap. Part of her cap was squished. Dida glided out from a nearby bush, fluffy white florets aflutter. The dandelion sprite's limbs may have been small and twiggy, but the violence promised as she shook her fists at Moyra was not to be mocked.

As Dida squawked and fussed over her friend's injured fronds, an apology rested on Moyra's lips. She almost didn't care what it would cost her to say it; she was an idiot for running after Cinn like that, and now Lula was hurt.

The pipes in the house behind them rattled loudly as Nena rolled through them, plopping out of the yard spout, pointing and wailing. It almost broke Moyra's resolve before she realized the lake sprite wasn't fretting about Lula; she was pointing at the lake.

An inky stain bloomed beneath the surface, color indiscernible in the waking morning light.

"Whose blood is it?" Moyra wheezed, wiping the tears leaking down her face.

Rather than answer, Nena splashed across the garden with surprising speed toward the lake.

"Nena, no!"

Dida leapt into the air with a battle cry, prepared to give chase, but as the lake sprite disappeared beneath the murky surface, Moyra grabbed the dandelion's twiggy leg and brought her to her chest.

"Stay. Please."

The stillness of the lake and the silence of the surrounding forest made the minutes last hours, the fear in her chest twisting into grief prematurely. Surely she would feel it if Gatty had perished, the way they had always been able to sense each other's pain. And Cinn had proved his ability to heal, but if something happened to Gatty, to Nena, then there was nobody to help them.

Placing the two sprites carefully aside, Moyra cried in rage as she pulled back her skirt to hit at the metal ring around her ankle. Being confined to the house was one thing but being unable to help people in trouble was a punishment she didn't deserve.

Her spell-cleaving power couldn't dent the magic binding the shackle, nor could Gatty's finessing. Regardless, Moyra found a nearby stick and shimmied it between her flesh and the metal, trying to wrench it off.

Lula mewled loudly, and Moyra looked back to where a soggy lump drifted across the lake's surface. With a shriek, Dida's head fluffed out to twice its usual size. Moyra was too slow to catch her again as the sprite flitted beyond the herb garden and spun her way across the lake.

"Please," Moyra whispered.

Letting her blessing swell, ignoring the twang in her ears as she pushed the limits of what she could accomplish without rest, Moyra sagged in relief to see the pearlescent fate line tying her and Gatty together, strong and clear. A second fate line throbbed in neon white between her and the floating lump.

Cinn.

Dida and Nena clutched strands of his hair, helping Gatty drag the limp body onto the sand. Bedraggled, his white eyes too large in his water-slicked face, Gatty shook out each bloodied paw.

"This one?" he asked, licking his chops.

"Thank you," Moyra choked as she dropped back to her knees in relief. "Thank you."

The fate lines faded away as Gatty dragged Cinn's mangled form across the beach to where Moyra could reach him. The strength of her familiar never ceased to amaze her, and once they were across the twine perimeter, she hugged him close, unfazed by how he drenched her clothes.

"Thank you," she muttered again.

"That's three times now, witch. I'll be calling in those favors sooner rather than later," he chided, but there was affection in his tone.

Releasing him, Moyra assessed Cinn's unconscious form. Wounds all over his body were closing quickly, patches of raw pink marring his freckled skin. But his chest was not moving. Turing him on his side, she beat at his back until he lurched, vomiting sludgy water all over her herbs.

"You're alright," she soothed as his fists clenched, shoulders tensing. "You're okay."

For a few minutes, Cinn continued to cough out lake water.

"I'm sorry. I should have warned you about the lake," she said when he finally stopped hacking.

Shuddering, Cinn shook his head.

"He should have known better. It is not the first time he's been taken by fae," Gatty said.

Cinn started, sitting upright and staring at the black cat licking himself on the porch.

Moyra smiled. "Cinn, this is Gatty. He can hear thoughts." Then to her familiar, "Cinn is kinner."

Gatty paused mid lick. "Interesting."

Rubbing his sternum, Cinn looked down to Gatty with a frown.

"What am I doing here? I could ask the same of you." The cat sith returned to cleaning himself, fur already drying under the fresh sun. "Your kind shouldn't be beyond the wards."

A brief pause, then Gatty scoffed.

"Of course I know of your kind. If there's one thing the fae deal more in than promises, it's gossip, and there has been little else to do the last half a century, stuck in this moldy shack."

"Nobody's making you stay," Moyra sniped, annoyed at being left out of half the conversation.

"Well clearly I can't leave you alone for five minutes without you putting clients in mortal danger," he bit back.

Moyra scoffed. "Five minutes? You've been gone for days."

"You told me to leave," he reminded her. "In fact, I believe your words were *get out of my sight right now before I turn you into a hat*."

"You destroyed the last of my tea."

"You forgot to leave out my milk."

Cinn spat out another mouthful of gunky water and cleared his throat. Taking his arm, Moyra helped him up the porch, giving Gatty a pointed stare as she went.

"Did it ever occur to you to just ask me for it instead of destroying the one bit of joy I have in my life?" she hissed.

"The fae do not ask for things," he growled, following. Finding a patch of sunlight warming the wooden floors through the glass windows, the cat sith stretched out to bask. "It suggests we are open for bargaining."

Getting Cinn settled at the table, she brought him a cup of drinking water and a spoonful of honey for his throat. He smiled shakily, taking the teaspoon before looking to where Lula was hugging Dida and Nena. He cleared his throat again before reaching over to place the spoon near them.

"They really didn't help all that much," Gatty said as he eyed the honey.

Moyra shook her head and went back to the kitchen to fetch a saucer of milk and another spoon of honey for her familiar. Cooped together for as long as they had been, they were bound to argue, but those days without him had been some of the worst of her life.

Then again, that might have been the lack of tea.

CHAPTER 19

CINN

HE WAS SICK OF FAERIES. SICK OF DROWNING IN LAKES AND rivers. It took every ounce of his self-control not to scream and spit because, damn it, he just wanted to go home and bury himself under blankets. But, instead of throwing his teacup across the room and shredding the remains of his ruined clothes, or running into the wilderness to scream and scream and scream, Cinn counted to ten. He gave himself exactly ten seconds to wallow in self-pity before he had to pull himself together.

Your mind will break before your body does.

Every day, he was a little closer to that edge. His body would exist forever, but he didn't know how much longer he could keep a grip on his mind. It felt like the sand that had slid through his fingers, desperate to find purchase on anything solid as the selkies dragged him across the bottom of the lake.

The sprites finished their honey treat quickly, flitting over to cover his face in tiny faerie kisses before zooming out the door again.

Gatty chuckled. "Sprites are such fickle things."

Cinn finished his tea, ignoring the large black cat. The mind-reading unsettled him, but more than that, he didn't want to remember the way it had become a true fae in the depths of the lake, ripping one of the selkies to ribbons while the other two swam off. Cats shouldn't be in the water. Cats shouldn't be able to swim and talk and grin so wide that, as Cinn slipped into unconsciousness, their rows of horrible teeth made him fear he would end up breakfast anyway. This cat only looked like a large companion for Puddles, but if Gatty came curling up on his chest in the middle of the night, Cinn would sooner wet himself in terror than scratch his belly.

"All done?" Moyra asked, taking his cup. She studied the remnants of tea leaves at the bottom for a moment before placing it aside. "I'll be back in a moment. I'll just fix up Jonah quickly."

His bleeding wounds had closed, but inside, muscle was still pulling back together, organs still shifting around. The tea sitting in his stomach, waiting for his kidney to be ready, was uncomfortable and it took a moment for Cinn to catch his breath.

Ten more seconds.

And when that was not enough, he put his head down on the table, covered it with his arms, and screamed silently into the wood.

It was too much. There was too much in his head. In his heart. So many things he needed to do, people he needed to help, but all he wanted to do was get the mark off the back of his neck. *Now.*

He didn't want to live forever at the bottom of a lake, an eternal feast for some faerie. Blank slate be damned, he didn't need to be a way-finder to know that as long as The Mark of One Unending remained, such agony was his destiny.

But there was a possibility that Moyra could remove it. She'd suggested as much when he first arrived, asking if that was why he had sought her out. And right now, that was the only thing he wanted. To be free.

Which was selfish.

Gods, he wanted to be selfish.

But if their situations were reversed, Eaon wouldn't run.

Sitting up, he looked to where Moyra struggled to get Jonah upright, whispering in his ear as she somehow convinced him to drink the tonic while still unconscious.

Eaon suffered in ways Cinn couldn't understand, but he would not run from pain if it meant abandoning his family. He was brave like that. Good, in a true, deep way that made Cinn ashamed.

Instinctively, he reached for the willow amulet hanging around his neck. The whole world stilled as his fingers brushed bare flesh. Looking down, he died inside at the poignant absence of Eaon's gift.

He was on his feet before he knew what he was doing, storming back outside, down the porch and beyond Moyra's herb garden.

"Cinn! What are you doing?" she called as she followed, stopping at the twine perimeter.

Once again at the lake's edge, his heart thundered. He reached for the dagger still at his hip. Among the dark blood dissipating in the lake, the tops of two heads drew closer, two sets of eyes glaring back.

"Don't be foolish, boy. It's just a necklace," the cat called. "I won't come after you again."

It was not just a necklace.

Taking a deep breath, knife in hand, he waded back into the lake.

Being underwater by choice was unnatural, but he tried to relax and let his body sink to the sandy lakebed. The sun was high enough to see the selkies' silhouettes slinking toward him, their humanoid figures hidden beneath seal skins they'd retrieved since Cinn's escape.

A thousand worries should be screaming inside his head—he was at a disadvantage in every possible way—but there was only silence, stillness, as he waited for the fae to reach him. His lungs did not ache for breath, his heart steady in his chest. The water did not burn his eyes the way it had only minutes before as he focused on the task at hand.

No excuses. He had to retrieve Eaon's amulet.

The selkies' eyes were just like the cat sith's as they grew closer, teeth bared. Their large seal bodies were liquid grace while Cinn's was slow and clumsy, so he tried not to move as they circled him, tracking their movements with his eyes.

Commander Porter had taught them on their very first day as cadets not to let the enemy get behind you, but if it couldn't be helped, at least be aware of their position. Cinn blinked at the memory, paying attention to the way the water shifted around him, silt billowing higher as the selkies' circling constricted.

They would attack from behind. Why wouldn't they? He would have to wait until they were close enough not to see him move. Too close and too fast to dodge the blade in their path.

Not yet.

Not yet.

The water swirling around him slowed. Frowning, Cinn turned to where the two selkies had stopped, blinking their too-large eyes at him.

Cinn knew he could hold his breath for hours and still

function, as long as he stayed conscious, but every minute he wasted would make him slower. Yet, to attack first would not end well, and he didn't understand the strange noises the two selkies made at each other.

One opened their mouth. Too wide. Far too wide. Cinn couldn't help but kick away as the selkie peeled off the top half of her seal skin, leaving it flowing in the water by her waist. Their eyes were still too big, mouth slit from ear to ear with rows of tiny teeth on display, but everything else about her appeared human. Black hair fanned around her pale face, and though her words were garbled underwater, he understood them when she spoke.

"You do not belong here, Marked One."

Instinctively, Cinn reached for the back of his neck.

"Our sisters sing to us from beyond the wards, their beastly cousins moving against your prison. Are you here to bargain for aid?"

A bargain. They had stopped their attack hoping for a deal.

Everybody knew not to make deals with the fae, and yet he had a suspicion that if he refused he would have to kill these two, and if they knew something about what was happening in the south, believed aid was needed, perhaps such an opportunity shouldn't be wasted.

He nodded.

The selkie still in seal form made more strange noises. Narrowing her eyes, the speaking one pushed through the water until she was within striking range.

Cinn didn't dare.

"You tried to capture our sister's skin."

Cinn shook his head adamantly. He honestly hadn't known what it was he tripped over.

"Is the cat sith a friend of yours?" she spat, a pulse going through her hair until it stood on end.

Again, Cinn shook his head. Absolutely not.

"Then I will make a deal with you."

She began to swim for the surface, but Cinn stopped her with a desperate wave. Reaching for the place around his neck where Eaon's amulet ought to be, he looked at them with pleading eyes.

Another strange exchange of sounds between the selkies before the speaking one nodded.

"Since you meant no harm and our sister attacked you first, we will fetch your amulet as a token of good will. But you will ask for no further compensation."

It had not occurred to him to ask for such, so nodding agreement was easy.

The seal-skinned selkie sped into the lake's depths while Cinn followed the other to the surface. Sucking down a deep breath, he paddled lamely while the selkie slicked back her raven hair. They weren't so far from the shore that Cinn couldn't hear Moyra's cursing.

Bristling, the selkie hissed. "We should have scalped her while the cat sith was away."

Cinn bit his tongue. Her voice was songlike above the water, light and whimsical. Absurd, considering how deadly she was.

As best he could, he mimed that he could not speak and hoped that would not be the end of this truce.

"Language is not a barrier in matters of magic. A promise is a promise."

The seal-skinned selkie poked their head above the surface, willow amulet hanging from between their teeth. Cinn took it carefully, dipping under the surface as he put it back around his neck before paddling back up.

"You require aid in the south," the selkie began immediately. "The waters are festering with mutation, the mer moving where they ought not be, their lethal brethren rising from deep slumber."

None of that sounded good. He couldn't know if it was true, but he nodded anyway.

"I will sing of our bargain to my sisters in the south and they will be your allies in the sea. This is no small offer, Marked One. We have no part to play in the blood about to be spilled, thus the cost of our assistance will be steep."

In Hyrsch, Cinn had listened to plenty of con artists hoodwinking unsuspecting shoppers. The selkie's sales pitch sounded a lot like exaggeration and doom-singing, and had Moyra not warned him about Chaos coming to destroy everything, he might not have believed a word from the selkie's mouth.

She eyed him, waiting to see if he would protest. When he held her gaze patiently, she continued.

"A vial of your blood."

With the amulet back around his neck, there was room in his head to think. Moyra said she'd traded a drop of her blood to Gatty for his familiaral guidance, and even that was not a risk all witches took. A whole vial of his blood, when he had forever to live with the consequences . . .

Glancing to shore, Moyra's thumb-sized frame was rigid, pale as fresh linen. She could see what he was doing as clearly as he could see the shaking of her head. But as their eyes met, her hands dropped from her mouth to her sides, her eyes closing. He waited, and after a moment she met his gaze once more, mouth popping open with surprise.

When she nodded, so did he.

Something akin to lightning clattered through his chest, making him gasp. His legs lost coordination for a moment, and he swallowed a mouthful of lake water before getting ahold of himself.

The selkie grinned.

"Return to the shore at sundown with the blood or discover the consequences of breaking a faerie bargain."

The water rippled as the two slipped beneath the surface again, leaving Cinn to swim clumsily back to shore. He swallowed three more mouthfuls before getting his feet on the sand, still gripping his knife in one hand and the pendant around his neck with the other.

"You might be the biggest imbecile I have ever met, but whatever you just did with the selkies . . ." She huffed as he dragged his waterlogged boots across the sand, meeting her at the twine perimeter. "Remember when I said there were moments in the timelines where your choices could take you toward one fate or another? This was one of them. I *looked*, and . . . What? Why are you looking at me like that?"

Cinn was too cold to know what his face was doing, but Gatty snorted from where he'd laid out across the porch. "He promised them a vial of his blood."

Moyra went from pale to grey.

Cinn grimaced.

"Well," she croaked. "We'd better get that sorted."

Putting the knife away, Cinn followed Moyra inside. At the sound of Jonah's snores, Cinn remembered what had started this debacle with the selkies to begin with.

Eaon needed help.

CHAPTER 20

MOYRA

THERE WASN'T A WORD TO DESCRIBE HOW BADLY SHE WANTED to scold Cinn's stupidity, all the while knowing that it had to be done. This path was written in the stars—stars that had almost swallowed her whole in their desperation for her to *see*. Which, considering her seer skills were not as honed as others, and considering Morvia's general disinterest in mortal lives, still had her trembling.

Whatever this all meant, she hoped it was worthwhile because an entire vial of kinner blood was a hefty price. It wasn't even her sacrifice to make, yet nausea turned her stomach as she emptied a vial of pepper and rinsed it.

"I've never drawn this much blood before," she admitted, sensing Cinn coming up behind her. "But I have some—"

Taking a knife from the bench, Cinn didn't hesitate to cut open a vein in his forearm. Blood pooled quickly, but not as fast as the skin was trying to pull back together. Moyra stared in shock as Cinn dug his fingers into the wound, holding it open and taking measured breaths as he held his arm over the vial in

Moyra's hands. Warm, bright red blood dripped on her fingers. Her stomach lurched, but she held steady until the vial was full, corking it and passing it to Cinn to pocket.

"Well." She gagged. "That's one way to do it I suppose."

As she washed her hands, Cinn wiped the stain from his skin. The silence was laden until Moyra finally said, "I'm sorry. I didn't know Jonah would upset you so much."

Shaking his head, Cinn took her wrist and led her to the table, glancing again to the male passed out on her couch. The freckles across his cheekbones were stark as his face paled, reaching for the necklace he'd risked everything to retrieve.

The willow tree amulet was rustic, unadorned, as if whoever had carved it lacked either the skill or intention to preserve it with resin. The kind of thing one kept for sentimental reasons rather than any inherent value.

Throat bobbing, Cinn offered it to her. Not the way he had offered her other things, as payment, but as if he held the secrets to the universe in the palm of his hand, terrified to show them to her.

Between the way Gatty drew closer and Cinn's trembling hands, she was almost too afraid to take it.

"What is it?" she asked warily.

Her familiar leapt onto the table, brushing his tail against her in a way that was both comforting and curious.

"He came for answers, and he has learned them." Gatty spoke with awe, answering without answering as he was prone to do. "They're just not the one's he expected."

Magic stirred in her gut, and though there was nothing special about the carving, no latent power within, she felt it call to something essential deep inside her.

Scraping out the sodden tea leaves from the bottom of her cup, she smeared them across her constellation tattoo and rallied the pool of power in her core. With utmost care, she took the wooden tree into her cupped palms.

Pressing it to her brow, then to her lips, she was barely capable of more than a whisper.

"Show me."

An unending cosmos exploded behind her eyes. Just as she had been trained to do, she threw down a mental anchor to her body and braced herself against the dreamscape, the stars, the lines of fate, as it all converged into a single vortex. All of time and space at her fingertips, Moyra's eyes rolled back in her head.

And then she *saw*.

Two young witches with mousy curls and golden-brown skin, eyes so like the color of honey. There was no mistaking who their sire was—the female had Kai's love of life shining in her pretty face; his fire and defiance, his determination and optimism. Light burned so deeply in her soul it radiated from every pore. And the male . . .

The Mother had made him the spitting image of Moyra's brother, breaking her heart into three dozen pieces. She could see in his aura that he was grounded and curious. Always watching, always listening, always learning.

He didn't just look like Kailevi, either.

Flashes of deep depressions and wild frenzies blitzed through the vortex. The edges of madness crept in as his suppressed magic grew too strong for the tonics Kailevi had taught his wife to brew. The terrible cycle Moyra had seen over and over in Qiri was being repeated—without access to an academy and faced with unending rejection, the unharnessed Morvish magic and his predisposition for mental illness would feed into each other until he succumbed entirely to madness and died.

Worse, Kailevi's son had no idea what was happening to him.

"Don't go too deep, Moyra."

Gatty's distant warning pulled her back. Reaching for her anchor, the willow amulet clattered to the table, the shack coming back into focus. Trembling, Moyra covered her mouth and closed her eyes.

Kailevi had found his destiny. Olyvia's sacrifice hadn't been for nothing. And Moyra had a niece and nephew trapped in southern Nir.

"You knew." Her voice shuddered, eyes welling. "As soon as you saw Jonah, you knew."

Her fear was mirrored in Cinn's face as he nodded. Quietly, he rose from the table and retrieved the worn-out scrap of parchment he had first shown her. Cinn's illegible scrawl was nowhere close to the elegance of the scrolling scripture.

"He wrote this, didn't he? I saw him briefly in your dreamscape, but I didn't realize . . ." She could barely keep her words above a whisper. "What is his name?"

Cinn looked to Gatty, who swished his tail and spoke on his behalf. "Eaon."

"And my niece?"

"Eavha."

Her chest ached so deeply she thought she might be sick. And in that moment, she knew—*knew*, the way Kailevi had *known*.

"They need me."

Her ankle tingled in warning. Fisting her skirt, nostrils flaring, she looked to Cinn. He raised his brows at the pleading expression she couldn't keep from her face.

She needed to see them. She needed to help them. But first, she needed to get this cursed charm off her ankle.

"I need your help."

Before she'd even finished speaking, Cinn nodded.

CHAPTER 21

MOYRA

"Moyra, you need to slow down." Gatty moved himself to the center of the table and sat, swishing his thick, muscular tail. "You have too many balls in the air right now. You're going to drop one."

"Kailevi has children. They need me," she repeated, bewildered that her familiar couldn't understand this.

"Jonah needs you. Your other clients need you. There's a mute kinner sitting at this table who needs you." Gatty's tail thumped on the table. "It is unbecoming of you to drop your responsibilities just because your brother procreated."

"Onribleq," Moyra scoffed. "That you have the audacity to say that after abandoning me for almost a week . . . over milk! That you have the nerve to assume I would leave the untrained depending on me with nothing!"

The cat sith didn't so much as blink at her outburst. In a low, silky voice that was pure threat, he said, "That you forgot your own shackle earlier and made me drop the juicy salmon I was about to enjoy is proof you are overwhelmed."

She was going to wring his neck.

"Ah." Gatty turned to Cinn, responding to one of his thoughts. "Moyra can explain."

Another throaty snore from Jonah kept the silence from growing too heavy as Cinn looked from the cat sith to Moyra, then back again. Sucking a tooth, Moyra leveled an impatient glare that went unnoticed for a full minute as Gatty picked a string of algae from his paw.

Finally, he said, "The boy doesn't know about your shackle."

"That was what I was going to explain to him before you decided to get on your high horse," Moyra ground out, rising stiffly from the table to brew another pot of tea before she murdered her familiar.

The sleepless nights were getting to her, as was the constant draw on her magic. She was a long way from burning out, but the constant dabbling was still more than she'd done in a long time.

After the tea was ready, she moved her chair to sit adjacent to Cinn and lifted the hem of her skirt just enough to expose the metal ring around her ankle. Cinn found a new shade of grey to turn, the yellow in his aura flaring brightly.

"What Olyvia did to the wards could not go unpunished. Since I was the only member of an unsanctioned coven left behind, the sentence fell on me. I'm to spend the rest of my life living here, in this shack. The twine perimeter is as far as I can go without this charm stopping me. Too many unifiers in prison to ally with, they said. They didn't want to risk a riot. Not with a coven's magic in my blood."

As she spoke, the dreamscape began to swirl over Cinn's head again. She kept an eye on it as he rubbed his wrists and scratched his neck. He did well to keep it at bay on his own, but when it was clear he couldn't push it away entirely, Moyra gave it a nudge.

"Unnecessary," Gatty scolded her, leaping from the table to his saucer of milk.

Ignoring him, Moyra went to the cupboard under the window and retrieved the few crystals she'd managed to scrounge up over the decades.

"Give me a moment, Cinn. I'm just going to cast something quickly."

Gatty's concerns be damned, Moyra arranged the crystals on the table along with a few candles before wiping The Seeing Mark of Truth Unveiled from her palms. The spell she was about to cast required no mark.

Her forehead tingled as she drew deep from the well of power inside again, sweat beading down her shoulder blades as she searched for the part that belonged to Olyvia.

For years, she had pondered over how her sister had done it. How she had hidden her intentions from the high seer. It was such advanced spell-cleaving that Gatty hadn't been able to find any information for her, and instead Moyra had to sift through the dreamscape for answers. Prying into people's heads without permission was not only extremely difficult, but it was unethical, and she had not enjoyed it one bit. But she found the spell she needed, and she had practiced it often so that, one day when she figured out how to get out of this shack, the high seer wouldn't see it coming.

"See no more, hear no more, know no more," she muttered, feeling for the threads of magic that held time and space together. "See no more, hear no more, know no more."

Over and over, she repeated the incantation as she cleaved through fate lines, barred the dreamscape entirely, shut out the stars, rearranging them until nothing could see the occupants of the shack at all.

It was only temporary and would only hold as long as Moyra

could focus, but it gave them privacy to discuss what had to be done.

"There is no mechanism to unlock the charm," she panted. "The only way to remove it is with a key. Not the regular kind. A crystal carved with one of the many Unbinding Marks, forged with intention to only work on this one charm."

Cinn held her eye, focused, as if he knew they had limited time to talk.

"The high keeper holds all the keys ever made in his office at the courthouse in Ahrenhale, which is heavily guarded both physically and magically. Gatty has never been able to get in, but his closest attempt was only thwarted because the ward would have killed him. That's less of an issue for you."

Before she'd even finished speaking, Cinn was on his feet, nodding vigorously. The series of motions he made with his hands was so impassioned that Moyra didn't need to know what he was saying.

Sagging, the spell-cleaving magic falling away, she managed to whisper, "Thank you."

Cinn waited for sundown.

All day, they had brewed suppression tonics for the untrained witches in preparation for if and when Moyra left, but when the cicadas started and the selkies returned to shore, Moyra waited on the porch as Cinn delivered his vial of blood.

The stars' whispering grew loud again, their urgency undeniable. Listening, she bit her lip at their approval of the exchange. The cementing of a fate Moyra hoped was not worse than the one they had promised if Cinn had refused the bargain.

Specifics weren't really the stars forte, but she knew a dire future when she saw one.

Once the selkies were satisfied, Cinn returned to shoulder his pack. There was a promise in his eyes, determination in the set of his shoulders.

"I'll wait here," she joked through tears she couldn't keep from welling. Hope was an evil little thing, but she clung to it more desperately than ever before.

Cinn smiled, then he leaned in and hugged her tightly.

"Oh. Oh, okay." Moyra sniffed.

She had not been hugged in a very long time. It took everything she had to keep her knees from buckling.

When Cinn let go, he took the willow amulet from around his neck and put it in her hands. It radiated an unnatural warmth so unlike the oppressive heat pushing down on them, even with the sun dipping below the horizon, that Moyra welcomed it against her skin.

"Thank you," she repeated for the thousandth time that afternoon.

Cinn gave a two-fingered salute before turning for the path that would take him to Ahrenhale. Gatty slinked to her side and brushed against her legs.

"Try not to get yourself killed while we're away."

Raising her eyebrows, she looked down at her familiar. "You're going with him?"

Gatty chuckled, turning into the shadows where he immediately became invisible.

"Obviously."

PART IV

PERIPETEIA

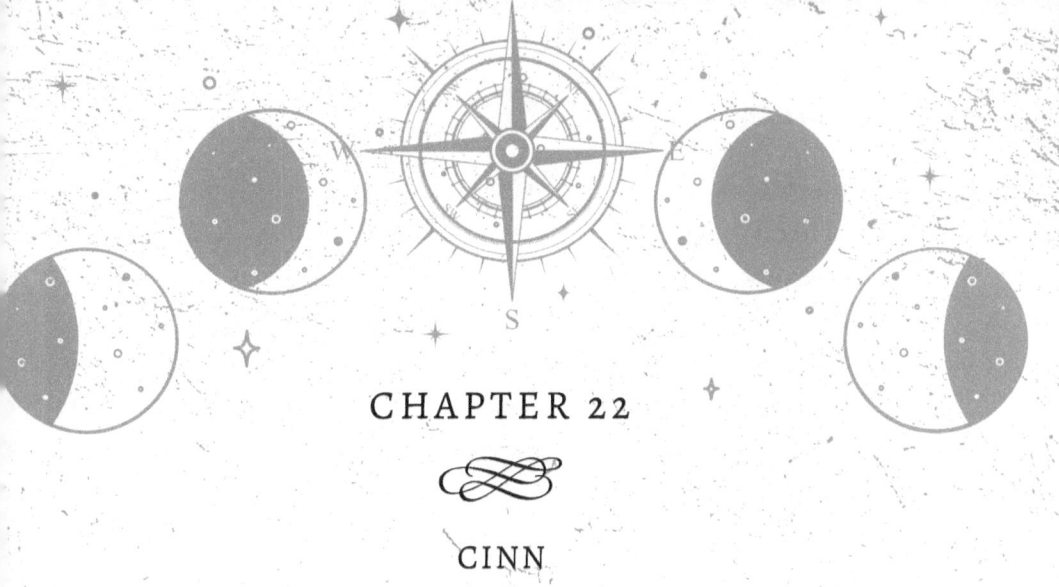

CHAPTER 22

CINN

THERE WERE A HUNDRED THINGS TO THINK ABOUT, A thousand problems to tackle, but the only thing running through Cinn's head was that *Moyra has a collar on*. The tightness around his own throat had been impossible to ignore since the minute he'd seen her ankle. So regardless of everything else going on, the metal ring had to go. Immediately.

The three sprites who'd snuck into his pack while Moyra wasn't looking clearly agreed. It was a miracle they'd stayed quiet as long as they had, their chittering growing louder by the footfall as Cinn climbed the hill out of the glen. He had to do this for Moyra, but he wasn't so confident that he'd turn away help. Even faerie help.

Without a pocketful of salt and rowan berries like he'd had while traveling with Eaon, he only had his knife for protection. Trees with faces watched him, whispering shadows stalking from behind their ghostly trunks. Nena crawled out of his pack, perched on his shoulder and hissed. Whether it was the sprite or the murderous intent Cinn was emitting, nothing sinister approached.

"Incorrect."

Cinn pulled his knife, flinching so hard Nena fell off his shoulder. Dida came fluttering from his pack too, hissing at the cat sith appearing from the shadows.

"Settle, thistle," Gatty purred as he fell in step beside Cinn. "Since I have gotten closest to retrieving Moyra's key in the past, I assumed you would need my guidance."

No doubt for a cost. He was still waiting to find out what the cat sith's price for rescuing him would be.

"No cost. Moyra asked me to help you with the lake, and if you can free her, it is I who will be indebted to you."

Crouching to scoop Nena from the dirt, who wailed as she picked soil from her liquid legs, Cinn cradled her and resumed his trek. His experience with the fae thus far had been overwhelmingly horrible, from those who wanted to eat him, to those with a vial of his blood, ready to use it for gods knew what.

Breeding purposes, Moyra had suggested.

Cinn froze. Was he going to be a parent?

Gatty began hacking with what Cinn slowly realized was laughter.

"Doubtful," the cat sith eventually managed. "Selkies tend to use more traditional ways of breeding, being mostly mammalian."

Cinn sighed in relief. Shaking his head, he returned to his point—the fae were awful, and yet Gatty seemed rather intent on kindness toward Moyra. He'd questioned what was so great about familiars that a witch would take such a risk, but now he was questioning what was so great about witches that a faerie would muster such devotion.

"It's not about greatness," Gatty answered his silent

questions, making Cinn scowl. If he wasn't holding Nena in one hand, Dida perching on his wrist to help clean out the dirt, he would have crossed his arms at the violation.

"There is a moment when you first see a witchling, their magic blossoming like a newborn star, and something intrinsic inside just *snaps* into place. You know that they are the one. Nothing feels as important as ensuring that witch grows into her full potential, and only when she stands before you in all her glory can you move on in peace. But the witch doesn't need to know how deep the drive to protect runs. Such knowledge could be abused, and so we bargain."

Cinn frowned, and before the thought had even finished forming, Gatty answered with a grin.

"I confess this to you, because you cannot tell anyone."

Scoffing, he urged the sprites back into his pack where Lula snored. While Moyra fussed all day, Cinn had watched the three of them arguing. Lula hadn't wanted to stay behind, even though her cap was broken, so now she slept inside his trinket box instead, safe from further harm.

"I confess this to you," Gatty went on, "because you need to understand that I will always be on Moyra's side. If she is at stake, you do not need to question my motives."

Somehow, that was comforting. Cinn nodded, retuning his attention to the shadows.

"They won't bother you as long as I am here." Gatty, too, surveyed the thinning bushland as the gravel solidified into a proper road. "I've had fifty years to assert my dominance. And they know if anything happens to Moyra while I am away, not only will I know, but I will make sure their deaths are excruciating."

~

It took longer by foot, but by dawn the city of Ahrenhale adorned the horizon. Whether it was the company or the information Moyra had given him about what went on here, Cinn approached with more confidence than he had last time. A little dusty but mostly clean, he blended in with the humans already preparing street stalls for the market. Wary glances were directed at the cat sith keeping easy pace beside him, but there were enough witches and their familiars wandering around that he wasn't out of place.

He hadn't noticed them before, overwhelmed as he'd been. Every witch with a constellation on his forehead had some kind of animal or fae creature tailing them, nodding their respect to Gatty as they passed by.

"They know who I am, and that I have remained with Moyra through her ordeal," Gatty murmured. "The civilians don't. Most witches, neither. If the public knew who Moyra was and what her coven had done, there would be a public crucifixion. It had been her fate for a little while, but the council chose to keep the public calm instead."

Calm was an overstatement. Packs of three or four protesters huddled in alcoves with their picket signs, whispering about whatever plans they had for the day. Unifiers or separatists, Cinn couldn't tell the difference. Didn't know which side he was on, either.

Was he a coward for wanting Qiri to remain a haven? For wanting to drag his family through the wards to safety and forget about what was brewing in the south? Probably. The idea of running from this conflict was increasingly uncomfortable, his conviction in past decisions wavering.

Glancing sidelong at the cat sith to see if he would respond to the direction Cinn's thoughts had taken, he was surprised to find the faerie distracted.

"That is where Moyra's parents live," Gatty spat. "I would kill them for abandoning her if Moyra let me."

The streets were lined with identical-looking houses, three stories high and crammed so tightly together that most shared a wall. Some of the houses had colored banners hanging over the doors, and one with a green thread-and-needle insignia had a line of despondent people sitting on the porch. A female had her head buried in her knees, rocking back and forth with her hands over her ears. Another sat staring at the cloudless sky, trembling from the weight of whatever she saw there, silent tears leaving tracks down her dirty cheeks. None had constellation tattoos and lacked the vibrancy most Morvish witches had in their hair or skin, yet Cinn knew they were still burdened with magic.

One thing at a time.

Free Moyra. Take her to Eaon before it was too late to help him. Then he could figure out what to do about this deity threatening everything.

Would it be so bad if the way things were . . . changed?

"Yes," Gatty said immediately. "Chaos may be forgotten in the south, but here, tales of what our world was like when he and Mother walked hand in hand are told freely. There are fae among us who still remember the days of war as Mother began her affair with Death, choosing their Balance over Chaos. If he cannot have her, he will destroy everything she holds dear and bask in a vengeance the High Spirits will deem petty. Mother can make a new world. Her Lover will be well fed, harboring the ruined souls of her creations. Morvia minds her own business. It is up to us to stop Chaos if we want to live."

As the cat sith led the way through the city to the council courthouse, Cinn frowned. If none of the other High Spirits wanted to intervene, then why did the Lover keep pushing Eaon back out of the void? What was the point if the deity knew all of living kind would soon be decimated? Why not just let Eaon rest in the afterlife?

The cat sith hummed, glancing up. "Curious."

Nena and Dida climbed out of his pack again, the lake sprite diving into a nearby fountain while the dandelion floated ahead. When Lula came huffing and puffing onto his shoulder, Cinn checked on the state of her cap. A chunk of it was still missing, but her tiny face beamed happily as she tried to climb up his ear for a better view. Sighing, Cinn helped push her on the top of his head like a tiny mushroom hat.

"We're getting close. Stay alert," Gatty warned.

He didn't really have a plan, but with Gatty by his side he supposed he didn't really need one. The cat sith would know what to do. Dida and Nena returned, the dandelion screeching in what could only be faerie curses as she hauled the lake sprite up into the air to perch on Cinn's shoulder. Shaking her head, tufts of Dida's waterlogged seeds flicked onto Cinn's cheek.

He didn't bother wiping them off as the road forked and an ivory structure rose before them. The courthouse spread across three city blocks with a single tower in the center, the top a glistening glass dome. Surrounded by a barred fence at least three men tall, guards held back the crowd camped along the road, more picket signs arguing against the continued separation of southern Nir from Tryce Point Bay.

"Blood on your hands, council!" someone shouted.

"Give up the moonstones!" another called. "Let the willing go south!"

"Hoarders!"

"Cowards!"

"Murderers!"

Gatty leaned against Cinn's legs. "This way, kinner."

Swallowing against the lump in his throat, Cinn kept an eye

on the guards as he followed the cat sith farther down the block. When they reached an area with few people loitering, Gatty walked into the shadow of a streetlight and disappeared. Stilling, Cinn frowned at the spot until the sprites started squirming, making their way down his body to the smooth road ringing the courthouse.

On the other side of the barred fence, Gatty stepped out of the shadow of a tree and grinned that horrible too-large grin. The sprites stopped at the trench of salt just inside the perimeter and squawked until Cinn knelt, scooping Nena into his palm and lifting her over first. She curtsied before rolling her way to Gatty's side. Only after drying his hands on his pants did Cinn pluck Dida up by her twiggy body, and Lula by her thick mushroom stem, placing them on the other side of the trench.

"Quickly, boy," Gatty called. "Before someone sees you."

Cinn flung his arms wide in a "what do you expect me to do" motion. The bars were too narrow to squeeze through. Even if he crushed his own ribs on purpose, his head was too big and he didn't have the means or desire to break his skull.

The cat sith just stared at him, blinking.

Seriously? You're not going to help? What happened to wanting Moyra freed? he thought with intent toward Gatty.

"You're too dependent on other people helping you out of situations. Do something for yourself, for once."

Cinn's teeth snapped, hands clenching around the bars. Not only was that unfair, but what would a faerie cat who could walk through shadows know about the shit Cinn had been through?

Gatty thumped his tail beneath the tree as the sprites gathered around him.

Moyra has a collar on, Cinn reminded himself. Memories of helplessness sucked the air from his lungs, but he couldn't deal with that right now. He needed focus, because Moyra was depending on him and so was Eaon. So was everybody.

Tightening the straps on his pack, he closed his eyes and pushed his forehead against the bars. He was not a witch, could not control the dreamscape with magic, but he could conquer his own mind. Despite the trembling and sweating that had nothing to do with Ahrenhale's weather, through the shadows of bruised knuckles as he pounded against the unbreakable barrier keeping him in the dark, the echoes of his panic-soaked screams, Cinn counted to ten. He breathed. He pushed the pain away and forced himself to think. Back before all of that. Back to Commander Porter and his training.

Through pursed lips, Cinn blew out a slow, forceful sigh.

He was not as fit as he wanted to be, but then again, he never had been. Gripping the bars, he pushed a leg through the gap and clenched until he could hold his whole body weight. Just to add to his motivation, he imagined Dearmead was here, watching. The witch made everything look as easy as breathing, and Cinn was determined to prove he was just as capable.

One hand over the other, Cinn pulled himself up, held his weight with shaking arms while he slid his leg up, bracing with his other ankle, until he could switch, holding his weight with his legs instead to reach farther up the fence. Inch by inch, he slithered, pausing to wipe the sweat from his hands but refusing to look back at the deserted streets. If someone saw him, they saw him.

By the time he reached the top, Cinn could hardly breathe. Every muscle in his body quivered, only his mantra kept him from slipping all the way back to the ground.

Your mind will break before your body does. Conquer that, and you will be unstoppable.

Ignoring the piercing tips of the gate as he dragged himself over the edge, Cinn didn't even try to lower himself with grace, letting his body fall to the ground. Something cracked, his vision spotting briefly as his forehead connected with the hard earth, but within seconds he was healing.

"Well, that took forever," Gatty purred, lowering himself so the sprites could climb on his back.

I hate you.

The cat sith chuckled as Cinn clambered to his feet, wiping the blood from his split eyebrow. Silently, the two snuck through the bordering shrubbery until a door at the back of the courthouse came into view.

"The high spell-cleaver has made sure that, once inside, magic cannot be used without an official exception," the cat sith explained, frowning at the heavy wooden door. "And there are supposed to be guards."

Perhaps they'd been called away to deal with the demonstration at the front gates.

"Or perhaps, despite Moyra's spell-cleaving, the high seer knows we are here, and this is a trap."

The sprites squawked and chittered for a moment before Nena slid off Gatty's back, leaving a trail of damp fur in her wake.

"Be safe, little one," Gatty said as Nena approached the door.

Cinn's heart squeezed as the sprite flattened herself and rolled under the door. Counting the seconds, the minutes, was all he could do as they waited for an alarm. How was he going to get back out of here in a hurry? How—

Nena rolled back under the door and squealed. With a high-pitched war cry, Dida shook Gatty's fur like the reigns of a horse and pointed at the door. Lula yawned.

"Seems clear." Gatty frowned deeper. "But I don't trust it."

What choice was there? He wasn't leaving without Moyra's key.

Without thinking too hard about it, Cinn ran for the door, twisted the handle, and pushed. He expected it to be locked, but it flung open with ease. Cinn's momentum sent him sprawling across the floor inside, staring back at Gatty, whose thick paws padded heavily on polished stone floors. The cat sith kicked the door closed with his back leg, leaving them in the dark silence of an empty hall, more doors lining both sides.

"If you get me killed, kinner . . ." Gatty grumbled, but Cinn shuddered as he climbed to his feet, running a hand over the back of his neck.

Something felt wrong.

For five long minutes, they stood frozen in the hall. There were voices in the distance but nobody close enough to see them. Cinn's body felt weird. Gatty must have been right; the quickening of his heart promised this was a trap.

"We are halfway there," the cat said softly. "At the end of this hall is a foyer and a staircase. On the fifth floor is the key room protected by a curse that would leave me dust in the carpet. You can survive it. You get through the door and grab Moyra's key, then we can leave."

Even the sprites had gone quiet, waiting for Cinn to blink. To breathe. When they got tired of waiting, Dida floated up to his shoulder, tickled her florets against his face before she bit his ear. Hissing, he flicked her away and wiped at the aching spot, fingers coming away bloody.

A door in the hall opened.

Without even thinking, Cinn leapt at the nearest doorway

and threw himself through. The cat sith followed, Lula still curled up on his back.

Nena and Dida stayed in the hall.

"Onribleq!" an exasperated voice called. "Someone call pest control, we have sprites in the building."

Tiny thorn's burst from Dida's body as, with a defiant cry, the disproportionately fierce sprite swarmed down the hall. Nena cackled, her liquid form rippling and bulging before, like a stung bubble, she burst, flooding the carpet. As whoever had called for help gave chase, Cinn slowly, so very slowly, wrapped his hand around the brass knob, closed the door, and counted to ten. His other hand was strangling his knife, but when the count ended and nobody came looking, he breathed.

"If there's one thing sprites are good at, it's causing tr—" Gatty began to promise, falling silent as his eyes widened.

Cinn stilled at the sight of blood spotting the pristine parquetry flooring. Reaching for his ear, his fingers came away bloody—again.

He was still bleeding.

CHAPTER 23

CINN

SECONDS PASSED, AND HE CHECKED AGAIN.

Still bleeding.

Again.

And again.

If a cat could turn pale, Gatty had. "The spell-cleaving is stronger than expected."

Ringing started in his ears, the entire world narrowing to the blood on his fingers. Leaning against the wallpaper, Cinn eased himself down and put his head between his knees. There was a time not too long ago that, had he suddenly become human, he'd have found the nearest sharp object to stick into his neck. But now . . .

"Breathe, boy. It's a requirement for mortals."

He was going to faint. He was going to die before he could free Moyra. Before he could help Eaon. Before he could save the Copelands. Before he could see Eddy and Rad. He was going to die.

"Pull yourself together," Gatty hissed.

For such a long time, living forever had been his worst nightmare—and he'd only just begun to taste all the horrors in store for his kind. It was a part of why he had come to Qiri. This was supposed to be what he wanted.

Instead, he was counting the steps back to that unguarded door; five to the room's door, six down the hall, one outside. It would only take seconds.

Soft mewling barely registered as Cinn's own ragged breaths filled his ears. Lifting his head, he found Lula at his feet. The sprite reached inside the fronds of her chipped mushroom cap, retrieving the shell she'd stolen from him that day by the lake. It too had cracked, but it was just as fascinating with its intricate, swirling grooves.

Lula held out the shell in her tiny hands. An offering. Though her face was the size of a fingernail, he could see sincerity etched there clearly. No strings attached.

The tremor that had plagued his hands during the early months of his escape returned as he extended one. Reverently, Lula placed the shell there. Cinn breathed the scent of fungus and algae as he brought it to his nose, taking him back to the lake. To Moyra. To the shackle around her ankle.

He knew what it was like to be a prisoner. Confined. He knew what it was like to wear a metal band that told the world your life was not your own. It was cruel, and he had once felt so strongly about such cruelty being abolished that he'd joined the royal cadets, despite the risks.

He was not a coward. He would no longer tolerate behaving like one.

The cat sith watched, tail swishing, as Cinn scooped up Lula, placed her on his shoulder and climbed to his feet. Pocketing the shell, he wiped his sweaty upper lip on the back of his hand and forced himself to notice the room and its grandeur.

He'd seen smaller houses.

Keeping his footsteps light, Cinn paced along the large mahogany table, running his fingers over the grain. At least fifty plush, velvet chairs surrounded it, a row of three at the head, behind which sat a rich wooden credenza. The variety of scented candles and perfectly round crystals were the only ornaments, but the deep emerald walls were adorned with paintings in gilded frames in lieu of windows, the largest of all depicting a glowing woman among a spattering of stars. A webbed galaxy of colorful lines surrounded her, but rather than mysterious or wise, the glowing woman seemed bored, body posed across a settee of clouds, the wine glass in her hand tilted and spilling onto a crowd of tiny figures below.

Gatty's cursing pulled him away from the artwork, and a moment later Cinn heard the problem for himself; the rumbling of voices outside was getting louder.

"It's too late to run," Gatty hissed, padding quickly to the credenza. "Get inside."

Cinn balked as the cat sith stuck a claw underneath the lip of the cupboard door and hooked it open. As the voices grew nearer though, he quickly climbed inside the cramped cupboard beside Gatty and Lula, pack poking into his spine. His fingernails were only just long enough to dig into the wooden door and pull it closed, the panel riddled with decorative holes large enough to see through.

"Ridiculous."

It was the first word Cinn understood as the door to the room opened and ten witches came inside. Each wore a colored robe with a different insignia on it, their large voices filling the vast space.

"It's just a couple of sprites," the yellow one said with a laugh, taking the nearest seat.

"This is a place of law. There shouldn't be fae running around at all."

"The guards will catch them eventually."

"And until then we are relegated to the back rooms? Disgraceful."

"It may work out for the best. If the demonstrators get inside, the first place they will storm are the courtrooms. It will take a while to find us here."

Cinn forced his breaths to be slow and silent as he watched the witches file inside. His neck was already aching from the twisted angle, but he didn't dare twitch a muscle as the last through the door paused, looking at the spot on the parquetry floor where Cinn's blood had fallen.

"The unifiers won't get inside," the male in orange said calmly as he approached the credenza.

Lula whined. Gatty smacked her with a paw and held his breath, but the witch didn't seem to have heard as he took a candle and round crystal to the head of the table.

"You hope," someone griped.

"Did you hear? They know about the moonstones."

"They heard *rumors* about the moonstones."

"Pearl, is everything alright?"

At her name, the witch staring at Cinn's blood looked up, eyes moving straight to the cabinet. A chill cooled the sweat on Cinn's body, hand once again on his knife.

"Everything is fine," Pearl lied. "The room is secure. Make the call."

"I think we should reschedule until the sprites are taken care of," the blue-robed male argued. "They could be spies."

"I would know if they were spies," Pearl argued. "Everything is fine. Let's vote and be done with this."

One of the others in a pale-green robe scoffed. "Like you haven't already *seen* how this turns out."

"I see many outcomes. A few are yet to make up their minds."

There was silence for a moment, tension rife in the air as the group took seats at the table.

"But the majority are in our favor, right?"

With an exhausted sigh, Pearl clasped her hands in her lap. "Make the call."

Muttering ensued among all bar the orange-robed one holding the crystal ball, who began to recite an incantation. A cloud of blue and purple mist bloomed above the table, tendrils seeping to the empty chairs and twisting into human-sized shapes. The gathering of ten witches was now one of forty.

"Thank you for finally joining us, Qiri," one of the smoke people said, their accent harsh and blunt in every way Ahrenhalish was long and lolling.

"Apologies for the delay. Our courtroom had to be evacuated." The orange-robed male who'd cast the spell spoke on behalf of all, their muttering now silenced.

"Has the civil situation there escalated?" another of the phantoms asked.

"It's manageable. How is that in Phara?"

"Also manageable, but the council is concerned it won't stay that way for long. Our border towns have the most at stake in this vote and they know it."

Again, the green-robed Qiri witch snorted. "Not more than us, I can assure you. At least you have the west to flee to if this goes badly. We only have the sea."

"Oh, please," another of the phantoms argued. "Everybody knows you have a hoard of moonstones ready to evacuate the elite at a moment's notice."

Immediately, a dozen voices rose in argument. Cinn couldn't pretend to have any idea what they were talking about, yet his heart pounded viciously, every word from their lips somehow the most important thing he'd ever heard.

"We were given the same allotment as the rest of you. It's not our fault Phara is plagued with thieves and Chaos sympathizers."

"Pah! Says the council who let a physical hole be blasted through the wards!"

"Enough!" Another of the phantoms rose from their chair, peering around at the large gathering. "Let us not devolve into squabble. Our seers say the final days are upon us—Chaos will rise, and we need to take a final vote on a course of action."

That silenced the room. At least briefly.

"Has everybody cast a silencing circle? We don't need word reaching the masses before we devise the best way to broach the news."

"Of course we have," the green-robed witch sniped again. Three others voiced their confirmation.

"Alright then," the Qiri witch dressed in orange rose. "I officially call this vote into action. Let the record show that the three councils of Tryce Point Bay and that of Yvar are gathered on this day to decide once and for all whether or not to remove the wards surrounding southern Nir."

Pain like a kick to the gut left Cinn breathless and nauseous, biting his own fist to keep quiet. He'd seen the unifiers and separatists on the streets, but that had been a hypothetical debate. This was real. If Moyra's sister alone could put a crack in the wards, the combined power of those gathered in this room, both physically and not, would be more than enough to tear it down completely.

And they were going to decide right now. To remove the only

thing keeping Chaos contained, or to leave the southern Nirnians to face their deaths alone.

Again, coincidence as a concept seemed laughable. There was no way Cinn could be cloistered in a cupboard at this exact moment with the exact knowledge he needed to understand the situation and not have it be divine intervention.

Gatty's claws extended as the cat sith's nerves matched Cinn's own, digging into his chest. Lula squirmed out from under the cat's paw and silently nestled under Cinn's chin.

Those standing around the table resumed their seats, a beat of oppressive silence ringing through the room before one of the smoke people at the far end of the table cleared their throat.

"I am Nistra, High Seer of Unsward, and I speak on behalf of Yvar. Our final vote is firmly *for*."

Cinn had no idea where Yvar was. Where any of these places were.

"I am Daan, High Seer of Diradale, and I speak on behalf of Phara. Our vote is firmly *against*."

His home and family were at stake, their lives in the hands of these strangers. The temptation to tumble out of the cupboard and beg left him trembling, except he had no idea what way he wanted this vote to go.

"I am Pearl, High Seer of Ahrenhale, and I speak on behalf of Qiri. Our vote is firmly *against*."

They'd said Qiri and Phara bordered Nir. It made sense they didn't want the wards taken down. But there was only one other seer standing. A vote *for* would make it a tie, and what then?

"I am Alissa, High Seer of Rothvale, and I speak on behalf of Erve." Time seemed to slow down as the room held a collective breath. Alissa's voice was low but steady as she announced, "Our vote is firmly *against*."

The representatives from Yvar immediately began arguing.

Loudly. The Qiri witch in the orange robes held up his hands, shouting over the cacophony.

"Yvar can count themselves lucky their vote was considered at all, given your barely appropriate position in this committee. The matter is now closed. The wards will remain intact."

Cinn shuddered, in relief or heartbreak, he wasn't sure. Maybe both. Maybe everything about this whole situation was devastating and there was no good solution. The arguing went on for a while, but the languages became mixed and he couldn't follow. Didn't need to. The others were not going to change their minds.

"The decision is final," the orange-robed male from Qiri boomed, more forceful than he'd been throughout this entire meeting. "Can we please move on to the next steps?"

"What of the gap?" a phantom asked tentatively.

"We have people scouring the mountains as we speak. It will be found and closed."

The tone left no room for argument and a fresh sweat broke out across Cinn's face. He needed to get back before he was stuck outside southern Nir forever.

"And the witch you have in custody?"

"Which one?"

"Moyra Thorne, obviously," the figure snapped. "Who else would I be talking about?"

At her name, Gatty's claws sunk deeper. Cinn repressed a growl but bared his teeth at the cat sith.

The green-robed witch stood, venom on his tongue, but Pearl silenced him with a gentle hand. Slowly, turning to the phantom in question, she assured them, "She has nothing to offer."

Disagreement came quickly.

"I still think Qiri could have done more to discover what she—"

"Yes, we are familiar with your stance on the—"

"—audacity to assume Qiri is not doing everything in our power to locate the gap—"

"Enough!" the orange-robed male shouted again, though this time it took longer for the crowd to settle.

Pearl kept her voice level and controlled as she addressed the committee. "Moyra Thorne is my responsibility, and the matter is closed. Let old matters lie. The bigger concern right now is that we have lost contact with our representative in Dusarn. Information about what is happening with the ruling clan inside the wards has stopped."

"When was their last report?"

"Two days ago. Her report stated that Jem's amulet is no more than a pretty trinket now the Sparrow Queen's pregnancy has reached term, and both Sanni's diaries are still lost. There seemed to be little hope for stopping Chaos's rebirth into mortal form. That Stephanya has not made contact again does not bode well for her safety."

The representative who'd spoken on behalf of Yvar slammed a hand on the table. "Two thousand years of spying, wasted."

"Not wasted," the seer from Erve countered. "We are as prepared for the disaster as we can be. It would be worse not knowing what was coming or when to expect it. *Seeing* inside the wards without a physical presence was too unreliable."

"Are we truly as prepared as we can be?" another phantom asked nervously.

"Phara should evacuate their border towns if you haven't already done so," Pearl spoke. "The unifiers will not take the news well, and they will make their own move on the wards soon. It's time to get the troops in position to defend."

"Erve will dispatch to Qiri immediately."

"And Yvar to Phara," their seer grumbled.

With a nod, the orange-robed male stood. "Then I declare this meeting concluded."

Waving a hand over the crystal ball, the magic died, leaving behind a blue-and-purple haze. The ten remaining witches all sagged in their seats.

"Did we do the right thing?" someone asked.

"Too late for that question now."

Unanimous nodding, yet there was a tangible sense of mourning that had Cinn's own throat tightening.

"May the Mother protect our brethren in the south." Pearl's prayer was mimicked by the others. It was too much for the white-robed witch, who burst into tears and stormed from the room.

One by one, the others left too. Only Pearl and the orange-robed male stayed.

"You alright?" he asked, squeezing her shoulder.

"I need a moment," she answered, patting his hand. "Thank you."

"Of course. I'll see you at the temple later."

His footsteps were even and steady as he left Pearl alone. When the door clicked closed behind him, the resounding silence rang like a death knell. His body cramped, but still, he held his breath.

"For months, I've been waiting." Pearl stayed in her seat, staring at one of the paintings on the wall. "The sprites. The spot of blood on the floor. Finally, it's time."

Cinn met Gatty's gaze, his panic mirrored.

From inside her robe, Pearl withdrew a chunk of rose quartz and a small velvet pouch, placing both on the table.

"Tell Moyra she needn't shield her conversations from me anymore. It's my turn to shield her from the others." Standing, Pearl looked to the credenza again. "The path will be clear. Use the full moon. And tell Moyra I am sorry."

Cinn wiped the sweat dripping down his forehead as Pearl left the meeting room. He waited another minute, just to be sure it was safe, before pushing open the cabinet door and rolling onto the floor.

Gatty wasted no time padding to the table, leaping atop it in a graceful bound.

"It's the key."

Shucking his pack off, Cinn stretched his cramped shoulders as he approached. The chunk of pale pink quartz was identical to the shade of Moyra's eyes, a gilded witchmark etched on its flat side. Lula pulled on the hem of his pants, so Cinn helped her to the tabletop before picking up the pouch. Small, perfectly oval stones no bigger than the copper coin in his pocket lay inside. Picking one out, it shimmered under the chandelier, but also emitted its own faint light, both opaque and translucent like frosted glass.

Lula cooed and made grabby hands, but Gatty knocked her aside with a brush of his tail.

"Moonstones," he breathed with equal fear and wonder. "How many did she give us?"

Peering inside the bag, he counted, Gatty reading the number from his mind.

"Seven. Mother above, *seven moonstones*. You can't possibly appreciate the weight of this gift, or what people would do to take them from you. Put them in your box, along with Moyra's key. We need to leave."

That was an order Cinn had no qualms following.

CHAPTER 24

MOYRA

SHE HAD NOT SLEPT ALL NIGHT. CHEWING HER NAILS DOWN to the beds, she watched the placid lake instead. The stars shone so brightly they may as well be screaming, but she didn't dare dabble in them. Didn't dare peek into the dreamscape or try to *see* what was happening in the city. If things were going well, she didn't want to jeopardize it, and if things were going poorly . . . she'd lose her mind trapped here, unable to help. Not just Cinn and Gatty, but the sprites had gone as well. It was the only explanation for the past thirty-six hours of peace.

By dawn, she'd wrapped her fingertips in cotton bandages and switched to chewing peppermint leaves instead. Her plant was almost bare.

"Moyra?" Jonah's voice croaked from the couch.

Swallowing a shriek, Moyra placed a hand against her heart to steady it. As lost in thought as she'd been, she hadn't even sensed the dreamscape easing.

"I'm here," she promised, leaving her spot by the kitchen window.

Friends weren't really something Moyra had. Allies in the unifiers, yes, but she'd spent so much time with her siblings growing up that she'd never felt the need to branch out further. Nobody had wondered after her when she'd been banished, and opportunities to meet people ever since were scant. Faeries didn't count. Most of the clients her parents sent couldn't hold a conversation for long enough, either.

Except Jonah.

"What happened?" he asked, rubbing the crust from his eyes, arms shaking with weakness as he pushed himself upright. "How long have I been here?"

"A full day and night." Crouching by his side, she checked his temperature with the back of her hand. His forehead was damp with sweat, but cool. "And I was hoping you could tell me what happened. You should have had enough tonic to keep you well for at least another couple of weeks."

Meeting her gaze and tilting his head, Jonah blinked rapidly. Even after guzzling as much tonic as she could brew on short notice, his magic still wasn't fully suppressed.

He'd first arrived nine years ago, barely sixteen and already homeless. It hadn't been her intention to befriend a child, but he'd needed one almost as much as she did. And he liked tea.

"I . . . I gave some away," he admitted, shaking his head as if trying to clear his vision. "I was trying to ration myself, but . . . I don't think that was a good idea."

"No," she agreed, not masking her stern tone. "If someone else needed a tonic, you should have sent them to my parents."

Jonah grimaced, chewing his lip as he began to rock back and forth. "Your parents are swamped. They couldn't help her for weeks, and I know you're stretched thin too, so I just . . . I thought I'd be okay. I've been feeling okay."

"You've been feeling okay because you take your dosage,"

Moyra scolded him again, but sat back on the floor and sighed into her hands.

She wished more than anything she could brew enough tonic to help everyone Ahrenhale had abandoned, but she was just one person. Her parents weren't enough, either, but she understood why they wouldn't share the recipe—the people of Ahrenhale were obsessed with money, holding it dearer than life itself; a decent magic suppressant could too easily be commodified, meaning the price of ingredients would skyrocket, and the medicine would become inaccessible to those who needed it most.

"I think we should talk about binding you again," Moyra pleaded.

"I'd rather die."

"Jonah . . ."

Eyes glazing over, his rocking intensified. "They're all going to die. We're all going to die."

Clutching his hand, Moyra reached a tentative tendril of magic into his mind. For once, it wasn't his way-finding that was running amok—visions of another place and time flashed behind his eyes. Not the dreamscape; this wasn't subconscious. He was *seeing*, but he had no control.

A city surrounded by grey desert and wind-swept trees. Living shadows and monsters unlike anything Moyra had ever seen slithered inside houses, ripping the buildings' occupants to pieces. A castle, crumbling. Inside, a queen writhed with labor pains on a dais. A king loomed close, murder in his eyes. And above it all, a winged beast.

With her own anchor firmly in reality, Moyra guided Jonah back out of his visions.

He was pale and panting when clarity returned to his dark blue eyes. "What's happening out there? I don't understand."

"Nothing that concerns you," Moyra promised, ignoring the churning in her own gut. "Come and eat something."

"I can't. I feel sick," he complained, wrapping an arm around his stomach.

Regardless, she left to make a simple soup on her hot plate; though if he was half as nauseous as she was, he wouldn't keep a spoonful down.

The world was ending. Just as she'd found something to live for, it was all going to be taken away.

The two of them suffered through breakfast. Getting something in his belly brought strength back to Jonah's bones, though; when he stood from the couch he only stumbled once.

"I need to get back. I've been gone too long."

"I don't have anything to send with you," she warned. Not to mention that if Cinn was successful in the city, she might not be around next time he came looking. "Please, Jonah."

Rubbing his temples, he shook his head.

"Have you seen what happens to a bound witch long term? It makes my worst days look like a blessing. I'd rather be raving mad than suffer that fate."

"I have seen it, and it's not always like that. You might be okay. And we can always remove the binding when more tonic becomes available."

His smile didn't reach his eyes, his aura dull and blue.

"When has a removal ever gone well, either?"

She knew the statistics. Suppression was like sedation—it wore off. A binding was a box, cutting the witch off completely. It was often described as trying to breathe with only one lung; trying to see with only one eye. Something important was missing, and while being bound wouldn't kill a witch—and many adjusted well, able to live a full life—there were just as many who struggled and suffered through every day.

Until the binding was removed. If the lid of that box was opened again, three things could happen. One, the magic would return the same as it had been before. It was what everyone hoped for, but for reasons not fully understood, it rarely happened. The second possibility was a surge; a spill of magic too fast, too hard, flooding the veins of the witch and killing them in an instant. It happened almost half the time. Techniques for controlling the flow were being developed, but advancements had fallen to the wayside these past fifty-five years. The third major possibility was corruption. The box was opened only to find the magic inside had wilted. Again, there had been investigation into why, but funding had come to a stall. It was impossible to know what would happen until the lid was lifted, but the rot was almost as likely as death.

So Moyra understood why Jonah was reluctant. Binding his magic would cripple him, and undoing it would be treacherous. Yet . . .

"You came to my door begging, Jonah. Ripping your hair and sobbing. You might not remember the pain you were in, but I do. Losing your magic altogether couldn't possibly be any worse."

Swallowing deeply, he looked toward the front door.

"You'd be able to keep track of the days. Of where you are and how you got there. You could get a job. A house. Give whoever it is you're sharing your tonics with a place to live, too."

Jonah didn't say anything right away, and when he finally did, she didn't believe him.

"I'll think about it."

She'd tried. It was the best she could do.

~

After Jonah left, Moyra sat on her rocking chair with a piece of parchment and a nib of charcoal, sketching selkies. One had come back out of the water, leaving her skin in the shallows again to sunbathe. The strange proportions of her limbs, the blubber rounding her body, the eerily long mouth—beautiful in a frightening way that was hard to capture on paper. But she spent the day trying, and when the sun once again set in a display that, after fifty years, was brain numbingly dull, she went inside.

A full night and day had passed since Cinn left, but that was okay. Over and over, Moyra reminded herself that everything was alright. She would feel it if something happened to Gatty, and so long as her familiar was safe, so was Cinn. They would all be okay.

~

The porch creaked.

Waking with a gasp, Moyra rolled out of bed and ran for the door. The night was deep, but moonlight illuminated a sweaty Cinn, her familiar by his feet with three sprites riding his back.

"Thank the Mother, her sister, and her Lover, too," Moyra wheezed, leaning in the doorframe with a hand over her heart.

"We come bearing gifts," Gatty purred, eyes shining.

Dumping his pack on the porch, Cinn pulled out his trinket box. From within, he brought out a chunk of rose quartz. The golden etching was so simple, yet so powerful. With anything less than the power of a coven, she would not be able to wield it.

A shudder rippled down her spine, heart stilling.

"Is that . . ."

"Yes."

She was dreaming. She had to be.

Cinn knelt at her feet and lifted the hem of her skirt, but this wasn't something he could do. Crouching low, she placed a hand on his wrist to stop him.

"May I?" Reaching for the crystal with her other hand, Cinn eagerly handed it to her, eyes wide as she placed the key against the metal ring.

Magic thrummed through her veins, waiting for direction, and though her throat was thick, lips numb and tingling, she gave it.

"Be it her tears, her wine, or her blood; however it is that Morvia's gift was bestowed upon me, let it save me now. Let The Key Mark for Those Unbound"—she grit her teeth as the words burned through her, so different to the magic she usually used—"*free me.*"

A pulse beat through the quartz into the steel ring. Spots darkened her vision and her stomach flipped, bile filling her mouth. The two halves of the shackle fell apart, the weight strapped to her ankle for fifty-five years thudding against the soggy wooden porch. Beside it, the quartz clattered as Moyra's shaking hands opened.

When her vision cleared, she couldn't stop staring at the blindingly pale strip of skin around her ankle. She pinched herself, and when she didn't wake up, she stood.

So did Cinn, and the relief in his eyes made no sense when she couldn't feel it herself. Not yet.

Each step was both heavier and lighter as she descended the steps and edged closer to the twine perimeter. She stopped just shy. The pain wouldn't kill her, but that didn't make it less horrid. Didn't make her any less afraid of it.

Cinn's hand slipped into hers, and when she looked up from

the toes of her shoes to his mottled eyes, he nodded in encouragement, other hand on his heart.

It was easier to take that first step with company. Together, they crossed the line.

There was no pain. There was nothing.

She brought her second foot over the threshold and collapsed to her knees. Cinn went down too, pulling her against him as the disbelief gave way to a tidal wave of relief, breaking out of her in wretched gasps.

Free.

CHAPTER 25

CINN

WATCHING MOYRA DANCE IN THE MOONLIGHT FOR THE remaining hours before dawn helped settle the twisting his heart had been doing since his own mark stopped working. Sitting on the porch with his legs splayed out, Cinn leaned on his elbows and smiled. Nena, Dida, and Lula danced with her, and at the edge of the bushland, other fae had stopped their prowling to witness the joy.

Beside him, Gatty thumped his tail in a slow, methodical beat. "How's the chest?"

Cinn glanced down and pulled his shirt aside. The stress punctures Gatty put in him had healed the second he'd stepped outside the courthouse, as had the faerie bite on his ear. He could count the number of times he'd been grateful for being kinner on one hand, yet the relief he'd felt at that healing itch, however fleeting, made him realize that he didn't want to die.

Was it self-obsessed that such a revelation felt as big as everything else he'd learned in Ahrenhale?

"A will to live is no small possession."

Cinn scowled. *Stop snooping.*

"I wasn't talking about you."

Moyra had stopped dancing, staring at the dusting of red on the lake as the sun once more graced the day. When she looked back, her grin was unlike anything Cinn had seen before.

Moyra yawned as she set the kettle on the stove, preparing two cups of tea along with enough honey and milk to keep her faerie family happy. The dawn light gilding her cheekbones couldn't hide the exhaustion lining her eyes. She leaned on the counter, frizzy straw-colored curls falling out from behind her ears as she shook her head.

"Pearl gave you seven moonstones? Actual charged moonstones? Pearl did?"

The stones in question were protected in their velvet pouch, locked inside the trinket box on the table.

"She did." Gatty managed to sound morose, even as he eyed the tablespoon of honey before him, licking his chops. "She also said to wait for the full moon."

Nobody had explained to Cinn what moonstones were. That Gatty hadn't already answered his silent question suggested this was not the time. He didn't need to see the dreamscape to know that something was haunting Moyra as she stared out the window, fingers clenched against the soft wood bench.

The kettle whistled. When Moyra didn't notice, Gatty cleared his throat.

"Oh." She blinked and turned to the stove to pour the tea.

Cinn watched her carefully. Watched the teacups trembling on their saucers as she placed them down on the table.

If she noticed the attention, she didn't let on. "Yes. The full moon. That's two nights away. There is a lot to prepare if we plan on leaving. A lot of work to be done."

Gatty shot Cinn a sideways glance before lapping at his honey.

The morning songs of swallows filled the silence. Cinn sipped his tea and watched Moyra's blinking slow until her eyelids closed and didn't open again, hands limp around her teacup. A light snore added to the birds' symphony.

Smiling, Cinn's own eyes ached.

"It is my professional opinion," Gatty said between licks of his treat, "that you both could do with a nice, long nap. We could *all* do with a nap."

At the correction, he glanced to where the three sprites had finished their honey and curled up in a pile on the kitchen counter. Each tiny breath from Lula's lips moved the seeds on top of Dida's head, both using Nena's body as a pillow. Watching them made him yearn for sunny afternoons lazing in the sun with Puddles.

"Hmph." Gatty scowled at him as he finished his honey and got down to find a spot by the window. "Domestics."

Puddles is worth ten of you. Cinn tightened his grip on his teacup and scowled back, admittedly, without vitriol. He couldn't have freed Moyra without Gatty, and though it went against all his instincts to trust the fae, there was something to be said for having a common goal.

With Gatty, it was Moyra.

With the selkies, it was Chaos.

Kaelean came to mind. She wasn't fae, but she was savage all the same. They too had a common goal; when it came to the others—Eaon, Eavha and Dearmead—he could trust her.

"Moyra," Gatty said gently. Walking across the table, he brushed against her. "Let's get you to bed."

Her next snore rattled the ceramic cups.

Cinn chuckled into his tea as he lifted it to his lips.

"Moyra." Gatty tried again.

Eyes still closed, she grumbled, "You're getting hair in my cup."

Cinn snorted tea out his nose, right back into his cup.

"And you"—Moyra opened an eye—"stop wasting tea."

Gatty's tail flicked. "I don't shed."

"Liar."

"Fae don't lie."

Moyra huffed and rubbed her eyes. "A nap is a good idea. I was up all night trying to figure out what to do about Jonah while I'm gone."

Startled, Cinn looked to the empty couch; he hadn't even noticed he was gone.

"I cleaned the couch," Moyra said as she stood, running her hand down Cinn's shoulder. "I promise not to drag you into my dream again, and I promise I will still feel it if you need me."

He didn't want to sleep.

Nodding, he let Moyra go, sharing a knowing look with Gatty as the cat sith followed her. With her bedroom door closed and the sprites asleep on the counter, he was as alone as he was comfortable being.

The quiet gave his mind room to breathe. Room to buzz like a hive full of bees.

None of this was why he'd come here. Deities and wars, unifiers and separatists, shackles and keys; all he'd wanted was a way to go home.

He could have died today.

Gently, he rubbed a hand over his chest again. The fabric of his loose linen shirt was scratchy and gross, but he had healed. Was he actually relieved? Or had he convinced himself he was relieved because dying wasn't a luxury he could dream of anymore? Not without being the kind of selfish worm he didn't want to be anymore. But trying not to be selfish was a constant battle, and surely if it was what he really wanted it wouldn't feel like fighting nature. Maybe selfish was just what he was. Maybe cowardice was his natural state.

Sighing, Cinn rose from the table and moved to the couch, massaging his temple.

Ten seconds. That's how long he was allowed to wallow.

But no matter how hard he tried to redirect his thoughts, they crept back in like smoke under a door.

He'd come here hoping for a way to make everything go back the way he wanted it. A pipe dream. Since finding Moyra, all he'd done was discover more problems. Those quiet months on the farm were never going to be anything more than another lost life.

As soon as the thought formed, it was happening. One by one, his memories of Belden became pictures on paper. He scrambled to keep them close, but they folded over and tucked themselves into blank envelopes, filed away in the dusty parts of his mind, ready to be forgotten.

Just like Edwina and Radley had been. Were becoming again. Blinking rapidly, the life he'd shared with his sister and brother once again felt foreign and hazy.

None of it was real.

He'd imagined them all—every pleasant thing in his life was just a dream. Perhaps even this moment. This house, Moyra, the sprites, her broken shackle by the lake . . . As false a reality as everything else.

Scrunching his eyes, he held his breath until his chest ached. Pain was real. A reassurance. But when he looked down through his spotty vision, the sight of his body confused him. He didn't know this body. It didn't belong to him. Tall and strong and whole—it was wish-fulfillment.

And if none of this was real, then he didn't know what was. If anything was. If it even mattered.

Tension left him at the idea, sinking into the comforting distance until his flesh was an empty husk. Every thought, every feeling, every memory . . . silent.

Numb. Void. It was as close to death as he could get. As close to peace.

Safe.

Inch by inch, the world disappeared.

Shadows grew longer.

Color dulled.

The air cooled, but it didn't matter.

Nervous chittering and padded footfalls were meaningless.

The movement in the shadows was irrelevant.

The deep feline growl.

The pressure of gravity swallowing the room.

Shtryg.

The word was meaningless, even as a memory blipped faster than a heartbeat.

It didn't matter. Shtryg weren't real.

Neither was the feral snarling.

The screaming rattling the walls.

The hot, wet splatter on his face.

The curdled-milk smell.

The sharp pinpricks in his side or the moon-white eyes filling his vision.

The gentle, warm hands on either side of his face.

"Is he hurt?"

"No."

"Mother above, what was that thing?"

"Shtryg," the cat spat.

He didn't know where he was or why a cat was talking. He didn't care.

"Shtryg? There haven't been shtryg in Qiri since—"

"Dryads have been gossiping. Beasts are gathering for the rebirth. I meant to tell you, but we were both distracted."

The cat left his field of vision and a woman's face replaced it.

"Cinn, I need you to blink or something."

When he didn't, she closed her eyes. An invisible pressure probed against his skull and color bloomed behind his eyes. Like the first breath after drowning, life flooded in, blowing all the envelopes from their dusty corner.

And there he was.

Eaon.

They were in their cottage at the farmhouse. Cinn had gone empty, so Eaon fetched a cinnamon biscuit from the house. Sitting on the floor, Eaon had forced Cinn's head to rest against his shoulder, coaxing him to eat.

As quickly as the image came, it was gone.

Fists clenching, he closed his eyes against the burning pain of *everything* coming back into focus.

"There you are." Moyra smiled down at him.

"Perhaps some fresh air," Gatty grumbled, licking his wounds.

Cinn blinked a few times, but the corpse on the floor didn't go away. In the moonlight—gods, an entire day had passed without him noticing—every grizzly detail of the beast still bleeding its putrid, lumpy white guts on the floor was stark: twig-thin limbs and knobby joints, flaccid grey skin and blackened bone claws in lieu of fingers and toes. Worst of all was its face. Two thirds of the flat plane hosted exposed, puckered muscle, a small opening lined in translucent needle teeth. Its eyes were still open, moonlight reflecting in their milky glaze. In death, the darkness it cloaked itself in had dissipated, the monster underneath naked.

He wished he'd never seen it.

"Come on," Moyra said softly, pulling on his arm.

Sweat slipped down his spine as he looked her over for injuries. Even a scratch from a shtryg was lethal.

"I'm alright. Sit up for me."

Gatty . . .

The cat sith glared as he cleaned his claws. "*Now* you're worried about us."

"Don't," Moyra warned.

With a sniff of contempt, Gatty thumped his tail against the floor. "Fae are not as affected as mortals by beast venom," he growled. "And self-preservation is a trait of sprites."

Cinn nodded his relief, but as he stood, the room tilted. Moyra's grip tightened on his arms.

"You're disoriented. It's alright. Just follow me. Slow and steady."

One foot in front of the other, he made it outside. She led him into the garden and made him sit among the herbs, their smells overpowering, the dirt under his clenched fists warm from the day's baking.

It shouldn't have shocked him how tactile it all was.

"I thought you were sleeping with your eyes open," Moyra told him. "Peacefully, for once, since I didn't see the dreamscape. I wouldn't have let you lay so long like that if I'd realized. I'm sorry."

Shaking his head to deny her guilt was too hard. The breeze on his cheeks, the starlight rippling on the water . . . Everything was too much. Too heavy.

"Breathe," Moyra reminded him. "And let me help you. Close your eyes."

He did as she said, back bowing as he put his head down on his knees. Color bloomed behind his eyes again. Waiting for it to take shape, he breathed through the onslaught of images running through his head.

One of them snagged.

A key with seven curling tree branches. *The* key—the chunk of rose quartz with that witchmark carved in gold.

He'd seen the mark before, tattooed with black ink on a pale palm.

A hook latched in his throat just as the dreamscape took shape, the blues and purples giving way to a hammock and a hot spring. One hand searching for a hook that wasn't really there, the other trying to hold onto a hammock that crumbled under his fingers, the pressure went taught as a fishing line. He heard Moyra's cry of alarm as the force ripped him from her arms.

The cave in the Northern Mountains disappeared from under his feet. Plummeting aimlessly through bursts of starry clouds, he couldn't breathe as a dark rift opened among the swirling purple and orange below. An open maw.

It swallowed him whole.

Emptiness rang in his ears as the plummeting slowed, then stopped. The darkness solidified beneath his bare feet and rear. Cold seeped down to his bones.

He knew for certain he was dreaming, yet it felt real. Cramped and sore, the tips of his fingers smashed against stone when he tried to reach out. His gasp echoed back too closely. Feeling around, there were walls everywhere, boxing him in.

No. No, no, no.

His bones already ached, joints grating as he shoved against the hatch door above with all the strength of his emaciated body. Railed at it when there was no give. No space. No air.

Ryson screamed. The sound of it filled the world as he thrashed—feet and hands and head and knees and elbows cracking against stone. His nails caught; ripped from their beds as he clawed at the walls, desperate to dig his way out. All the while, he screamed, over and over until he tasted blood, but nobody could hear him. Nobody was coming.

"Tell me where the Kinner are and I will let you out. Tell me, and you can go home."

He'd loved her.

She had saved him, and he had loved her.

Until she'd done this to him.

When he was finally too tired to continue beating at the walls, he heaved emptily, limp in his cell. His mother had warned him this sort of thing would happen one day. That he would have to be strong, steeling his mind to keep it whole despite what they did to his body. With nothing but eternity ahead, the only thing of value was sanity.

But his mother was gone.

Everyone was gone.

He was alone, and it was *her* fault.

Days.

Weeks.

Months.

Years.

Time went by, and there was only the dark and *her*. The only part of him that mattered was breaking. Every second he spent in the dark, he forgot a little more—who he was, why he was there. What lay beyond the room of blood, bile, and pain.

It didn't matter.

Nothing mattered.

No, that wasn't true.

One thing mattered.

Pressing his fingers to his mouth, he shook his head.

"You're alright." The words came from nowhere. "You're alright."

He was not alright.

"Come on, Cinn. I'm here."

Nobody was here.

"Remember me. Please. I'm here. You just have to let me in."

He couldn't get himself *out*, let alone help someone *in*.

But the door over his head cracked open and moonlight came pouring in.

"That's it. Good boy."

Hands reached into his cell and pulled him out. Something was lodged in his throat, but Cinn opened his eyes to Moyra cradling him on her lap. Rosemary and lavender filled the night air, and high above, masses of pale white stars dominated the sky.

"You're here. You're alright. I found you." Moyra trembled, voice cracking on every word. "I found you."

He blinked, and the dark was back. Moyra's grip tightened. He was aware of her, but he couldn't see.

"I'm still here. I've got you," she promised, though it sounded like she was trying to convince herself more than him. "I've got you anchored. I won't let go again."

He couldn't do this anymore. He couldn't be in this place.

"Gatty!" Moyra screeched. "I don't know what to do!"

The cat sith's deep, lazy voice was born of this darkness. "It's the blockage."

"The dreamscape *took* him, Gatty. I couldn't find him anywhere," Moyra cried. "I don't know what to do. I can barely hold on. I don't know how to help him."

The silence lingered, but her grip did not waver. The darkness couldn't take shape so long as she was with him.

"You can't," Gatty said softly. "Look at his past lines. See there? He made a choice. Now the path is forked again, this choice a mirror of the one he made before. He has to help himself, Moyra. He has to choose differently. Right now, or never."

"What choice?" Moyra begged.

"He knows."

Vague Morvish nonsense.

Except, deep down, he did know. He just couldn't do it.

His body jerked in small, involuntary movements as he tried to shake his head.

"He's stuck," Gatty continued. "His instinct to run has left him stuck."

"Please," Moyra whispered against his forehead, her warm breath a relief from the bone shattering cold. "You can do this."

He shook his head again, more fiercely.

"I'll give you a moment," Gatty offered.

Only Moyra's ragged breaths filled the silence. Not even the cicadas were out.

"He's gone, Cinn." Moyra spoke against the shell of his ear this time. "There's nobody around for miles and miles."

He was alone.

"I'm with you," she insisted, as if she'd felt the terror locking up his body. "I'm here. It's you and me. Whoever it is you're running from can't find you here."

Relief.

Short lived.

Everything was so heavy.

"You can give it to me. Let me hold it with you."

Squeezing his eyes shut, he shook his head again, chest

heaving with panicked, desperate breaths. Not because he didn't believe her, but because he was so close to caving in. Everything he'd endured, everything that happened . . . he couldn't let it be for nothing.

"It's okay," Moyra soothed. "It's okay. You can let it go."

Everything was breaking. He couldn't pull it back together fast enough. Pain had never been enough to draw it out of him, but this . . .

His voice cracked as he let out a sob. Moyra curled over him, hands smoothing back his hair, magic a gentle caress against his blistering mind. A promise that there would be peace as soon as he let go of the strangling darkness in his throat. A promise of cinnamon and a warm blanket.

His breath trembled as he inhaled.

And then he spoke.

"I know where they are."

The sound was a broken rasp, his voice so foreign he wasn't sure it was him who'd said it. Dizziness told him he had; the panic threatening to drown him.

He wanted to suck the words back in.

He couldn't face what would happen now.

He wanted to die.

Moyra stroked his hair once more.

"Okay."

He opened his eyes, vision spotty, body wracked with violent waves of hot and cold. But nothing happened. He'd said it, and nothing happened.

"I know where the Kinner are," he said again, choking.

"Alright," Moyra promised.

Alright.

He was alright.

CHAPTER 26

CINN

HE COULD STILL SMELL THE HERBS AS HE SPRINTED THROUGH the forest. Rough undergrowth tore at his bare feet while thorny shrubs drew blood from his arms and neck. A monstrous roar shook debris from the highest tree branches, warning him the beast was not too far behind.

What kind of bullshit dream is this!

"I didn't make the dream, I'm just here to guide you through it," Moyra answered.

Heart acidic in his chest, Cinn ran without thought to where he was going. Though he pushed his body to its limits, the beast's hot breath down his neck would not relent.

Bursting through a cluster of shrubs, Cinn skidded to a stop at the edge of a cliff. Spinning back, he raised his arms in preparation for the collision.

Only the cicadas met him, the night damp against his skin. Shaking, he dropped his arms. There was no sign of the beast.

He didn't trust the stillness.

Did you get rid of it?

"No."

Huffing, Cinn scowled at the shadows. *Feel free to do something useful.*

"Who knew you had such an attitude," she quipped back.

A branch snapped to his left.

Nothing could really hurt him here—he was lucid enough to know that—but the scrape of his breath was still painful in his ragged lungs as the shrubbery rustled and *she* stepped out.

Cinn stepped back, the cliffside crumbling under his heels.

Moyra, get me out of here. Now. He wasn't afraid to beg. *Please.*

She didn't answer. She didn't pull him out.

Desperately patting his sides, he was surprised to find William's dagger strapped there. No shoes and dressed in the rags he'd escaped in, but he had the knife.

Did you give me this?

Once again, Moyra didn't answer.

Pulling the blade free, he moved into one of the few defensive positions he remembered from his cadet training.

She stepped closer.

In the dungeon, she'd always worn dark pants and tunics, a dark mask over her lower face, but that wasn't the version presenting herself now. Standing there in all her majestic glory, gold-and-purple dress enormous, dark-grey hair coiled neatly beneath the ruby-encrusted crown balanced on her head, she didn't appear to have any weapons bar the sweet, blood-red smile plastered on her stiff face.

This was the princess he had sworn to serve and protect. The one he had adored. The one who had betrayed him.

She stepped closer and held out a gloved hand, crooking a finger for him to approach.

He never dreamed of her like this. It was a version that had ceased to exist the first time she took a blade to him. But as he dared to meet her gaze, shaking so hard he nearly dropped the knife, he saw it: the monster lurking beneath her skin.

Red lips pulled back to bare pointed teeth, snarling as her outstretched hand grew claws. She lunged for him, and Cinn slashed his blade across her palm. The ground beneath his feet crumbled as his weight shifted, gravity threatening to drag him down into the ravine below.

As she shrieked with pain, he scrambled away from the edge. The blood dripping from her hand was putrid, and as the princess's body morphed to something hideous, her dress ripped to ribbons, Cinn knew running would be useless.

He had to fight instead.

Vaguely resembling a skinned bear, the creature she'd changed into barreled toward him. It was Dearmead in his head now as Cinn moved his feet, bracing himself. Not the guardian's words—they'd never exchanged any that the other understood— but the technique he had taught him.

Timing was everything. He faced down the lumbering bear, and at the last second, in the same movement, Cinn dropped to the ground, rolled to his back, and stabbed up into the bear's gut. The beast's momentum forced it to gut itself, blood and bile spraying everywhere, but as the bear collapsed and Cinn rolled back to his feet, spitting bits of flesh and ready to attack again if needed, he saw it was unnecessary

The bear was gone. *She* was back.

She was dead.

Was . . . Was that even possible?

Warily, keeping the knife angled, Cinn crept forward. She was a witch, but she was still mortal—yet he had never thought of her so. She was too powerful, too horrid, too much. She was a mountain, and he was a pebble.

As he drew close enough to hear the rattle in her chest,

innards soaking the soil, it dawned on him how very wrong he had been.

She could die.

He could kill her.

Moyra's hands were on his temples as Cinn woke from the dream. They had not moved from the garden all night, and they had not been disturbed. Not as he'd passed out over and over. Not as Moyra had anchored him in the dreamscape, helping him navigate the horrors in his head. Not as the sun rose on their last day in Qiri and Cinn thought he might finally be able to keep his grip on consciousness.

He had spoken. The words lodged in his throat for years had finally come out, and though he had not uttered another sound since, there was an easiness to his silence. It wasn't because he couldn't speak, but because he didn't know what to say.

No, that wasn't true.

Watching the colors of dawn dare to compete with those of the dreamscape, Cinn took Moyra's hand and squeezed. Parting his lips, it took a few seconds to convince himself he could still do this.

"Thank you."

Habit saw him sign with his free hand as he said it. It would be a long time before he was comfortable enough with speech again to give it up altogether.

Moyra returned the squeeze.

"You're beyond welcome, Cinn." She rubbed her ankle as she added, "At least we're even now."

Forcing his aching body to sit up, they watched the sun paint the woods in green and brown, far more vibrant than the forest of his dreams. A part of him was still there, standing over *her* bleeding corpse.

Until that moment, he hadn't known what he wanted to do about the Sparrow princess. Eaon had thoughts on the matter, and Kaelean had said . . . something. He'd been so numb he couldn't remember. But now, the metallic residue on his tongue was all he needed to know.

For what she might have done to Edwina and Radley, for the trouble she had caused William and Sarah, for the pain inflicted on Siobhan and the rebels, he wanted her dead.

And for what she had done to him . . . he wanted to kill her himself.

"You alright?" Moyra asked.

Swallowing down the violent tang, he nodded. Then he jerked his head toward the shack and mimed her going to sleep.

"Only if you're sure you'll be alright."

Not only had she been awake all night helping him, but they had another big night coming up. She needed the rest.

He nodded insistently, pointing to himself then to the porch. He had no intention of going anywhere.

Covering another yawn with the back of her hand, Moyra stood and succumbed to her exhaustion. Once the door was closed, Cinn stood too, glancing around the glen. The wildlife was out, drinking from the still water of the lake, but he didn't see any fae. No beasts, either.

He still couldn't believe he'd been so detached from reality he hadn't even noticed the attack. The only evidence there had been a shtryg in the house was the stain on the floor. What Gatty had done with the body, he didn't want to know.

That couldn't happen again. He needed to be ready.

He wasn't a scrawny seventeen-year-old boy anymore—*she*

would not get the upper hand on him again. The next time they met, he would be ready.

Summer was beginning to cool, a breeze blowing back his hair. Tightening his laces, Cinn found the strongest bit of deck he could and got down on his hands and toes.

One, he counted silently as he brought himself down, nose to damp wood, then pushed back up again.

Two.

Recalling his cadet routine was easier than expected, as if his mind and body were eagerly in sync for once. It was tougher than it used to be though, which was embarrassing. Considering he'd been working with William all summer, he hadn't thought he'd be so out of shape.

Your mind will quit before your body does.

He'd had to repeat his mother's mantra over and over just to get through it—his body would not fail him if he didn't let it. The hour he spent on the porch was as much an activity of mental training as physical. He'd grown too used to quitting.

Never again.

By the time he was finished, his hunger for revenge burned as deeply as that in his actual stomach. Creeping inside as quietly as he could, he used the small washtub to clean himself before finding clothes to wear, leaving his sweat-stained ones to soak. In the kitchen, he pulled a handful of jackfruit jerky from the nearly empty traveler's rations he'd had in his bag since leaving Wyldeden, snacking on it as he hunted through Moyra's kitchen supplies.

She didn't have much. Cinn was practiced at surviving on less, but he wasn't trying to simply survive anymore. If he wanted to be strong, he needed to eat, and no doubt Moyra could use something hearty after expending herself in his dreams all night.

The elder slaves in Master Ackford's house had taught him a recipe for nutrient-rich bread, made with scraps from the master's meals and the very few provisions they were allowed for themselves. Cinn's ability to slip his shackles and sneak into the city to steal a bit more had been a boon, and the recipe had developed until a single slice was enough to fuel a body for most of the day. When freedom came, Edwina, Radley, and he had continued to experiment as they found their feet.

It was disorienting as Cinn made a mental list of what he needed, and he warred with the part of himself that still wanted to run from who he used to be.

No.

It was his own voice barking in his head. No—there were not five different versions of himself taking turns with his body. He was all of them.

He was Ryson Tacenda, the wild kinner child attached to his mother's hip. He was also Ryson, the slave with no surname. He was the cadet, and he was the thing in the dungeon. He was Cinn, the boy who'd grown up in the dark. He was all these things at once. The barriers between them had kept his sanity intact, and for that he was grateful, but it was time to take them down. He could be here in Qiri, missing Eaon and both of his families, and he could also train like a cadet again, make the slave bread, without having an existential crisis.

He could.

There was no booming crash, no dust and rubble as the walls crumbled down. Only a breath, pulled in through his nose and held for a moment, the mildewy air permeating cracks that had been forming for months, then released through slightly parted lips.

Hello, he greeted each isolated part of himself as he felt them crowding in.

The pain and sadness they brought with them was uncomfortable. Cinn's hands trembled as he measured the flour into a mixing bowl, but the recipe didn't call for precision—a hodgepodge of whatever they could get their hands on, only working by sheer willpower and hope.

A lot like himself.

Hunting through cupboards and foraging through the garden, it took hours of chopping, grinding and kneading before the dough was ready for the oven. By then, he had drawn the attention of the sprites. He gave each a drop of honey with a wink, but as they chittered their glee, he hushed them with a finger to his lips.

The oven made the room stuffy, his heart heavy. He could almost hear Edwina telling him he'd kneaded it wrong while Radley complained about the rosemary making his clothes smell. Letting himself love them again was torture. The grief at what had been taken from him.

Taking a deep breath, he went to his pack and pulled out his trinket box again. Moving the moonstones aside, he brushed and smelled each beautiful thing, but he didn't push the grief away. He sat with it until he was dizzy and retching, clutching the paper fox to his chest.

The creak of a door registered a moment before Moyra's bare feet padded across the wood. Her bleary eyes were bloodshot as she sat beside him, placing one hand between his shoulder blades and the other on his sternum.

"Healing hurts," she whispered. "But the pain will lessen, and one day your wounds will be but a scar."

He nodded, focusing on the pressure of her hands. The control they gave him over his own breathing.

Sniffing deeply, she turned toward the kitchen. "It smells nice in here. What are you making?"

He made the sign for bread, even though she wouldn't understand.

"Don't want to speak today?" she asked.

Cinn shook his head. Not yet.

"That's alright. How about I make some tea?"

A smile broke across his face. Always with the tea.

As if she knew what he was thinking, Moyra smacked his shoulder as she got to her feet. Cinn only grinned wider. Tea and bread did sound like a good breakfast.

CHAPTER 27

MOYRA

Watching Cinn run himself ragged was as much exercise as Moyra ever planned on doing. He'd been outside sweating all day while she sat at the table with another cup of tea and a bowl of crushed herbs. There was a song she'd learned at the academy, and as she marked her face and hands with ground lemongrass, applied with a point of lapis lazuli, she hummed it to herself. So much more effective than a pendulum, her mind, body, and spirit settled into the meditative calm needed for effective *seeing*.

What she'd done by the lake when the selkies had offered Cinn that deal had been messy. The stars had been screaming and she'd been anything but calm—all she'd been able to *see* was a path of desolation and another of hope. This time when she drew on her magic, Olyvia's and Kailevi's magnifying her maladroit skills, she had clarity.

Show me where to go, she prayed, forehead tingling where her tattoo gleamed. *Show me what to do first.*

As soon as night fell, she would use the moonstones to go

south of the wards. She would find her niece and nephew and do everything she could to help them. She just needed to *see*. Colors burst behind her eyes; pink, red, and golden stars, and at each core, flashes of futures. Moyra sank farther into her pool of power in a bid to control the visions.

Finding Eavha was easier than finding Eaon—her niece's potential futures burned inside the brightest stars. What played out inside them, however, left Moyra frowning.

The witch haunting Cinn's nightmares was softly tending to a sleeping Eavha, the two of them swaddled in silk linens. All the harsh lines of the grey-haired witch's face were soothed as she stroked Eavha's sweaty curls from her forehead. The image only lasted a moment before the star wobbled and the vision changed. Eavha and the witch stood in a marble room, the balcony behind them lending a view to a comparatively small city. Both witches were grief stricken over a leaking box on the table, a decapitated head inside. A snake lunged from the open mouth, but the grey-haired witch caught it in an impossibly quick movement, her grief giving way to utter rage. The vision shifted again; a grand council room, the table laden with dead bodies as the grey-haired witch stood above them. Eavha was still at her side, along with four others, but only her niece was crying as a portal opened, calling the witch's name over and over.

Aisling. Aisling. Aisling.

Moyra pulled herself from the vision, humming her song as she asked the stars to show her Aisling. Clearly this witch was important to her niece despite Cinn's history, but whether Aisling would lead to Eavha's survival or destruction, Moyra had to know.

Princess Aisling Aurnia. The stars sighed her name with a reverence that turned Moyra's stomach cold. She didn't know what it meant as they eagerly offered a collection of burning red stars. *Soon to be Queen of the Sparrow Coven.*

Moyra raised her brows at the word "coven" before realizing it was another appropriation. There was no pool of power the princess drew from, and Aisling's own store was mediocre at best, even as she stood in a foreign throne room and faced down the most terrifying things Moyra had ever seen.

Monsters.

Rabid and crafty, they swarmed. Teeth and claws, wings and tails, they would not stop until they drew blood. Aisling met each with a silver axe, and though she was covered in witchmarks, she could barely use them. An ethereal presence cried in the corner and Moyra startled at the constellation tattooed on the ghost's forehead.

As if time and space, the veil between Mother's and the Lover's realms, meant nothing, the Morvish ghost turned to Moyra and wept.

"Help her. She's the key to all of it. Please."

Trembling, Moyra left the vision as quick as she could. Others took its place. The cries of war as white flecks fell from the sky. A dark-skinned male with a long black braid, standing in a field with only a wooden staff to protect him.

And Aisling. Alone, standing on a bridge suspended between two towers, an endless pit below and mountains to either side. Climbing up the exterior of one tower was a gargantuan beast unlike any other. Glistening eyes of fire trapped in ruby, they found Aisling waiting and grinned. It spoke her name with the same reverence as the stars, its voice everywhere and nowhere all at once.

There was no doubting who the creature was. Only one being could emanate such violence.

Moyra's knees buckled at the sight of Chaos approaching the princess.

"*One thing at a time, Moyra,*" Gatty's calming tone filled her head, pulling her away from a future that seemed so much more concrete than the rest. "*Focus on Eavha.*"

"Thank you for finding me."

"*You should have fetched me before doing this.*"

Ignoring the scolding, Moyra turned her attention back to Eavha. Riding on the back of a majestic, winged horse, she approached a cliff-top city, a swamp beyond and the sea below.

The name shuddered through the realm of stars.

Pirevia.

Seeing Chaos in mortal form had shaken her. As the vision shifted quickly, the sun baking a dirt-floored arena, Moyra could not focus enough to see what was happening. Only that Eavha and Aisling were there, as was the dark male she'd seen before. Another male—*Prince Nevan*—stood beside Death, reaping hundreds.

With a gasp, Moyra opened her eyes. The force with which she pulled herself from the visions sent her reeling, the chair beneath her balancing precariously on two legs. Grabbing the edge of the table, she righted herself.

"Eavha's going to die," she wheezed.

"When?" Gatty demanded from where he sat on the table beside her bowl of herbs.

"I don't know. I didn't—"

"Go back and find out."

Steeling herself, controlling her breaths, she tried to *see* again. Only vague nonsense greeted her, too much frantic energy pounding through her body to focus.

"Tomorrow, I think." Frowning, she pushed harder. "Even if I go to her first thing tonight, it won't make a difference. In fact, it might make it worse."

Standing, nails between her teeth, she paced to the kitchen window to watch Cinn running back from his lap around the lake.

"Aisling is with her, and Cinn's presence . . . the two of them in the same space is not a good idea."

"Talk to him. Make him see reason."

"That's not fair. You haven't seen his dreams—"

"Your niece's life is at stake. Talk to him."

Gripping the crystal pendant around her neck, she rallied her magic. She might not be able to *see* well right now, but her way-finding skills were easier to handle.

Fate agreed with Gatty.

"Alright."

"Cinn." Moyra stepped onto the porch.

At her call, he slowed his running and changed direction, bounding up the stairs with more energy than he had business having while so sweaty.

By the wariness that came over his face, her own must have betrayed the panic taking root.

"I've been looking into the future to plan for tonight, but Eavha is in trouble. She's gone to a place called Pirevia."

Cinn stiffened, stepping closer to clutch her wrist. The way he paled through his flushed cheeks was indicative of how bad this was.

"It can't wait. She needs us." Moyra's throat had swollen, her voice strained.

Fate and Gatty be damned, she couldn't tell him about Aisling. Not when he was just starting to feel better.

But she had another idea.

"We won't make it in time to help her, but I . . . I'm going to try something. I need to borrow your amulet."

Without hesitation, he pulled the willow tree carving from around his neck. At the tight grip Cinn kept on her wrist as she hung the carving beside the lapis lazuli, Moyra explained.

"She needs help we cannot give her, but that doesn't mean we abandon her. Eaon's Morvish, so I'm going to try and contact him through the dreamscape. We learn how to do it in the academies, but . . ." She fondled the two pendants. "He's untrained. It could be dangerous."

Cinn bit his lip. When words didn't come right away, he cleared his throat and wiped the sweat from his forehead. Moyra waited patiently, and when his breaths stopped shaking, he managed to speak.

"He would want to know."

It pained him to say it. To let her take this risk with Eaon's life.

"It's not just Eavha," Moyra tried to justify it. "There are so many people in danger, and she has company—"

"Who?" Cinn asked, pulse throbbing in his neck vein.

"A male witch. Dark black hair—"

Cinn scratched at his collar, shaking his head. "Dearmead."

"Is he important?" He must be if the stars had shown him to her.

"To Eaon."

A tangled web of fate lines. This Dearmead was with Eavha and Aisling, both he and Eavha connected to Eaon, who was connected to Cinn. As was Aisling.

"This could go so wrong. Eaon could get really hurt."

Cinn closed his eyes and let go of her wrist, tucking his fists under his arms. Rocking on his heels, it took a long time for him to finally look at her.

"I know him," Cinn croaked. "He would want to know."

Moyra shook her head. Not in refusal, but in disbelief that she was even going to attempt this.

"If I sense things going badly, I will pull right out," she promised herself as much as Cinn.

Taking her hand, the two returned to the table inside. Gatty narrowed his eyes but didn't say anything about her decision not to tell Cinn the truth, watching stoically as Moyra ground a fresh bunch of lemongrass. She took the time to brew a cup of mugwort and ginseng tea as well—this past week had been a nonstop drain on her magic, and though she had the strength of a coven inside her, she was beginning to feel the fatigue.

"Try and keep your head empty," she told Cinn as she resumed her seat. "I don't want any distractions."

He nodded, so Moyra placed her elbows on the table, clasped the amulet hanging around her neck between her palms and laced her fingers. Eyes closed, she called on the dreamscape, and as it always had, it answered eagerly.

For the first time since she was a witchling, she was nervous. The dreamscape had always been her favorite of all Morvia's realms; a boundless place where the subconscious of every intelligent thing could rest. Dreams had so many uses, and when the realm was calm like this, they were a pleasure to walk through. It was unfortunate that whenever it came to Cinn, the dreamscape turned rabid. It had whisked him away and hidden him from her. Every trick she'd ever learnt at the academy had been useless.

As if in apology, violet clouds drifted by peacefully, inviting her in. The dreams inside were mellow. Gentle. It would have been a pleasant place to linger, but she was not here to snoop on the subconscious of any old Ahrenhalian.

Eaon, she called. *Take me to Eaon.*

Eager, a hook sunk into her heart and tugged her through infinity. Colors flew by at an alarming speed, but even here the wards around Nir had a hold. A ring of fog approached, and as she passed through it, the dreamscape obscured. Muddied and vague, it was no wonder the council had sent spies to Dusarn to keep track of the situation—all normal methods of communication were unreliable.

The colors slowed and Moyra came to a still. This was the place where Eaon's subconscious would normally take shape, but the dreamscape didn't form a scene.

He wasn't asleep.

She was already risking a lot by attempting to contact him, but to force the dreamscape on him? She wouldn't do it to a novice, let alone someone who had no idea he was even Morvish.

Do it.

The command came from everywhere and nowhere.

Moyra flinched as it filled her head. Looking around, there didn't appear to be anyone else conscious in the dreamscape.

It took a moment to realize who it was, but . . . No.

There was no way.

Morvia didn't intervene.

Morvia minded her business.

Except today.

Steadying herself, clamping down on her magic, Moyra sent a tendril through the veil to where Eaon's consciousness waited on the other side. Slowly, carefully, she wrapped the dreamscape around his mind, the way an octopus might gently grab hold of its prey.

The moment he slipped inside, the dreamscape came alive,

crackling with undiluted energy. Without so much as a day of training, the dreamscape wanted to obey him over her.

But it couldn't.

Since Eaon couldn't manifest a physical form, his soul was a ball of shimmering light, and Moyra blanched at the sight of it. In all her years, she had never seen one so burdened. Four large leeches suckled greedily, their lengths fading into a gaping void that hovered nearby. What they were and where they had come from, she didn't know, but Eaon's soul faded slightly with every hungry draw, tainted with a frigid darkness.

It wasn't just the leeches that horrified her, though. A coil of foreign power was wrapped tightly around Eaon, binding his own magic—a golden aura that strained inside. And *that*, she recognized. The binding was rudimentary, unskilled and unpracticed, as if the witch who'd cast it didn't really know what they were doing. Had never graduated an academy. Had no constellation tattoo.

Moyra knew whose power bound him. She'd know the hue of it anywhere.

Kailevi, what have you done?

There was too much magic going to waste in Eaon's soul, the coil constricting it too tight. Moyra doubted Eaon had more than a month before something broke irrevocably.

She needed to go to him—help him.

Soon. Right now, she had to send him to Eavha.

Fear and curiosity tinted the dreamscape in the same greyish-yellow surrounding Cinn most of the time, and as Eaon noticed Moyra manifesting a body for him to interact with, she heard his internal questioning in her mind.

He didn't have the control to keep his thoughts private, and he did not recognize her.

"*Because we've never met,*" she said directly to his mind. "*I'm sorry I had to drag you here when you've had no training, but it's urgent.*"

His lack of form disturbed him, but the abstract nature of existing in a spirit realm was familiar. He'd been in the void with the Lover many times, and he assumed she was another spirit, too.

"No," she answered. "*My name is Moyra Thorne. Cinn is here in Ahrenhale with me. I am Morvia-blessed and I have seen something in the stars that Cinn said you needed to know urgently. It's about Eavha.*"

His relief about Cinn quickly gave way to the bright flare of panic. She moved closer, trying to keep the dreamscape wrangled as it attempted to take shape. Eaon wasn't even aware of his influence, but now was not the time to teach him.

"*She's followed Aisling Aurnia to Pirevia to fight Prince Nevan. Dearmead is with her. The stars show a massacre.*"

The panic swelled so ferociously that, despite Moyra's steely grip, the dreamscape almost took form.

"*I know it is a lot, and it is confusing. I warned Cinn this might be too much for you, so try to put this out of your mind. When we meet, I will explain as much as I can. Just focus on Eavha. She needs you. Dearmead needs you.*"

The Morvish ghost's plea replayed in her mind.

"*And Aisling. You must protect her at all costs.*"

His soul shuttered and twisted, flaring hotly. The binding around his power groaned at the strain, threatening to snap. If that happened, the surge would kill him. There was no doubt in Moyra's mind.

A thin whip of power escaped Eaon's bindings. It struck her like a whip to flesh, and it was all Moyra could do to keep control.

She had to leave. Now.

Withdrawing the tendrils of magic from his mind, she

pushed him back out of the dreamscape as gently as she had reeled him in.

Let him be okay. She had not prayed to Morvia since the temple, but she did it now. *Let them both be okay.*

Opening her eyes, she returned to her kitchen table.

Exhausted, she drained her tea and put her head in her hands. Cinn gently rubbed her back.

"It's done," she told him. "We just have to hope it is enough."

When she looked up, Gatty's eyes were wide as the impending full moon, as if he had seen how close to a disaster the conversation had been.

"Cinn, I think you should make Moyra some more tea."

Taking her cup, Cinn left for the kitchen. It spoke legions that Moyra didn't even have the energy to scold him about how he brewed it. The dreamscape clung to her, and the harder she tried to fight it off, the deeper it seeped into her mind.

"I don't feel well."

"Let's get some fresh air," Gatty suggested, jumping from the table.

She didn't think she could do it, but she gripped the table and stood anyway.

A flash of pain behind her eyes had them rolling back in her head, the world exploding with color. A single word became the only thing that mattered.

"Seven."

CHAPTER 28

CINN

"SEVEN. SEVEN SEVEN SEVEN. SEVEN."

Cinn left the kettle, skidding to his knees to catch Moyra before her head hit the floor. Gatty froze by the door, staring in shock.

"Seven. Seven seven seven. Seven."

The whites of her eyes quivered, lips drained of color. Cinn held her tightly as Moyra's body began to convulse, yet she continued to repeat the pattern over and over.

"Seven. Seven seven seven. Seven. Seven. Seven seven seven. Seven."

Cinn turned to Gatty, heart galloping in his chest. At least with the cat sith he didn't have to speak.

Get help!

"Seven. Seven seven seven. Seven."

Rather than run or dissolve into shadow, Gatty just stared.

What are you doing?!

"Seven. Seven seven seven. Seven."

The word had lost all meaning. Carefully, Cinn lowered

Moyra to the floor, preparing to run all the way to Ahrenhale and back if he had to.

Before he'd taken a step, Moyra fell still. As quickly as it had happened, it was over, her eyes returning to normal, her body going slack.

"Moyra?" Cinn croaked, frozen mid lunge toward the door.

She lay dazed, blinking rapidly before pointing to the kitchen. "Tea."

He wasn't in the mood to mock her for her addiction, running to the kitchen to finish. The kettle had been left on the stove and was about to boil over, so he grabbed the jar of tea leaves and herbs she'd left out and made up a cup.

By the time he returned to her side she'd managed to sit up, Gatty acting as a support. She thanked Cinn with a weak smile as she took the tea.

"As soon as the moon rises, we need to go."

"Eaon?" he asked, heart aching.

She didn't answer, grabbing hold of the tabletop to pull herself upright. When he refused to stop staring, she nodded to the chair he'd been sitting on before.

"We have to believe he will be okay," she said, draining her tea. "But we need to finish getting ready. Make a plan."

"Find Eaon and Eavha," Cinn declared, throwing a hand to the door. As far as he was concerned, that was all the plan they needed.

Resting her head in her hands again, Moyra stared at the bowl of herbs, lost in thought. Gatty padded over, rubbing himself on her legs. Mindlessly, she reached down a hand to scratch under his chin.

"They need us, yes," she said softly. "But Chaos is coming. So is the Lover—Death. Morvia spoke to me in the dreamscape, and . . . Nir needs all the help they can get. More than just you and me, Cinn."

Gatty purred. "You don't need to ask, Moyra. I will follow you to the grave."

"Thank you." She smiled fondly at him before turning back to Cinn. "But it will still take more than the three of us. We need all the help we can get. Even that you don't want to give."

There was nothing he wouldn't give to protect his family. He didn't understand what she was so insistent about.

Except, then he did.

He shook his head.

"We need them, Cinn. You can trust me with this," she began, but he shook his head again and took her hand.

It wasn't that he didn't trust her, but what he had already told her and what she was asking of him were two different things. He knew where the Kinner were. He had admitted that much. It had hurt, but it had helped too, and all his fears about what would happen if he let those words out had borne no consequence. But telling Moyra where they were . . . No.

His people could not help them.

"Why not?" Gatty asked.

Cinn scowled. *Stop it.*

"He thinks the Kinner cannot help," Gatty told Moyra.

"Why not?" Moyra repeated gently.

He didn't want to talk about this.

He couldn't talk about this.

Moyra and Gatty both stayed quiet as Cinn's throat tightened, head swimming. He couldn't talk about this, and yet he had to.

Eavha was about to die. They had just risked Eaon's life to help her. Chaos was coming. Death was coming. The world was literally ending . . .

And he couldn't open his mouth to help?

Unacceptable.

Keeping his people's most guarded secret was a rule beaten into him since the day he was born, but what good was it doing? It didn't help the Kinner. It hadn't helped Cinn. He could not think of a single reason other than his mother's order that this secret be kept.

And Moyra was not *her*.

Gatty smiled, and for once it wasn't a threat.

"I can't . . . explain," Cinn whispered. "But I'll show you."

Dusk brought forward the moon. As if every creature in the glen knew Moyra and Gatty were leaving, the forest was a hive of activity, eyes watching the three of them descend the steps to the soggy porch one last time.

Moyra's bag was full of herbs and crystals, while Cinn's own was stuffed to the brink with all the food he could carry.

Lula, Dida, and Nena waited in the garden, mewling.

"You've been wonderful company," Moyra lied as she crouched, offering them an entire jar of honey. "I'm trusting you to keep an eye on this place while I'm gone. If any of my clients come looking for me, I want you to take them back to my parents, okay?"

None of them were interested in the honey. Nena outright wailed, while Dida clung to Moyra's boot.

Cinn crouched down too, stroking Lula's cap gently. She peered up at him with the saddest eyes a mushroom could make, tiny crystal tears dripping down her thumbnail-sized face.

From his pocket, he took out the blue-streaked pebble.

Kissing it one last time, he placed the rock in her hands and kissed the top of her cap, too. She didn't whoop in glee; she simply stared at him and hugged his gift to her chest.

"We must go," Gatty reminded them.

Cinn stroked Lula's head one more time before getting to his feet, offering Moyra a hand.

"Be good," she said, plucking the dandelion and lake sprites off her shoes.

In the shallows of the lake, two selkies stood with their seal skins wrapped around their waist. When Cinn caught their eye, they nodded, and though he didn't know what it meant, he nodded back.

"Ready?" Moyra asked, palm sweaty in Cinn's.

From his other pocket, he pulled out the pouch of moonstones. Moyra fished one out and held it up to the moon.

Between the glow within and the moonlight illuminating its cloudy surface, it could have been a drop of celestial glass.

"It's a soul," Gatty said, sitting by Moyra's feet.

Cinn dragged his gaze away from the stone to blink at the cat sith.

"Now is not the time," Moyra muttered.

"Now is exactly the time. That inner glow is a soul. The last remnants left behind by a Morvish witch who denied the Lover's embrace to linger in the void. They trade their soul to the moon so a stone can be used like this. Once."

Cinn looked back to the moonstone. To the pouch, with six more stones inside. Six more sacrificed souls.

"We go south of the wards with respect," Gatty continued.

Nodding, he looked to Moyra. She spared him a tight smile before turning her face to the moon.

"In she comes, there she goes. Master of Tides, let us be thy sea tonight. In she comes, there she goes."

Moyra brought the glistening stone down between them, a tiny moon inside.

"So, where are we going?" she asked. "You need only say."

He nodded, closing his fingers around the frosty moonstone. Gatty jumped into Moyra's arms.

She would not know. This would be okay. His lips felt numb as he parted them, sucking down a breath that didn't satisfy.

"Orhn."

PART V

CORDOLIUM

CHAPTER 29

CINN

ONE MOMENT HE WAS IN QIRI, A DEEP VACUUM FROM ABOVE dissolving his essence to dust, but no more than half a heartbeat later the moon washed him out on a very different beach. The unrelenting song of the stirring sea hit him like a hammer to the head.

The salty air drying his eyes had Cinn feeling five years old again. His parents' large hands clutched his tiny ones, lifting him out of the puddle of puke at the bottom of the rowboat.

"It's time you saw something," his mother told him.

"I'm not sure about this," his father muttered over Ryson's head. *"He's still a child."*

"Childhood is a luxury our kind don't get to have."

Moyra clung to him anxiously as Cinn took in the island he'd only visited that once. Their family was nomadic, so he was used to wandering, but drawing close enough to humans to rent a boat was strange. That his parents had gone to such effort to bring him to a beach just like any other in Nir was stranger.

His mother had stood in the shallows, staring back across the strait, black hair slicked back by wind. She often did that. At two and a half thousand years old, she had many memories to get lost in.

Cinn cleared his throat, shaking the ghosts from his mind. Wherever she was, wherever his father was . . . it wasn't something he had mental space to think about.

"This . . ." he started, lifting a hand to indicate the island.

Both his voice and his gesture fell flat when his throat clogged. His blood quickened, breaths growing thin. Moyra waited patiently for him to decide whether what he wanted to say was worth it.

"Sacred place," he managed, shivering. The summer nights were cooling, meaning autumn would be back soon.

"To the Kinner?" Moyra asked, giving Cinn the option to simply nod. "And nobody ever looked for them here?"

Cinn grimaced as he nodded again. They had looked. *She* had looked before Cinn was even born, or so she'd said during one of her frustrated rants, rattling off all the places she'd already scoured.

"Any other lies you want to try?"

He shivered again and clenched his fists, crossing his arms. The things he had endured to keep this place a secret . . . and here he was, about to give it up.

It was the right thing to do, but that didn't make it easier.

Just before he and his parents had reached the fishing village to rent the rowboat, they had stopped. Holding his face so there'd been no choice but to meet his mother's too-intense stare, her nails in his cheeks had been painful, words brutal and promising consequences.

"Never, ever, tell anyone about what we are about to show you. Never speak the island's name. You take this secret to your grave, Ryson, and you know how far away that eventuality is for our kind. I expect

*you to cut out your tongue before you speak of this place, and when it
grows back, you cut it out again."*

She'd waited for a nod despite her grip on his face. He
remembered the itch in his cheeks as the cuts her nails left
healed.

"It's just you and me, remember," Moyra said, putting down
Gatty so she could take his hand, forcing his arms to relax.

In this one instance, perhaps his mother would approve. He
had not brought Moyra on a whim. He'd brought one of the only
witches in the world who could possibly help his people.

"I will wait here," the cat sith announced, planting his behind
in the sand to stare across the strait. "Something feels strange. I
will come find you if I need to."

"Are you sure?" Moyra asked, frowning as she followed his
gaze.

Gatty scoffed. "Don't ask such ridiculous questions."

Shaking his head at the over-sized feline, Cinn tugged on
Moyra's hand. Their boots sunk in the soft sand as he led her
across the beach and up a dune so tall it obscured the palm trees
on the other side. The shallow wheezes as Moyra crawled behind
him ended in a sharp gasp as they reached the top and the bulk
of the island lay before them.

Everything was exactly as he remembered it.

Stone rubble lay as far as the eye could see, overgrown with
flowering sedum and other greens. Every hundred feet or so, half
an intact wall protruded from the destruction like a lone hand
reaching from under a mass of corpses.

The history lesson his parents had given him as they took
him through the ruins stuck in his mind—he dared not forget a
word of it. Before the Sparrows had risen into power, this was
the city from where the Kinner had ruled all of Nir. Or at least
the parts inside the wards. As they'd picked through it, his father

had poetically described the ornate bridges once crossing the strait, the architecture so impossible many considered it magic. No witch had played a hand in the construction though.

Now, there was less evidence of the bridges than there was of the once towering city. At five years old, Cinn had not possessed the imagination to picture the structures his parents described, but he kept their words preserved like winter rations:

"This is where the rebellion both began and ended. Where we were transformed from human to unending. It was only right that we pay homage to all that happened here by appointing it Nir's capital. We called the city Kin in honor of the founding rebellion camp, because during the war, no matter what species you were, we had one cause. We were one people. We were kin. Our kind were named after it, and now this is all that's left. Because of witches. Because of the Sparrow Coven." His mother had spat on the ground. *"Come, Ryson. Let us show you what they're capable of. Let us show you what will happen to us if we are found."*

Down the other side of the dune, Cinn had to focus on every breath, every footfall, as he kept hold of Moyra's hand and retraced his steps from fifteen years ago.

It took hours to reach the place Cinn wanted to take her. Seven majestic temples had once adorned the center of the city, or so his parents had told him, and every single day there had been a line five blocks long of people wishing to leave tribute. Out of all seven, only one remained partially intact. The front wall was high enough to bear a vacant doorway, an inscription Cinn couldn't read just above the opening. He stopped to look at it, remembering the way his mother had shed an actual tear, but neither she nor his father had explained why, or what the inscription said, or who the temples were for.

Moyra did.

"Patron of blood and breath, bless-ed Sanni."

The name stole both the blood and breath from Cinn's body. His mouth popped open, eyes wide as he turned to stare at Moyra.

It took her a moment to remember.

"Witches call her the Spirit of Healing," she recalled, then frowned at the look on Cinn's face. "What's wrong?"

Until this moment, he hadn't put it together—why the Sparrow Coven had chosen this place, in all of Kin, to punish his people. Now that he knew more about the spirits and how his kind were made, knew the mark on the back of his neck was just a spell, one cast by Sanni . . .

Backing up a few steps, he turned away to empty his stomach behind a pile of rubble. Moyra didn't crowd him as he leaned on his knees, trying to catch his breath.

"We don't have to do this." Moyra spoke softly, edging closer to lay a hand on his back. "I shouldn't have pushed. If you say they can't help, I'll believe you."

Wiping his mouth on the back of his hand, he straightened, taking even, measured breaths. He did not want to do this. There were very few things he wanted less, especially when they still had six moonstones, the one they'd used to travel to Orhn dull in his still-clenched fist. It would be so easy to leave. To go back to Eaon. To go home.

Without a word, he turned from Moyra and walked beneath the arching doorway. There wasn't much left of the structure beyond that, and with the vegetation climbing over the rubble it took him a while to find the spot they needed to uncover. His hands shook as he began to move loose stones, Moyra close behind. Together, it didn't take long to clear away the piles, revealing a wooden door laid into the ground.

A steady, high-pitched hum left him dizzy. Cinn reeled back from the door, shoving his fists into his eyes. Before he knew what he was doing, he was back through the archway.

"Cinn!" Moyra called, chasing after him.

It was different now he knew how it felt to be locked beneath a door like that. He flinched as Moyra's boot caught a stone, all his instincts screaming to knock her to the ground and run. *Run, run, run.*

He was alone on a deserted island with a female witch he didn't know but admired, being led to a door in the floor where only pain existed. He didn't know what look he had on his face, but as Moyra reached him, she stilled, raising her hands.

"It's alright."

Lies.

His face tingled, hands cold even as the rest of him broke into a sweat. The knife at his hip was a solid weight.

"What do you want to do?" she asked. "We can leave right now. Try again another time."

His brain couldn't comprehend what she was saying. They could leave? Just like that?

"I promise," she added. "I'll swear a binding oath if you want me to."

The screaming in his head stuttered, the prickles under his skin warming. The next breath he took was easier. He could leave. Simply having the option steeled his spine.

"Do you want to know the very last thing my parents said to me before my exile?"

Blinking, he turned to face her, desperate for anything other than nausea to focus on.

"They meant to encourage me to tell the council where my

sister and brother broke the wards, but . . . it's stuck with me for different reasons. I think you need to hear it."

He wiped the sweat from his lip, and she waited for him to nod before placing both hands on his shoulders, rose-quartz eyes staring hard into his own.

"Only stupid people are without fear, and you are not stupid. You're afraid and it's okay to admit that. We're all afraid. Courage is a choice, and we have to make it over and over." Moyra's hands slid from his shoulders to his face. "And Cinn? It is *your* choice. I will not think less of you if you cannot choose courage this time."

Waiting to see if she was finished, he held her gaze another moment before pulling away.

Maybe she wouldn't think less of him, but he would. Not that it had stopped him from running before; shame had never stopped him from abandoning people he cared about in moments of crisis. But he wanted to be different. Better.

Choose courage.

Arms crossed as his cheeks blushed bright, Cinn planted his feet and refused to move until his body realized he would not obey the instinct to run. Unaware of the internal battle happening, Moyra continued to watch him cautiously, hands twitching at her sides as she resisted the urge to reach for him again.

"It's alright," she repeated.

He nodded. This time it was true.

One step at a time, he made his way back to the door and pulled it open to show Moyra the winding staircase that led deep underground.

CHAPTER 30

CINN

THEY STOPPED TO REST THREE TIMES DURING THE DESCENT. Every footfall echoed, and if it weren't for the occasional cluster of bioluminescent fungi spreading across the clay-brick walls briefly illuminating their pale faces, there would be nothing to differentiate the stairwell from the Lover's void. Around and around in a never-ending spiral, Cinn was sure hours had passed, his hand increasingly sweaty in Moyra's steady one. Without her to hold onto, he would have lost his mind. One step he would be alright, but the next would have his head spinning, skin crawling with how close the walls were, how cold the air was, the absolute darkness of it.

But he was not alone. Whether Moyra was working to keep the dreamscape from swallowing him whole, he didn't know, but he appreciated her being with him either way.

Exhaustion and leg cramps were inconsequential compared to the spike of panic as they finally reached the bottom. Moyra stumbled over her feet at the sudden lack of another step, and though Cinn's grip kept her upright, her other hand reached for the wall. At her touch, a patch of moss began to glow with the same pale blue of the fungi, letting Cinn see that—while her hands may be steady—her eyes were just as wide in fear as his own.

Her handprint stayed on the wall for a few minutes, allowing the very barest of views down the impossibly long hall. The two of them could barely walk side by side, elbows scraping more moss to life and leaving an eerie trail behind them.

The light should have helped, but the shiver running down Cinn's spine had nothing to do with being so deep underground

"What's that sound?" Moyra whispered, steps slowing.

He couldn't hear it yet, but he knew what she meant. He remembered freezing up the first time he'd heard it, heels digging into the stone floor and refusing to go farther. His mother had stared at him in that expectant way she'd had, letting the moss go dark until he took the next step forward. When he was five, he didn't know what the sound was. After spending years trapped in a cramped cell, he did.

It was misery.

At the end of the hall, the moss stretched around an open cavity where a door ought to be, and beyond, the dark was seething—a gaping mouth yearning for life to consume. Along the threshold, deep gouges in precise designs bled into the stone.

Witchmarks.

"What in the world . . ." Moyra whispered as she crouched to inspect the marks. She reached to touch them but scrambled back at the sudden *crack* from deep in the dark.

Cinn urged Moyra to back away, heart stopping dead in his chest as a *bang* echoed, followed by an inhuman screech. When the rapid padding of bare feet began, growing louder, faster, Moyra unabashedly put herself behind Cinn, grip white-knuckled on his shoulders as she peered around him.

A shadow darker than the rest barreled toward them. He knew what was coming, but he still flinched as hard as Moyra did when a body slammed against the empty threshold and ricocheted off nothing. Moyra screamed, and the *thing* picked itself up off the floor, whipping its head at the sound.

Pale lips pulled back to bare, bloodstained teeth. Its jaundiced eyes were all pupil, not an ounce of recognition within. Body mere flesh-wrapped bone and white as winter, it threw itself against the invisible barrier again. Again and again.

No food. No water. No light. They could not die, but they could waste. Waste away in the bowels of the temple they'd built to honor the spirit who'd made such agony possible in the first place.

There was no way to know how big the pitch-black room beyond was, but there had to be thousands of kinner inside. After fifteen-hundred years, only this one still knew that light meant *out*.

Cinn remembered wetting himself. His parents had explained how they used to come as often as they could in the early years, trying to help, but eventually those inside gave up and a new era arose. Those unable to defend themselves were claimed by stronger kinner. Hoarding the weak as a personal source, they used them, fed on them, whatever they had to do to remain strong.

That this one had the sense to know light meant visitors, had the energy to run, to fight and scream, meant they had a food source. Meant the hunger in their eyes was not just about getting out, but of wanting fresh meat.

When he was five, he had not been able to sleep for days. Now, Cinn found he could not judge them.

"They can't help," Cinn said softly, turning his back on the rabid kinner.

"No," she agreed breathlessly, a hand at her throat.

"You can help."

She shook her head. "Even if I could figure out what had been used to seal the door, even if I could break it . . . I can't help them. There's no . . . there's no healing from . . ."

Cinn knew that. He knew they could never let the kinner out. They would be a plague on the world, unkillable and unstoppable, rampaging in their madness. It was one of the many reasons he would not tell *her* where they were. At first, it had been his promise to his mother, but after seeing for himself how ruthless *she* was, he knew she would find a way to release them. To harness them. And when she failed . . . he would be responsible for unleashing a beast upon the world worse than any other.

No, the spells on the ground keeping the kinner locked away weren't the ones he'd wanted her to break. Turning his back and moving aside his shirt, he tapped on the back of his neck, then pointed at the kinner still clawing at thin air.

"Break."

His people's pain wasn't the kind he could explain. She'd needed to see it, so when he asked her to break the spell giving the Kinner unending life, she would not fight him.

"Oh," she said softly.

The two of them stared as the rabid kinner screeched, bashing its head and fists against the invisible barrier. Beyond, in the dark, a sickening symphony of crunching bones and pained moans.

"Leaving them like this . . . would be cruel," Moyra began, voice thick. "But what you're asking me to do is genocide."

Cinn didn't know what that word meant. He said nothing, trying not to think of the magical barrier between him and the

255

kinner as a mirror. Trying to shake the idea that this madness was his destiny.

"I don't . . . I can't . . . We are not qualified to make this decision."

The snort that raked Cinn's throat was unintentional. Moyra turned to stare, wide-eyed, but all he could do was raise an eyebrow. As if *anybody* was qualified to make a decision like this.

The words wouldn't come to him, but he knew in his soul that putting the Kinner out of their misery was the right thing to do. They could not be saved, and as someone who had a modicum of an understanding of the suffering they endured every moment they continued to exist . . . If anyone should make this choice, it was him. The kinner were humans, blessed or cursed with unending life, and they had enjoyed the benefits for centuries. Two years of enduring its more painful consequences had left him almost beyond repair. A millennium was unimaginable.

"If it was me—" He almost said '*when it is me*' instead. "—I would thank you."

Covering her face with her hands, Moyra swayed, probably wishing he had never shown her this.

After a moment, she dropped her hands, eyes closed as she said, "Okay."

Relief shuddered through Cinn's chest, burning hot and wet down his cheeks.

"Okay," Moyra said again, shaking herself and turning back to the moss-shrouded doorway. "If I go near the witchmarks on the floor, will . . . I mean, could I get hurt?

Cinn shook his head and wiped his face on the back of his hands. "In, but not out."

So the Sparrow Coven could shove new kinner in when they

caught them without having to lower the barrier, his parents had explained.

Inch by inch, Moyra crept to the line of witchmarks. The back of her shirt was soaked with sweat as she peered at them, muttering to herself; not a spell—it wasn't the kind of inflection for that—but something that sounded a lot like cussing in a language he didn't understand.

"Damn it, Olyvia. I kind of hoped I wasn't going to be physically able to do it," she finally said in Nirnish. Then to Cinn, "Keep back. I don't want the spell to accidentally break your mark too."

As Moyra dragged her pack closer and began unloading the candles and crystals she'd brought along, Cinn's heart began to race so ferociously he thought he might vomit. If this worked . . . *she* would have no use for him. There would be no information to leak.

The kinner battered at the barrier with vitriol as it watched Moyra light a match and set it to a white candle. Fire. Warmth. Cinn remembered how hollow his own longing for such a thing had once left him.

Trying her best to ignore the screeching kinner, Moyra lay out a piece of parchment and began tracing a mark of her own with charcoal—a key, the top of which splayed in a pattern of curling tree branches. The same one used to break Moyra's shackle. The same one inked on *her* palm. Nausea sent Cinn to his knees, shutting his eyes.

"It's called the Key Mark for Those Unbound," she said. Cinn didn't need an explanation since he didn't understand magic anyway, but he got the feeling Moyra needed a moment to compose herself. "It's common, and suitable for a broad range of things depending on a witch's power and their intention. I watched my sister Olyvia use it to channel her spell-cleaver gifts many times, and as you know, our coventry has heightened my own capacity for spell-cleaving. I simply have to be clear with my intentions, and project the magic through this mark and into that . . . cavern. I've seen Olyvia do it so many times. So many times."

Cinn opened his eyes. Moyra hung a crystal pendant around her neck.

The only sign that magic was being wielded was the raised hair on the back of his neck and the now-familiar cadence of incantation as Moyra held her hands above the flickering flame. Her body rocked back and forward, and Cinn could have sworn the charcoal branches of the key began to writhe, flexing toward the kinner still slamming its head against the barrier between them. The dull thud of it was almost hypnotic as Moyra continued chanting, hands trembling over the candle until, finally, she turned them over, palms facing up. Keeping her fingers pointed to the kinner, Moyra leaned down and blew out the candle.

Cinn held his breath.

The kinner slammed his head against hard air again, and again, and again; and then stopped. A visible shudder ran through him, head back, shoulders scrunched, as if the back of his neck tingled.

His skin yellowed quickly, eyes widening in shock. Clarity shone briefly in his eyes as he looked from Moyra to Cinn. His shoulders sagged, hands falling limp at his sides before his eyes finally fluttered closed. Blood pooled between his lips, but the kinner's knees collapsed from under him before it stained his chin.

Within the space of a single heartbeat, the tunnel fell silent. The cavern beyond the doorway seemed to wheeze with the death rattle of thousands within.

The earth should have shaken. The moon should have cracked in two. Seas should have boiled, mountains caving in on themselves. The world had changed irrevocably, and yet nothing was different at all.

His people were dead. The Kinner were dead. The end of forever.

Cinn stared at the body crumpled at the threshold.

Rest in peace.

The silence was palpable as Cinn and Moyra climbed their way back to the surface. Frequent rests were needed as the hours wore on. Cinn's legs were jelly, but he only needed a few minutes to rest before he was ready to climb again. Moyra took longer. Breathless and unable to keep in her complaints, she couldn't handle more than fifteen steps before needing to sit again.

If he were stronger, he would have offered to carry her. If he'd begun training again sooner instead of letting his body stay weak, he could have helped her. As it was, all he could do was keep her hydrated and let her lean on his shoulder as she dragged her feet up the steep, spiraling steps.

When they finally crawled out into the sun, Moyra's face was blotchy, eyes red with unshed tears. She made it onto a flat bit of dirt just beyond the rubble of the temple and collapsed, rolling onto her back and wheezing loudly. Cinn started to say something, but the words got stuck in his throat. He sat beside her, legs splayed out, and just stared at the late-summer foliage. The strong breeze was a gift, cooling the sweat on his skin.

"Thank you," he finally croaked. Judging by the ache in his chest, the heaviness of his tongue . . . they'd be the last words he spoke for a while. With his wounds open again, it was too hard.

But he owed her those words. As she pulled off her boots and bloodstained socks, exposing the raw blisters on her feet, he owed her more than gratitude. Owed her everything.

Because of her, he would be safe. At least from Sparrows.

So would the Copelands.

Edwina and Radley—he could find them.

The thought took his breath away. He could see his family again without putting them in danger. He could kiss his sister, who'd begged him not to go to the palace the last time they'd seen each other. He could hug his brother, who'd sacrificed so much in the name of protecting him, just for Cinn to throw it in his face by walking right into trouble. He could apologize for abandoning them. They could be together again.

"Where have you two been?!"

Cinn flinched as Gatty appeared from the shadows.

"What's wrong?" Moyra panted, forcing herself to sit up.

"You've been gone two whole nights. I couldn't find you anywhere!"

Never had Cinn seen such fury on a cat's face. The time lapse surprised him. Walking through the city to find the temples had taken a while, sure, and the climb had been long, but it didn't seem right for more than thirty hours to have passed.

"We were—"

"I don't care. Come. Now."

The urgency in the cat sith's tone left no room for debate. Leaving their packs, Cinn helped Moyra stand and slid an arm around her waist, half carrying her as they hobbled back through the ruins to the top of the dune.

"What is that?" Moyra wheezed, shielding her face against the sun.

Far in the distance, a pillar of black smoke rose into the sky.

"Fire," Gatty breathed.

Cinn liked fire. He liked sleeping by the hearth and toasting marshmallows. The word didn't make sense with the growing cloud of soot in the sky. Yet a chill spread from his brow to his toes as he realized what territory lay directly across the sea.

He'd left the Copelands in Anfar.

Wide-eyed, Cinn turned to Moyra and pointed to the shoreline far across the strait. His family needed him.

"I can't," she said, face paling. "The stones only work under moonlight."

Then he'd swim.

"The water is swarming with merfolk," Gatty warned, tail swishing. "They're waiting for survivors to flee for the water. Then they'll feast. You won't make it beyond the shallows before becoming fish food."

An eternal feast at the bottom of the sea while everyone he loved burned.

Cinn dropped to his knees, clutching the willow pendant around his neck. He couldn't get to them. He couldn't help.

Not for hours.

CHAPTER 31

DEARMEAD

DEARMEAD COULDN'T HEAR HIS OWN SCREAMING OVER THE dragon fire blistering toward Eaon. Clutched tightly in the beast's talon, there was nothing he could do as the phouka banked, putting himself between the flames and the witch riding his back. Nothing but shove his stone blade deeper into the delicate skin around the dragon's claw, desperate to force it to let go. But the stone was chipped, the blade close to breaking. Argo-blessed silversmiths were rare in Wyldeden, and it didn't make sense to forge weapons from silver in a place where beasts would never reach them. But that's what he needed.

The dragon relented its white-hot barrage and the blood drained from Dearmead's face at the sight of Eaon's body plummeting lifelessly through the sky. Nothing was left of the phouka except burning black feathers and chunks of scorched bone.

The surviving members of the sky coven still rode their cunae mounts nearby. Dearmead screamed for them to catch Eaon, but they were too far away to hear him, having taken the dragon's distraction as an opportunity to race farther over Anfar, battling the blaze devouring the forest.

Screeching its victory across the mountains, the dragon turned, and for a fleeting moment Dearmead hoped it would grab hold of Eaon the way it had grabbed him. But a booming flap of its wings sent them gliding over the Womb instead.

"No," Dearmead croaked, twisting as much as he could.

There was nothing he could do. Eaon was lost to the haze of smoke below.

Between the altitude and speed, Dearmead could barely get down a breath. He fainted at some point, but his new kinner body woke him in time to see the mountains give way to rolling dunes of white sand, freckled with tufts of black foliage and wind-blown trees growing at fierce angles. His heart flipped over at the land's strange beauty, but as the pins and needles flooding his limbs reached his hands, he gasped, flexing his empty fingers.

"Looking for this?"

He jerked his head toward the rider crouched on the dragon's other talon, flipping Dearmead's dagger. The mutant witch's posture suggested he was not disturbed by the whipping wind, utterly relaxed against the dragon's ankle.

"Where have you been for the last two-thousand years? Even humans outgrew stone weapons; a kinner like you should have something a bit more . . . well, *more*."

Dearmead snarled, but the sound was pitiful; there wasn't enough air in his body. But that wasn't what made his chest ache. Just that morning, he'd woken up at peace for the first time in months, the sound of Eaon's steady heart beating in his ear. Now . . .

"And that armor!" The rider cackled. "Were you hiding among those simple tree-hugging witches all this time? How dull. Unlike the story of how one of the Kinner befriended a phouka and a Sparrow, of all things."

It took too long to realize the rider thought Dearmead was one of the original Kinner, and Eaon a part of the Sparrow Coven. So much had happened so quickly, there hadn't been time to think, to process. But now he remembered the blast of necrotic magic Eaon had used to try and save him. The way the rider had simply *pushed* it away. The three cunae and their riders, who'd died in an instant.

A familiar swelling in his chest as the images played over in his mind gave him something to hold onto. When Eaon had been branded and thrown out of Wyldeden, Dearmead's fear had paralyzed him. He'd drowned in it.

It had taken his ma's death to learn how to swim.

For as long as he could remember, Bayfield family dinners had been filled with talk about the battle for the Boab, the rogue who'd scarred his ma's face, and the internal struggle she'd faced when the clan's belief in Balance clashed with her guardian duty to protect. His bedtime stories were lengthy descriptions of the quiet calm that came over Calla Bayfield when the time to kill arrived.

She'd tried to train that calm into all her children, and when Dearmead had tracked Eaon all the way to Pirevia last spring, he'd felt it. What it had let him do in that city had scared him. Now, he was thankful. All the rage and fear billowing in his chest didn't swallow him whole. Instead, it forced survival to the forefront.

There was nothing Dearmead could do as the dragon glided over the strange colorless desert. To the north, a city came into view. Smoke billowed there too, though there were no flames.

"We'll have plenty of time to discuss your hiding places and how many more of your kind are still roaming around," the rider continued, following Dearmead's gaze and narrowing his eyes. "Later, though. My master beckons. We'll have to make your initiation to the harbingers a quick one."

The rider clambered back up the leg of the dragon, the claws he had in place of fingers and toes finding easy purchase in the beast's thick skin.

They banked south, and a single mountain came into view, it's surface like shards of slate cutting into the cloudless sky. There was nothing natural about its loneliness in an otherwise flat expanse of land. A mountain should not exist there.

As the dragon descended, Dearmead's stomach fell too. The harsh surface was crawling with beasts—dragons nestled into crevices, protecting eggs from packs of lurking lupani, while flocks of cawkers and harpies plucked six-legged salamanders from their sunbathing spots, ripping into them with abandon. At least they did, until a pack of impossibly giant salamanders slithered out of their caves, scattering the winged beasts.

At the base of the mountain was a large opening where a dozen mutated witches waited with loops of rope and shining silver weapons.

"Put him with the others!" the rider shouted as the dragon's talon finally opened.

Dearmead fell a hundred meters to the ground and landed with a loud *crack*, pain fracturing through his spine. For a fleeting moment, his limbs wouldn't work, but the healing itch was quick to flood his veins, radiating from the mark on his neck. Not quick enough to return movement before the mutants descended on him though. One tied a rope around his ankles while two others searched his armor for weapons. The rest had gone inside the mouth of the cave, shouting in Nirnish.

"Back! All of you! Your turn to eat will come!"

As they dragged Dearmead by his ankles, his body went cold. It was so sudden and so drastic his muscles spasmed. There were no drawings of shtryg in his textbooks back home—since they were mostly mist and shadow—but the way the air thickened, gravity pushing down as creatures crowded in, left no doubt in his mind as to what dwelled inside the mountain.

As the healing magic fused the broken parts of his spine back together, Dearmead lashed out at anything he could reach.

"That's it, get the blood pumping," one of the mutants mocked him. "The shtryg will thank you for it when they come to feed."

He caught someone by the ankle and pulled. The mocking turned to cursing.

"Damn meat sack," the mutant hissed, followed by the sound of a metal weapon sliding against a scabbard.

"Let him fight while he can," another muttered. "He'll grow boring soon enough, just like the others."

Others. Dearmead latched onto the word. The possibility of allies in this cesspool was a hope he didn't know he needed as the mutants dragged him deeper.

They reached a tunnel. Lighting the way were glass lanterns with hissing fire sprites trapped inside, pounding on the walls of their tiny prisons.

The flickering firelight let Dearmead see the mutants clearer; all were similar in that their skin was partially scaled, but while some had clawed feet or hands, others sported curling horns or spiked tails.

Dragon-like, Dearmead realized as he twisted at the waist, throwing a fist into the back of someone's knee. The mutant crumpled and snarled, once again drawing his weapon.

"Don't—" the one dragging his feet started, but Dearmead

didn't hear the rest as the pommel of the sword smashed against his temple.

~

Pain.

Laying on his back, his eyes flung opened as he reached for his gut. The metal stake protruding from his bare midriff sent tremors of agony radiating through his entire body, vision spinning and darkening at the edges.

"That should keep him down." A mutant laughed, driving the six-foot stake deeper into the stone beneath Dearmead with unnatural strength. "Round up the cawkers first. They're overdue."

Spasms of hot and cold flushed his skin as the mutants left. A newly familiar itch began to burn as The Mark of One Unending replenished the blood seeping from his wound, keeping him alive. Time and reality ceased to exist as Dearmead's entire world shrunk to the acute pain in his gut. Wrapping his shaking hands around the stake, he took as deep a breath as he could manage and pulled.

Screamed.

The stake didn't budge, but every muscle and organ in his body convulsed at the pain. Dearmead let his dizzy head roll to the side, hands falling limp as he fought unconsciousness again.

A dying fire sprite lay limp in a filthy glass jar suspended from the ceiling, still emitting enough light to see there were others in the small, carved-out pocket deep inside the mountain. Three of them; naked, filthy, and emaciated, but otherwise in perfect health. A male, pale and freckled, was sitting unconscious against the wall, a similar stake through his chest pinning him upright. The second kinner—because that was what they had to be—

stared vacantly at the floor, shallow breaths whistling through chapped lips. A chain was wrapped so tightly around her middle the flesh was split around it, the end of the length bolted to the floor.

The third kinner was different. Her mottled blue-green eyes were trained on Dearmead; gaze harder than the cave wall the chain around her neck was bolted to. Her lips had a blueish tinge, the rest of her so pale Dearmead doubted she'd seen the sun in years. Black hair fell in ratty tendrils to her hips, small bugs crawling among it.

"You . . . will not . . . break," she wheezed as rasping squawks echoed in the lone tunnel branching into darkness.

Dearmead turned his head toward the tunnel just as a dozen cawkers—in all their four-foot, red-and-brown feathered glory— came barreling in. Intelligent eyes latched onto his prone form, their sharp bony beaks opening to reveal rows of tiny, sharp teeth.

CHAPTER 32

EAVHA

AISLING AND KAELEAN WERE GONE. THE MOMENT THE PORTAL closed, Eavha's knees gave out. That spurt of healing she'd given Aisling was pathetic, but it was all she had left. The nice demi-kin woman who'd stepped up to rule Hyrsch in Aisling's absence helped Eavha down to the floor of the throne room, unperturbed by the filth now staining her dress. Sweat and soot and muddy river water, blood and burnt flesh; there wasn't an inch of Eavha that was clean. Everything she touched was soiled, but the demi-kin woman crouched down in her simple but elegant gown and took her hand.

"What can we do to help?"

Swallowing thickly, Eavha looked to where Lorelei had moved to the wall of stained-glass windows, looking down on the mayhem outside.

"Kaelean left her in charge." And maybe that was for the best. Lorelei had more power than Eavha. Understood more and spoke better Nirnish. She had centuries of experience, and even if she hadn't been a fair ruler, she was no Nevan.

She was no Sparrow King.

Rich, dark blood pooled from King Phineas's body, but it was slowing. Even if she could rally the strength to try to heal him, there was no life lingering. As for performing necromancy again, that was well out of her league.

In Wyldeden she had been a big fish in a little pond, but now, out in the world . . . well, now she was a guppy in a depthless lake.

"Help *you*," the demi-kin woman—*Edwina*—insisted. Eavha wasn't sure why it took so long to recall the new ruler's name. Cinn's sister. "What can we do to help *you*."

It was more than a kind offering. Eavha's fear of her own ineptitude was mirrored in Edwina's face. They were both too new at this. Both out of their depths.

"Fetch all the ginseng root you have in this . . . building," Lorelei interrupted, waving a dismissive hand around the throne room as if it were unpalatable. "Chamomile, echinacea, and aloe vera too. Take it down to our healers. That's what you can do to help."

The raw plants wouldn't be enough. They needed salves and poultices, blessed bandages and creams. They needed healers who knew how to apply them, how to check for infection. Eavha had been down in the streets helping Yvette organize the few healers remaining, but ever since Aadya had decimated the Wyldeden Sanni-blessed, only the medicalists and the brewers were left, forced to learn and apply trauma triage in the same heartbeat.

Edwina's face had gone blank, lips silently mouthing the names of the plants Lorelei had rattled off. She didn't know them.

"Help me up," Eavha asked quietly. Then to Lorelei, "I'll get the supplies to Yvette, then I need to go to Pirevia."

With her power unbound, Lorelei didn't deign to look at Eavha, waving in dismissal. Maybe that was for the best too. Eavha didn't know how to be around her old high priestess without trembling.

Edwina held onto Eavha's hand as she climbed to her bare feet, looking back to the spot where Aisling and Kaelean had disappeared. They would be okay.

Cinn's brother had remained silent through all this, arms crossed and glaring at the dead king.

"Rad," Edwina called. "Are you coming?"

"I'll find you later. I'm going to take care of *that*." He lifted his chin, still glaring at Phineas.

"I think we should leave him for Aisling—"

"Go rule the city, Red."

There was no room in his tone for debate. Edwina left her brother to do whatever he was going to do; whatever a once enslaved demi-kin felt was justified for the witch-king who'd deemed their people undeserving of basic dignity.

In the infirmary, Eavha took a moment to wash her hands. The rest could wait, but if she was going to handle healing materials, she didn't want to risk contaminating them. The contrast of the empty infirmary to the overflowing one she'd abandoned in Pirevia gave her a second to breathe. Just that morning she'd been curled up in bed beside Aisling, grateful they had survived Nevan's arena. Laying together, basking in the morning warmth and the perfect symphony of their beating hearts, had been their sole moment of bliss before the world began burning.

She hadn't had a second to breathe since.

"I'm so sorry about what's happened," Edwina said softly,

filling as many sacks and crates as they could carry with whatever looked useful. "There are a few servants in the palace that are adept with medicines. Would they be any help?"

Eavha nodded as she splashed some cold water on her face, taking a bite of bitter ginseng root to rally some energy. "Anyone. We need all the help we can get."

While Edwina gathered the servants, Eavha packed the herbs. As soon as they were ready, the small group hurried out to the frightened and pained wails of her people.

Humans and demi-kin alike came from their homes with pitchers of water and cleaning rags, fresh clothes and blankets. One witch was pulling rose bushes out of someone's garden, burying their hands in the fresh-turned soil to coax large aloe plants to maturity, while a human woman stood by, sobbing over her ruined garden.

Edwina and the servants dispersed as Eavha squeezed her way through the crowded streets.

"Yvette!" she called.

The new elder healer was exactly where Eavha left her, surrounded by desperate people begging for help. Two young healers in training sat on the ground, blessing bandages as fast as they could. Between them, a witchling no older than ten wiped his tears on the back of soot-stained hands, ripping donated shirts to ribbons and adding them to the pile.

"Eavha," Yvette panted when she caught sight of her. "Quick."

"Eavha!" someone else called. "It's Eavha! Please, save my sister!"

"My da is burned! Please!"

"Won't Sanni help us? Can you ask her?"

"Eavha, over here! My baby! Please, my baby."

"Give her some space!" Yvette shouted at the crowd. "Give us all some space!"

"I can't," Eavha whispered as she reached Yvette, barely able to see the elder through the tears blurring her vision. Through the specks of cool ash still falling like snow over the city. "I'm . . . I'm . . ."

"One thing at a time," Yvette said, voice low, rummaging through the supplies in Eavha's shaking arms and pulling out a reel of stitching thread. "Think back to your training. We're in a mass casualty situation. What do we do first?"

"Damage control," Eavha answered. "Isolate the critical and stop as many deaths as we can."

"Yes," Yvette answered. "So, wipe your bloody nose, grab those bandages and get cool compresses on the worst burns."

Rubbing the heel of her palm under her nose, she was surprised by the dark smear of blood. Was she that close to burning out?

"They want more than that from me," she said. "And Aisling . . ."

Yvette had stopped listening, stitching a gushing neck wound someone had received while running through the Oford forest.

"Eavha! Help!"

"Over here! Please!"

Her hands were shaking as she grabbed some blessed bandages from the trainees, too focused on their task to see who took them. A man shoved a pitcher of water in her hands, barely cool under the summer heat. Night was on its way, but it wouldn't bring much relief. Not with the fire still raging across the Dividing River.

Dousing a bandage in the water, she took the nearest person with a severe burn and pressed the compress to their blistering flesh. Screams of pain weren't foreign to healers, but here, so far from the tranquility of the clinic, it was too raw. Too real. The smell of singed hair, of sweat and piss-stained clothes, was too hard to ignore. She could barely hear her own prayer as she begged Sanni for help. To give her more magic. More strength.

The spirit wasn't listening. Wasn't here.

"Eavha's blessing is dry." The whispers started. "She can't help us. Mother of all, we're going to die."

"Nobody's going to die!" Eavha snapped, which was stupid. Death hovered everywhere. "Come here."

She grabbed the next person with a burn and soaked another bandage in water. It wasn't going to be enough to help them long term. Maybe not for more than a few minutes. Another healer was flustering over a scraped knee a little farther down the street and Eavha wracked her brain for their name.

"Shanna! Come here!"

The healer's head whipped up, leaving her patient, desperate for direction. Eavha knew the feeling.

"Come and do this." She showed her how to make a compress. "Start with the most severe. I'm going to blend an antibiotic salve."

"Yes, Heir."

"Is mine severe? It hurts!"

"Mine too!"

"Over here! There's more bandages!" A call from farther down the street.

Eavha forced herself to control her exhales. Back at the supplies, she ripped at the herbs she needed, pulling out jars of aloe jelly and poppy milk to blend into a paste. She couldn't stay —Aisling needed her to go north—but she couldn't leave, either. She couldn't walk away from this, even if she may as well have been human for all the magic she had in her veins.

All the Sanni magic, anyway. Her kernel of Terra-blessing was enough to draw out the herbs' potency as she blended quickly.

Through all the noise, a tiny voice caught her attention.

"Ma, wake up."

A shudder ran down her spine. Looking up, she peered through the crowd to where, across the street, a young witchling hovered over their ma's limp body. Even from so far away, Eavha could see the blue tinge of her bloodless face.

Leaving the pestle, Eavha pushed her way through the crowd.

A year ago, she had said those exact words. A year ago, she had been home alone with her ma while Eaon and Da were traveling. She'd dragged herself out of bed and into the kitchen where breakfast had not been prepared. Ellissa had still been in bed, blue-lipped and pale.

"It's okay," Eavha said as she reached the witchling, pulling them away. "I'll help."

The female wasn't sporting any burns as far as Eavha could see, but as soon as she checked her airway, the problem was evident. Soot lined her throat, so swollen it was restricting airflow.

"She's dead, isn't she?" the young witch asked. Not a single tear dampened their cheeks, a somber *knowing* in their eyes.

Resting two fingers against the mother's wrist, Eavha waited for a heartbeat. "Not yet. Wait here."

It pained her to leave, but she needed supplies. In school, she had been so cocky that she would never need to know how to do these things that she'd barely listened in class. Why learn how to heal the hard way when all she had to do was lay a hand over someone's throat and they'd be fine? But the hard way was on the exams, and it was Eaon who'd made her study. Eaon who'd made sure that, when a day like this one came, when she was spent and desperate, she would know what to do.

"Give me that." She snatched a small dagger from a nearby civilian's belt, then a damp bandage from Shanna and a thin bamboo reed from a pile Yvette was using to tighten tourniquets. The elder frowned as she stole the reed but didn't stop her.

Eavha ran back to where the witchling stared vacantly at their dying mother.

"Hey." She tucked the supplies under her arm and placed a scarred palm against the witchling's face. "Do you think you could help me?"

Direction. Distraction. The witchling nodded.

"You see that rose bush over there? The one pulled out? I need fifty crushed petals. Can you fetch them for me?"

The witchling nodded, running for the bush.

Dropping to her knees, Eavha cleaned the blade with the bandage. Then with the other side, she cleaned the mother's throat. Feeling down the column of her airway, Eavha forced her hands to steady. This had to be perfect. Too many important arteries lay in the neck and nicking one would kill this witch faster than the lack of air.

Lucky she'd made a habit of being perfect. Of refusing death at every turn.

The Lover could not have this mother, too.

Slicing into the witch's airway, she held pressure on the wound and slid the hollow reed into the hole. Tying the bandage around the mother's neck, Eavha stabilized the reed before blowing gently into it.

It only took one breath for the mother to respond.

Undiluted panic was also not a novelty to healers. Holding down the witch's wrists, Eavha used her body weight to force her still, keeping her voice low and urgent.

"You need to calm down. I am helping you. Breathe through the reed. It's hard, I know, but you can do it. Your witchling isn't watching right now, but they're close. Do this for them."

The mother stared up at her, bloodshot eyes wide, dry lips parted to speak.

"Here." Eavha gently touched the red skin beside the incision. "Breathe here. Don't try to talk. As soon as I can, I will heal this properly for you, but for now, I need you to breathe."

A crumpled rose petal fell beside the mother's face. Eavha turned to see the blackened feet of the witchling beside them.

The mother breathed.

"Good. So good." Carefully, Eavha stood and smiled at the witchling. "It looks scary, but your ma is going to be okay. Do you know how to pray? Rub those petals into your hands and pray with your ma. That will help."

It would do absolutely nothing, but they didn't need to know that.

Fondling her once-again-broken Blessing Charm, Eavha knew she needed to be here. To do what she could until her Sanni-blessing had a chance to grow strong again. Not strong enough to bring back the dead—she didn't think she would ever be that strong again—but enough so to help ease the swelling in this mother's throat. Strong enough to mix up a decent salve. To clear the infection from septic burns.

She could not leave.

Aisling had asked her to rally the people in Pirevia, but she wasn't an army commander or a soldier. She didn't have the undeniable authority that Kaelean or Lorelei could emanate.

She was a healer, in her heart and soul, and that's what she needed to stay and be.

Jogging to the rose bush now speckled with white ash, she plucked a leaf and brought it to her lips. Wracking her brain for the right name, she pushed a little Terra magic into the silky green leaf.

"*Killian, it's Eaon's sister. Listen.*"

CHAPTER 33

KILLIAN

As Killian flew home from Pirevia on the back of a cunae with one of the sky witches who'd come to Eaon's aid, he prayed to every single spirit that his clan was not behind the fire growing in Anfar. The monstrous plumes of soot rose so high into the sky it was a veritable wall along the Southern Spine. As far away as they were, not much of the blaze itself was visible bar the smoldering edges creeping steadily east.

Miika's new union-bound companion, Yasmin, kept her cunae north of the Vein snaking far below. Dozens upon dozens of witches stood barefoot along the banks, hands raised to the sky. Their indiscernible voices rose in unison, coaxing tiny droplets of precipitation from the river and guiding them into the sky. Gusts of wind pushed waterlogged clouds southward toward the fire in a feat of magic that left Killian nauseous and would leave many of those casting spells below burned out. Or whatever the Mare-blessed equivalent would be.

Killian had never come close to using more magic than he was physically capable of, but he'd seen it. Just the other day,

Tomaii and Reigan had let the flame Ignatius left within each of them burn too hot, too long. They were taught in school to know their limits, to not ask the Spirits for more than they could handle, lest they spontaneously combust. Perhaps the Mare-blessed melted, or maybe they were like the Terra-blessed, whose bodies just gave out and died.

His heart ached as he watched a number of river witches collapse to their knees.

When it came to protecting the land, all elemental witches were one. Killian was singularly blessed by Terra, but he sent up a prayer to Mare, the water Spirit, as well as Celeste, the sky Spirit. Neither would listen, but it couldn't hurt. The river clan needed all the help they could get as they prayed for rain.

By the time the cunae reached the gorge, the Northern Mountain Clan had rallied in the bordering fields. Every Ignatius-blessed witch was painted with ash, hands joined around a bonfire, swaying and chanting in unison—a large scale version of the flame-control spell Reigan and Tomaii had performed to save Eaon from burning to death the other day.

Killian looked for his friends among the clan but didn't see them. As Yasmin landed her cunae alongside the rest of her coven, he immediately dismounted.

"One hour," she warned in her thick, rolling accent. "Then I go back, with or without you."

Nodding, they parted ways. The high scout working as Miika's second-in-command was giving instructions to a large group preparing to head down the mountain. They wouldn't get to the border for at least a week, but a fire this size could easily burn that long. It would be too late to keep it from ravaging the forest, but though the Heart Lake and the Vein connecting it to the ocean ought to protect most of Vertlyn from any spread, it only took one lucky ember to raze the northern territory as well.

Eyes widening as Killian approached, the high scout pulled him aside and kept her voice low. "Where is Elder Miika?"

"Still in Pirevia. What's going on?"

"The high priest is communing with Ignatius. The heat is off all known scales and the blaze burns at unprecedented speed. Our best Igni have gone with some of the sky coven to see what can be done until our forces reach the demarcation line with the alchemists' salamander solution."

"So, this wasn't us?" Killian sagged in relief.

"Of course not! A threat from Kaelean Caesarea isn't reason to incite war against Wyldeden, and never like this."

"Giselle!" one of the alchemists called for the high scout.

"Go." Killian lifted his chin, backing away.

The high scout didn't hesitate, rushing to where barrels of salamander solution were being loaded onto a cart, two of the few enormous horses the clan had tamed armored and ready for their journey south.

Neither were Daani, Miika's horse. That beautiful beast had come sprinting back after Eaon abandoned her—a sign that something was very wrong. The Wyldeden clan held animals in a higher regard than any other witch community he knew, so for Eaon to have left Daani in the wild . . .

Calming the horse had been difficult when Killian could barely stay calm himself, and he hadn't quite gotten her back in the stable before someone tattled to Miika. Convincing his brother to move on Pirevia, to trust Eaon's frantic premonition, had cost Killian a month of chores, but it was worth it.

Running as fast as his tired legs would take him down into the ravine between mountains, the path to the warren crowded with witches focused on getting supplies out, the endless drills they'd run in case of such a disaster weren't a relief. Everyone knew what to do, everyone knew their role, but nothing could have prepared them for a bushfire of this magnitude. His ma and da were among the group filling canteens with water for the Igni-blessed, none of whom would leave the bonfire above until the last embers had cooled.

Killian would join his parents soon, but first he had to find his friends.

They were both exactly where he'd left them, though the healer was gone. Tomaii was guzzling a bucket of water, blond hair dark with sweat and plastered across his forehead, while Reigan leaned against the wall, flushed and breathing hard.

"You alright?" He went to Reigan's side and rested the back of his hand against her forehead. She was still hot, and when she looked up at him, the dark brown of her eyes was molten lava. Utterly bewitching, had the Spirit of Flame's touch not been so deadly.

"I'm alright," she managed, voice both hard and breathy.

"I'm alright, too, you know." Tomaii dropped the empty bucket and sighed. "Fuck, water is so good. Where'd you run off to? How's Eaon doing?"

Killian shut his eyes. The world had gone to shit since the two of them had saved Eaon from burning at the stake. He didn't know how to begin explaining everything.

Reigan's hand on his arm was clammy. "Did the containment spell work? Is he okay?"

"It worked." He met her gaze and took her hand. "But nothing is okay."

CHAPTER 34

KILLIAN

"Tomaii, stop!"

It didn't matter how loud Killian shouted after his friend, Tomaii was a bull through the tunnels. Those gathered in the warren twisted out of the way in a well-practiced maneuver when they saw him coming, barely sparing the trio a glance.

"Tomaii," Reigan snapped, panting as she hurried alongside Killian. "Neither of us are in any shape—"

All three of them froze—the entire warren froze—as a scream echoed through the cavern. Not of pain, but grief. Everyone stared at Selena, the Wyldeden witch who'd come with Eaon, as she collapsed to her knees in the middle of the cavern, burying her face in her hands. Her boyfriend Brach crouched by her side, slowly coaxing her to her feet and back down one of the tunnels.

"Yeah," Tomaii hissed quietly as the hustle of the crowd began again. "Let's just sit on our asses while hers and Eaon's home burns."

There were a lot of things Tomaii was flippant about, but fire was not one of them. The Igni-blessed were raised with a healthy respect for the Spirit of Flame's element and the duality of its nature. It was warmth and life. It was destruction and death. The flame that burned inside each of the Igni-blessed could take them either way.

"Has your flame even replenished?" Killian challenged, reaching for Tomaii's arm. "Will you actually be able to do anything?"

"It will buy time until the alchemists get there." He pulled his arm from Killian's grip and broke into a jog.

"I'll kill him," Reigan hissed as she struggled after him. "I'll fucking kill him."

"Wait." Killian pulled her to a stop. "You're not well either."

"I can't let Tomaii go off by himself. You know the kind of shit he'll end up in."

"I'll go after him. Just . . . stay here. Help here."

He knew the suggestion was a mistake the moment the words passed his lips. Reigan was the molten lava to Tomaii's wildfire, and the look she leveled at him for suggesting she stay behind boiled him from the inside out. Normally he relished that look, especially when followed by a crooked smile that promised trouble, but there was only rage in her face today.

Today, her glare had him sweating. "I don't want you to get hurt, is all."

"I'm going after my cousin," she said stiffly.

She would not be dissuaded. Killian's choice was made for him.

"Then we'd better hurry."

Night was falling, but across the heather fields and sparse bushland, the burning forest lit the horizon in golden reds. Yasmin was mounting her cunae again, but paused when she saw Killian, Reigan, and Tomaii running into the bonfire field.

"Cutting it close, Killian." She frowned. "And I cannot carry three."

"Tomaii, please wait," Reigan tried again, lunging for her cousin's arm and digging in her heels. "Think!"

Yasmin didn't want to wait, but as the two Igni-blessed witches argued, a breeze blew through Killian's thick black hair, bringing with it a small green leaf. Not something he would usually be distracted by, except this leaf was full of whispers, loud and urgent.

Plucking it from his hair, he held it close to his ear. Listened.

"Guys," he called, feeling the blood rush from his face.

"I'm going," Yasmin said with a huff.

Lover spare him, she was the perfect fit for Miika.

"Would you fucking wait?!" he roared at her.

Wide-eyed, she raised her brow. Even Tomaii and Reigan shut up. Throat growing thick, the look on Killian's face, the tone in his voice, held their attention.

"It's Eaon's sister." He held up the leaf. "Serious shit is going down and she's begging me to go back to Pirevia."

"The Sparrow City?" Reigan frowned, still clutching Tomaii's wrist. "Is Miika in trouble?"

Killian's older brother could handle things just fine. He'd said as much when Killian had expressed concern at leaving him alone in that disgusting city. He was an *elder*. He didn't *need* help. He was too good to need anything from anyone anymore.

"Probably, but that's not why I have to go."

And he did have to go.

Tomaii turned away from the bonfire to meet Killian's eye. "Of course serious shit is going down. The forest is burning!"

"Yes, it is, but the world is also ending."

"What?" Yasmin snapped. "Speak plainly."

"Have you heard the legend of Chaos?"

The minutes he wasted catching everyone up were minutes they didn't have. Eavha needed every Pirevian willing to sail south mobilized. Now. With Yasmin, it would take all night to get there. On foot, weeks. He could send a message to Miika, but his brother was so fucking pig-headed . . .

Reigan turned her back on him and forced Tomaii to look at her.

"You and I both know we are not helpful here right now."

"But—"

"I have always followed you, but right now, I need you on my side. I am going with Killian."

Both the males flinched. Never in a million years would Killian ask Reigan to choose between them, and never would he expect her to choose him. It was one of those unspoken things that all three of them understood.

"We'll take Daani," Reigan continued. "But you should go with Yasmin."

The sky witch balked. Killian, too, wasn't sure what Reigan was planning. But she was the cleverest of them, and if she had an idea, he would listen.

"Do what you do best, Tomaii. Make Miika listen to you. Make him begin preparations, and then make him wait for us."

There was none of Tomaii's usual joviality as he shook his head, uncomprehending. "Killian's his brother—"

"When has that ever made a difference with Miika?"

Nostrils flaring, Killian crossed his arms. It was true.

"Yasmin is his—"

"We're talking about *Miika*."

Sparing a look to the sky witch, Killian's lip curled in amusement at the snort and eye-roll she gave.

"Now, I mean this with love." Reigan grabbed her cousin by the scruff of his neck. "But nobody is more irritating than you, so go annoy the shit out of our elder until we get there."

Tomaii blinked—twice—before a mischievous grin once more graced his face.

CHAPTER 35

EAON

IT WAS NO LONGER A SURPRISE WHEN EAON WOKE TO THE bone-deep blistering cold that meant he'd been in the void again. He was so tired of it. Whatever bliss had burned in his soul as his blessing—*the seed*—took more lives hadn't lingered, so there was nothing to dull the bitter edge of disappointment twisting in his chest.

He was so tired of all of this. The death staining his hands, his failure, the pain—and Mother knew he was in so much pain he could barely breathe—but more than anything, he was especially tired of the Lover's insistence that he could not rest. The High Spirit of Death had ignored his demand for answers about the seed. Ignored his begging not to be pushed back into his body, too.

Finding the will to blink, the only reason Eaon knew his eyes were open was the speck of red light so high above him it might as well have been a star. The ground was sticky; spongy enough to have cushioned his fall but not so much that he survived it. Legs twisted awkwardly beneath him, a wire of agony coiled around his spine and neck. The familiar creaking of his ribs as he tried to draw a satisfying breath told him most were broken.

His scattered brain found enough sense to put together where he had to be; what he had been flying over, the absolute darkness, and that singular speck of red light so far above there was no possibility of ever reaching it. There was nobody to nurse him back to health at the bottom of the Womb.

He should be goop. That his head was intact was a miracle.

That he was alive at all was a punishment.

"Phouka?" Eaon's voice cracked in the dark.

Only when it stopped did Eaon realize there had been whispers.

He couldn't see anything, but the Lover's magic perked up as living shadows came closer, investigating what had fallen into their nest. The sentient seed's hunger for souls signaled how many surrounded him.

A dozen. Two. Fifty. A hundred.

They were not bright the way the fae were, nor were they dense like humans. The closest thing he could compare them to was the harpy, but far less substantial. The promised flavor coated his tongue in static.

The air became vacuous and heavy. Smothering. He recognized the sensation from his time traveling the Oford forest. Kailevi had never let one get close, leading Eaon away from the lone beast stalking among the lifeless trees, but there was no mistaking it.

There were shtryg at the bottom of the Womb.

"Tasty witch," a breathy voice whispered.

"Poison," another hissed.

"Can we eat it?"

"Kill it."

"Take it to Master."

The words brushed against his face. Eaon tried to lift his arm, to bat them away, but doing so twisted the broken bones in his chest and a soundless scream tore through him.

Gravity incarnate descended until there was nothing but that impossible weight. He could not move. Could not fight. The Lover's blessing ached for the shtryg to touch him, and right now that magic was all he had.

The phouka was not there to stop him.

Nobody was coming to rescue him.

You are exactly who you need to be. Stop fighting it.

The leather cuffs around his wrists were scraps.

Eaon let go.

Sinking into its cold depths, the seed swelled, its magic washing across the bottom of the Womb with a heavy sigh.

A dozen—two—fifty—a hundred shtryg souls winked out, the crash of them into Eaon's own a rush like nothing else. It was darkness and lust and power, and in the blink of an eye, his pain vanished.

More.

The darkness was starting to open. He could see shadows within the shadows, hints of souls lingering in nearby caves, singing to his blood like a siren.

More, the magic begged. *More. All of it.*

All of it.

PART VI

METANOIA

CHAPTER 36

CINN

FINALLY, *FINALLY*, THE MOON SHOWED ITS FACE. GATTY HAD walked into the shadows hours ago to investigate and not returned, but they knew better than to wait. The cat sìth would find them when he was ready.

Moyra's hand was already in Cinn's as they stared across the strait to where Nir was burning.

"Where to?" she asked solemnly, watching the halo of red and gold grow steadily brighter.

There was only one place to go.

Hiking his pack higher, Cinn pulled the willow amulet from his neck and passed it to Moyra.

"Eaon," he told her.

Wherever he was, that was where Cinn needed to be.

During the hours they'd been waiting, Moyra had fashioned a belt of twine and tied the velvet sack of moonstones to it. Priming three with that same whimsical spell, she passed him one to keep in his pocket.

"In case of emergency," she said, placing a second in her own pocket. "And in case we get separated."

Cinn took a steadying breath as they joined hands. Clutched in her other, Moyra held the amulet and third moonstone.

The world went white.

Then it was black.

Heat blasted his face, sucking the air from the world. Embers rained down. Cinn threw himself over Moyra, screaming in her ear in the hope she could hear him over the roaring forest behind them. She didn't hesitate, fumbling for the emergency moonstone before disappearing from under him in a flash of light.

On his hands and knees, Cinn choked out the black smoke consuming the world. If Eaon was here, he was dead. Knowing that didn't stop him from calling out.

"Eaon!"

He could barely hear himself as he crawled across the soot-dusted grass. A tree snapped and cracked, the *whoosh* of swelling flames brightening the burning scene enough for Cinn to spot a charred body laying nearby.

Still choking on hot soot, Cinn crawled toward it, stopping abruptly when he realized how close to a cliff's edge he was. The body was half slung over the precipice, and as Cinn crept carefully forward, he also realized that it was not Eaon. Too tall, too big.

"Eaon!" Cinn called out again, voice coarse as coals.

The body moved.

Crawling faster, Cinn pulled them back from the edge, cringing at the burnt flesh sticking to his palms. He didn't have long to fret over it. Right before his eyes, the flesh was reborn. Muscles and veins duplicated, repairing a body that had once been destroyed.

Stunned, it took Cinn a moment to coordinate himself enough to turn their head to the side. To spot the iridescent mark glowing on the back of their neck. A rasping snarl that was decidedly *not* human made Cinn flinch.

Pained yellow eyes peered up fearfully.

Cinn knew that fear. The dread that came with being discovered.

Hacking out another lungful of soot, he turned his own head to show his mark. The creature clutched his wrist, anxiety replaced with desperation as they pointed back toward the cliff's edge.

He loved Eaon, but he couldn't just leave this creature to burn indefinitely. Staggering to his feet and apologizing in advance for the pain he was about to cause, Cinn grabbed the creature under the arms and began dragging them to safety.

"*No!*" they cried in a voice so broken it bled.

Then he felt it.

A waft of frigid cold, emanating from the cliff. It reeked of rot and decay—a smell that had no right to cause Cinn so much relief. He knew exactly what, or who, was causing it.

"Leave . . . me," the healing creature gasped. The kinner that was not a kinner. "Help . . . him."

Gently, Cinn lowered the creature to the ground before covering his mouth and nose with his forearm. The smoke wouldn't kill him, but every breath burned, his body quickly becoming heavy and useless. He did not want to leave the creature, but he was only one man. He couldn't save everyone.

"Go," the nonkinner rasped again.

Nodding, Cinn approached the cliff's edge once more. It was a different kind of blackness to the smoke-filled night. The kind moonlight couldn't penetrate.

As the glow of the fire spread, tinging the remains of the

forest in red and gold, Cinn noticed the tower nearby. They had seen that tower while traveling to the Northern Mountains.

"That's both the safest and least accessible way to cross the Womb," Eaon had told him. *"Climbing the mountains will kill you—well, not you per say—and the climb is horrific, but the bridge between the towers has Sparrow gatekeepers. Without official permission, they won't let anyone cross it. I swear, one day someone will remind that coven they don't own everything and everyone."*

Another waft of that familiar, deadly magic blew up from the famed pit. The moonstone had taken him as close as it could.

Looking down into the endless depths of the Womb, Cinn grimaced.

This was going to hurt.

Cinn took a deep breath and closed his eyes.

Then jumped.

CHAPTER 37

EAON

PEARLS OF ECSTASY WERE BECOMING HARDER AND HARDER TO find, but his reach was limitless as the magic seeped into every crack, searching for its next meal. Every time he found something to consume, bliss rumbled down the tendril back to his soul, eliciting a pleasure that cancelled out the pain of his broken body arching off the ground.

Farther and farther the insatiable beast inside him reached, until something new grabbed its attention. From above, a bright life force barreled toward him.

Salivating, he reached for it.

The ravenous fingers may as well have not been there for all the effect the magic had on the delectable, plummeting soul. Blistering in cold rage, the fingers shifted into claws that swiped again and again, yet they could not grab hold. When the body finally splattered on the ground a dozen feet away, the life force continued to burn.

Ugh. It was *them*.

A growl curled his lip as he abandoned them in search of easier prey.

The crunch of shifting bones was easily ignored. So were the gasping breaths and agonized whines. The squelching of the ground as the immune creature crawled toward him.

What was not easy to ignore was the mad thrashing of his magic's temper as a hand found his, fingers intertwining. A gasp of pain fractured from the untouchable soul as the seed lashed out. Fingers, warm as a fresh brand, smoothed away the sweat and soot-matted hair from his forehead.

He leaned into the touch, somehow craving the agony of that caress more than the famished seed craved another soul.

Lips found the shell of his ear, the whispered voice unfamiliar as it uttered a single word.

"Eaon."

And that word meant something to him.

Something important.

The death spilling from him in a torrent of need turned inward, furious that anything other than its hunger had stolen his attention. It drove into the impossible person now laying their head on his shoulder, who groaned at the onslaught, their fingers tightening around his own.

"Stop." The word was a sob against his chest, each one after it growing quieter. "I need you to stop."

He was good at that. At doing what had to be done. For Eavha, who he wanted to throttle at least as often as he wanted to hug, loving her dearly enough to suffer for. It wasn't his da talking to him now, asking him to stop. Asking him to do what needed to be done. A deep, buried part of him ached. It wasn't fair that his da wasn't here to help him anymore, but Eaon knew he still had to do this. He had to rein it in. To stop the taking.

For Eavha.

For Dearmead.

For . . .

"Cinn?" Eaon's voice cracked as he reached weakly for the mess of knotty hair at the back of the head resting on his shoulder.

A pained, shuddering breath was his only answer, and Eaon grit his teeth, trying to spool back the magic.

He couldn't find the edges of it, and as it sensed Eaon's changing intentions, it railed. His back arched again, this time from pain as claws sunk into his spine, the movement sending waves of sickening agony cascading through his broken legs.

"Shit," Cinn wheezed, digging his fingers into Eaon's arm. "No. It's okay. Give it to me. I can take it."

Giving the seething entity somewhere else to go beside the shredded remains of Eaon's insides was the sort of typical generosity Cinn had always offered him, but even through the haze of pain in Eaon's head, he remembered Cinn begging him to stop.

He couldn't hurt him anymore.

With every ounce of willpower he had, Eaon drew the tendrils of death back into his body until it felt like his skin was going to burst. He had never been in so much pain. His teeth rattled, the bitter taste of blood in his mouth as acid burned behind his eyes, burrowing into every pore.

He was going to die again.

Or at least he hoped.

CHAPTER 38

TOMAII

A PART OF TOMAII SANG AS HE CLUTCHED YASMIN'S WAIST. Flying was not an adventure he'd dared hope for, and under better circumstances, he may have crowed into the clouds. Staring back at the fire, the thrill banked in his chest.

It was beautiful and terrifying in the worst way. At night, the blaze's power couldn't be denied, the vast majority of the Anfar forest visible from its light. The flame that had burned inside him had nearly gone out during the control spell with Reigan the other day, but now it surged to life again, so fiercely that Yasmin hissed.

"Sorry," he called over the buffeting wind, keeping his head low behind the sky witch, her veil a shield.

"Burn me again and I will drop you into the river."

At least that would be an exciting way to die.

"You know what's weird?" he said instead. "The smoke."

"Smoke from fire? So very strange."

Snorting, Tomaii shook his head. "A natural forest fire should burn white. But it's black. It doesn't make sense."

Yasmin didn't answer as she shouted a command to her giant moth creature, its delicate wings fluttering quicker. Ahead, silver in the moonlight, a heavy raincloud floated from the Vein on an unnatural wind toward the forest. The wafting magic turned Tomaii's stomach, but it didn't stop him from marveling at the feat of the witches far below. Knee deep in the river, their dance was smoother, slower than the wild stomping of the mountain clan; the way most things between the Mare- and Igni-blessed were oppositional. But for every difference dividing them, there was one thing they had in common: the fluxing state of flame and water was a beauty felt in the soul, and Tomaii grinned at the synchronization managed.

Except then the cloud broke. In unison, half the witches in his view collapsed into the river. Tomaii watched the plummeting water fall faster than his grin could dissipate.

"Oh, fuck."

One who was still on her feet tried to drag another to shore, but as the deluge hit them full force, it forced them both below.

With the water so clear and the moon so bright, Tomaii could see their unconscious forms drifting in the easy current. Other, bigger shadows moved in as the fae and beasts dwelling in the Vein scented blood.

"Yas—"

"You can't help," she interrupted.

He was sick of hearing that.

Not just today, but every damned day of his life. It was what made Eaon open up during his first visit to the gorge; Tomaii knew what it was like to feel unwanted. The Northern Mountain Clan worked around his inability to focus on a task long enough to get good at it, but they didn't trust him with a lot of things. Too unreliable. Too easily distracted. Finding something to do was half the battle because nobody thought he could help. It didn't bother him much; Tomaii liked to think of himself as the spice in everybody's bland day.

And he hadn't listened to anyone's opinion on what he could or could not do in years.

Removing the bow slung across his back, he plucked an arrow from its quiver and—with the flame in his soul dancing freely—prayed for Ignatius's permission to use it. When he blew on the arrow's tip, the flint began to burn.

"What are—" Yasmin began before Tomaii took aim at one of the merfolk creeping toward an unconscious witch and let loose.

"Yes!" he crowed as the arrow hit its mark, blood blooming through the water.

"Save your arrows, you idiot," Yasmin hissed. "The night is long, and who knows what we'll run into."

"This flight is going to take all night?" Tomaii complained.

"And then some."

"What if I have to pee?"

The Celeste-blessed witch didn't laugh. To be honest, Tomaii was forcing the joke anyway. Looking back again, he could almost hear the screams of the Anfar dryads, burning inside their trees.

"Do you hear that?" Yasmin asked.

Tomaii raised his brows. "I'm not imagining it?"

But then he heard something else—whispers, drowning out the distant roaring of flames. Louder and louder, voices closed in on all sides. The cunae trembled beneath them, the sky-witch's grip tightening on the reins as the clouds undulated, wispy faces peering from within.

"What—"

"Sprites," Yasmin cut him off.

"In the sky?"

"Mother made the fae to care for the world she created. The sky is a part of it."

"And that?" Tomaii asked, swallowing as he eyed a larger form breaking through the wall of a dense cloud. Yasmin hissed. The creature was as insubstantial as the cloud sprites, but its size was enough to make the cunae swerve away. It's snake-like body writhed through air currents, in sync with the slow flap of wings, scales for feathers. Face like a horse, it speared toward them.

Tomaii prepared another arrow.

"That's no way to make friends."

Yasmin stiffened against Tomaii, who held his bow steady. He tried to remember the last time he'd ingested one of the hallucinatory mushrooms that grew in the damper caves of the gorge, but it was long enough ago that the large black shadow-cat riding on the back of the cloud-beast had to be real. Eyes like two moons stared at him as the creature sidled up beside the giant moth.

"Witches talk so loud," the shadow-cat continued, "and the fae are very good listeners. Lucky for you, I intercepted chatter about your dire need to reach the city east of here."

"You're fae?" Tomaii asked, refusing to lower his bow.

"Quiet, fool. Do not engage," Yasmin hissed back.

The too-wide grin of the shadow-cat was an omen of death.

"I commend your intelligence, but you'll find the fae make more benevolent bargains when we face a common enemy."

"We won't bargain with you," Tomaii warned, arms beginning to ache from holding.

"Even if I can assure you that you'll reach the city before dawn?"

Time was of the essence. Eavha had made that clear. A few hours could make all the difference.

"Okay, I might bargain with you," Tomaii hedged, relaxing his hold slightly.

"Idiot," Yasmin hissed again.

"A small favor," the shadow-cat purred. "And I will ask the sky-dwelling sprites to aid you."

"Why would they listen to you?" Tomaii asked, risking a glance to the dozens of tiny cloud faces keeping pace, skipping along the updrafts.

"Because a favor from a cat sith is no small token."

"Do not do it," Yasmin warned under her breath.

He truly hated being told what to do.

As if the cat sith heard his though, it grinned that feral smile again.

The world was ending. What was a small favor to a faerie at this point?

"Deal."

Even Yasmin was breathing hard, veil askew, as the cunae finally slowed. Tomaii's heart was beating harder than it had in a long time, and it took a minute to smother the grin creeping across his own face. If for no other reason, he was glad he'd made that deal with the cat sith for the sheer thrill of it.

There wasn't much to smile about in Pirevia, though.

Tomaii only knew the cliff-side city by reputation. Unlike Killian, he had never ventured farther than the bleeding mountain, and he didn't feel like he'd been missing much. The bog surrounding the city smelled like rot, a sea of flies ravaging propped-up corpses. Typical Sparrow bullshit. Death might be a natural conclusion, the Lover's embrace a beautiful reward for a life well lived, but to worship the High Spirit above all others, to revel in its ugliest faces, was blasphemous. It was a slap in the Mother's face for the gift they were given. The Sparrow Coven might own the land the Northern Mountain Clan called home, might demand their everlight and other resources as payment for allowing them to remain independent, but they were a stain on this world Tomaii couldn't wait to see wiped out.

Killian said the city was under control when he'd left. It wasn't now.

With the sun still an hour away, he'd expected Pirevia's occupants to be sleeping soundly, not barricading their houses and battling against rampaging faeries. Green-skinned swamp nymphs and pixies rioted through the streets alongside ragged, filthy demi-kin. Everything was a weapon, and everyone was a target.

Lurking among them was the kind of fae warned about in old folklore. Seven feet tall while hunched over, prowling along with too-long, double-jointed limbs that reminded him of a spider's crawl, walked a swamp hag. She grinned with needle-sharp teeth, face sallow beneath her limp swamp-reed hair as she hunted an injured woman dragging her wounded leg down a red-stained street.

"Ah." The shadow-cat, who'd rode alongside them the whole way, seemed delighted at the sight. "One of the Old Ones. I must speak with them."

Tomaii snorted as the cunae banked, preparing to land within the palace walls. "Go right ahead, Mr. Cat. Feel free to get yourself eaten."

Tsking, the shadow-cat leaped from the cloud-creature's back, solidifying as he landed atop the palace wall. The flying creature dissipated into mist, and Tomaii shook his head as the cat sith dropped down to the street and padded off after the swamp hag.

"You are a fool," Yasmin scolded, landing her cunae artfully.

"And you're a killjoy," Tomaii countered as he slid down, bare feet silent on the smooth stone. His body ached and he couldn't quite stand straight as he waddled a few feet away to stretch his legs.

The sky witch didn't seem to have the same trouble as she secured her mount and stalked gracefully toward the palace doors.

"You, uh, keep Miika busy. I'll catch up." Tomaii grimaced, massaging his numb buttocks.

"You'll find us in the council room, discussing his brother's poor choice in friends," she sniped back before climbing the steps and disappearing inside.

Rally the troops, Eavha had asked them. Looking around, Tomaii didn't like their chances. Even less so as he finally managed to shuffle into the foyer to find demi-kin sitting in clusters, backs to the wall, staring vacantly at the door. Some were so gaunt he could see the shape of their skulls beneath their faces, skin so pale and thin a harsh wind would probably split it. A few flinched as he came inside, others baring their blackened teeth.

Tomaii tried to smile as he hurried after Yasmin, still visible at the top of a grand staircase. Again, he'd only heard of such structured architecture from Eaon's stories. The stairs in the gorge were rough stone, the clan's interference with the natural land kept to a minimum. These halls, the carpet and chandeliers and railings . . . it was all so forced.

Yasmin led the way to a room high up in one of the palace towers. Windows adorned two of the three walls, a large hole busted through one of them. The broken glass had been swept into a pile in the corner, the broom still in Miika's hand as he stood at the head of a large table occupying most of the floor space. His back was to them, watching the mayhem outside.

"What happened?" Yasmin asked, voice low.

The elder's shoulders dropped in relief at the sound of her voice.

"What remained of Prince Nevan's guard abandoned their posts when Princess Aisling left. The humans began to organize. I considered abandoning the city, but—" Miika turned, sentence forgotten as his eyes widened, mouth agape.

Tomaii grinned and leaned against the open doorway. "Speechless suits you."

The elder's face reddened as he hissed, "What the actual fuck."

Yasmin released a long-suffering sigh as she approached, running a slender hand down Miika's now tense shoulders. "It's a long story, and believe me, I wouldn't have brought him if it wasn't important."

"Where's Killian?" Miika snapped, narrowing his eyes.

"Oh, unclench, Miika," Tomaii chuckled. "He's on his way. I just missed you so much I opted to fly with Yazzy instead."

The sky witch bristled, turning her head slowly to glare at him. "Don't make me regret not dumping you in the Vein when I had the chance."

"Stake and burn me, I can't deal with this right now," Miika muttered, massaging his temples and turning back to the window.

Tomaii stiffened at the words. *Stake and burn me*. It was a saying they all threw around so carelessly, but now, all he could see was Eaon bound to the pyre. His friend had not been present at his own trial, unable to defend himself or explain why he let the phouka loose. The elders had voted on the punishment. Miika had voted.

"Don't fucking tempt me, you miserable piece of shit," Tomaii hissed. Smoke curled from between his teeth—an effective party trick.

Scenting it, Miika and Yasmin both looked to him warily.

"Let's keep to the point," the sky witch said, pursing her lips. How she could stand the male, let alone form a union with him, Tomaii didn't understand.

He let her explain everything that was going on with Anfar while he simmered. Explain Eavha's whispering leaf and her request to organize whatever forces they could and send them south to Hyrsch.

Miika balked, throwing a hand toward the window. "Organize this?"

Swallowing his rage, he twisted it into a cruel smile. Killian would have argued with his brother until they were both blue in the face, but that had never once worked. Yasmin was still too new, her gentle urging and encouragement falling on deaf ears.

This was why Killian had asked Tomaii to come instead.

"It's fine, Yazzy. Miika probably couldn't do it anyway. Can't stake and burn an entire city. I'll do it myself." He shrugged and turned around. Took exactly one step before Miika snorted.

"You couldn't organize a brunch if someone handed you a schedule."

"Oh, how you wound me!" Tomaii called back, winking to a human servant who stood in the hall, watching wide-eyed. He switched to Nirnish, though his fluency was poor. A little gossip couldn't hurt. "I'll just make another faerie bargain with the swamp hag. She'll wrangle everybody to Hyrsch."

"No you won't!" Yasmin shouted.

"*Another*?!" Miika was right on his heels.

Tomaii waved a dismissive hand as he hurried his steps down the hall. "It's no big deal. With the beasts and Chaos on the way, what harm can a little deal do? If we don't make our stand in the south, we'll all be dead soon anyway!"

"I command you to stop!" Miika hollered, chasing Tomaii, who broke into a jog.

"Oh, you *command* me?" Tomaii laughed. "Forgive me, Your Haughtiness, but I bend only to the will of the Spirits!"

Spitting curses, Miika chased Tomaii down the halls and staircase. If he wasn't Igni-blessed, the elder probably wouldn't try so hard to stop him. Would have likely shoved Tomaii off the edge of the gorge a long time ago, Balance be damned. But the magic the Spirit of Fire had given him, what Ignatius permitted him to do with it, was too rare a gift to waste.

"Get back here, you little shit," Miika snarled, catching Tomaii by the collar and hauling him to a stop.

"So handsy," Tomaii panted, grinning from ear to ear, knowing his amusement would only rile Miika more. "I didn't know you felt that way about me."

"You are not to engage with the fae. Do you understand?" Miika ignored Tomaii's ribbing.

"Well, what's your suggestion for rallying the troops then?" he prodded, aware of their demi-kin audience. Miika noticed them too, sighing through his nose.

"Not that I'm required to answer to a civilian like you," he hissed in their native language, "But I'll prepare something to say to these people. Something to minimize panic, but motivate them to cooperate. Just *stay put*."

Tomaii saluted him mockingly, resisting the urge to punch him in the face for sentencing Eaon to death. Later, when the world wasn't in quite so much danger. "Let's go write a pretty speech then."

CHAPTER 39

OWEN

OWEN SAT ON THE FLOOR OF PRINCE NEVAN'S BEDROOM, staring at the splintered door. Kicking it down had done nothing to relieve the tightening ache in his chest. Neither had pissing on the bed or setting it on fire. He'd have done the same to the prince's body, but he hadn't thought to grab it before leaving the arena and he wasn't about to go back out there now.

The smoke from the burnt linens lingered, no doubt worsening the ache in his chest as he coughed again into the crook of his elbow, but he didn't care. It was a shame the whole room hadn't caught alight. A shame he hadn't thought to throw himself on the fire, too.

Nevan was dead, the city collapsing in on itself without leadership; he'd gotten what he wanted, yet none of it made him want to get up off the floor.

Not even unlocking all those cages in the sewers had made him feel anything. The demi-kin wanted him to join them, rioting and rampaging in the streets without consequences, but Owen didn't care.

Nora was gone. Nothing fucking mattered anymore.

Their home in Hyrsch could fall to ruin, he didn't care.

Their staff could starve without their employment, he didn't give a shit.

The family they'd wanted to raise together . . . Siobhan was pregnant, and he didn't care anymore. What was the point of it without Nora? They were supposed to do it together. They had promised each other they were in this *together*. But where the fuck was Nora now?

She'd left him. She'd chosen the *cause* over him, knowing damn well he had never been as strong as her. Knowing damn well he couldn't do this without her. He'd have suffered any torment, would have given anything to keep her safe, and she had thrown it in his face.

His anger and bitterness made him sick with guilt. None of the vitriol in his head was fair, but that didn't stop it festering anyway. He had no control over his thoughts, just like he had no control over anything in his life. The few choices he'd made had led him right back here.

Maybe he could see the sun, but, deep down, he would always be in the sewers.

"Excuse me?"

Owen stiffened. On his way up the tower, he'd taken a sword from a fallen guard who'd dared refuse Aisling's claiming of the city. He reached for it as he got to his feet.

The woman standing in the doorway to Nevan's bedroom took a step back, raising her pretty, manicured hands. She had no weapons or armor. In fact, the flimsy dress she wore was practically transparent. Her button nose wrinkled, baby-blue eyes darting between the sword in Owen's hand and the charred remains of the prince's bed.

He should lower his weapon. She was vaguely familiar and

unarmed. She was also very clearly not a witch—he could tell just by looking at her.

"Are . . ." She swallowed nervously, keeping her hands in plain sight. "Are you Owen?"

His eyes narrowed. When he said nothing, she continued. "Nora—"

"Don't talk about my fucking wife," he spat, stepping forward, fingers twitching on the blade.

"Oh gods, please don't kill me. My name is Rhosyn—"

That was all it took for him to know exactly who she was. Their entire plan had rested on Rhosyn Shaye's love for a demi-kin pirate. It failed because of her. Nora was dead because of *her*.

"Get out!" he roared. He'd kill her. He knew it. He could feel the urge in his veins. And what was one more innocent woman's blood on his hands at this point?

"I . . . I . . ." She wanted to flee, but she managed to stutter out a coherent sentence before she did. "I wanted to help, so I . . . In the throne room."

She was gone before he finished taking a full step toward her. It took every bit of willpower Owen had not to chase her down. Blood thundered in his ears, every breath filling him with need. Maybe he should be down on the streets with the other demi-kin, slaughtering any human stupid enough to look at him. But once she was out of sight, the red haze faded from his vision. It took a minute longer for him to comprehend what she had said.

He almost didn't care, but something nagged at him to see what Rhosyn had done.

Edging through the door, he stopped dead in his tracks at the sight on the dais. Wrapped in white linens, a body lay prone across the marble. Numbness spread from his face to his hands, sword clattering to the floor.

Even wrapped, even from across the room, even dismembered, he knew it was Nora. He'd know her anywhere.

He didn't want to see, but his feet took him closer anyway. Linen wrapped her body like a swaddled baby, the bouquet of flowers tucked among the layers almost masking the scent of decay. Kneeling beside her, his hand moved without consent to rest upon her still chest. Empty and hollow, the corpse was a husk. Her softness was gone. Stiff, as if the marble of this cursed palace had seeped into her bones.

"Nora."

Her name was a whisper, as if he were afraid to wake her. But she wasn't here anymore. That had never been clearer. Her body was here, most of it at least, but her soul, whatever it was that made her *Nora* had departed. The only thing left was the grief in his heart—the love that would never die but had nowhere left to go.

It hurt, this grief. This excess of love.

He would bury her. Not in this fucking city. Somehow, he would get her home. He would bury her, and then he would force himself to bury his grief, too. Bury his love. He had no use for it anymore. All it did was hurt him.

Made it hard to breathe.

A long, low whistle echoed through the throne room. Owen's spine straightened, hand reaching to his hip for a sword that wasn't there.

"Maybe I just been living underground too long, but why'd his Royal Jackass have such a big room for a fucking chair?"

There were very few people he wanted to see less right now than the demi-kin who'd occupied the cell beside his underneath the arena. However long he'd spent down there, waiting for the signal to stage the breakout—a breakout that was doomed to fail before it even began—was already more time that he ever wanted to spend in her company.

"Fuck off, Cecelia."

"Overheard some of them witches running around the castle like they own it now. Sounds like some shit is going down out in the big wide world."

Removing his hands from Nora's corpse before clenching them to fists, he shut his eyes and growled through his teeth. "I don't give a shit."

Cecelia snorted. "Me neither."

A long silence sat between them. Owen had no intention of breaking it.

"It's just . . ." Cecelia's voice wavered. And that was enough to make him turn. She was staring at Nora's linen-wrapped body, chewing her lip, arms crossed tightly over her chest. She had not changed from the filthy, bloodstained clothes she'd worn in the arena. Hadn't washed her face or brushed her hair. "I just . . . don't know what to do now."

"You could start by leaving me alone."

His dangerous tone didn't disturb her. She barely even noticed he'd spoken. "Some of the demi-kin from the sewers are blubbering in the infirmary, others just wandering around in shock. Most are with those from the arena, killing whoever they can get their hands on. I'd join them, but . . . Them witches are gathering anyone willing, sending them south. I don't know what a dock is, or a ship, or a war, but it sounds violent and . . . that arena is all I know. I'm a fighter, and now I don't know what to do."

Owen was about to snap at her to take her existential crisis somewhere else, but something she said snagged. "Did you say there's ships going south?"

Cecelia lifted her brow, but otherwise didn't answer.

Turning back to Nora's body, Owen didn't have to think about what his next move was. Gently, carefully, he lifted his wife from the dais, cradling her against his chest.

"Pick up my sword," he said to Cecelia. "I'll show you what a dock is."

CHAPTER 40

OWEN

CECELIA WAS RIGHT; PIREVIA WAS IN CHAOS. NOT ONLY WERE the demi-kin healthy enough to swing a weapon rampaging through the city, there were fae alongside them. Knee-high nymphs, mud-sprites, goblins, and pixies screeched with glee as they chased terrified humans into their houses, maiming any who ran too slow. A swamp hag's ghastly face was lit only by the occasional candlelight from unboarded windows, the lamplighters clearly and fairly having abandoned their nightly duties.

There was no sign of Aisling anywhere, nor any of her companions. They'd left the city to fold in on itself. Left him behind.

Clutching Nora to his chest, he moved quickly. Cecelia stuck close by, sword at the ready, teeth bared at the pixies who noticed them. The two moved like an arrow through a swarm of bees—direction among the madness—following the familiar path to the city's eastern gate and the scaffolding lining the cliffside.

"Stay behind me," Owen told Cecelia, placing each foot carefully, clutching Nora's body so tightly he'd have bruised her if she were alive. Whispering to her as if she could hear him kept him focused. "I'm taking you home now, my love."

The docks were only slightly more organized, though just as crowded and hurried. No guards minded the docked ships, plain-clothed civilians free to load supplies. Two older humans, sea-weathered and grey-bearded, stood on a pile of crates, shouting over the mayhem to direct traffic.

"She can't hold the weight, lad! Put the metal on *Siren Song*, she's built for heavy cargo! And move the people onto *Airbreaker*!"

Owen shuddered at the name.

"What are those things?" Cecelia asked in awe, taking in the armored ships floating on the black sea, the full moon mirrored on its choppy surface. "Is that water?"

"Stay close." This moment, the first time Cecelia saw the world, should have been beautiful. With the rot of his wife's body burning his nose, Owen didn't care.

Nobody else did either as they pushed their way through scurrying dockhands.

The *Airbreaker*. The slave ship he and Nora arrived on, along with the rest of the rebels Aisling had sent away, was still docked. The desire to spill a barrel of oil and set the thing on fire burned deep and deadly, but that would not help him get his wife home.

A human woman stood on the gangway, counting heads as masses boarded. Out of fear for what was happening in Pirevia or a genuine desire to go south, Owen didn't care, only that there was room for him.

"Owen?"

Standing onboard the ship, a silhouette waved to him. In the dark, he couldn't see who it was, but logic suggested it was probably a demi-kin from Hyrsch. Another survivor of their failed coup.

The woman on the gangway didn't stop him, and Cecelia stayed close as they boarded the ship. He would not go below deck. He would not take Nora back down there.

"You made it," the silhouette said, coming to meet them. His face was vaguely familiar, but Owen couldn't name him.

Words ceased when the rebel soldier looked to what Owen was carrying. No platitudes were forthcoming, thankfully.

"We just going to stand around or we going to do something?" Cecelia broke the silence, lifting her chin to the soldier she didn't know.

"Nothing to do. There's a couple of Sparrow-witches on the ships. Celeste-blessed. They'll put wind in the sails. Should halve the time it takes to get back to Hyrsch."

"Don't know what a Sparrow is, but I heard there was fighting to do in the south," Cecelia continued. For once, Owen was grateful for her ceaseless chatter. The weight in his arms was growing too heavy.

The soldier nodded, taking her in. "Don't think you're going to need to know what Sparrows are anymore. Those here said they've lost contact with the king and queen. Everything's going to shit. Princess crying about the end of days. Going to be a lot of fighting before this is over."

Cecelia grinned.

Owen eased himself to the deck, sitting against the railing between two cannons. He didn't care about any of it.

CHAPTER 41

MOYRA

The moonlight spat her out onto a crowded street, smoke curling from her singed clothes. Tossing her pack aside, she knelt to pull off her boots, the soles melted and sticking to the road beneath. Her escape from the fire had been quick enough to avoid burns, but not to walk away unscathed.

She'd just left Cinn there.

Shocked, she fell back to sit on the cobblestone road. She'd just *left* him.

"Oh!"

The cry came a second before a knee connected with the back of Moyra's head. Chin bashing into her sternum, she gagged on the bile suddenly in her throat. A whole person tumbled over the top of her head, sprawling across the road, the ceramic pitcher in their hands shattering to a million pieces.

"Ow," the young woman sobbed quietly as she rolled onto her back, blinking in confusion at where Moyra sat rubbing the back of her head. "Where in the Mother-made world did you come from?"

The flickering yellow light from the streetlamps was plenty as Moyra took in the girl. She was filthy. Hair wild and wrapped in knots atop her head, as if she didn't have time to tie it back properly, clothes stained, her face streaked in soot and dirt, spattered in blood and ash . . .

Moyra knew exactly who she was.

Even if she hadn't screamed the name over the roar of the inferno, knowing the moonstone would take her directly here, even if she hadn't already seen the young witch's face in visions and dreams, Moyra would know this girl.

She had Kailevi's eyes.

"Eavha . . ."

Picking dirt out of her scraped elbow, the young witch wasn't fazed by a stranger knowing her name.

"Burns over by that yellow house, smoke . . . breath—" She stumbled over her Nirnish "—by that lamp. My blessing is still . . . tired, but I will see you as soon as I can."

Before Moyra could say anything else, Eavha was up on her bare feet, soiled dress torn, racing to intercept a man carrying more pitchers of water. Which is when Moyra noticed everybody else on the street. People coaxing exhausted, injured witches inside houses while others simply curled up in garden beds or under streetlamps. Huddled under a blanket, a child no older than five sat alone, staring vacantly at the sky while cradling an inconsolable infant.

Following their gaze, Moyra's lips parted in a silent gasp at the aura in the night sky. An aura that tinged the city in flickering red, ash settling on rooftops, scuffed into the sidewalk by rushed feet. Bushfires were known to happen in Qiri from time to time, but this . . . The burning was visible as far as she could see in either direction.

There was nothing she could do for Cinn. He had a

moonstone to get him out of there, but she had a feeling he wouldn't use it until he found Eaon. Spitting the bile from her mouth, Moyra removed her melted boots from her blistered feet and hobbled after her niece.

Eavha had taken another pitcher of water and dropped to her knees beside a couple nursing deep burns on the soles of their feet. Reaching inside her chest binding, Eavha pulled out herbs and small glass vials of what looked like aloe jelly.

"Eavha," Moyra called again, coming up beside her.

"What?" Her niece didn't look at her as she tried to balance the vial between her knees and crush herbs between her fingers, while at the same time pull bandages out from her chest binding, dipping them into the pitcher.

Dropping to her knees as well, Moyra took the vial. "I can help."

She needed to help. After what she had done under the temple in Orhn . . . She couldn't think about it yet, but she needed to help heal.

And she really could. Her parents had specialized in magic-suppression, but they had made all kinds of things at the apothecary. Including simple burn treatments. Things Moyra had thought beneath her. Things humans could do themselves.

She silently thanked her family for having forced her to learn anyway.

Even as Eavha used both hands to prepare the bandages, carefully cleaning the burns, she kept one eye on Moyra's busy fingers. Not even the broken cry cracking from the burnt witch distracted her.

"Bless the herbs before you mix them," she said.

Moyra paused, frowning. "What do you mean, bless them?"

Eavha spoke again in a language Moyra didn't understand,

and when she stared at her blankly, their frowns of confusion matched.

"You're not from Wyldeden," Eavha realized.

"No," Moyra answered.

"Switch with me then."

Moyra took one look at the blistered, raw flesh Eavha was cleaning and felt her face go numb.

"You're not a healer, either." Eavha pursed her lips.

"Not . . . not that kind. But I can blend a salve."

"It's no use if you don't bless the herbs."

"The spell I use works just fine where I'm from."

Eavha blew out a frustrated breath but let Moyra continue her work. "Where are you from?"

". . . North."

Now was not the time to explain, even if Moyra couldn't stop staring at features that were so clearly Kailevi's. A stare that only made Eavha's eyes narrow further.

"Now is not the time to be . . . what is the word . . . vague. You're not from Wyldeden but you knew my name."

"Yes." Moyra nodded, meeting her gaze.

It was the first time Eavha had truly looked at her. Moyra could tell, because her eyes widened, her breath leaving her quickly.

"You're Morvish."

The constellation tattoo on her forehead gave her away.

"Yes," Moyra repeated, finishing the salve and offering it to her niece. "I only just arrived. My name is Moyra Thorne."

So still she could have been one of the fae, Eavha stared. Finally, voice quieter than a mouse, she whispered. "Cinn found you."

"He did. Here, take this." She placed the vial in Eavha's hand and forced her fingers to close around it.

Distracted, Eavha looked around the dark, miserable street. "Is . . . Is . . ."

"He's with Eaon," she reassured her, hoping the sick twisting in her gut wasn't evident on her face. Cinn had called Eaon's name, and the moonstone had taken them into the depths of an inferno. It couldn't mean anything good.

Whether her facial control failed or whether Eavha already knew, she looked back toward the red aura in the sky. "Eaon . . . He went to see what . . ."

"Eavha." Moyra took her hands. "We are here. They are there. Let's do what we can, and not worry about what we can't."

Nodding quickly, she turned back to the witch who had passed out from the pain, carefully slathering the salve over the burns.

After another moment, Eavha muttered, "My da used to say that."

Moyra only smiled.

CHAPTER 42

CINN

BY THE TIME EAON'S SURGE SETTLED, THE CONTACT BETWEEN their skin nothing but a tingle, Cinn was numb with cold. It could have been minutes, or it could have been hours since Eaon had fainted from the pain he wouldn't share, no matter how Cinn begged. It was so much worse than before Cinn left.

Without light, the only sign that Eaon had not actually died again was the shaky rise and fall of his chest, the stuttering pulse under Cinn's hand. Relief was fleeting. The red speck that flickered as black smoke consumed the world above may as well have been a star, unreachable in every way. If firelight couldn't grey the endless shadows at the bottom of the Womb, then moonlight certainly wouldn't find them, meaning the spare moonstone Moyra had given him was useless. But Eaon needed help. If Cinn couldn't get them out, his friend very well might die again. And one day, the Lover might not send him back.

Cinn ran his hands softly over Eaon's face, around the back of his head and down his neck, looking for injuries. Exploring the planes of his collarbones, then over the shoulders and down his arms, Cinn found them: dislocated elbow, shattered ribs . . . his legs below the knee were splinters.

Moving him was impossible but staying where they were was a death sentence. At the bottom of the deepest ravine in Nir with an inferno blazing above, nobody was coming to help.

There was just Cinn.

If he could rip the mark off the back of his neck and put it on Eaon, he would. If he was a witch instead of an oddly durable human, he could do more than just stop Eaon's surge; he could do something to actually help.

Stop it, Cinn chastised himself.

There wasn't time to spiral. To be mad at himself for not being a healer like Eavha, or powerful like Kaelean. Being kinner would have to be enough.

Feeling his way back to Eaon's face, Cinn checked he was still unconscious. Skin cold and clammy, eyelids closed and still, only the fluttering pulse in his neck was a comfort.

Cinn smoothed back Eaon's hair, promising silently, *I'll be right back*.

Leaving his pack, he counted each step as he reached blindly for a wall. The spongy ground was unstable and made it hard to keep track of which direction he'd left Eaon, but with the dark so complete it was easier to make a mental map.

When he realized that's what he was doing, he froze. How had it taken so long for him to realize how sempiternal the dark was? In those early days . . . weeks . . . in that cell underground, he'd made escape plans. He mapped what he knew of the palace in his head, mapped the city beyond. It was so real in his head that he'd envisioned finding Eddy and Rad in their apartment; pictured their faces when he came bursting through the door and begged them to run with him.

"Stop." His voice was still so strange but hearing its smallness in this grand cavern reminded him that he was not *there*.

His foot kicked something hard that rolled and clacked loudly against something else. Crouching low, he felt along the porous ground until his hands brushed against what was distinctly bone. Small spinal bones, longer limb bones, and a skull that was not human. It was wide browed with long horns curling out of its temples. Of course things had fallen and died in the Womb before, but the fact of it, the tactile death in his hands, only fueled his urgency to find a way out.

~

There was no way out.

Hours passed as Cinn felt blindly along the sheer wall of the Womb, finding nothing but sharp juts that cut open his hands and smaller bones that crushed easily beneath his boots. Hours that Eaon didn't have. The small rousing noises he'd begun to make urged Cinn back, once again tripping over those thick, hard bones.

Looking up to that unreachable speck of flickering fire, a small part of him regretted jumping. He'd put himself back in an inescapable darkness.

But this was different. He was not chained down. Not sealed within. A human body would never reach the opening of this gaping chasm, but Cinn's body was unstoppable. Or so he'd been told.

Eaon needed him to be.

The breath he loosed trembled as he knelt by Eaon again, assessing his injuries by feel alone. Then he crawled across the spongy ground to the bones nearby and dragged them over.

{Sorry,} he signed as he picked up the large horned skull and eased it over Eaon's head. If they fell, hopefully the skull would protect him somewhat.

Pulling his shirt over his head, Cinn ripped it into long strips. The longer bones would work as splints, keeping Eaon's bent and broken legs as stable as possible. His friend groaned as Cinn tied his ankles and knees.

He was going to wake up.

Nausea threatened to empty Cinn's stomach as he rest his forehead against Eaon's and whispered, "I'm sorry."

Panting as his pain registered, Eaon's voice cracked. "Cinn?"

Pressing a kiss against Eaon's forehead, he wrapped one end of the last strip around Eaon's bicep and tied it off, then the same around the other arm.

There was no graceful way to do this. There was no way to get Eaon on Cinn's back without causing him immeasurable pain.

Scooping him under the arms, Cinn pulled his friend into a sitting position. Eaon didn't scream the way Cinn braced himself for; the sound was a quiet crack at the back of his throat as Cinn slipped his head and one arm through the loop of cloth and twisted around. Holding tight to the knots he'd tied, Cinn lifted. Stood.

Eaon was dead weight, silent as he slipped back into unconsciousness. Cinn's knees buckled, every muscle in his body straining. Taking a single step towards the wall of the Womb seemed impossible, let alone climbing it, but his only other option was to lay at the bottom of this dark pit and succumb to whatever nondeath both he and Eaon would endure. To become one of the rabid things locked under the old city of Kin on Orhn, feasting on his own flesh, on Eaon's, to ease the endless hunger. Eaon, who was too hurt to protect himself from the monster Cinn would become.

One wobbling step. A second. Adjusting Eaon on his back and tightening the strip of cloth binding Eaon's arms until Cinn's sternum groaned from the pressure, he took a third. Laying a hand against the wall, he searched for an outcropping to haul himself up with.

Breathing took concentration. He didn't dare look up again to take in the enormity of this task. One step at a time, forever, until they got to the surface.

Finding a handhold, he jiggled it to make sure the rock would hold. Then he braced a foot against the wall, wobbling under Eaon's weight. In one jerking movement, he pulled himself up the wall. Immediately they slipped back down.

Gritting his teeth, he waited for the healing itch in his scraped palms to ease before he tried again.

A screech echoed through the empty cavern.

Cinn closed his eyes. Of course there were beasts to contend with.

A second shriek. Cinn noted the sound came from above. Pulling his silver knife, Cinn debated whether it was worth the effort of putting Eaon down. A shadow blotted out the speck of fire, the feathery flapping of the beast's descent warning their speed. Putting his back, and Eaon, against the wall, Cinn faced the dark with his knife, waiting.

The creature landed with a dense thud. "Eaon? Kinner?"

Cinn sagged, recognizing the voice of the burnt figure he'd left on the surface. Without having to speak, it managed to find them.

"Is he alright?"

"No," Cinn croaked. "I . . . I have to climb."

A beat of silence, followed by a dark chuckle. "I may not know you, but you are a true kinner. I commend you."

The flap of wings tousled Cinn's hair, and before he could

bring himself to ask what the creature meant—what it was or what it was doing—huge talons sunk into Cinn's shoulder. Gritting his teeth against the bite and reminding himself that climbing would hurt worse, Cinn held onto the muscular leg as his feet were lifted off the ground.

The fall had lasted an eternity and going up seemed to take just as long. The winged creature panted hard, but with as much determination as Cinn had mustered to climb the Womb, the nonhuman kinner creature matched it, continuing to flap. To rise.

Darkness gave way to shadow, then to dim orange light. Sweat beaded across Cinn's forehead as the bone-chilling cold of the underground gave way to blistering heat, fire still raging above. As they finally emerged from the Womb, Cinn's scream was lost among that of the creature—of that of the forest—as they burned.

The itching began anew as they climbed above the flames, half gliding half crashing toward the top of the nearest tower.

There were no guards. Bleeding and burned, splayed across the flat of the turret, the two immortals coughed the soot from their lungs. Silent on Cinn's back, Eaon was in bad shape.

"His sister is a healer," the creature wheezed. Black as night, it resembled a horse-sized raven. "I'll take you both there . . . in a minute."

A thousand questions sat on the tip of his tongue, including how this creature knew who Eaon's sister was, but Cinn couldn't bring himself to voice them. He could speak. He knew he could. That physical block that swelled in his throat whenever he'd tried before was gone, and yet, words wouldn't come.

He lay still as the creature rose onto taloned feet, then *popped*. Where an enormous black bird had stood, a hairy man with the head and legs of a goat stood, yellow eyes peering down at him. Somehow, this form was more terrifying. And it had nothing to do with the curling black horns or its towering height.

Carefully, almost tenderly, the black-furred goat-man untied Eaon from around Cinn's chest and got him slung across his own. Then it held out a hand. An offering.

"I thought I knew all the kinner, but I don't recognize you."

Taking his hand, Cinn climbed to his feet, still trying to catch his breath. He pictured the two words he wanted to say in his mind, then forced his mouth to move.

"Second generation."

"Ah. Who were your parents?"

Two more words. He could do that.

"Ru." His father's name was foreign on his tongue. His mother's even more so. "Vy."

The creature's face broke into a grin. "Now I know where your gumption came from, Son of Ru and Vy."

Only the fae could stand there and hold a conversation about lineage at a time like this.

Swallowing, Cinn looked out to the forest. At a guess, a fifth of it was aflame, and in the middle stood a tree, so much taller than the rest. Or what used to be a tree.

Eyes too dry for tears, Cinn counted to ten. That was how long he would let himself panic for. Then he had to move.

"Get Eaon help," Cinn panted, pulling his spare moonstone from his pocket. It hummed with cool power in his hand, waiting for direction. "I have to go."

The amusement left the fae-kinner's face. "I hope we meet again, soon."

Undoubtedly. Eaon was as safe as he could be right now, and though it felt like ripping half his heart from his chest, Cinn would have to find him again later. The rest of his family . . . He'd left them with Kaelean.

Clenching his fist around the moonstone and picturing the shrew-eyed witch in his mind, her name was barely past his lips before the world went white and Cinn disappeared into moonlight.

PART VII

QUERENCIA

CHAPTER 43

CINN

MAYBE HE WAS DOING SOMETHING WRONG WITH THE moonstones, because when he stumbled from the moonlight again, Kaelean was nowhere to be seen. Maybe wishing his way to people was less precise than a specific place. And maybe he should have asked for one of the Copelands instead, because he had no idea where he'd ended up.

Only that, if the Copelands were here, he needed to get them out. Now.

Standing in the center of a mosaiced courtyard, the black-and-grey tiles chipped beyond recognition, Cinn tried to orient himself in the crumbling ruins. Polished grey sandstone towers were all that was left of what used to be a palace, the walls latticed with cracks. One swayed on its foundation as a howling wind tore through the courtyard. Cinn stumbled from the force of the gale and tucked his hands under his arms, missing his shirt. Small fires smoldered among fresh rubble, but aside from the flickering shadows they cast, there was no movement to indicate life. But something was out there. The roar of the forest fire had been replaced by the screeching cries of lurking beasts and the distant screams of terrified people.

Carefully, Cinn approached a nearby wall that was half collapsed, clambering over the piles of stone and brick to get a better view. His breath left him in a shudder, stomach dropping to his feet. It wasn't Hyrsch, the city was too large and too old, but something about its inherent regality and grey sandstone architecture tugged at his gut. But that could have been the nightmare come to life taking place within. All the wild things that thrived in bloodshed crawled across rooftops, plucking civilians off the streets. Potential victims were running low though, packs of indiscernible beasts fighting over a mangled corpse.

Turning back, he hissed into the dark. "Kaelean!"

Nothing.

Slipping back down the wall, he crept through the courtyard, peering through breaks in the wall. Like with Eaon, the moonstone must have taken him as close as it could, which meant she had to be around somewhere. Maybe injured. Maybe it would be his turn to save her skin for once.

His mouth was dry as he hissed her name again. What would he do if she was injured, though? He didn't have another moonstone to get them to safety, and . . .

He'd left his pack at the bottom of the Womb.

Holding onto the wall, Cinn forced himself to take a deep breath through the ache in his chest. It was just stuff. It was just a feather, and an eggshell, and a little paper fox. The shell Lula had given him.

"Kaelean!" he spat through gritted teeth.

A faraway battle cry.

Cinn turned in the direction of the swaying tower in time to see a shape climbing the exterior. A familiar shape. Body of a wolf, scales of a lizard, its frill was tucked back against its neck as the lupanis sunk its claws into stone and hauled itself through a gaping hole. A large part of the tower had fallen away, the remnants of stained glass barely visible in the moonlight.

A howl broke the night. Slithering up the side of the tower behind the lupanis were roiling shadows, darker than night itself.

Sucking down a breath, Cinn leaped over piles of rubble and skidded for the charred doorway of the servants' entrance. The howling wind and groan of the walls as gravity threatened to pull it down masked his heavy footsteps pounding down the hall, past kitchens and washrooms, and out to the main foyer. A once-elegant stairwell took Cinn to the upper levels and a grand set of doors.

Shoving them open, he froze.

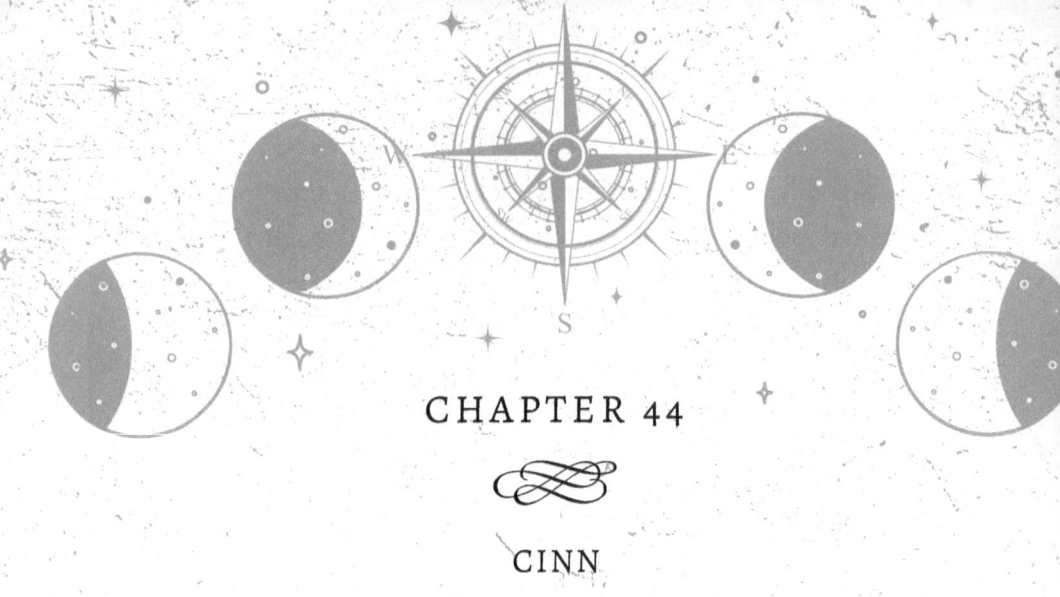

CHAPTER 44

CINN

CINN'S BODY LOCKED UP.

It wasn't the shtryg darkening the corners of the decimated throne room, waiting for their moment to strike, nor the deeply scarred lupanis that was definitely not Kaelean, circling their prey; it wasn't even the two eight-foot-tall monsters, beetle-shelled and prong-limbed, teeth glinting under the glow of everlight sconces, that plunged his heart into cold, cold fear.

Grey hair stained with blood and soot, she wielded a battle-axe against the nearest monster, teeth bared behind broken lips. Her black leather bodysuit was torn, the skin beneath seeping red, and when the monster raised its forearm to block her blow, she cried out in pain from the reverberation. Stumbling, she barely had the strength to raise her axe against the swiping claw of the second monster, its throaty chitter crawling down the back of Cinn's neck.

Through some witch sense—because gods knew he wasn't so much as breathing, let alone making any noise—her head snapped up. Shock widened her eyes, her flushed cheeks draining.

He couldn't move. Every muscle frozen stiff, his heart stuck mid beat, as if this moment, seeing her again, would be the thing that somehow killed him. He could only stare back. Stare at the scar marring her cheek, pointing toward her ear.

The beasts crowding the room didn't care that he'd arrived—one sweeping, pincered arm knocked her off her feet, her pained cry weak as her head hit the obsidian dais. The lupanis crouched back on its haunches, eyeing her throat, but a screech of denial, of possessiveness, from the nearest monster halted it. Joints clicking with every step, its hard outer elytra sliding against the muscle beneath, the monster stalked to where she couldn't quite rise to her knees.

It was going to kill her.

Cinn's fingers twitched toward his silver dagger.

The fear soaking his body dissipated at the realization that Princess Aisling Aurnia was about to be killed. The world blurred and sharpened all at once until the throne room, the dais, the bloody corpse spread over it . . . disappeared. There was only him and *her* and all the blood and pain and fear she had ripped from his body, soaking his vision in red.

He could not let the beasts have her.

This kill was *his*.

The slide of his dagger from its sheath drew the nearest shtryg's attention. Avoiding the light of the sconces, the creature was a blur of shadow as it rushed him, the hair on Cinn's arms rising as gravity increased. He forced himself to stay upright as the beast lunged. Forced himself to keep his eyes open as shadow enveloped them both and a spindly grey body, its whole face a puckered muscle, nothing but rings upon rings of needle teeth, became visible. The invisible weight it exuded was too immense to lift his arm, so Cinn let the shtryg collide into him. Let it run itself through on his dagger. It screeched in shock, and the pressure in Cinn's head eased enough for him to withdraw the blade and aim higher.

As his knife pierced its heart and the shtryg shriveled inside itself, a second took its place. A third. Teeth and claws sunk into every limb, his lungs, his guts, his throat, over and over. Venom burned through his veins, and Cinn had never been so grateful for the healing itch that followed it. For his new-found health and the speed it allowed his mark—his curse and his blessing—as it soothed away the dissolving tissue. A feral grin broke his face as he pushed the pain into the dark recesses in his mind. The shtryg had teeth, but so did Cinn, and through sheer luck or force of will, his knife arm was never pinned down for long.

The next few were more cautious, holding back long enough for Cinn to get to his feet. Staggering away from the smear of blood on the marble floor, he glanced to where *she* was still managing to fend off the beetle monsters. She couldn't keep it up for much longer.

Turning his back on the shtryg, he ran for the nearest sconce. At the quick movement, the lupanis turned for him, racing the shtryg who were braver with his back turned. Smashing the glass encasing the everlight with the hilt of his knife, Cinn ducked.

Everlight was made by Igni-blessed witches, Eaon had told him. Little balls of fire that burned indefinitely and kept shape through magic. Usually. Cinn had guessed—hoped—the need for glass to contain the flame meant that magic wasn't doing so, and as it exploded from the sconce above, he smirked.

The shtryg shrieked, fleeing to any shadowed corner they could find. The lupanis skidded low, unbothered by the light and heat.

Rolling aside, Cinn kept his dagger angled. The everlight fire had caught hold of the dead shtryg bodies nearby, surprisingly flammable, and as the lupanis growled and leaped for him once again, Cinn threw himself into the blaze.

He'd been burned before. *She* had done that to him. He knew what it would feel like, and though he couldn't help but scream as his flesh melted and healed and melted and healed, it was worth it. Pain meant nothing if it would get him a shot at *her*.

The lupanis didn't know what to do as Cinn dragged himself, clothes and hair alight, to his feet and threw himself at the beast. Lizard scales might be heat resistant, but they still burned, as the beast roared and rolled, trying to get him off, Cinn plunged his knife into its throat over and over.

The beast fell limp beneath him, and when there was nothing left to burn, his body began to itch.

He turned back to the shtryg.

Realizing what he was, what he was capable of, what he would do to defeat them, they ran. Raced across the walls and ceiling for the safety of night.

And those two monsters, who'd cornered their exhausted prey, paused.

Cinn could feel the metal of his knife's hilt malleable in his hand. The fire was not good for the silver, either. He didn't trust it to pierce that shiny black shell encasing the monster.

The battle-axe lay an arm's length away from where *she* was pressed into the wall, desperately reaching for it, a crab-like pincer pinning her waist. It was silver tipped—he could tell even from halfway across the room—and if he could get rid of those two creatures, one now turning in his direction, it would be poetic justice to kill the princess with her own weapon.

Sheathing the dagger, Cinn took a few deep breaths to make sure his still-itching body was ready. He had never been so focused, so unstoppable, in all his life. This was what his mother had meant when she'd told him to conquer his mind. To find this place of bloodlust and hatred that made everything else inconsequential.

Pain didn't matter. Only the pain *she* had caused.

His clothes, the knife, whatever else he lost in this fight, none of it mattered. Only what *she* had taken from him.

Only the pain he wanted to inflict on her. Only the life he was going to take from *her*.

The gods themselves could not stop him.

Not this night.

One of the monsters stepped forward. Cinn's shadow blended back into the dark as he ran from the everlight fire, melted boots leaving bloodied prints in his wake. The monster speared one long, clawed limb for him, but he dodged to the side, skidding to his knees and sliding under the creature's legs, scrambling for the axe.

He could smell her. Could hear her heavy, labored breaths.

The axe was heavier than he thought it would be, but he ignored the strain in his arms as he lifted the weapon and brought the blade down on the pincer pinning *his kill* to the wall. A good blade. Sharp. It easily cut through the hollow bone, the pincer falling into her lap. The beast screeched and stumbled away, waving its dismembered limb in the air.

A blow to the back sent Cinn sprawling face-first onto the floor, unable to draw breath through the pincer, cold as death, inside him.

A grunt of pain, and *she* crawled to him. Took the axe back and staggered to her feet. Swung.

The creature pinning him roared and lashed at her, pulling the pincer from his body. As soon as he could move, he grabbed the dismembered claw from the ground.

The first blow cracked its exoskeleton—and brought its attention back to him.

Rather than attack, it dodged aside as Cinn made a second swing. A third. The stump where it had lost its claw was still bleeding a lumpy white goo as it dodged again. Hesitated, turning its sharp antennae between Cinn and the princess, who engaged its brethren.

With a single, cracked screech, it limped toward the broken wall where the shtryg had escaped. Cinn didn't care. He let it go, turning his attention to his primary target, who'd finally managed to sink her axe into the monster's forehead, cleaving its skull in two.

It crumpled to the floor, and she sobbed. One foot braced against the monster's head, she yanked on the handle of her weapon, trying to get it unstuck.

Without a word, without a sound beside his footsteps on the marble, he drew his knife.

Pulling her axe free with a cry of pain, of relief, of sheer exhaustion, she turned to face him. Took in the cold wrath written on his face. The knife clenched so tightly in his fist it had molded to it.

"Wait," she croaked, climbing up on shaky legs.

Wait.

He had begged her.

Wait.

Within reaching distance, he spat at her, lashed out, swinging wildly for her head. She arched back, the tip of his blade scraping along the base of her throat.

Raising a filthy, ungloved hand, she muttered a word, but only a breeze blew against him. He slashed again, matching every retreating step she made with a stride of his own. He wanted her bleeding. He wanted her begging. He wanted her dead.

Knees hitting the dais where a chewed-out witch-corpse lay seeping blood and shit across the marble, she rolled over the body and scrambled back.

"Please stop. I don't want to hurt you," she said.

Laughter burst at the words, but it died quickly as all the pain she'd already caused washed through his body. He leaped upon the dais and swung for her again, but she ducked under his arm and kicked out the back of his knees. He dropped, but managed to draw the blade across her thigh.

She didn't react to the pain, clenching her fist and jabbing it into the side of his neck.

Weak. The blow knocked him off balance, but he was sure she could hit harder than that. Snarling, he threw his body weight into her and plunged the knife for her chest. Fast as a whip, she dropped the axe and put her hands between the point of the blade and her heart, the silver blade sinking through flesh like butter.

Now she screamed.

Cinn salivated at the sound of it, driving every ounce of his weight down harder. She squirmed, pushing back with her mangled hands. He didn't notice right away that she'd also hooked one leg around his back, foot planted against the marble stone; not until she flipped them both over. Bone snapped against his back as she rolled them on top of the corpse on the dais, blood cloying the air as he lurched and smashed his forehead against her nose.

Her cry of pain and the blood splattered across her face as she reeled back, the slick of it across his own face as he pulled the blade free from her hands, filled him with vicious glee. Grabbing a fistful of loose hair, he ripped her head to the side, rolled back on top of her and aimed the knife at her throat again.

Raw power exploded between them, throwing him back. His head cracked against one of the thrones and the red in his eyes went spotty with black.

Panting on the ground, she didn't get up. Didn't speak. Hands shaking, she clutched them to her chest.

"I'm sorry."

Blinking until his vision cleared, he pushed himself back onto his knees. Those words, especially from *her* mouth, left a hot, bitter taste on the back of his tongue, filling his head until it felt like it would explode.

Staggering to his feet, he crossed the dais in four quick steps. She rolled away and clambered up, wheezing hard.

"I don't want to fight you. I'd let you do whatever you want to me if I could, but Chaos is coming—"

He didn't care.

The world could end, and he didn't care.

She stopped talking, shaking her head at his utter lack of interest in anything bar pulling her intestines out through her teeth. Slashing with his knife again, she ducked and rolled, retrieving her axe in the process. It hung in her bleeding hands, face paling and flushing simultaneously at the pain.

"Don't make me do this. Please," she begged.

As if it was his fault. As if he'd brought the years of torture on himself. As if he'd given her no choice. As if she didn't have a choice now.

He didn't hesitate, stepping once more into her space, plunging the blade toward anything that would make her bleed. He knew she would swing for him, and he raised his arm to shield his chest as she brought the heavy blade down. It hit the bone—cut *through* the bone—but as the dismembered limb thudded to the floor, he barely felt it. He was too far gone to feel anything.

She stared at him in horror as she yanked back, a significant chunk of his arm ripping away to thud on the floor. It didn't stop him as he aimed his knife for her face. She ducked and swung again, her axe imbedding itself deep in his side. His body crumpled from the blow, but as he wrenched himself off and the itch began to knit the wound closed, his stump on fire as it tried to heal too, he went for her again.

She blocked his next swing with the handle of her weapon, but the force of the impact on her hands was too much. The axe clattered to the floor.

The soot and dirt and blood on her face became streaked with tears as her knees buckled. Mouth opening and closing over and over, she debated what she could possibly say that might give him pause. But there was nothing. There would be no mercy.

"I . . . I'm sorry," she panted.

Shaking her head, raising her wounded hands, a dribble of blood leaked from her nose. Her lips. Her ears.

"*Cons e fractu osza.*"

Pain shattered through his body as every bone fractured to splinters.

He was unconscious before he hit the floor.

CHAPTER 45

AISLING

"Aisling, wake up."

Too hot. Too cold.

"Please," someone sobbed. "Aisling, please. Please, please, please."

Davina. She would know the sound of Davina crying anywhere.

Slowly, Aisling became aware of her body. Of the pain. Of her head throbbing against the hard marble, every fiber of her being burning, as if everlight was consuming her from inside out.

She couldn't open her eyes. Couldn't move her fingers. Blood coated her teeth, and she knew it was a miracle she had not burned out.

She should have burned out.

Opening that portal in Anfar had sapped every iota of magic her Celeste-blessing provided. Fighting off the mutant witch and that *thing* that had come out of the queen's womb had dried up the little strength Eavha had gifted her. Then the beasts had come, and she had scraped every drop of power from her veins, but there had been almost nothing beside her Lover blessing.

She did not have Nevan's ability to dole out deadly curses, nor her mother's poison lips, or her father's ability to curse objects. No, she could see the dead. She could see through the veil between the Mother's realm and the void.

And when it was clear Cinn would not stop until he'd killed her, she had done what she had been warned to never do. She had breached the veil. Not just with her sight, or her voice—she had wanted to *feel* Davina. She had reached for her, taken her hand, and cried at the chill piercing Davina's very soul.

Her lover had reached back. Reached into Aisling. Had used her hands, her mouth, to command a spell she'd never heard before.

"I'm sorry. I'm sorry. I couldn't let him . . . I couldn't . . . Please wake up. Please."

The world rested on her eyelids, yet she lifted them.

Davina hovered nearby, transparent and sobbing into her hands. On the other side of the dais, Cinn was still unconscious. Mangled, but slowly healing. He wouldn't stay down forever.

But she couldn't get up.

Unlike him, she would not heal. So many of her tattoos were shredded, her hands useless, ribs broken, guts bleeding.

"Davina," she croaked, voice barely a breath.

But Davina heard her.

"Bless the Lover," Davina gasped, coming closer. "You're alive. You're awake!"

Barely.

The panic filling her dead lover's face said she knew it, too.

"Eavha," Aisling croaked. "I . . . need . . . Eavha."

Davina gaped, shaking her head, not understanding what Aisling wanted her to do. Swallowing thickly, closing her eyes against the pain bursting behind them, Aisling managed a few more words.

"Again. Take . . . me. Take . . . him."

Desperately, she scrounged her soul for a speck of magic.

"No," Davina whispered. "It'll kill you."

"Eavha."

"What if I can't get you there in time? What if she can't—"

"Eavha."

She found it. Just enough strength to reach for Davina again, the veil between them a ripple of space, of time. It was her only hope of surviving this. Of warning people against what had happened in this throne room. She simply didn't have time to die right now, but even if it happened, even if Davina's other visions of the future had been wrong as well and these were her final minutes, she could hold on long enough to see Eavha one last time.

Shudders rocked through her body, pain giving way to numbness. It wasn't a good sign. But her determination must have been evident on her face, because Davina nodded. Chin wobbling, she let a few more tears fall before forcing a smile.

"I'll get you to Eavha."

That last scrap of power flared and died in Aisling's chest. For a moment, a blip of a second, there was nothing at all between them.

Davina lunged.

Aisling burned.

Inside, she was screaming. Outside, her body stood. Moved. Cried at the pain as she grabbed Cinn by the arms and heaved him over her shoulder. Rifled through the melted remains of his pant pocket until she pulled out a colorless stone.

"Knew it." The words were not hers, though they used her voice.

Limping to the destroyed wall of King Phineas and Queen Tallula's throne room, moonlight spilling in, Davina lifted Aisling's shaking, bleeding hand, the moonstone stained red.

"Master of Tides, our nightly light, I beseech thee to see this offering new once more. Take from me and give to it what has always been yours."

Aisling knew those words. Back when this city had been whole and Davina had been bright and warm, their love still a young bud, they had traded secrets. Davina had told her how she'd travelled from Qiri using moonstones. What they were. How they were made.

Aisling's internal screams grew louder. This was *not* what she had in mind. This was *not* what she had wanted Davina to do.

Years in the void, suffering, so she could stay with Aisling and see their plan through . . . all of it came to an end as Davina traded her soul to the moon. Aisling could feel it withering inside her, seeping into the stone.

With the last of her hold on Aisling's body, Davina prayed.

"In she comes, there she goes. Master of Tides, let us be thy sea tonight. In she comes, there she goes."

The stone twinkled.

Aisling dropped to her knees, Cinn's weight crushing. Her body was hers once more.

Davina was gone.

Yet, she could almost see her. Like a memory of a painting of a moment lost to time. A sad smile as she encouraged Aisling, despite the pain, despite the grief already choking her, to go.

One more time, Aisling choked on her destination.

"Eavha."

CHAPTER 46

EAVHA

A DEAFENING SCREECH FILLED THE NIGHT. THOSE SLEEPING ON the streets startled awake, and Eavha joined them in looking to the slowly sinking moon. A large shadow flew toward them—too large to be a regular bird, the word *beast* began to echo among those climbing to their feet.

"Get inside," Moyra, that strange pink-eyed Qiri witch who'd appeared out of nowhere, wheezed. "Everybody needs to get inside."

But as the shadow pierced the dense smoke smothering the early morning hours, a second desperate shriek called down, and Eavha recognized it.

"No." Her stomach fell into her feet. "No, no, no. Eaon."

That was no beast, it was Eaon's phouka friend. The one her brother had rode on the back of toward a ravaging fire. The one now screaming with urgency as it hurtled toward the palace.

Breaking into a run, Moyra chasing closely, she could not stop the word from wheezing out between every pounding step.

"No. No. No, no, no."

ALEX CLIFFORD

Not a plead or a prayer for the Lover to spare her this pain again, but absolute denial.

Refusal.

And if the High Spirit of Death wasn't careful, the word was also a threat.

~

A small crowd had gathered in the courtyard outside the palace where the phouka had shifted back into its fae form, easing Eaon to the ground. Eavha buried her internal screaming beneath the calm, collective front of her healer training as she saw the state of her brother's broken body.

"There's not much left in the infirmary, but someone get down there and bring more thread. Some bandages," she managed as she skidded to her knees.

The phouka's heavy hand landed on her shaking shoulder. "You cannot touch him."

"I know that," she snapped.

A human woman broke from the small crowd, running for the grand doors of the palace. Long dark hair and a swollen belly was all she needed to identify Siobhan, despite only having met her briefly in Wyldeden. The rebel who'd tried to kill Aisling. The woman who had freed Cinn. Which meant . . . There. Two of the faces peering down with horror were also familiar: the farmers Cinn and Eaon had stayed with over the summer. Grimacing, she shook her head to clear it.

"What happened," she demanded from the phouka, laying her face as close to Eaon's as she dared, listening for breath sounds.

"There was a dragon," the phouka said lowly, kneeling beside her to untie the old bones stabilizing Eaon's shattered legs and neck.

Muttering broke out above and Eavha snapped again, "Everyone back off!"

"Give them space," the male farmer said, turning his back to guide people away.

"That's what burned the forest," the phouka continued, trying to keep his voice down. "It was going after the Ignatius-blessed witches attempting to control the blaze, so we tried to stop it. Failed. It took the kinner who rode with us, and Eaon . . . fell. From the clouds to the bottom of the Womb, he fell."

He had died, Eavha realized. A fall like that could have no other consequence. He had died *again*, and the Lover had given him back *again*. Put him back in a broken body, breaths rattling in his chest.

Just this morning, Eaon had been hand in hand with Dearmead, smiling his first true smile in Mother-knew how long. Now . . .

"Someone get me some leather gloves, damn it!" she screamed, pulling out the last bandage she had shoved in her chest binding and tossing it at the phouka. "Put this around that wound."

And Dearmead. Gone. Not dead, but she didn't want to imagine what kind of fate she had destined him to by putting The Mark of One Unending on his neck.

Finally, Siobhan returned with a handful of supplies. Not enough. Not nearly enough.

Damage control. His femur was sticking out of his thigh, so much blood still seeping from the wound he would likely die again if she didn't get it under control. With steady hands, she threaded a needle.

"Phouka, I'm going to need your help."

"You have it."

"We have to get that bone back inside his body, and then we have to get the wound to stop bleeding."

In her periphery, Eavha noticed Moyra kneeling by the discarded bones, eyes vacant, the constellation tattoo on her head shimmering. "Seven. Seven."

"Someone shut her up. I can't deal with that right now," Eavha snapped.

It was the female farmer who came forward, gently placing a hand on Moyra's shoulder.

Blocking out the rambling and hysterical conversations about dragons and burnt forests, Eavha used what little magic she had recuperated during the night to assess Eaon's internal damage. It was bad. The kind of bad that left her hands shaking, sweat soaking the back of her dress.

One thing at a time.

Nobody had brought her any gloves yet, so all she could do was direct the phouka. The moment the Old One got hold of the protruding femur, Eaon began to stir. She didn't have any poppy milk to dull the agony he was about to be in. And maybe it made her a coward, but as the phouka began to twist and push the bone back into place, she covered her ears and shut her eyes against the raw, broken screams her brother made.

When she let herself look, Eaon was still conscious—pale as a wraith and shaking from shock, but conscious. The phouka was pinning him down with one foot while stitching the wound. Steady, as if he had experience with such things.

"Hey, you're alright," Eavha promised tearily, moving into his line of sight. Sweat dewed his face as his vacant, pained eyes met hers. "I'm going to make sure you're alright."

"Not too close," the phouka ground out. "The seed has

grown and is trying to feed again. I am absorbing the wafts, but be wary."

As if in response, Eaon's eyes darkened, the amber of his irises disappearing into the void blooming from his pupils.

To her left, a beam of pale moonlight brightened the dark dawn, and in its wake stood a ruined Aisling.

For a heartbeat, Eavha could only stare.

Then Aisling dropped the lump on her shoulder—an almost naked, filthy and unconscious Cinn. The shock of him being here, of seeing him and Aisling in the same space . . . she couldn't feel it. Her mind was racing, but her body was frozen, unable to pull her eyes away from where Aisling swayed. Slowly, it dawned on Eavha that Kaelean was missing. That the high priestess had gone to Dusarn and not returned.

Pins and needles flooded her skin as her stomach curdled.

Aisling's knees buckled. Her lips parted, but no words came. Only a deluge of blood. It brimmed in her eyes before spilling down her cheeks.

Eavha dropped the bandage she'd been about to bless. It was useless.

She was useless.

It was a truth that rang like a death knell as she hovered between her brother and her . . . Aisling.

Aisling, who was burning out before her very eyes. Eaon, who was drowning in the void and may never walk again. She couldn't help either of them.

But there was no one else.

No one here, anyway.

Closing her eyes, Eavha put her head to the ground, turned her palms to the sky and let go of her corporeal body. She had never been good at separating her soul, at turning the pages of the book of realms Kaelean had tried to teach her about. Terra had been waiting as she had flown over the forest with Aisling, as if hoping she would come looking.

Just as Sanni now stood expectantly in the doorway to her own realm.

All her life, Sanni and Terra had been something abstract. Deities that had touched her in the womb to leave their mark and been nothing but a vague presence over her shoulder ever since. They had refused her requests and constricted her access to magic at times, as was their right, but otherwise they had not interfered.

In the forest, she had not had time to marvel at Terra's beauty. She did not have time to take in all Sanni's glory now, either. Her tutors at the Sanctuary for the few months she'd trained as a priestess had warned her to be reverent when she eventually contacted the spirits, but there wasn't time for that either.

"Please," she begged. "What you gave me is not enough. Help me save them. I'll give you anything."

Sanni had ignored her prayers all day. Had ignored the cries of the Wyldeden clan as they lay dying in the street, the pleading of the healers who had nothing but herbs and cloths. Eavha did not expect this to go well, but she had to try. She could not stand there and be useless.

Sanni's voice was clipped and curt.

A favor.

Eavha didn't hesitate. "Anything."

Magic snapped against her heart, so forceful she flinched back into her body. A binding promise. Her racing pulse thundered in her ears, heart swelling as the overwhelming presence of the Spirit of Healing invaded her.

I was right to choose you, Sanni said inside her mind. *This is what it is to be a true priestess.*

The Spirit's power flowed through Eavha, their wills one and the same. Without hesitating, she crawled to Aisling and lay her hand on the torn flesh of her shoulder. Shredded flesh, bleeding organs—none of it compared to the damage Aisling's soul had taken from the burn out, balancing on the edge of the void. Eavha grabbed hold of Aisling's soul with a strength that wasn't hers, keeping it from tipping over as Sanni's power pulled at the worst of her injuries.

There would be a price for this. Without her Blessing Charm, this power did not come from within. She was a conduit, but as Sanni said, that was what it was to be a true priestess. To commune with the Spirits themselves, to work with them, to sacrifice a part of herself so that she may wield a greater power. For the clan. For her family.

Aisling would live. She had to live.

Even as Eavha's own body began to grow weak from the sheer power running through her veins, she knew she would risk her own burnout to ensure the people she loved would endure.

Not under my care, you won't, Sanni promised, pulling back.

Just enough magic to heal the worst of Aisling's injuries. Just enough to move her safely to the infirmary.

"Thank you," Eavha sighed, then looked back to her brother.

Rest, first.

An absurd notion. There would be no rest until everyone was okay.

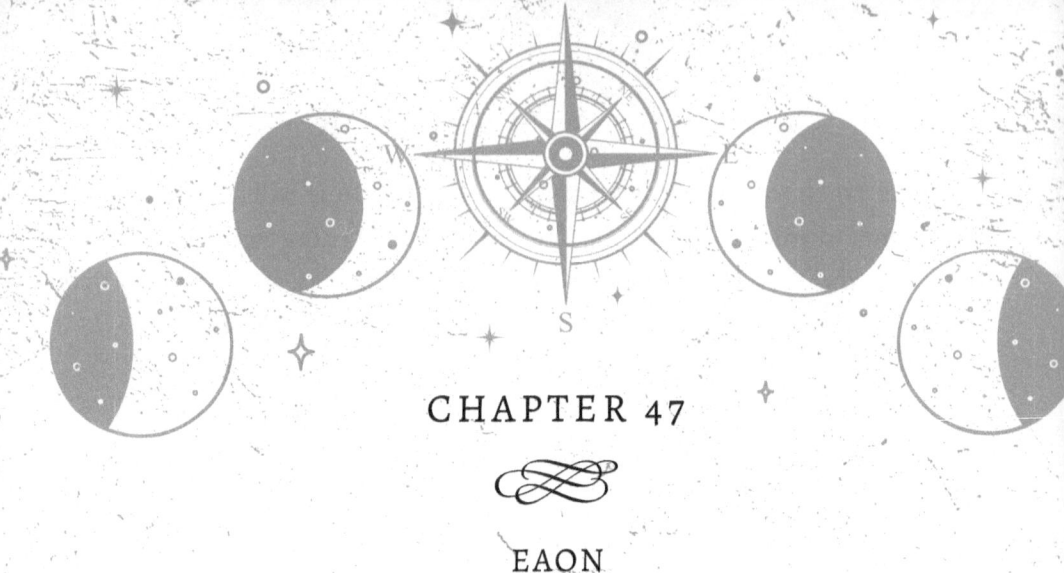

CHAPTER 47

EAON

"Look at me."

The command in the phouka's voice was undeniable, even as Eaon burned and burned and burned. Not even the chill of the seed inside him, clawing desperately to get out, to feed, could cool the pain he was in. The pain of his body, the pain of the sentient necrosis taking its wrath out on him, the pain of knowing his sister would be the first to die if he couldn't get it under control.

The phouka's command held such power that it broke through Eaon's will to remain absolutely still. Moving his head just enough to meet the phouka's goat-slit eyes was almost too much. Another waft of death tried to spill from him, but the phouka absorbed it without flinching.

"It's grown too strong. You cannot bury it. Give it to me, Eaon. I will not let you hurt anyone."

Relief shuddered through him, but he still couldn't let it go. Down in the Womb, Cinn had said a similar thing. Cinn had spoken. The memory was so jarring he lost focus for a second, a small wave of power seeping from his skin.

"That's it, witchling. Let it go."

Not with Eavha so close. He would burn and burn and burn forever rather than risk her.

She couldn't help him. Not the way she was helping Aisling.

The princess was in bad shape, and beyond her . . .

Eaon's vision went red. Every muscle in his body tensed, his back arching, teeth snapping so hard one of them cracked.

"Get . . . him . . . out . . ." Eaon hissed.

Even out of his mind with pain, he could put together why the princess was in such bad shape. Why Cinn lay in a crumpled heap behind her. Death poured from him gleefully as Eaon turned his attention from Cinn's healing form to the wretched hag who'd hurt him. Again.

"Get him out of here," Eaon managed as the tension eased inside him, every wave of poison the phouka absorbed giving him another breath of relief. "Get him away from her! Get him out of this city! Now!"

"Easy," the phouka remained a pillar of calm above him. Only the slight shudder at each deadly wave of Eaon's surge gave away that he felt anything at all.

But someone listened. Eaon almost passed out from relief as the Copelands reached Cinn's side. William gathered him up easily, and soon, the humans were all out of sight.

"She's stable," Eavha said, as if she hadn't heard his screaming. "Let's get her to the infirmary. Phouka, can you bring Eaon?"

"Yes," he told her. Then to Eaon, "This is going to hurt."

⟳

Someone had brought Eavha a pair of leather gloves, but Eaon growled every time she came too close. He didn't want her touching him.

A servant who'd remained in the palace brought some pain relief, which Eaon drank down quickly, hoping it would knock him out again. The sight of his twisted legs, the rib poking through his torn shirt . . .

Dizzy, cold, both numb and in blazing agony; he was still in shock.

Eavha tried again. "Let me—"

"No," he snapped.

"I've treated you before—"

"*No.*"

"The gloves—"

Eaon took a deep breath in preparation for the fight he was about to have when Yvette and a trio of witches came stalking into the room.

"I heard there was an emergency." The high healer took in the room, took one look at Eaon, and sagged. "You're either the unluckiest witch in all of Nir, or you must really like my company."

Be it the shock, the pain, or the poppy milk slowly working its way through his system, Eaon couldn't help but chuckle. Eavha gaped at him, but the sound was cut short by the ache in his chest, every rib a burning iron.

"Can it be both?" he wheezed.

"He won't let me work on him," Eavha said.

Eaon winced through another laugh. Even the phouka raised his brow. He couldn't explain why it was so funny that, right then, with that tone, Eavha had slipped back into her bratty teenaged self, dobbing on him to their ma. It was ridiculous. He'd fallen from the clouds into the Womb, his sister was bringing back the dead, and it was all just so . . . ridiculous.

Eyeing him warily, Yvette took Eavha's leather gloves.

More footsteps pounded down the hall. A dark-haired girl tried to run through the door, a blond man on her heels, but one of the other witches who'd come with Yvette stopped them.

"Is it true? Is Aisling dead?"

"If only," Eaon laughed to himself, blinking against the spinning ceiling.

"No," the witch whispered. "But . . . It's Edwina, isn't it? And Radley? I recognize you from . . . Never mind. I need to tell you . . ."

The conversation fell into whispers.

"Eavha?" Aisling's tired voice called. "Why are we in Hyrsch? I . . . I told you to go to Pirevia."

"Really? That's what you have to say?" Eavha snapped, leaving Eaon's side to go back to the princess.

Eaon snorted. Why was his sister always where she shouldn't be?

"We're out of time." Aisling trembled while Eavha took her hands, inspecting the damage. "Chaos has been born into a mortal body and his acolytes are on their way to this city. We need the Pirevian troops."

"*What?*" the phouka growled, its grip on Eaon's wrist becoming painful.

Eaon didn't care what they were talking about. Streams of color danced along the ceiling in an intricate web. He'd never seen anything so beautiful.

"I took care of it," Eavha said softly. The promise didn't seem to settle Aisling any.

"Kaelean's missing," Aisling continued. "A . . . a dragon showed up. She attacked it."

That sobered Eaon a little. "A dragon? Was . . . was Dearmead there?"

Aisling shook her head, face reddening as Eavha began stitching closed the gaping wounds in her palms. "Why would he be?"

Eaon closed his eyes. *Because he was trying to save me. I failed him.*

"He lives," the phouka tried to comfort him. "We will find him."

From across the room, a voice called, "I can help."

The witch who'd turned the nosy humans away stepped forward. Eavha looked to her and scowled, but Eaon's head emptied. The constellation on her forehead, the strange pink eyes . . . He recognized her from that vision he'd had in the Northern Mountains.

Moyra Thorne.

"Later," Aisling hissed through clenched teeth. "What part of *'there's an army of beasts on their way right now'* did you all miss?"

Ignoring her, Moyra stepped up to Eaon's bedside, eyes glassy and red with unshed tears.

"I'll help you," Moyra promised. "When you're well, we have much to talk about."

CHAPTER 48

WILLIAM

EYES STRAIGHT AHEAD, WILLIAM KEPT CINN TUCKED TIGHT against his chest as Siobhan and Sarah led him through the crowded city streets. Word of the dragon and the princess's return had spread, rousing the masses who'd only recently gotten to rest, and reawakening the fear that had soaked the air from the first whisper of fire.

"This way," Siobhan panted, guarding her swollen belly.

Puddles the cat trailed her closely, winding between her feet and meowing silently. That the damned thing hadn't fled already wasn't a surprise; it had grown attached to Siobhan in Cinn's absence.

William didn't know where they were going, but he was grateful for Sarah's hand on his elbow. There was a reason he'd retired from smuggling demi-kin from Kerveda all those years ago; the feel of Cinn's broken body in his arms quickened his blood in a way that wasn't good for his heart. The pain in his head was growing unbearable, the throbbing in his ears making it difficult to hear much beyond Siobhan's muffled instructions.

"Just a little farther. Down this way."

"Breathe, honey." Sarah's grip tightened.

All he could do was grunt as they made their way down another inner-city street. The houses were pompous, their human occupants patrolling the lawns to defend against refugees. If he had the energy, he'd have glared right back as they rushed toward a double-story bluestone house with high, wrought-iron gates.

There were no lawn guards. In fact, the gates were wide open, along with the front doors.

"Paulette?" Siobhan called, voice breaking. "Aria?"

"Put him down, William," Sarah said as soon as they were in the door, that hard calm in her voice that meant business. "You're turning blue."

A wide hall opened on the left to a sitting room where witches dozed fitfully on every flat surface. A barefoot child with daisies still braided in her hair sat up with a start at the new voices, tiny fists clenched in the cushion she'd curled up on, but a human boy about the same age came out from under a blanket nearby and soothed her with a stuffed rabbit doll.

William lowered Cinn to the rug but couldn't get back up. Letting himself drop, he shut his eyes and sucked down stale, humid air.

"Oh, Siobhan!" a woman cried out as she ran in from the hall. "You're alive! We've been so worried!"

Sarah's gentle hands were on his back as he peeled an eye open, watching the rebel they'd housed for months break down in a maid's arms. Ever since they'd been told about Nora's death, she'd been fighting tears—tears she could let go of now they were safe in her home.

Now they were *all* safe in her home.

Puddles trotted to Cinn, meowing and licking at his blood-splattered face. He was soaked in it, blackened with soot and bruises that were still healing. But he was safe. Their boy was safe.

From where he'd been resting on an armchair, a male witch rose, limping warily over. The fireplace hadn't been lit, nor had the candles on the mantle, but an enclosed glass lantern sitting centerpiece on the coffee table emitted enough light for the frown on the witch's face to shadow his eyes. He glanced at Cinn, whose bones groaned and creaked as they shifted inside his body, before turning to William. The witch language was jarring, and it only took a few words for the male to realize talking wasn't going to work. With a hand against his bare chest, he pounded on it quickly, a question in his eyes.

Nodding hurt, so William did it slowly. The witch limped urgently out the front door.

"She's dead," Siobhan cried, holding onto a stunned maid. "Nora's dead, and I have no idea where Owen is, and . . ." Backing away, she pulled her soot-stained skirt taut around her belly.

"May the gods have mercy," the maid managed, chin wobbling.

The witch returned with a handful of herbs, twisting the leaves together as he muttered under his breath. Opening his own mouth, he demonstrated to William where to place the herbs beneath his tongue before handing them over. Bitter and grainy from the fresh soil still clinging to them, William nodded his gratitude anyway.

"I think all the witches have finished in the washroom for now. Let's get you cleaned up and into bed," the maid said, taking Siobhan's hand.

The rebel looked to the Copelands, to Cinn, and wiped at her red eyes. "Are you okay?"

"We'll be alright, lovey. Take care of yourself," Sarah told her, continuing the soothing circles on William's back.

Cinn's chest crunched as his ribs slid back into shape.

Covering her mouth, Siobhan let the maid rush her from the room.

CHAPTER 49

CINN

THE TASTE OF HER BLOOD ON HIS TEETH CURDLED HIS stomach. A running tap sent a chill down his spine, and he woke with fists flying.

"Whoa, easy."

The hands around his wrists were firm and large, the voice gentle and familiar. It took a moment for his eyes to adjust to early morning darkness, but as he recognized William's concerned, heavy frown, Cinn relaxed a fraction.

"You're alright, kid. Come on. Sit up."

Everything ached. Itched. Who groaned louder as William hauled Cinn upright was a coin toss—as the dawn glow greyed the room, the sheen of sweat and exhaustion on William's features became stark. Sarah was there too, face fresh and wearing strange clothes. They both smelled like soap and lemon, though the pile of filthy rags in the corner of the washroom belied their state. A washroom he didn't recognize. A luxurious ceramic tub was filling with steaming water, gloriously soft towels folded neatly atop a footstool. A window dressed in lacy curtains gave a view of the dark morning, clouds awash in golden red.

The fire. It was close enough to cast its light on . . .

Hyrsch.

Cinn told himself the steam from the tub was the reason his eyes were welling up. The reason his breath was stuck in his chest, his skin balmy.

"It's alright," Sarah said as she shuffled closer, keeping a firm grip on the back of his shoulders. "You're alright. We're alright. Siobhan and Puddles too. Everything's alright."

He was in Hyrsch; nothing was alright.

"We're not in the palace. This is Siobhan's home. Owen's home." Sarah continued her attempts to reassure him, but it was only William's unbreaking grip on Cinn's wrists that kept him from sprinting for the door.

He'd rather face the fire than be here.

He'd rather burn to dust.

He . . . He'd had her. Right there in his hands, her throat, her life, and she had gotten away from him.

And . . . Cinn looked around again, his inability to draw breath giving way to panicked ones.

"Eaon."

William and Sarah jerked back.

"He's . . . Gods, you just spoke." Sarah clutched her throat. "Eaon's being treated. He's with his people. He's safe."

If Eaon was in Hyrsch, he was not safe. None of them were safe, not if *she* knew they mattered to him.

"I'm going to keep a hold of him," William said to Sarah from where he sat on the floor beside Cinn. The words were muffled and far away, a hollow ringing filling his ears.

Distantly, he was aware of Sarah dampening a cloth and taking the stool to sit across from him. She gently wiped at the dried blood on his hands, then his neck. He couldn't close his eyes as she washed his face, staring at the ghost-white flesh of his wrists as William kept his grip tight.

Instinct made him tug, but William would not release him. In fact, the stern look the man gave him warned that even if Cinn put effort into an escape attempt, he would not let him go.

"I know you're scared," he said. "But nothing is going to happen to you as long as you stick with me. That's not a suggestion either, kid—you stick with me, end of discussion."

Cinn held his gaze, unable to think. Scared didn't begin to cover it. Angry didn't brush the surface. Confused was the world's biggest understatement.

"Let's get you in the tub, sweetheart," Sarah soothed.

There wasn't much left of his clothes. Or his boots. William carefully released one wrist to help peel the remains off, but it took the both of them to get Cinn to his feet and in the tepid water.

He couldn't feel it. Couldn't feel the Copelands' gentle hands as they washed away the blood and soot and gore staining him to the bone. Sarah filled the silence with a mild retelling of what happened since Cinn left them—their time in Wyldeden, the people they met, then the fire and their mad ride on Kaelean's back as the entire clan fled for the Dividing River. It was the realization of how close he'd come to losing them that brought him back to his body.

Kaelean had saved them. And he . . . he hadn't found her in that other grey city.

Where was she? Was she alive? Would he ever be able to repay the debt he owed her?

And how had he gotten here?

What had become of *her*?

What had she done to him? In all their time down in that cell, she had never used a spell like that on him.

Choose courage. Moyra's words were an anchor as his thoughts spiraled.

A month ago, he would have fled without looking back. Now, Cinn knew nothing would ever be that simple again.

"Siobhan found these for you," Sarah said, shaking out a dusty pair of trousers and a too-large linen shirt. "She said Owen wouldn't mind you borrowing his clothes, but the trousers were never going to fit so they found an old pair the gardener had left to be laundered."

Refusing to be useless, Cinn forced himself to get out of the tub on his own. William stood nearby, ready to grab him if need be, but after toweling off he took the clothes with a strained smile and got himself decent.

Hyrsch.

Everyone he despised was here, but so was everyone he loved. With the world burning to the ground outside, he might not get another chance to tell them.

Cinn reached for William's hand. Then Sarah's.

He walked the city streets like a ghost. At some point, his grip on the Copelands' hands became less about guiding them and more about needing their strength to keep him upright. Westgate was like a dream. A place he'd made up in his head, come to life around him.

"What is this place?" Sarah asked as they came to a stop outside a fruit store.

It was closed, barred shutters padlocked over glass windows, but Cinn wasn't interested in shopping anyway.

He didn't know what he expected to find—corpses hanging from the gutters, blood coating the upstairs windows, a platoon of armed guards waiting to arrest him—but there was none of that. The apartment above the fruit store was dark and quiet, not even a candle burning.

William followed his gaze to the second floor and tightened his grip on Cinn's wrist.

"You used to live here?" he guessed.

Cinn nodded. He hadn't spoken another word to them since Eaon's name fell from his lips, and they hadn't pushed him to. He was grateful for it. Grateful they were here with him as he turned to the alley beside the building.

Choose courage.

Sometimes courage meant letting people help, because he couldn't do this alone.

Down the alley, at the base of the rickety wooden staircase leading to the second floor, Cinn looked up to where the familiar shape of the wonky door sent him to his knees. William hauled him upright and Sarah wrapped a hand around his waist.

He didn't think he'd ever be back here. He had shed this place, his family, his life, his *self*, for fear of the grief breaking him. It was the only way to keep his mouth shut against Aisling's torments.

But he was silenced no more.

He was tormented no more.

Each step felt like shrinking, until he was fourteen and following Radley up the stairs for the first time.

'Our very own home,' his brother had promised.

The lock had always been flimsy at best, but now it was broken. Maybe the bodies hadn't been strung up outside for all to see; maybe they'd been left in here for when he returned.

No. He had to stop thinking of them as dead. He had been

careful—so careful. He'd never alluded to their existence, and if *she* had known of them, she would have used them against him before now.

It would be fine.

"Do you want me to . . ." Sarah offered.

Cinn shook his head. Pushing the door open, he peered inside the apartment. It still smelled of mildew, the early daylight filtering dully through dirty windows. The furniture was mismatched and falling apart, clothes and discarded papers scattered about.

It was exactly the way he remembered it.

He couldn't get down a deep enough breath as he stepped inside. The floorboards creaked, and he almost chuckled as he remembered the way Radley would try to sneak in after a wild night out. Edwina would berate him for ruining her sleep when she had an early shift at the palace in the morning. Radley would apologize and collapse on the floor in front of the fireplace—the one they could only afford to light on the coldest winter days. Cinn would throw him a blanket from the couch and grin, looking forward to the day he'd be old enough to go out drinking with Radley. They would run wild in the streets, causing trouble everywhere they went with no master to beat them upon their return. There would only be Edwina, until Cinn convinced her to come with them, of course.

Except they would have called him Ryson. He didn't know if he was ready to use that name again.

The apartment felt too small now, and this time when Cinn's knees buckled, William lowered him to the floor.

"Deep breaths."

Cinn tugged on his wrist, and this time William let go. Perhaps he knew Cinn didn't intend to run, but rather drag himself to the fireplace where he could lay down and pull a musty old blanket up to his chest.

It smelled of stale ale and smoke.

Just as he took his first easy breath in what felt like days, clomping footsteps rushed up the steps outside.

In the same moment that Cinn sat up, Sarah dropped to the ground and put herself between him and the door. William pulled a knife similar to the one Cinn just now realized was not at his hip.

A man in Hyrschian colors practically fell through the door, his wide eyes quickly scanning the Copelands before moving to Cinn on the floor.

As they locked gazes, the man froze.

It took a moment for Cinn to realize that the whiskered chin and sunken eyes staring back at him were familiar. Older, sadder, but familiar.

"Ry?" Radley's voice broke.

Behind him, Edwina pushed through the door. "Oh gods, it's true."

A wash of pins and needles flooded through Cinn's body as William moved aside and Edwina half-ran, half-crawled across the floor, flinging herself into his lap.

This was real, Cinn realized as the solidity of his sobbing sister barreling into him sunk in. The warmth of Radley as he collapsed to his knees beside them, pushing Cinn's unruly hair out of his eyes.

"Holy fuck," Radley choked.

Cinn snorted, then choked on it, unsure if he wanted to laugh or cry and finding that only a bit of both would do.

He clung to them as they lay in a heap on the floor, sobbing together in front of the fireplace. This was better. This was right.

Edwina's voice cracked against his chest. "You're home."

EPILOGUE

THE HARBINGERS

MORE CAREFULLY THAN HE HAD EVER HANDLED ANYTHING IN his life, Byron placed the shifting mass of mist and claws in the crib he and the other harbingers had prepared for their master's birth. Still adjusting to the weight of the wings gifted to him, the mutant witch stumbled back and clutched the wall of the cave. Every bone and muscle ached from the transformation, but pain was secondary to his awe at the power his master had shown barely an hour after being birthed into mortal form.

The red eyes staring at him from the crib held an ancient intelligence. Only his shifting body was young—Chaos, in all his glory, lay within.

Dropping to his knees, Byron bowed. He would have to fetch a kinner soon, clean it up, to present his master with a worthy meal.

A gasp at the entryway.

"It worked," Urian breathed, dropping to her knees as well.

Byron grinned. "That it did."

"And Queen Tallula?"

"She didn't survive the process. Her sacrifice will be honored by history. Did you get the book back from her prayer room?"

"I . . ." Urian swallowed. "I tore the palace apart, but I couldn't find it."

Byron tensed. "You *lost* one of Sanni's diaries?"

Before Urian had a chance to defend herself, before Byron could threaten a punishment, the atmosphere rippled with power again and Urian burst into red mist. The writhing mass of shadow and flesh flopped out of the crib and rolled across the floor to where Urian had been, lapping at the mess.

"Allow me to fetch you some food, Master," Byron said reverently, hiding his shaking hands.

Chaos growled, a sound that reverberated down Byron's spine.

"Now." The command was all consuming.

Byron lurched to his feet and jogged from the room. The new kinner. Nothing else would do. If Byron had taken the time to think upon delivering the fresh meat, he would have told the others not to let the flesh be tainted by the teeth of servants. To keep him pure for their Master, whose birthing call had been felt in the bones of all who'd pledged themselves to him.

In the main den of their mountain-side hideout, the other harbingers were waiting. When Byron emerged, they followed him, full of questions.

"He is born?"

"Where is Urian?"

"He gave you wings? I want wings!"

"Is it true you met one of the variables? Did you kill the princess?"

He should have. Aisling was obviously not a threat to their master, barely a threat to Byron, but he still should have killed her. The Morvish witches who'd joined their cause had seen her as a potential threat to Chaos's rise—one of several—but if he had killed the pathetic witch, he wouldn't have learned that Aadya lived. That she had not been killed during her last mission to Wyldeden after all.

She waited for him. In Hyrsch.

The torment he would rain down on that city would make what he'd done to Anfar look like a slap on the wrist. And if he could retrieve Aadya . . .

It shouldn't be a priority, but she was. To him, she would always be a priority.

"Shut up," he spat at the others. "I need to tend to the Master. Denyse and Roal, prepare the troops to march on Hyrsch. Wert, scope the city out. And Pryll, I want you to go back to Dusarn and find Sanni's diary. Urian failed and our Master was *displeased*."

Pryll paled and immediately sprinted for tunnel that would lead her to the dragon nests.

"Hyrsch?" Roal questioned as the others left to do what had been ordered. "The wards are weakest in the north. We should be going that way. There's nothing in Hyrsch."

Byron clenched his teeth. "Aadya is there."

Roal was silent for a long while. "Don't take this the wrong way, but we all knew the risks when we chose Chaos as our master. Aadya—"

"Is worth rescuing. We need to know how many of the variables she got rid of." It was the least of the reasons why Byron wanted that city ruined. "Besides, it is the princess's city. She . . . got away from me in Dusarn. You've seen Morvia's pathways—killing her and collecting Aadya reduces our failure risk significantly."

"True," Roal admitted. Then nodded. "Alright."

Roal turned to chase after Denyse. Moving their army would

take weeks, so they needed to get moving soon. Byron rolled his shoulders, straining under the new weight on his back.

"I'm coming, Aadya," he whispered to himself as he stalked down the hall toward the kinner pen.

He had promised Aadya they would rule the world together, and never, in all his long life, had he broken a promise.

CHAOS IS COMING

WHO WILL SURVIVE THE BATTLE FOR
HYRSCH?

THE MARK OF THINGS UNLEASHED

ARRIVING

2023

ACKNOWLEDGMENTS

I hate cliffhangers, but at the end of The Mark of One Unending, I wrote one. It was during the drafting process for Book 2 that I realized Cinn's journey into Qiri was about more than fulfilling a prophecy or searching for answers; it was a story of healing, and deserved more than to be squashed into what was becoming a very large book. So I split the novel, allowing The Mark for Those Unbound to be born. Thank you to everyone who waited so patiently for me to finish this part of the story. I hope the wait was worth it.

This story would not be what it is without the incredible work of Kat Betts from Element Editing Services. Going on this journey with Cinn was incredibly taxing, and every time the physical, emotional, and mental toll this book was taking on me became evident on the page, she caught it. There is as much of Kat's blood, sweat, and tears among the words as my own, and I am forever grateful to have found someone so passionate and dedicated.

As always, I have to thank my family for their unending support. Not just with these books, but in life. No matter how far from the path I may have strayed, they've always been there to guide me back.

At the point of first publication of this book, I am lucky enough to have a few hundred readers, and I am so very grateful to each and every single one of you. I wish I knew each of you by name the way I do Logan and Emma, who I have had the greatest of pleasures talking with via social media. Both of your enthusiasm and love means the world to me, so thank you.

Finally, a special shout out to coffee and the magical Melbourne Breakfast tea blend by T2. Let's face it, you guys are the real MVPs here.

See you all again soon.

ABOUT THE AUTHOR

Alex Clifford has spent the past decade studying creative writing, interior design, sociology, psychology, and secondary education, bringing it all together to do what they have always loved to do best—tell stories. As a neurodiverse, queer, widowed, single parent, Alex is excited to bring their perspective and experience to the fantasy genre for many years to come.

For more on Alex Clifford's upcoming work, visit:
    www.alexclifford.com.au

You can find them on social media at:
    Facebook: facebook.com/AfsCliffordBooks
    Twitter: @AfsClifford
    Instagram: @almost_alex
    TikTok: @alexcliffordwrites

www.ingramcontent.com/pod-product-compliance
Lightning Source LLC
Chambersburg PA
CBHW050114120726
47904CB00004B/1344